*"There's something timeless about Yakov's journey,
one that has the simplicity of a folktale
and the weight of a vast Russian saga."*

— Kirkus Reviews

The Tinker's Son

This is a work of fiction. The appearance of historical figures is based on the author's best understanding of their lives and attributes. The interactions of these figures with fictional characters spring solely from the author's imagination. Any resemblance of a fictitious character to actual persons, living or dead, is purely coincidental.

Albion-Andalus Books
P. O. Box 19852
Boulder, CO, 80308
albionandalus.com

Design by Albion-Andalus Books

Cover design by Pascale Hutton

ISBN-13 (PB): 978-1-953220-42-4

The Tinker's Son

A Novel

Paul Horvitz

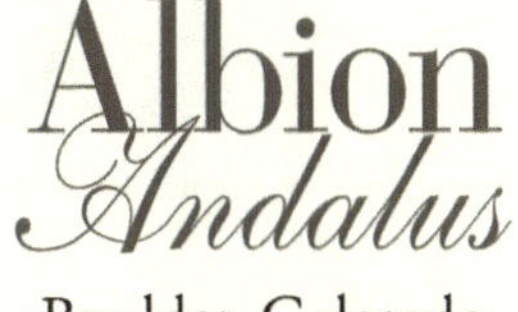

Boulder, Colorado
2024

For my children,
Eva and Zach

Acknowledgments

I am indebted to five readers of the early manuscript. Lesley McDowell in Glasgow made brilliant recommendations on behalf of Jericho Writers. David Lerman's nuanced and detailed comments saved me from errors of fact and judgment. My son, Zachary Horvitz, vetted the more esoteric aspects of the novel's basis in Jewish thought and was instrumental in connecting me to Albion-Andalus, where my editor, Daniel Jami, added astute suggestions and deft copy edits. Over several months, Nan Hayes employed an incredibly keen eye to spot flaws in the characters and story. Her insightful ideas for improvements and her unflagging encouragement made this a much better book than it would have otherwise been. I have tried to avoid historical inaccuracies, but it is likely that some have crept into the manuscript. Those errors are mine alone.

1

The November night is desolate and cold. In the darkness, I rise from my bed, shivering, and push open the shuttered window to investigate a persistent scuffling that has jarred me awake. Mist floats over the street like a wintry ghost. Across the way, I sense penned geese waddling in the mud, but my eyes are focused on the source of the scraping sound directly below. Under the half-moon, I see a figure who moves with an aura of moisture hovering about him. He turns his back to me as he shuffles down Maya Street in his bulky wool coat and fur hat. I can make out one leathery hand and the mud-caked boots. The rumor is that he delivers his documents in the dead of night to avoid confrontation. I can see exactly who it is. The limp gives him away.

Everyone in Navahrudak — all the Jews in this shtetl, at least — know the Conscription Officer, Ivan Ivanovich Rybakov, and his telltale gait. I never expected to see him outside my home. At best, it was a remote possibility. There is only one explanation for his presence now: he has just affixed to our door a draft notice with my name on it, acting on behalf of Russia's Imperial Army. When I registered for the draft lottery in the spring, as the Tsar had mandated, I believed that my luck across twenty charmed years of life would hold. Tonight, I feel the knife of failure in my gut. My luck has burned away like morning dew. It will make the coming day one of heartache for my parents. I watch Rybakov's shimmering figure fade into the shadows.

And here is the other shame of it: until the interruption, I was immersed in an erotic dream, caressing a young woman. They weren't the breasts of Zaltsman's daughter Mindl; she is as flat as my father's workbench. Over my objections, the marriage brokers — they are all spongers — convinced Father and the jeweler Zaltsman to strike a deal, and I acquiesced. As I say, it wasn't Mindl in my dream but the poor Jewess I've seen scavenging in Market Square with the confidence of a lioness. She is barely literate, I imagine. But how alluring this mysterious girl is!

To explain my fascination with her is impossible. I have watched her move and seen her hazel eyes and the dark curls of her hair. She has smiled at me — at least I think she has. In my dream, I trembled when I touched her. I want to return to her and dream of her again.

I admit that such nocturnal diversions are the full extent of my intimate experience. I am no different from any other rabbinical student in the Minsk region. We are all taught that our loyalty must be to Torah alone. Most nights, I would like to think I reside solely in the comforting embrace of the Scroll of the Law, falling asleep to the seductive charms of a prayer, not those of a female I barely know. To have the Almighty in my heart should be my one constant desire, though I confess it doesn't always seem that way. At times, I feel the pull of cosmopolitan ideas that I know are inconsistent with the serious spiritual life that my learned rabbi requires. But I cannot help myself. I have an insistent urge to know everything about everything.

I have many other flaws and weaknesses as a human being, and God knows them all. Though my parents think they understand me, they don't. We all harbor secrets, and I have my share. Apart from the pleasures that lure me toward forbidden knowledge, one of my most closely guarded secrets is that, at the age of twenty, I still don't know how to fully be an adult. I seem to accept all authority. Everyone thinks I am confident, but inside I feel fear, and I know how absent-minded I can be. I get lost in the beauty of pure knowledge and sometimes forget the practicalities of life. Everyone, especially my father, believes I will become a revered rabbi, like his own father, and that the clay from which I am being molded is setting properly and will harden smoothly at just the right time. Yet inside, deep within, I still feel dangerously unformed and malleable.

None of this has tarnished my reputation in Navahrudak or at the synagogue and the *beit midrash*, the yeshiva where I pour my energy into Torah and Talmud nearly every day. Many here agree that I, Yakov Leibovich, am a serious young man and that avarice and conceit do not live within me. Mother proclaims with pride that my Good Inclination dominates my Evil Inclination. I must live as a paragon of Good, as every rabbi should, preparing myself and my followers — how many will there be? — to greet the Messiah. Without any other discernible path before me, I do what I must. I prepare myself for the arrival of the Messiah, whenever he might show himself. Now, though, a new path has been thrust upon me. What choice do I have? It leads to the army of the Russian Empire, the army of the Tsar, and perhaps to great suffering.

It is still the middle of the night, though, and I am cold. I don't want to think about this alternate future. I climb back into bed and pull the quilt up to my chin so that my shoulders are covered, hoping to revisit the stimulating warmth of the scavenger girl. I will retrieve Rybakov's document in the morning and worry then about how to break the news to Father. I try to fall back to sleep, but nothing works. The scavenger girl will not return to me this night. I am reminded that some things cannot be imagined away and that dreams are a fleeting escape.

At first light, when the roosters begin to crow and the goats begin to stir and bleat, I rise, adjust my skullcap and sidelocks, and wash myself while offering praise and thanks to Almighty God. Little Moyshe, my brother, is stirring in the bed nearby. I can feel the acid in my gut. I consider pausing to write an entry in the journal I keep beneath a floorboard under my bed, reflecting on this moment of fear and confusion. But I decide against it. Moyshe might see. Besides, there isn't enough time to indulge my desire to hear my own distressed voice as I contemplate life as a soldier. I must retrieve Rybakov's notice at our door before my parents find it. I quietly descend the narrow stairs and glance toward my father's workbench, a well-worn table strewn with gadgets, watches, small mechanical appliances, and tools of every sort waiting to be revitalized. I thought he would still be asleep, but there he is, the Tinker of Maya Street, toiling away before the morning meal.

Mother has a habit of entering the kitchen each morning and throwing open the front door to sample the weather and expel the stale air that gathers in the house overnight. But I am up before her, earlier than usual, and the door is still shut. I pull it open to reveal the notice tacked to the wooden frame, just as I expected. Its color, a mottled light brown, confirms its official origin. The wax-sealed envelope bears a scrupulously penned address, "Y. Leibovich." Each letter is the size of a postage stamp. My father is Yehudah, but I am certain the document inside is for me, summoning Yakov Leibovich to service in the army. My midsection tightens and my breathing quickens.

Like many functionaries in the Russian Empire's western borderlands, conscription officers tend to be discharged soldiers. During daylight, when Officer Rybakov moves among the vegetable carts and butcher stands in Market Square to stock his cupboards, the hitch in his walk is as obvious as a cow's tail chasing flies. Everyone knows his handicap is the result of a wound from the last Tsar's humiliating war in Crimea the year before I was born. Around here, people say that when Rybakov rises before dawn and nails an induction notice from the Imperial Army to a weathered wooden door in the Jewish quarter, the Great Abyss fractures and all the malevolent spirits ascend through the floorboards, lodging within the parents' hearts like burning splinters.

Today's victims are my father and mother, my Tatte and Mameh. I am resigned, believing that I must do what I am called to do. As soon as Father learns of Rybakov's delivery, however, he will curse our family's bad fortune. With justification, he will launch into a harangue about the plight of the Jews in the Pale of Settlement, this vast ghetto where we struggling Russian and Polish Jews scratch out a living under stifling restrictions.

When I turn back inside, Mother has entered the kitchen and already noticed the open door. She begins to light the lamps and the coal stove to prepare tea and buckwheat groats. Then, she spots the envelope in my hand.

Before I can say a word, she asks, "What do they want from us? Did your Father forget to pay a fine?"

"Wait, Mameh."

"Did he underpay the rent? Is there a new tax?"

"Just wait, Mameh." She cannot help herself.

"Will they force us to move? Is there another epidemic? Are we quarantined?"

"It's for me, Mameh. Let me open the envelope. Please."

"Alright, my dear Yakov. Just open it."

I sit at the table under a dim morning light that filters through our dusty kitchen window. Outside on Maya Street, a pushcart is groaning and squeaking. As I break the seal, I find myself whispering the psalm: "The Lord is my light and my help; whom should I fear? The Lord is the stronghold of my life; whom should I dread?"

Mother stands a few respectful feet away, visibly suppressing waves of apprehension.

Inside the envelope is a flawless example of Imperial bureaucracy. I have read pretentious state declarations before, and I expected no less from this one. These documents are always meant to command absolute obedience. At the top of the notice is the Russian Empire's impressive Coat of Arms, an eagle with spread wings. At the bottom are two red-ink impressions, stamps that frame the conscription officer's meticulous signature. As I read, I silently mouth each Russian word.

The Pale of Settlement originated in the late 18th Century and defined areas in the Russian Empire where Jews were permitted to settle following an edict by Catherine the Great banning them from Russia's interior.

"What is it, my son?" my mother asks again nervously.

I don't look up. "Do you remember I had to register for the draft lottery last spring?"

"You did?"

"My name was drawn, Mameh."

"What are you saying?"

"It's an induction notice, Mameh. I have to go into the Imperial Army. I have to be fitted for a uniform and try to be a soldier now. I'm sorry. I suppose my luck has abandoned me. God willing, it will all be fine."

A pause, an open palm to the mouth, wide eyes, tears welling, trembling. "Oh, Yakov, Yakov . . ." She turns urgently toward my father's workbench, wiping her hands on her apron, and shouts, "Yudel! Come and look!"

Is there a prayer to reverse bad fortune? Or was this event preordained by some cryptic numerology of Kabbalah? I know my father. When he sees the draft notice, he will rail against all of the powers of the State and the Heavens, be they tangible or mystical. I await his verdict. One thing he will surely say: I warned you.

Heeding my mother's vehement summons, Father huffs into the kitchen and immediately sets his eyes upon the mottled brown envelope in my hand. Already, he knows. His chin rises, his head hinges back, and his eyes close. Then he grunts as if choking on a chicken bone. He looks at my mother. "Why?!" he shouts to the Heaven beyond the ceiling and pounds one open palm on the wooden table, causing everything upon it to rattle.

When the table comes to a rest, I apologize, as if all of this is my fault. I tell Father that I saw Rybakov deliver the notice during the night.

"I'm sorry, Tatte. I will face this. Don't worry. I'm sorry."

"Give it to me." He points to a chair. "Galya, sit down." As my mother resentfully complies with Father's barked command, he slumps into his chair and holds his forehead in one hand and the government notice in the other, reading.

After the seething subsides, he explains in a calm, professorial voice, "When you were born, Yakov, I made a promise to myself. I would never allow you to join the Imperial Army. Never. Do you know why?"

"Your own experience was not good," I reply softly, my head down.

"More than that! More than that!" He looks at me and insistently points one finger toward the ceiling. His tone is suddenly boiling. "You will be cannon fodder, Yakov! Is that what you want to be? Do you want to die in a frozen trench so the Tsar can beat his chest and draw bigger maps of the Russian Empire? You want this? I don't!"

Mother is choking back tears. She has lifted her apron to her face. "I will pray to God every day and every night." Then she blurts, "What about the wedding?!"

I had considered this question while lying awake last night. I knew it would surface. "How can it possibly go forward?" I reply, my shoulders shrugging and my palms begging toward the sky. "The wedding must be dropped, unfortunately, mustn't it?" Though I am not the slightest bit sorry about the prospect of this wedding's collapse, I again add, "I'm sorry."

Father sighs. I can see he has capitulated. "For now, anyway, until we can fix this situation. What else is there to do? I will explain to Zaltsman. But we will work something else out. I'm not sure what, exactly, but we will. Then, we can have a wedding."

"The poor girl. It will break Mindl's heart," Mother says, as if Zaltsman's daughter is already part of our family. "It is breaking my heart."

I can only sit somberly, pretending to be aggrieved and wondering what Father means by "fix this situation." He repairs everything that passes through his hands, but "this situation" is different.

Father tosses the document onto the table like a heel of stale bread. "The Pale of Settlement is a prison," he declares. I am certain he is about to launch into a familiar speech. "No Jew can work as a professional. It's forbidden! No Jew can own a house. Forbidden! We can't own land.

Forbidden! We can't live in St. Petersburg or Moscow if we want to. Forbidden! Ah, but the army? The Tsar's army can come into any shtetl it wants and take you off to fight, as if you owe some allegiance to this despot, this dictator. One war after another, Yakov. It never ends!"

"The reform law . . ." I begin softly, crossing a forbidden border into muted praise for the Tsar's attempt to modernize his military and make conscription more equitable.

Father interrupts, "The so-called reform law! Don't be fooled, Yakov. Law or no law, you are cannon fodder. Believe me!"

I cannot deny or diminish my father's motivation. Yehudah Leibovich wants me as far away from the army as possible because he believes he is protecting his first-born from certain death. His father was a rabbi and he would have been one, too, had he not been conscripted and wounded in the Russian retreat at Sevastopol. The family story is that Father's main role in the army was repairing muskets, pots, canteens, lamps, belts, knapsacks, and makeshift stoves for an entire company in the field. But he also carried a weapon and fought, heroically, I imagined. After he recovered sufficiently from his shrapnel wound, the Imperial Army sent him home, and he married my mother, a young bride handpicked for him by his father and the elders. Mother explained to me privately that, by then, my father's desire to return to the worn texts of the *beit midrash* and pursue a life of devotion to Torah was a dying ember. Bitterness does not inspire a love of God.

So he set up shop at 57 Maya Street as a tinker, working from a room inside our timber-and-mortar home. I should note that he is unusually skilled at his work. As I say, he can repair anything, from kettles to clocks. Clocks bring in the money, not kettles, but he feels a sense of obligation to help customers stretch the value of their most utilitarian goods. Mother told me the war diminished my father's faith and left him depressed. It was her way of excusing what she knew were his excessive efforts at controlling my destiny. And it was her way of asking me to excuse him, to forgive him.

Forgiveness is important to the Jews, important to our relationship with God, and important to our relationships with each other. It is sacred. So, I tried hard to forgive my father. But it was never easy.

At the table, I can sense the coarse anxiety in Father's voice. He reminds me that when he was drafted, the Tsar's service requirement was twenty-five years. I have heard this many times. Even the new service minimum under the reform law — six years in uniform and nine in the reserves — sounds harsh to him, not so much because of the years taken but because of the conditions of service that he presumes are as denigrating today as they were when he served. I've heard that conditions have improved, though I would never say this to his face. Yitzchak Levin, a schoolmate whose older brother Kalman was drafted a year ago, told me as much. The family gets letters from Kalman saying the commander is a decent man who doesn't hate the Jews. The division is twenty percent Jewish. Can you imagine? Twenty percent!

The Jews in Kalman's unit keep the Sabbath. They even have a small Torah scroll with them. A Torah in the Tsar's army! They aren't forced to eat non-kosher food, at least in their barracks. They can use their own pots. They don't pay the kosher-meat tax like other Jews. The Jewish conscripts have an association to earn extra cash, and they pool their resources for items they need. According to Kalman's account, they stay together and pray together and train together. This is what Yitzchak Levin told me, at least. I believed him then and I believe him now.

But I don't divulge any of this, lest I be accused of romanticizing army life. I know when to keep my mouth shut.

My father also rails against Officer Rybakov, his latest proxy for the despotism of the Russian State. "The limping Rybakov brought it in the night? He doesn't want to face us! I know his type. To him, the Jews are separatists and parasites. He has no inkling what the Chosen People means. They mock us. They call us arrogant! They think that because we maintain our spiritual traditions, we are anti-Christian. They think Yiddish is a bastard language, an affront to Russian. Imagine that!"

"Calm down, Yudel," my mother enjoins.

"Calm down? Stop telling me to calm down, Galya! I'll calm down when I want to calm down!"

I shift backward. My father frightens me at times. I have seen him push my mother, shove her, in fact. She doesn't deserve this. She would do anything to keep us safe and preserve harmony in the family. Sometimes, Father becomes impossible, physically imposing his will. Oddly, though, I know that Mother doesn't fear him. She seems to understand her husband and tolerate his excesses, I suppose because she knows that at his core, he is a good man. This is my mother's strength: to absorb slights and insults in order to maintain marital peace.

"Yudel, please," Mother says softly.

"Please, Tatte," I say, briefly trying to protect my mother from an instinctive surge of resentment.

You see, we Jews are forever viewed in Russia as a problem that must be solved. This new Tsar seems to want to solve what everyone refers to as "the Jewish question" by requiring us to conform to a supposedly benevolent new Russian system and way of life. This Tsar sees himself as a reformer, and in some ways I think he is. But it is mostly a matter of perception. The reality is far less clear. Many Jews see nothing new or benevolent at all about Emperor Alexander II. As for myself, I have no firm opinion on the best way forward. I rarely make choices boldly. I take one step at a time and hope for the best. But I have navigated these recent months thinking that maybe the Tsar should enjoy at least some benefit of the doubt.

Yehudah Leibovich strenuously disagrees. In fact, my father's determination to protect me by keeping me out of the army was evident long before we discussed registering for the lottery. More than a year ago, as I recall, he suggested we alter my official birth record to place my name outside of the draft group. It instantly felt corrupt.

"It can be arranged with a few clever disbursements of cash," Father explained at the time, as if such a step required nothing more than a routine business arrangement that he could consummate during an hour's errand.

"Wait, Tatte. You mean you would pay someone to secretly change the record books?"

"So?"

"Where do you go to do this and whom do you pay?"

"For now, I only know it's possible. I can find out from the beadle at the synagogue. He is very clever about such things."

"But where would you get the money? We don't have it, Tatte, do we?"

"Maybe we do. Maybe we don't. There are ways, Yakov. It won't be a big sum, anyway. You just arrange a loan if you have to."

"But where do you get such a loan?"

"Stop with the questions! Take my word for it, it is not impossible!"

In that moment, I felt myself leaning toward what would have been my earliest contrarian act — outright disobedience. But I pulled back from the edge and instead offered an argument that my father himself had handed me: fear of retaliation.

"We will be found out and betrayed," I said firmly and dismissively.

"Maybe so and maybe not," he mused.

"Of course we will, Tatte. Some functionary turns us in and the consequences will be devastating. Falsifying official documents? You could go to prison!"

Father was silent. Sometimes he acts so rashly, I thought.

"Surely they would punish all of us or find a way to block my path to the rabbinate," I argued.

This struck a nerve, because Father was fixated on my path to becoming a rabbi. I can't say exactly why he backed away from the idea of altering the records, but he simply dropped it. I love my father, but when he forces me into situations that I'm unprepared for or ones he hasn't fully assessed, anger and resentment not unlike his own grip me, and I want him removed from my life. I worry that this burning feeling in my gut will consume me one day. Even though I lack confidence and have no strong sense of my own will, I know when Father's schemes exceed all reason. I know when he ventures into utter fantasy, and I try to save him from himself.

A few months later, he put forward an even more outlandish scheme to keep me out of the draft lottery. Thank God it was more of a raw notion than a fully considered plan: he mused about a sham adoption for Moyshe. He was thinking aloud, speaking earnestly to his own ears, it seemed. If some other family adopted little Moyshele, just on paper, I would legally become the family's sole son and therefore exempt from service under the new conscription law. For an instant, Father beamed at his own brilliance.

"I could pay Zaltsman to adopt Moyshe," he said in a whisper. "Zaltsman needs us."

I was momentarily confused.

"Why?"

"Why? Because he is desperate to have the finest young man in all of Navahrudak marry his daughter!"

I countered: "You can't be thinking of Moyshe at all, Tatte. Don't you see what might befall him?"

"Moyshele will be fine. He would stay with us. Zaltsman just has the documents, not the boy. Maybe it could work." I recall thinking that nothing he said made sense.

"He will be fine? This violates God's laws, Tatte! Are you thinking at all of Mother? She will collapse! Forgive me, but it's just madness, a crazy idea."

I remember his head falling to his chest as he let out a long exasperated sigh. He knew it was crazy. Finally, he said to me, "I doubt your mother will allow it. So be it. You are right, Yakov. I let my zeal get the better of me. The price is too high, and there will be other ways to keep you safe."

Last spring, when it was time for all twenty-year-olds to register for the draft lottery, he thought I could just refuse.

"Every Jew must boycott the annual draft lottery!" he spat. "We were expendable in Crimea and you will be nothing less, Yakov."

"It's not as bad now as it was for you," I ventured. "And my chances in the lottery are good, Tatte, don't you think?"

"Not as bad today? Don't speak foolishness, Yakov. How do you know this? You have experience?"

Nothing about the Tsar's army was tolerable to my father. Should I have seen it any other way?

"Well, no, of course I don't have experience, Tatte. But you know they don't draft every registrant. And it's by lot."

"How are you so sure you won't be picked?"

"Um, I've always been lucky, Tatte. You know that. Don't worry. I heard at yeshiva they take less than one-quarter of the registrants."

"Don't be so sure you won't be among them. They always find a way to take the Jews. Always."

It wasn't that I felt an overwhelming desire to comply with the draft registration rule, though I felt inclined to obey. It was more that I feared what might happen if I didn't register. So many times, Father had explained the vindictiveness of the Russian state. Why wasn't he listening to his own words? Why was he overlooking the threat to our family? Again, I felt I had to rescue him from his own worst instincts.

"What if I refuse to register?" I asked at the time. "Can you imagine? We will be inviting the worst form of retribution. You told me this. They will take it out on little Moyshe when he comes of age. They will punish me and you and Mameh and Moyshe. All of us. You told me this is how the system works. Didn't you? Don't you remember?"

"Okay, yes. You can be punished by the State bureaucracy. They are petty. They love to make you suffer. I told you this, and it's true. Especially if you adhere to the Jewish faith."

Again, I couldn't let Father's indignation blind him. After I reminded him that the entire family might suffer, he softened, reconsidered, and eventually relented, but I could see how much anger and concern he harbored, anger at the state and concern that his eldest son would go to war and return in a coffin.

I should acknowledge that another factor influenced my decision to participate in the lottery: my aforementioned tendency to be obedient. I was an obedient child and I suppose this extended beyond my father's commands to those of the state itself. Perhaps I should call it a naive sense of civic duty. One thing that influenced me was an essay published by the wealthy Jew Horace Günzburg — Baron Günzburg, as he is known in St. Petersburg, where he is said to live in opulence and grandeur. My father calls Günzburg and his ilk "collaborators." Maybe so, but he is also the most generous philanthropist in all of Russia, and the object of his largesse is Russia's vast community of Jews.

Günzburg argued in the essay that Jews must participate fully in Russia's civic life, including serving in the army, to prove themselves worthy of full emancipation. Does the Almighty want me to run from civic responsibility? Does a good person let others take up arms while fleeing to the safety of academic arguments about justice and equality? It is a paradox. Are the downtrodden better off if they gradually earn their emancipation by submitting to the Empire's rules, even the unjust ones? Or should they boldly insist on immediate and full emancipation as a natural right, even if it leads to rebellion, retribution, and delay?

I don't know the answer, but I thought a good person should do responsible things and that following the rules of the lottery would keep everything calm and unthreatening. So, I registered for the draft. I didn't know if it was the right thing to do, but I prayed that God would find favor in my choice. For reasons I cannot explain, God did not find such favor. He does test us.

Do not conclude from my recounting that Yehudah Leibovich is a simple man with simple passions. This is not the case. He is a literate man who once aspired to the rabbinate himself. He reads all the newspapers, front to back. I rarely pick them up after he folds the pages and drops them to the floor with a sigh, as if he has just witnessed the seams of humankind's fabric ripping apart. As I say, the practicalities of life don't seem to penetrate my world very deeply. Father, on the other hand, feels the sting of every harsh new political machination.

Lately, he's been telling me that the territories of the Ottoman Empire to the south and west of Imperial Russia are aflame and that the Tsar wants to expand his borders so that the Russian Empire can be truly pan-Slavic. I have heard this term but am not sure what it means. Father says the

Christian Slavs in Bosnia and Herzegovina have risen up against Ottoman rule, and the Christians in Serbia and Bulgaria are rebelling as well.

I barely know these places, but it looks as if they are roiled by the most inhumane acts. If the latest war correspondence in the newspapers is to be believed, the rebellious Christians are the victims of savage attacks by Turkish gangs and army irregulars. No wonder the Christians are rebelling. Wouldn't anyone under such awful conditions? At least it's not the Jews who are under attack. The Ottoman Jews have their own challenges, as they live in a no-man's land. Amid these sectarian clashes, Father says, the Jews are forced to make a narrow calculation of the lesser of two evils. Where will survival be better assured, among the Christians or Mohammedans? The Jews often take refuge in Turkish-controlled towns, but it is not a clear choice.

Rybakov certainly knows his induction notices draw blood in Jewish homes. The latest Tsar has just mobilized Russia's Army of the South, and the Yiddish newspapers are full of bad omens, according to Father. Just last week, as I sat on the wooden study benches at the *beit midrash*, which adjoins the stone synagogue on Minskaya Street, the rabbi warned all of his rabbinical students that another war with the Turks was brewing. The Crimean conflict two decades ago was the latest in a series of such wars. There have been other bloody clashes with the Turks during what Father calls "this ghastly century." Now people are on edge. The current Tsar has signed a mobilization order, and no one takes it as a bluff, certainly not Father. He is a veteran of the Crimean War, after all, though he never speaks of it to me or little Moyshe.

In the kitchen, holding my draft notice in his hands, Father is trying to calm himself. I can see he is thinking. I feel sadness descending. I assume I will enter the army, but I can see that Father is still determined. He stares at the table, clenching one hand in the other. He looks away and lowers his voice.

"I'm going to talk to the rabbi about getting you out of this conscription situation," he says gravely. "The rabbi knows people, Yakov, influential people. Reb Epshtein will have ideas, I assure you. His brother lives in St. Petersburg. We can work something out. Mark my words: you will not be going into the army."

His chair scrapes the floor as he rises. I have heard an iron finality in his voice many times, but this time sounds more like a sacred promise to himself.

When I was younger, I believed that every turn in my life was the result of God's plan and that God loved me. Lately, though, whenever I reread my private journal, I can see the subtle changes in my awareness of my father's power over me. I now see the Almighty, the Omnipotent One, as more of a steady hand on my shoulder, a wise and trusted confidante, but one who cedes primacy to Yehudah Leibovich in matters of life's practicalities.

That doesn't mean I am ready to stand up to my father. I remain hopelessly obedient, destined to be a mere bystander to whatever new gambit he pursues with Rabbi Epshtein to keep me out of uniform. My powers of rebuttal are nearly exhausted, and I feel creeping dread. Father is fixated on my survival, and he will conjure anything to get his way. Besides, I know it would kill him if I became a soldier and returned home maimed or dead. He would blame himself, and it would devastate him.

All I can do is walk each day to the *beit midrash* and lose myself in study. At yeshiva, I can read Torah and Talmud, debate the meaning of each passage, probe the rabbinical commentaries, and argue with the other students about which great rabbi presented the most convincing interpretation. I can escape to the purity of Torah and the uncontaminated haven of intellectual discourse, perched on my wooden bench amid the splendidly carved timbers of the study house, snug in my frock coat and rubbing my hands occasionally to ward off the cold.

Of life outside these walls, I really know nothing. So what can I do? I will remain cloistered in the oasis of yeshiva as I await the unfolding of my new path. This state should not be mistaken for blissful calm. Inside, I feel a looming crisis, and fear rises in my throat.

2

Twice already, I have veered off course on my way home from the *beit midrash* to wander into Market Square, drawn by an unquenchable need to know whether images of the scavenger girl, locked in my memory during the interrupted dream, come close to matching what my wide-awake eyes might see. Both times, I departed the synagogue and searched, only to surrender to a throb of disappointment inside my gut. As I walk again for a third time to find her, a drizzle descends through barren trees, coating the roofs of the surrounding houses and the shawls and wool coats of the shoppers picking over leftovers. I scan the market hopefully, wondering if I can rekindle something from that reverie. My persistence is rewarded; she is here, holding her canvas sack at her side while haggling with an itinerant merchant. It seems to be over the value of a stack of dull second-hand pots. I must act, but I am not sure how, so I whisper to myself, offering pitiful encouragement: stop lurking and step forward, you fool.

The day-old vegetables are opposite her, and I position myself so that we are facing one another. We will see each other if she should happen to look. And I want her to look, to see me, to rescue me from my awkwardness. I glance first. She is dressed neatly, but her clothing is worn and the leather of her shoes cracked. I see the dark curls of her hair flattened beneath her scarf. In the chill air, her cheeks and the tip of her nose are rose-colored. She is younger than me, seventeen perhaps, and the picture of beauty. My forehead wrinkles. As she looks up, her eyes meet mine for an instant. In the late-afternoon light from a retiring sun, they gleam with an intensity that is impossible to ignore. She sees me watching, and I am emboldened. With my heart thumping in my chest, I inhale and address her, gesturing to her sack and wondering if she will notice that my voice is trembling.

"May I offer you a hand carrying your goods, Miss?"

The vendor, whose back was to me, pivots and flashes a look of annoyance at the intruder who has interrupted his private business

transaction, his face a weathered gray that matches the worn condition of
his pots.

The girl, who hasn't lowered her eyes for an instant, replies quickly,
firmly, and with a brief smile.

"I am stronger than I look, Yakov Leibovich, but thank you."

What? What did she say? I am dumbstruck. Her words reverberate
through me as she purposely lifts her sack and turns to walk away. How
does she know my name? I want to speak urgently and loudly enough to
reach her, but instead I hear myself stammer.

"Are . . . are we acquainted?" I say this to her back while desperately
probing my memory to place her in my past. How can she possibly know
me? Is there an underground gossip network in Navahrudak, or a demon
who reads minds? Clearly, the scavenger girl is amused, for when she
glances back, her alluring face projects more than a hint that she is toying
with me and enjoying it. The teasing continues.

"We were acquainted," she remarks, maintaining an ironclad grip on
the mystery she has created and nurturing it with pinpoint effectiveness.

I must walk briskly to catch up to her, the soles of my shoes grinding
through the dirt on the path to the street. From a few feet behind, as I
watch her long skirt sway with the cadence of her stride, I blurt, "I'm
sorry, but may I ask your name, Miss?"

She looks straight ahead and keeps walking, but I hear her faintly
mocking reply, "I see you have forgotten."

"If we have met, please forgive me . . ."

"It doesn't matter." She still does not break stride or turn. Her shoulders
are square. Her scarf is easing back as her sweeping curls bounce lightly
with each step. Turning abruptly, she looks straight at me and admonishes,
"If you are marrying Mindl Zaltsman, you should not be seen with me,
you know. People gossip."

This arrow pierces me with stunning force. She knows about Mindl?
But how? I am anguished now, searching every corner of my memory, but
I cannot place her. Do I tell her the wedding is postponed? Do I tell her I
am a conscript now? Do I say that my father and Reb Epshtein are working
on a way out of military service for me? And if I say nothing, what then?
What will she think? She will have to conclude that I am indeed marrying
Mindl Zaltsman, which I have no intention of doing! One doesn't speak of
such private affairs in public, a convention she blithely ignores. My God,
this brazen girl knows everything about me, and I know nothing of her.

I am in a vise. Since my future is in limbo, there is little I can say that I know to be true, so I hold my tongue, feeling trapped and bewildered. I will be leaving Navahrudak soon and, in my mind, I should be separating myself from this town and its residents. Yet I am drawn to this girl, even as confusion and self-doubt envelop me. She is more captivating than my dream ever suggested, more captivating than any song in praise of the King of Kings Himself.

"Good day, Yakov Leibovich," she says with a parting smile.

To her back, I reply, somewhat hopelessly, "Perhaps I can help you some other day!" I barely hear her response, "Perhaps."

I have felt humiliation and clumsiness before, but not to this depth. Fortunately, she does not turn to witness my reduced state. My shoulders have sagged and my chest has nearly collapsed. Did she say, "Perhaps?" I think so. It wasn't, "No." I'm certain of that. I vow to find her again. I must find another opportunity to satisfy my curiosity, which is now burning out of control.

A day after my encounter with the mysterious scavenger girl, Reb Epshtein pulls me aside as I enter the *beit midrash*.

"Peace be upon you," he says buoyantly. "God has heard our prayers!"

The rabbi tells me he has received a letter from his brother Pinhas in St. Petersburg.

"Pinhas has connections inside the Ministry of War, you know, good connections, very good connections in fact. He sent me a detailed letter, and the news is good, Yakov."

"Have you spoken to my father yet?"

"Of course, we've talked, but he doesn't know the outcome yet. You can tell him the good news yourself! You won't have to go into the army, Yakov. Do you understand? This is a blessing. Pinhas has arranged everything."

Before I can pose another question, the rabbi is reminding me that his father used to sell construction supplies to the Tsar's army, and that Pinhas is now managing the family business. The brother knows many officers in the ministry, even generals. Pinhas is well respected, a man who can get things done.

I should be relieved, I suppose. Instead, I am wary. The rabbi's praise of his brother is excessive, even fawning. Something about it makes me suspicious. Should I take all he has to say at face value? Does Pinhas Epshtein, this Jewish merchant from St. Petersburg, work miracles such that a conscript in Navahrudak is suddenly relieved of his responsibility to the Tsar? It can't be possible, can it?

"Did we make a gift to someone?" I inquire, cautiously pushing the boundaries of diplomacy between student and teacher. "I mean, make a payment in return for special treatment?"

The rabbi scoffs at my insinuation, shaking his head. He flips both hands in the air dismissively and lets them drop onto his desktop like stones. "Of course not, Yakov. But listen, my son. There is one condition attached: you must agree to work for a company that will supply everything the Imperial Army needs in the field and at the barracks. It's a transport and supply enterprise, an extremely big operation to supply Russia's army, Pinhas tells me. And it is run by Jews, so don't worry."

Because of his father's business with the Tsar, Reb Epshtein is well-informed about such matters, and he begins to explain the context in detail. He is a storyteller by nature, and sometimes there is no denying him. This is one of those times, so I listen.

"The Imperial Army commissariat is a den of corruption, and the Tsar knows it," the rabbi begins. "It was only a matter of time before the work of the commissariat was placed in the hands of experienced merchants and middlemen, in other words, Jewish businessmen. The firm you will be working for is called Greger, Gorvits, Kogan & Company. It is new and being managed from St. Petersburg by Andrei Moiseevich Varshavsky, whom Pinhas knows. You will have to drive a team of horses and haul military supplies here and there for the enterprise, Yakov. Pinhas tells me the job will last two years. That's far shorter than army service, mind you, and safe—nothing dangerous. In addition, you must agree to handle some accounting ledgers so they can monitor the disposition of the supplies they're hauling. It takes an hour of training. Simple. You won't have any trouble at all, my boy. And you will be paid."

Importantly, the army has approved this job, the rabbi tells me, to my astonishment.

"How is that?" I ask. "They have already approved it?"

"Calm, calm, my son," the rabbi replies, his hands smoothing what must be wrinkled air in front of his chest. "The Ministry of War is going to inform Rybakov. The conscription officer won't bother you. Rest assured, everything is in order."

I am to start the job in January, less than a month away. Pinhas will soon forward to the rabbi a letter of instruction from Varshavsky. The rabbi tells me he will pass along the letter as soon as he receives it.

Suddenly, my confidence drains away, and I am frightened. There is so much to absorb. Drive a team of horses? I know nothing of horses — or donkeys or oxen, for that matter. I only know how they smell. I haven't slept outdoors a night in my life, or eaten wild berries in the field, or slaughtered a chicken. I know the Torah, Talmud, and Kabbalah as well as anyone. I know the teachings of the ancient rabbis with unrivaled recall. Furtively, I have even read the poems of Goethe to satisfy my thirst for new ideas. But I haven't smoked tobacco, like so many soldiers seem to do, or carried a flask of vodka in my breast pocket, or survived on black biscuits, or experienced enough intimacy with a woman to convincingly tell boastful stories. How will I survive as a teamster and an accountant? What do I know of manual labor, and travel to distant cities, and the vicissitudes of the weather? I know nothing.

At home, when I disgorge the rabbi's news about the supply job, my parents are overjoyed. I will not have to fight, but must work bringing the army all that an army requires, I tell them. Mother throws her arms around me from the side and smothers my cheek with kisses, then cradles my face in her thick hands. I can smell the onions on her fingers. "I prayed every day!" she exults. In my father's eyes, too, there is relief. A generous smile of satisfaction and happiness escapes the wild underbrush of his mustache and beard.

"I knew the rabbi would succeed," he says, nodding approvingly. "I knew it. You see?"

Although I complain mildly about the prospect of tending horses, my father is positive that supplying the army will be far less dangerous than serving within its ranks.

"Unless there is a war," I say.

"Especially in war!" he cries. "Dear God in Heaven, especially in war, my son!"

The idea of packing a few personal things and reporting to this supply company reminds me that I have heard nothing from Father about the wedding to Mindl Zaltsman.

I ask him cautiously, "Did you talk to the jeweler Zaltsman?"

"Not yet," he replies with a wrinkled frown, "but now it is imperative. I thought there might be a way to keep our arrangement, but now I do not. It would be wrong to subject the poor girl to a wedding a week before you leave on a journey whose end date we cannot know. I will speak to him. I have to think about how to convey this news without causing shock. Maybe it's impossible."

I think of the flat-chested Mindl and silently rejoice. Then, my thoughts veer to the enigmatic girl in Market Square, the scavenger who seems to know me like a sister. It is not that I am obsessed with her. But I do harbor an insistent urge to know who she is and how she knows me; anyone would. She must live in the poor neighborhood north of Market Square, where ghost-like Jews take jobs pushing carts for half a day's wage to survive until the next morning. This is the lot of more than a few Jews in the shtetl. It is said that they survive on little more than air. The word in Yiddish that my father uses is *luftmensch,* a dreamer with no means of support, living on nothing.

I wonder what this girl's circumstances are. I have already learned conclusively that she is not shy. Indeed, she is clever, and must live by her wits. And now, having heard her speak, I sense that she must be literate after all, perhaps even educated, though I haven't a clue how. That is unusual for a Jewish girl, for any Russian girl. I wonder if she will still be in Navahrudak and unwed in two years' time. I wonder, with a pang of jealousy, whether she has already experienced a man in some stolen moment of passion that I cannot yet imagine, having not had experience with such things. I wonder if she already belongs to someone and plays at teasing and torturing other men for sport.

Nine anxious days pass, and there is no letter from Varshavsky. I can tell that my father now believes that the arrangement with Pinhas Epshtein is evaporating. Daily he inquires, and daily I reply by shaking my head. On the tenth day, his anxiety and mine coincide. I must know. After study that day at the *beit midrash*, I find Reb Epshtein sitting on a synagogue pew. He is not alone, unfortunately, but in the middle of consoling Aharon Botvinik. The congregant is the older brother of Minda Yankielovich. I overhear their conversation from a nearby bench. It seems that Minda Yankielovich was widowed just hours before, when the main gear of the town's grist mill caught and crushed her husband, Mendl Yankielovich, as he was trying to shoo out a trapped mouse. I can hardly believe my ears. Being utterly faithful to the One God, as Mendl Yankielovich was, is not enough to make it through this life? One perishes trying to save a mouse? I listen to the rabbi's soothing words. When the downcast Botvinik departs, I rise from the bench and gently intercept the rabbi on the way to his study.

"Forgive me, but it's important, Reb Epshtein. Is there any word yet from your brother or the supply firm?"

"Patience, patience," the rabbi advises, looking at me with a soft smile. "Believe me, Pinhas has all of this under control. He will not let us down. Pinhas deals with people who keep their word, Yakov. Wait a few more days. The mail is slow. I'm sure we will hear from him. Just be patient. And tell your father not to worry."

My hands are pushed deep into the pockets of my frock coat as I make my way home, doubting that Father will be reassured by the rabbi's words. What can I do but tell him that the rabbi doesn't seem to be worried? The sun is low. Down the street, I see an old man walking slowly toward me. Like an aging ox, he is bent, head down but eyes forward. His coat is too large for his frame, and he is limping. He sees me.

Before I can veer away to avoid Ivan Ivanovich Rybakov, the Conscription Officer lifts his head further, raises a summoning hand, and calls to me in a rusty but sharp voice.

"Leibovich!"

I stop in my tracks and wait for him to come closer, knowing it is too late to avoid an encounter.

"I had some trouble finding you," he says accusingly, nearly out of breath.

Fear is racing through my veins. What does he want?

"I have an important matter, Leibovich," Rybakov says, his icy eyes narrowing. "The Ministry of War informs me that you will be working for a new supply company. But the Ministry has also told me that I must fill my entire conscription quota for Navahrudak. The quota doesn't just go away, you know. And I will comply."

"Why does this involve me?"

"Why does this involve you? Simple, Leibovich. You are required to help me fill my quota. That's how it involves you. You have made a special arrangement, and I need a new conscript to replace you. If you are not entering the army, I must find someone who will take your place. And it must be a Yid, a Jew for a Jew."

"But the lottery . . ."

"The lottery is over, boy. If you wish to escape army service — I know this is what you are doing — another Jew must go in your place. All you need to do is tell me which Jew. Do you understand, Leibovich? Find me another Jew to take your place and everything will be fine. Very simple."

"No, no, no, I don't understand," I blurt, trying to deflect what I know cannot be deflected. "The Ministry approved the supply job!" But of course I do understand. I understand with excruciating clarity. Rybakov is exacting his revenge. That is it — revenge. It can be nothing else. Panic rising in my chest, I begin to feel nauseated. How in the world can I hand this man a replacement soldier?

"You have five days to give me a name, Leibovich, no more. I need a name, and you must supply it."

"I don't know anyone!" I protest. "How can I give you a name that I don't have?"

Rybakov is sneering now, glaring, seething. "You know, you Yids are all leeches. You want the Empire's protection but refuse to serve the Tsar. You refused to attend the lottery drawing. Why? It was disrespectful!" He points a crooked finger at me, his back bent and eyes aflame. "And I'm sure your father paid someone for this exemption. Am I correct? Of course, I am! It is a smelly situation, Leibovich. Repulsive."

"But I don't know anyone," I say desperately. "You cannot . . ."

He cuts me off.

"How you get a name is your concern, Leibovich, not mine. When you deliver a name to me in person, you can go off to the comfort of your little supply job. Or if you wish, you can avoid giving me a name by entering the army, like you were supposed to. It is entirely up to you. If I don't have a name in five days, mark my word: everyone will learn about this scandal — everyone. I can get all of this rubbish into circulation and into the newspapers quite easily. Everyone will know what you and your meddling father have done. Five days, you hear?"

Raising his finger, he mouths the words slowly, as if I am deaf, "Five days!"

Rybakov turns slowly and hobbles away. I am shaking, unable to move a step, my eyes brimming with tears. I begin to regret everything: listening to my father's hectoring about the army, allowing him to conspire with the rabbi, meekly going along with both of them. Look what we have done! I am horrified. The army can take me. My father and the rabbi can explain to Varshavsky. I have never felt such defeat, such humiliation. My head drops back, and my eyes close. I exhale and the mist from my breath falls to the frozen street.

At home, when I slowly recount the conversation to my father, I can see a curtain of dark pain descend. He stews, sitting at the table with his head down, saying nothing. He rubs his head, adjusts his skullcap, strokes his beard and mustache, and pulls at his sidelocks. When I see that the initial shock has worn off, his expression changes. Now, he is calculating. I look down and wait, measuring the permanent cracks in the floor.

Finally, he clears his throat. "Do we know someone?"

"How can we possibly do this, Tatte?"

"Maybe there is an alternative."

"What alternative?"

"For one thing, my son, you could have an accident. Do you know what I mean? It happens all the time. It's nothing at all."

"Tatte, what are you saying? You're saying I should hurt myself, aren't you."

"Small, nothing important."

"You want me to cut something off my body to get out of the army? This is the course you would have me take? Self-mutilation?"

"It's nothing dramatic. Don't make it more than it is."

"No, no, I'm sorry, I will not do that. You can't make me do that." Listening to my own words, I know how shocking they must sound to Father. Defiance is a foreign tone to him. It is to me as well. But I have now defied him.

"It's not as bad as you think, Yakov. You adapt quickly. They won't take you if you've lost two fingers — just two. You've seen Skolnik's missing fingers? And Margolin's eye? They had accidents, that's all. And the army rejected them. It's not the end of the world. They live quite nicely. They are alive and married and have children. They live like everyone else."

"I can't do this, Tatte. I won't. You want me to be a coward and a cheat and, and . . . cut my fingers off? How can I do that? Am I to submit to your ax?"

I can tell these words sting him: "coward" and "cheat." They sting because they imply he will be an accomplice bearing as much guilt or more than my own. This is the inescapable truth.

I continue, "Yisrael Tsipershtein, at the *beit midrash*, told me yesterday that he was drafted from the lottery the same day I was. I won't say he's happy about it. But he is going, Tatte. He's not resisting. I know his parents are worried. But they're not trying to secretly arrange some other result."

"Tsipershtein? The short one?"

"Yes."

Father looks to the side, shaking his head, annoyed. He strokes his beard.

"Okay, Yakov, okay, I'm not going to force you to cut yourself. There won't be any self-mutilation, as you put it. It means we have to come up with a name though. Do you understand? That's the only way to give Rybakov what he's demanding. And before you say anything, an idea just came to me, a good idea."

"Tatte, I can go into the army. You survived; I can survive."

"Stop this right now and listen! You're not going into the army, Yakov! Listen to me!"

He lowers his voice, as if someone might be eavesdropping through the walls. "There's a vagrant who lives on the north side of town — a dirty kid who steals from carts the farmers use to come to market, maybe your age or a little older. I've seen him on my deliveries. People talk about him. When I first saw him, he had sidelocks. He's got no family, nothing to live for. He's a troublemaker, a lost soul, but a Jew. You see? Being in the army would probably do him some good."

I am shaking my head. All of this is wrong. "No, no, we can't, Tatte."

"Can't?" Father raises his voice to an insistent rasp. "Here's what we cannot do, Yakov. We cannot let Rybakov have his way! Don't you see? He wants us to give up. He thinks we won't give him a name. He wants to force one more Jew to grovel to the Tsar and go into the army! We can't let him win, Yakov! It's out of the question."

His words and demeanor are ironclad and immovable. My shoulders sag. As my father frames it, this is our choice: lick the boot of a Jew-hating Russian bureaucrat and agree to enter the army, or violate all the tenets of goodness, compassion, and mercy and hand up an innocent, nameless boy as my draft replacement. His life for mine. His blood for mine. His future for mine. I know in my heart that this mustn't happen, but I feel trapped. How can I deny my father's absolute need to protect me?

Tatte knows what I am thinking.

"Yakov, the name doesn't matter. Just tell Rybakov where the vagrant lives. I don't know the name. You don't know the name. And we don't want to know the name! Everything can be anonymous. Give Rybakov his quota, and give yourself a chance to survive."

Then he deploys his most powerful weapon: "If you go into the army, you will kill your mother. Do you understand that? She will not survive."

Operating now on instinct alone, without looking at my father, I shove my chair back and walk out the front door into the frigid night, swearing under my breath — just loudly enough for him to hear my blasphemy. I take God's name in vain and curse my father and the rabbi. But here is the raw truth: I could walk to Kirova Street right now, knock on Rybakov's door, and tell him, "I will be a soldier. Forget the replacement. I'll go into the army. Take me."

Why can't I bring myself to do this? My father's admonishment is ringing in my ears: "You will kill your mother." What Father also means is, "You will kill me." I know this. But he is right about Mother, too. He is right, I can't deny it. I know her, mother will be torn to pieces. Never have I felt such an unsettling burden.

The next day, Father and I slip out shortly after dawn and walk to the poor Christian quarter. Winter has closed in on the town. Patches of mud on the street have iced over during the night. I am propelling myself as if in a dream, meandering purposelessly through thick gauze. Father discreetly asks passersby if they know where the neighborhood tramp sleeps, the young one who steals from farm carts. A dusty woman hauling coal turns and points to an abandoned shed at the top of Sverdlova Street. The vagrant is camped behind the shed, she says. We follow her directions and easily find him. The vagrant is on a straw mattress under three worn coats arrayed like blankets, asleep, most likely, or dead. He is on his side, his dark brown hair matted, and his beard wildly untended. We can barely see his face. I see no sidelocks or skullcap. It is difficult to make out much more except that we are looking at a human form, a young man no doubt struggling to survive.

"It's him! The same one!" my father whispers to me excitedly, as if discovering a diamond in the mud beneath his shoe. "I'm sure of it!"

I am torn. I keep thinking: what we are about to do is a violation of everything I know to be good and every teaching of our faith. But what if I enter the Imperial Army with a war looming and never come home? Where does my family find peace? How does my mother go on? How does my father live with himself, after trying so hard to help me avoid army service? I can feel the cracks in my Good Inclination widen. My father's rationalization — this lost soul will be better off in the army — becomes my rationalization. It creeps up and begins burrowing into my soul, and I cannot help it. I cannot stop it. I can taste the cowardice in my throat, and I hate myself for it. But I know how devastating it will be to my family if I turn myself over to Rybakov to end this farce. I feel utterly defeated.

The next morning, on Kirova Street, I stand facing Rybakov's thick door for a long moment before the old man answers my weak knock.

"You can fill your quota," I tell him, glancing at his drooping face, then turning to stare off into the mist. "There is a young vagrant who lives in the poor Christian quarter. I saw him there yesterday. People in the quarter know him. You will probably be doing him a favor by taking him. We know he is a Jew."

Bile enters my throat. The betrayal — that is what it is — tastes like a self-induced poison, and I feel like retching.

"What is the name?" Rybakov demands gruffly.

"I don't know the name. I only know that when he appeared there a year ago, he wore the skullcap and sidelocks of a Jewish boy. My father saw him. Neither of us know his name."

Rybakov asks for an exact location and I give him directions to the makeshift shelter.

"You have what you need," I say, turning to leave. "I've met your requirement."

"We don't take drunkards!" Rybakov shouts to my back. "If he's unsuitable, you will hear from me! I will be back!" I listen for the door to shut, but I cannot make it out, so I just keep walking.

I know nothing of the vagrant's health or habits, but I keep telling myself the army will save him. As I walk home, I wonder whether Rybakov will go to the poor quarter to search for this boy, and if he does, what he will find. I feel drained. Silently, I ask for God's forgiveness. My vision blurs as I walk. I wipe my nose and cheeks with my sleeve. "Stop it," I tell myself. Taking a deep breath, I beseech the Almighty to bring this new conscript, whomever he might be, home alive.

"Merciful God . . ." I mutter. I don't know where God's mercy should be directed, to the vagrant or to me. But I beg nevertheless for the God of Mercy to hear me.

When I show up later at the *beit midrash*, drained and weak, the rabbi hands me a sealed letter. Finally, the message from Varshavsky. In an alcove, I tear it open and read carefully. I must take the train to Odessa and arrive by the fifteenth of January with warm clothing, warm boots, and a small knife if I have one. Anxiety surges through me. I know so little about what I will face, but my fate is now sealed, and I need to reconcile myself to this strange new chapter in my life. For better or worse, the choice has been made. I can't say it was my own choice, but I have allowed it to happen. I am being propelled forward by my acquiescence, my weak character, and my inertia. It is a pitiful version of myself. As the psalm says: "All who see me, mock me. They open their lips; they shake their heads."

Before departing to Odessa for training as a teamster, I decide to seek out the scavenger girl again. Two days before the Christian New Year, I find her on a street just off Market Square, one that I rarely travel. Providence is with me. Her sack seems heavy.

"Peace be upon you," I say in a strong voice, trying to sound cheerful. She looks up. All of her full curls are visible, as her scarf has slipped down around her neck. How flawless she is. I lock onto her arresting eyes as I walk toward her.

"Today, I insist on carrying this heavy load, Miss. Are you headed home?"

"It's a long way. Thank you just the same."

"No, no, I have time."

"You'll be late. It's almost the Sabbath."

I force a quick smile. "God will forgive me. The Book of Splendor says, 'If a man does kindness on Earth, he awakens loving-kindness above.'"

Cocking her head to the side, she quips, "Well, Yakov Leibovich, I suppose it is only fair, as I am just a girl and you are a man with the strength of Samson."

I can't help but be amused. Good-natured banter is a staple at the *beit midrash*, and I will surely miss it. I manage to smile at her weakly as I hoist the bulging sack over my shoulder with one swiveling motion. I tuck my book of commentaries under one arm.

"At least let me carry your book," she insists, taking it from me, almost touching my arm. "A girl is allowed to carry such a book, you know."

We walk north. When I am certain she is in a fair mood, I ask, "You do have a name, don't you?"

She breaks into a charming, girlish laugh. "So, I have succeeded in torturing you."

Her face is mesmerizing and fine-featured. Her cheeks are pink from walking, and her eyes seem like emeralds lit from within.

"I'm not sure why you're laughing," I reply. "Torture is not pleasant, you know."

"Don't be dramatic." She pauses. "I really don't mean to torment you. Do you remember the name Rivkah?"

Rivkah. It comes to me instantly. It is not an unusual name; I have known several. But this Rivkah suddenly attaches to a face in my memory. Yes, of course, it is Avram Eizenberg's younger sister. The last time I saw her, she was was just a girl waiting outside the *beit midrash* for her brother to exit so that she could walk home with him. Avram was my friend, a yeshiva schoolmate, a fellow seeker of knowledge and commandment. When the lessons were done, we would emerge together, often joking and shoving each other, as I recall, and she would always ask her brother what he had studied that day. This was remarkable behavior. Girls aren't meant to seek knowledge or to care about Torah and the volumes of rabbinical commentaries, but she did.

"Rivkah Eizenberg," I pronounce triumphantly.

"So, you do have a memory after all!" There is a prankster's edge to her voice. "But I forgive you for forgetting me."

"You are not the same Rivkah I met years ago," I say resolutely. "You must have been twelve when I last saw you. You've grown up." I try to make it sound like a compliment.

"I hear growing up happens to girls from time to time, and to women," she says, smiling at me in a way that tells me she is pleased with herself.

When Avram drifted out of my life, Rivkah disappeared as well. She is no longer an awkward younger sister, a slender girl tagging along with her brother and his yeshiva mates. She must be seventeen now, with a bright smile when she allows it to be seen. I take note of the shape beneath her coat and shawl.

"I am glad to be forgiven, and I am sorry that I didn't recognize you, Rivkah."

"If you are studying Talmud day and night, I'm certain you know how special forgiveness is," she tells me.

"It is. Did you know that Rabbi Moshe Cordovero describes thirteen levels of mercy? In truth, I'm no longer studying, though. In two weeks, I have to go away. It's my time to serve the Tsar."

"The army? I hope not."

"I was drafted a few weeks ago, but my father arranged another job for me. It's with a private firm, a Jewish firm, that will be supplying the army. I have to work as a teamster and an accountant. Can you imagine? I don't know anything about either, but at least I won't be in uniform."

"Thanks be to God," she responds. "I don't have a good feeling about the army."

Rivkah turns a corner into a poorer quarter of the city, one I know little about. The odor of waste and offal is strong. Lamps flicker in a few of the ramshackle tenements, and I detect faint Yiddish conversations through the windows.

"There always seems to be a war, and too many soldiers don't come home," she says.

"Was your father conscripted?" I ask.

"No."

We walk in silence for a moment. I sense there is something more she wishes to say, and in five or six steps, she does.

"He died in the cholera epidemic when I was thirteen."

I stop. "I'm sorry. Blessed is the Name of God. I didn't know." It is only now that I realize I haven't inquired about Avram. We continue along the street.

"Did Avram leave town? How is he?"

"I will tell you, since you ask. It isn't what I would wish to say, but he is not with us. Avram is a lost boy. We don't see him. It is as if a dybbuk leapt into my brother's soul when my father died. We love him, my mother and I. And we pray for him. But he doesn't want to listen to us or be with us. It's been months since I last saw him. It's tragic. A friend told me she saw him living on the street in the poor Christian quarter as a squatter. How he survives, I don't know. I barely have the strength to look for him, but have tried a few times. He saw me once and ran away. I live with my mother and bring in a little money buying and fixing kitchen pots and pans, as you can see. That is my trade, now, which is why my sack is heavy today. My mother has survived so much hurt. Did you ever meet her? Her name is Shayna."

"No, I'm sorry, but I would like to." My mind is racing with her words: living somewhere, a squatter, the poor Christian quarter. I am moving along the street but feel numb and lost. How can this be? Did I hear her correctly?

"The Community Fund keeps us alive, thanks be to God," she continues. "We don't like to take charity, but since my father died, it's almost all we have. He was paying a tutor for me so I could learn to read and write Yiddish and Hebrew, but after he died, we couldn't afford to continue."

Her words stab me. A lost boy. The poor Christian quarter. It can't be; it mustn't be. But my memory of Avram confirms everything Rivkah is saying. In my mind, I retrieve a picture of his face, a good and handsome face when I knew him, with distinctive eyebrows drooping to the sides. We were yeshiva mates. He could have been my brother. He struck me as intelligent, inquisitive, and fearless, but also a bit reckless. Avram was outspoken, as if he couldn't regulate his thoughts.

I recall thinking years ago that something odd must have happened to Avram. When he stopped attending the *beit midrash*, I remember rumors circulating about strange and rude behavior, vodka, and a malevolent force, a dybbuk, that seemed to possess him. The boy had brushes with the town elders and the rabbi — a different rabbi then, an older one — over petty thefts and foul language. At the time, I knew something was wrong with Avram. But I assumed he was just unable to manage life at the *beit midrash*. I assumed he had taken up a trade or moved to Minsk. I just assumed, and never asked.

I had no idea that Avram's father had died or that Avram had left home. I vividly recall the nameless tramp huddled under shabby coats on a bed of straw. No family and nothing to live for? That's what my father said. I see the outline of the figure, the dark brown, matted hair. It wasn't that I couldn't see the face of the vagrant that day. I didn't want to see it. It would have been too much. The boy's anonymity gave my father and me a ready excuse for our behavior. We didn't want to see the person beneath the coats, especially the face. We didn't want to be haunted by it.

I can barely believe the awful result. Could it be a mistake? There must be more than one vagrant. At this moment, I truly despise my father, and retain only a remnant of love for myself. It is not a mistake, no. Nearly a week has passed since I told Rybakov where to find the nameless tramp. If the Conscription Officer has acted, this tragedy cannot be undone. I feel profound alarm.

"Avram was sixteen when your father died," I manage to say, seeking confirmation.

"Yes."

"And that's why he left the *beit midrash*."

"Yes. He told me once that God had abandoned him. I have to think he was right." She stops and hands me the book of commentaries. "I will carry the sack from here, Yakov Leibovich. You have done more than enough. It's getting dark."

Rivkah Eizenberg has not been shielded from suffering. She speaks without shame or reticence or self-pity. Her beauty and her pain seem inseparable to me. I can see now that her eyes reveal more than an alluring glint. They also reveal maturity and the determination to go forward in the face of hardship, to survive. It is striking and sad and enticing all at once.

I also see that despite all the constraints on her life, she is a free person in that she controls her life, makes her own decisions, plots her own course, and speaks her mind. There is no other choice for her. I envy her independence. But I am overwhelmed by shame at the damage I'm certain I have done to her, of which she has no idea.

I place the sack on the ground softly to muffle the clatter of its contents. The thought of telling her what I know, what I have done, is fully suppressed.

"I'm sorry about your brother," I say quietly, still looking down.

"If I see Avram again," she says, "I will tell him you are going to be Navahrudak's greatest and most handsome rabbi."

It isn't until later that this generous flirtation registers. For now, I only want to slip away. I force a smile. "It's not likely our paths will cross. May God give you peace, Rivkah."

"I'm sure you will come home one day," she says cheerfully. "You will probably find me at Market Square, still selling second-hand pots."

I want to say something more, but the words are stuck. I am shaking, holding the book of commentaries close to my chest, while watching her carry her wares into the gathering shadows. It is the Sabbath, and I should be home. Part of me wants to be there instantly, to exit this dark and painful corridor. Instead, walking quickly, I make for the shed near the edge of town on Sverdlova Street. I am drawn to the straw mattress and the pile of coats, hoping beyond reason that my dread is merely a garment woven by the Evil Eye to deceive me and that I can summon the will to throw it off, and everything will return to normal.

Darkness is falling. I must step nearly to the edge of the shed and kneel on the ground to see inside. There is only debris. Someone clearly lived there. But the mattress is gone, the coats are gone — Avram Eizenberg is gone.

3

The Imperial Army's abduction of Avram holds a sad and embarrassing irony for me, for in the months leading up to what they would arrogantly call an induction, I was studying Jewish ethics. It seems I never took the lessons to heart.

I was exploring the ideas of Reb Yisrael Lipkin of Vilna, who teaches that studying Torah, even diligently, doesn't necessarily make a person morally strong. It isn't guaranteed that your soul will improve; you must tend to that directly, on your own. Every act and every episode of inaction changes the world, Lipkin believes. People must attempt to correct their flaws in order to perfect themselves. God doesn't do that for them, which in my case is unfortunate.

My own recent moments of inaction are startlingly instructive, a slap in the face, really. I admit I am frightened knowing that this stain of poor judgment will remain with me until I provide a satisfactory remedy. It is as if I have slipped to the bottom of a glorious mountain and am now peering up a steep slope that must be scaled anew to reach the level of goodness I require of myself. As for the level that God requires, well, that lies far beyond. When I discovered I had inadvertently hand-picked Rivkah's brother to take my place in the army, I not only understood how grievously I had acted, I also knew how blindly naive my mother had been to believe that Yakov Leibovich's Good Inclination dominated his inner adversary, the Evil Inclination.

For as long as I can remember, life in the *beit midrash* has centered on the dissection of Torah and its commentaries. But we also learn to undertake earnest examinations of our own thoughts and actions to understand if we are virtuous and worthy. I wouldn't know what a Russian Orthodox house of study is like, but I imagine that, for a student to be looked upon as a good and faithful Christian, he has to make vows and affirmations of the Christian way. That's not quite what we do.

In my own faith, the most important vow seems to be to oneself. Though Reb Epshtein hasn't put it quite this way, it is evident self-scrutiny is a cornerstone of Judaism. God's commandments guide us, but we are also taught that our thoughts, emotions, desires, and motivations must adhere to the set of ethical and moral principles that the commandments imply. To look inward and judge oneself seemed to be a necessary excursion on the journey to righteousness. And for better or worse, I do look inward.

It took time for me to understand this. As a young boy, all I wanted to do in *beit midrash* was please the rabbi and play at righteousness. Apparently I succeeded in the former, for it wasn't long before Reb Epshtein told me he had discussed with my father the course of study required for me to become a rabbi. Why would they ask for my consent? Every step along the path was set before me.

Nonetheless, with the rabbi's guidance, I grew to enjoy self-examination. It suits me, for it opens the door to contemplation — about everything, from the depths of the soul to the vastness of the universe. It was the rabbi who urged me to keep a journal of my observations and thoughts about what I was learning, though he couldn't have known at the time that its pages would become a secret refuge to reflect upon topics and tendencies that he would undoubtedly see as heresies

I remember him telling me, "It is good to question and good to seek answers. You can meet God wherever you are, so it is good to know where you are."

And so I have become comfortable with self-awareness and think often about what I see when I look in the mirror. I can't say if I am a harsh judge of my own character or a naive one.

In the days following my encounter with Rivkah in which I learned of Avram's fate and my role in it, I thought this process of self-reflection might shatter me. I know I have to seek forgiveness to repair the wounds I have caused, but given I am about to board a train for Odessa and a temporary new life, I am not sure where or how to begin. I desperately want to turn back the clock, to begin my life anew, only this time with the knowledge and experience of painful errors.

Thinking back, I don't recall ever facing anything like the turmoil I now feel. I must have been obedient and intelligent enough as a boy to give my parents confidence that I would fulfill my role as the eldest son: carrying on the family name and traditions in a way that will be respected in the community, bringing forth grandchildren, honoring the Jewish faith, succeeding financially so as not to be a burden on them. I wanted to be good, and I think for many years I was.

They said I favored my *zeyde*, my father's father, who was tall — at least until the old rabbi entered the bent and stooped phase of his life. He died when I was ten, Moyshe's age. I had a strong constitution as a boy and was rarely ill. I took to reading early and quickly grew to love books. I was curious about the world, more curious than my parents knew. From a young age, I loved to ask big questions. Father encouraged me to discover the teachings of all the esteemed rabbis in history, even the most revered mystics. There were rabbis he disapproved of and said so. All of them led Hasidic sects. In his opinion, too many Hasidic rabbis pandered to the weak and confused, hawking foolish magic and turning ancient Kabbalah from a profound exposition on the Universe, Creation, and Man into a populist liquor.

It was at this age, ten or so, that I realized I was on a path toward the rabbinate. It seemed to be in the natural evolution of my life, though I eventually realized how much my father had influenced my steps and direction. If there were other possible paths, I wasn't made aware of them. Reb Epshtein placed rabbinical commentaries in front of me at the *beit midrash*, and the truth is that I found them fascinating, not so much out of a duty to Torah but out of an insatiable curiosity about the invisible vectors within the human heart and mind. I began to think about the nature of knowledge and existence. Then, I learned that the Greeks had a word for this: "philosophy." Torah is full of such examinations. But I privately sensed that Torah could not be the exclusive vessel of human understanding and wisdom, even though the rabbis treated it as such.

All of my reading quickly turned me into a lover of language, and the more I read, the more proficient I became at Yiddish, Hebrew, and Russian. My parents were unaware, but I was also teaching myself German.

When I was fourteen, the eccentric Jewish coachman who worked the Minsk-Navahrudak road took a liking to me because I was one of the few people, child or adult, willing to engage in conversation with him. His appearance — the discolored teeth, the foul odor, the way he talked and sang to himself — neither shocked nor repelled me. One day, as a gift, he handed me a novel by a German rabbi, Ludwig Philippsohn, that had been translated into Russian. The book was a vivid historical novel about the heroism of Jacob Tirado, a migrant from Spain to Holland who established a synagogue in Amsterdam in the 16th Century.

I fell in love with this book, and when I told the coachman how much I enjoyed it, he started bringing me copies of a Jewish monthly that the same Rabbi Philippsohn edited and published. It was called *Die*

Allgemeine Zeitung des Judenthums. The coachman explained that the journal, available in Minsk, was a feast of ideas about religion, morality, and political events across Europe written expressly for Jews. Its essays, he said, often challenged the supremacy of rabbis in ways that I could never have imagined while sitting in Reb Epshtein's yeshiva.

I do not know how the coachman came to be so learned while transporting travelers along the Minsk-Navahrudak road with a team of horses and a simple enclosed coach. Perhaps his horses knew the way, and he rode atop the coach reading the entire way. How would a passenger know? This much was clear: the old coachman was an iconoclast, even a heretic. On the whole, he distrusted rabbis, and let me know exactly how he felt.

"It's not poison, what these rabbis are teaching," he told me once in a whisper, drawing me close to his weather-beaten face and stale breath. "But it's not necessarily good for you, either. Be careful what you consume, young man."

Unlike his novel, Rabbi Philippsohn's *Die Allgemeine* was published only in German. When the coachman fulfilled my request for a German-Yiddish dictionary, which he obtained used, I created my own German lessons in private moments. My goal was to make sense of Reb Philippsohn's articles, and I improved month by month, disposing of each edition of the journal after I had translated what I could.

When I was sixteen, I discovered Goethe, who wrote poems and essays at his home in Weimar. "Try this," the coachman commanded, handing me a thin volume. "It will be easy to translate." A new word entered my vocabulary: *"intelligentziya."* I was driven to understand Goethe in the original German. It was a challenge and a feast. Little by little, forbidden ideas beyond those of Goethe entered my realm. I secretly borrowed or purchased any secular journal I could get my hands on, especially those containing essays on philosophy, culture, science, and politics. I discarded them when I was done, or passed them to a schoolmate whom I could trust and knew had a taste for some of the same ideas. I especially enjoyed reading about life in the large cities of Europe and the new production centers called factories. My schoolmate, in return, surreptitiously passed articles to me about the new theorists of evolution, Darwin and Spencer. These two thinkers shocked me, but I found their arguments persuasive. New worlds suddenly sprang up, if one was open to listening and seeking.

I was keenly aware that none of these intellectual meanderings would meet with my father's approval. If I should even mention a reformist rabbi in Germany like Reb Philippsohn or a wealthy Jew in St. Petersburg like

Baron Günzburg, he would launch into a bitter harangue. Günzburg, in particular, triggered Father's outrage.

"I've been warning you about him!" he'd say. "He and his ilk believe in the so-called Enlightenment, the Haskalah, the Jewish Renaissance. Jews so modern they forget they are Jews! Integrationists! Assimilationists! Apologists! They dress like Europeans, as if they were dandies in Berlin or London. They forget God's commandments — how convenient! They have broken with our traditions. They have forgotten Torah, Talmud, and Kabbalah. Their religion is the state! They worship the Russian Emperor or Otto von Bismarck. They hardly speak Yiddish anymore! It's disgraceful." And so on.

It was about this time that I saw I was attracting the attention of females, eligible girls and their mothers, when they found themselves close enough to size me up. I heard their comments and learned to read their expressions.

One day, I overheard a marriage broker at our house trying to sell Father a match — "the perfect girl for such a handsome and intelligent young man." It irritated me. The concept of marriage entered my world when I was sixteen, after a growth spurt and the flimsy beginnings of a beard. I understood for the first time that my mother wasn't the only woman who considered me to be an attractive male or even what true "maleness" meant. Father listened to the most interesting dowry proposals, and more than once suggested I joyously embrace the enterprise of marriage.

"You will take a bride just as I took your mother as my bride, and just as Zeyde took your grandmother as his bride," I remember him telling me.

"I don't even know how to think about this," I said. "Is a young man not supposed to have a mind of his own? And is a girl not supposed to have a mind of her own?"

"There is no thinking, Yakov. We do according to tradition. You will see, it is a blessed event."

I resisted as much as I could. I'm certain that one reason Father initially decided not to pressure me is that he didn't want to interrupt the exceptional progress I was making in Torah and Talmud studies under Reb Epshtein's tutelage, not to mention the fact that the dowry offers kept improving. More than once, I heard him explain the terms of a proposal to my mother in great detail, as if he were about to negotiate to acquire a valuable gem. And like a gem, provenance was important. They talked as much, if not more, about the parents of the would-be bride and the family she came from as they did about the attributes of the potential bride.

Then I heard the name Mindl. I can only assume that Zaltsman the jeweler, one of Navahrudak's wealthier Jews, made an especially attractive offer in return for a commitment to wed his daughter. Like me, she was tall, but that seemed to be the only attribute we had in common. I might have seen her twice and had only the barest memory of her when my father informed me that I was to wed her, love her, and bring forth grandchildren with her. It seemed so odd.

Fear of women had nothing to do with my reluctance to marry. Why fear those who by nature and commandment are subordinate to men? Even the great teachings of Kabbalah describe a divine concept with masculine and feminine attributes in roughly equal measures, but the woman serves the man. This is an immutable pillar of God's plan. I admit, my interest in the opposite sex was brimming. I had no shortage of fantasies about climbing beneath the bedcovers in a darkened room and directing myself to the sacred fissure to fulfill God's commandment to be fruitful. But I was training to be a rabbi! Didn't passion for God and His Word come first?

At the not-so-subtle suggestions of Reb Epshtein, I came to believe in a lofty goal: not merely to be ordained, but to rise to a station of honor in the community as a wise and compassionate spiritual leader, the only individual capable of convincing the Jews of Navahrudak to remain observant and adhere to Judaism's essential commandments in the face of burgeoning modernity.

I also fell in line with my father's long-held desire to somehow hasten the emancipation of Russia's beleaguered Jews. This is a topic Father spoke about with indignation for as long as I can remember. Though we disagreed about the best way to achieve this end, I absorbed and accepted his view that emancipation was an absolute and essential ambition for Russia's Jews. In fact, I wasn't propounding original ideas when I debated Father but borrowing from Reb Philippsohn and others whom I was reading in secret. I absorbed their original thinking and passed it on.

Nostalgia for one's youth solves nothing, of course. One cannot turn back the clock to live again on a different path. The only choice is to go forward. Yet in the aftermath of the Avram Eizenberg episode, the future looks ominous to me. I am careful to tell no one the truth about Avram's sudden conscription and my role in it. How can I? I need time to make amends. I cannot imagine persuading either of my parents that I should take responsibility for what I have done and simply agree to join the

Imperial Army. If I reject the supply job my father has arranged, I will infuriate him and, as he has warned, break Mother's heart.

But there is something else behind my self-imposed silence: I mustn't do or say anything that might cause Rivkah Eizenberg to learn the truth. Not yet, at least. I am not prepared to accept the possibility that she will forever despise me for what I have done. Whatever my relationship with her might be or might become, I feel a strong need to protect its fragile threads. I must carry my betrayal of her brother deep inside, shielding it from the light.

In my heart, I don't want my tenuous connection with the scavenger girl to end. Yet my rational self tells me there is little hope that I will see her again. At times, my mind conjures images of a hurt and tearful young woman cursing me, closing her hands into fists, and beating my chest for what I have done to her brother.

Five days before I depart for Odessa, Father presents me with one of his satchels and a new pair of wool-lined gloves to take on my journey. I have little else to pack: two changes of clothes, winter boots, my small prayer book and prayer shawl, and the little leather boxes I strap to my arm each day — *tefillin*, which contain Torah passages; I will wear my ritual undergarment, the white cotton *tallit katan*, with its knotted fringes, as a reminder to "not go about after your own heart" but only to do God's commandments; and the last items to go in will be my journal, a fountain pen, and a small bottle of black ink. Does ink freeze? I wonder.

One cherished item must remain, the pocket watch my father bought for me second-hand on a trip to Minsk, which I take a moment to cradle. It is my most valuable and beloved possession — a dozen jewels inside a gold case, made in America. Nearly every night before I sleep, I study the sweep of the small second hand, silently meditating on the passage of time until my eyelids begin to fall. Sometimes, I mark time silently, with my eyes closed, then quickly glance to see whether my cadence matches the watch's, as if this device were somehow connected to a heavenly form of perfect time.

Father told me the watch was crafted in a place he pronounced "VAHL-tem," near the city of Boston, in America. The brand name, Waltham, appears in small black letters on the face of the watch, which I keep in a blue velvet pouch at the back of a drawer in my bedside table. It was my reward for succeeding in a study challenge that Father arranged with Rabbi Epshtein as an incentive for me to become the finest scholar in Navahrudak, apart from the rabbi himself, of course. But I cannot take the watch with me into the wilderness, it would never survive. Besides, I don't feel I deserve to have it with me — not now, not after my most un-rabbinical moment on Sverdlova Street.

The incident exposes my self-doubt, which in turn seems to fuel a wider sense of anxiety. I worry I won't be able to control a team of horses, and complain to my father about it. I need to feel confident I can surmount obstacles and survive whatever circumstances arise while working as a teamster, but on the eve of my departure, this confidence is still missing. It is odd to think of myself as a twenty-year-old man setting off into the world while knowing I harbor such fears. Am I a man? I'm not so sure.

Father sees all of these anxieties as inconsequential. He scolds and reassures in one breath, but these tacks seem to negate one another, and in the end, they do nothing to ease my agitation.

"You are making more of this than it warrants," Father scoffs. "It's not difficult, Yakov. You teach a horse to obey and it obeys! So stop this nonsense."

"I have no experience with accounting either," I grumble. "What made them think I know accounting? Did the rabbi lie to them about that?"

"They'll teach you. It's counting and writing numbers — child's work! Don't worry, you don't need to be a professional. They picked you because you are highly literate. In the army, you don't know how to do anything at first, correct? No one knows; take my word for it. I am sure the supply company will train you, just as the army trains its soldiers."

"How can I keep the Sabbath and the kosher laws?"

"It's a Jewish firm, Yakov!" This is true, but it does not seem to satisfy me.

One evening at supper, after listening once again to my own immature squeaking, I relent, if only to end Father's pique.

"Alright, blessed is God, I will learn to drive horses."

"Yes, blessed is God," my father replies firmly. Mother rises from her chair and embraces me from behind, pressing her warm cheek against mine. In the last several days, she has often offered this expression of love that for years I have taken for granted.

Later, after Moyshe has fallen asleep, I quietly twist four rusty nails out of the floorboard, two on each end, and remove my journal. Eventually, I will wrap the journal in cloth and place it at the bottom of my satchel. For now though, I need it to draft a private letter to Rivkah Eizenberg. I have considered this for many days. My plan is to inquire in the poor Jewish quarter about Rivkah's whereabouts, locate her dwelling, slip the sealed envelope under her door, and quickly disappear.

There are many reasons for my decision to write to her. I am troubled about the way she and I parted when I realized I had turned over her brother to the mercenary Rybakov. I need to show her that I don't wish to discard the seeds of our relationship, and that I genuinely care about Avram. The problem is that I must write with the utmost tact, navigating the dangerous terrain between truth-telling and prevarication, between sincerity and disingenuousness. What is left to offer her? Only well-crafted half-truths. Using the scratchings in my journal as an outline, I carefully transfer the finished letter onto fine paper by candlelight.

> *Dear Miss Eizenberg,*
>
> *I trust you will not find this note intrusive. I write to convey how much I enjoyed your company when we walked from Market Square earlier this month, and also to deliver news concerning Avram.*
>
> *After we spoke, I happened upon the Navahrudak Conscription Officer, Ivan Ivanovich Rybakov, who mentioned that he intended to persuade a vagrant living off Sverdlova Street in the Christian quarter to enter the Imperial Army. I did not inquire as to the vagrant's name, out of concern that Avram might prefer to conceal his true identity, but it could be none other than your brother.*
>
> *I am certain this turn of events will cause you much worry. I offer you my profound assurance that I will do my utmost to find Avram and offer appropriate care should I be fortunate enough to locate him during my travels. I cannot say if his path and mine will cross. Surely, though, he is worthy of every consideration. If I should meet Avram, I will convey your affection for him, and his mother's, and bring word of his situation to you.*
>
> *When we parted, I implied, perhaps hastily, that we would not have the pleasure of seeing one another again. Although my wedding obligation has been erased, I have a new employment obligation, and I cannot say where it might*

take me. Please know, however, the depth of my regard and admiration for you.

> *Most sincerely,*
> *Yakov Leibovich*

As I carefully fold the letter, I realize that Rivkah Eizenberg now sits squarely at the center of my private, inner world, both an object of my desire and a wellspring of my fear.

⁓

The odors of livestock surround me as I search for Rivkah's residence, or perhaps it is just a room. What else can I do but return to the spot where we last parted and inquire of someone there? The neighborhood changes from street to street. The closer to the town's fringe, the poorer the homes — patched roofs, rickety foundations, the windows in dire need of repair — and the poorer the people in them. Without paving stones, the streets accumulate layers of dust. Dogs bark as I pass.

"Do you know Shayna Eizenberg?" I ask a woman peering out from her front door. "She has a daughter named Rivkah with green eyes and dark hair?"

"Ask the tailor," she suggests, nodding her head toward a storefront across the street. "He knows everyone."

I pull open the door and lean into the narrow tailor shop. From the back, an old man glances up, peering over the rim of his spectacles. His fingers are bent with age, and I can see the needle he holds is shaking.

"I'm looking for Shayna Eizenberg, sir," I say. "Do you know where she lives?"

"She's not a customer, I don't think. You should ask Miryam Steklov, two doors down. She knows everyone in this quarter." So, Shayna Eizenberg cannot afford a tailor. I hadn't thought of that.

Mrs. Steklov isn't at home or does not wish to answer the rap at her door. I begin to waver. Maybe this letter to Rivkah isn't a good idea after all. I think about turning for home but am interrupted.

"You are looking for someone?" The woman who addresses me is thin, old, and bent, and carries a covered basket that looks heavy. I explain that I am trying to find a girl named Rivkah. "Do you know her? She has green eyes and dark hair, and carries a sack. Have you seen her?"

The old woman rests her basket on the ground, but doesn't seem to be able to stand erect, though she lifts her face to look at me. "The unwed girl? She cares for her mother. I know her. Her father was a carpenter, God bless him. He died in the epidemic. The girl carries junk all day and sells it in the square. I know her."

"Seventeen years old or so?"

"She stays in the alley off Volkava Street, upstairs with her mother. Sweet thing, she has such a smile. And who are you? A suitor, perhaps?"

"A friend. Where is Volkava Street, please?"

"Very close. Keep going straight. It's two blocks before the town ends and the pasture begins." Her hand shakes as she points. "You have to look carefully to find the alley on the right side, though. She is beautiful, isn't she? I wish you the very best, young man." She looks at me the way a tailor examines a customer to estimate his size. There is a glint in her eye. Somehow, she knows.

"Such a handsome young man," she adds before turning away, bent again by the loaded basket but smiling just the same.

The alley is not difficult to find, only dim and narrow. Ten steps in, on the right, is a tall storage-shed. A set of steps rises to what looks like a second-floor portion of the shed, which is attached to the back of a narrow house facing the main street. I can see a small window and a stovepipe at the upper level. It is the only dwelling in the alley. Is it even a dwelling? This must be it, as there is no other door. Someone must live here. I creep up the stairs as quietly as I can, halting with each creak of the wood and nails. At the empty landing, I slip the envelope under the door and quickly retreat, hoping I have found the right residence. The old lady seemed to know the right place.

On my way home, I ruminate on the sentiments I have expressed to Rivkah. My letter represents a crude attempt at a cleansing, an inadequate effort to begin securing what the rabbi calls in Hebrew *"selichah,"* forgiveness. I know it is woefully insufficient. True *selichah* must be sincere, yet the letter leaves so much unsaid. Still, it is better to begin the process of forgiveness, even in a small way, than continue to hide everything. This is how I rationalize it.

Years ago, Reb Epshtein introduced his rabbinical students to the concept of *selichah*. I admit, my grasp of it is far from solid, for until now I have had few reasons to consider its nuances. The rabbi has summoned me for a conversation before I depart for Odessa, and I consider whether I should seek his guidance on *selichah*'s finer points, assuming I can do so without revealing too many details about my misdeeds, or sounding accusatory of his role in them.

As I wander toward the synagogue, I recall the first time I stood before the rabbi inside his sacred, imposing study. It was when Avram Eizenberg was still at the *beit midrash*, and the two of us were forced to endure a long lecture from the rabbi on the sanctity and proper handling of prayer books. The rabbi didn't summon, but literally dragged, us to his study, grabbing our collars and pushing us forward. We were just children. We had been joking about kissing the prayer book after dropping it on the dusty floor and before placing it back on a shelf, as custom demands for a holy item that has been misused. At the back of the room, Avram touched the corner of his prayer book to his rear end, then kissed the volume with naughty irreverence. Oh did we roar with unbridled laughter! I, of course, had to mimic Avram in this sacrilege, so as not to allow him to be the exclusive source of such ribald fun. I touched the corner of my prayer book to my own backside, and we laughed even louder. Unbeknownst to us, the rabbi was watching from the classroom doorway, and both of us were caught in these sordid acts. I remember the two of us standing before the rabbi with waves of horror cascading over us.

This is what I am thinking about as I sit down across from Reb Epshtein for a farewell discussion. Books and scrolls surround the table where he writes his commentaries. Some are well-ordered and gathering dust, like an ageless monastic archive; others are open and assigned a leather marker. Two lamps and a large ink well rest on the dark wooden desk. A shaft of grayish light captures a shower of minute, sparkling aerial debris as it angles toward him from a high window cut into the thick stone wall. The rabbi's spectacles rest low on his nose.

"Well, Yakov, praise be to God. I am greatly relieved that you will not be forced to put on a uniform. It is a blessing."

"Yes."

"And I want you to know when you return, I will have a place for you here, and you can resume your studies. You mustn't lose sight of your duty to God and the Jewish people."

"I won't, Rabbi."

"Good, good. You know, you will be exposed to many things in the coming year that you are not used to here in Navahrudak. We are protected here, a sheltered people."

I say nothing. Perhaps my face registers some incomprehension, because the rabbi quickly expands his comment.

"Trying moments, you know: exposure to coarse language, temptation, alcohol, tobacco, certainly exposure to women from time to time. You understand, I'm sure."

Again, I say nothing.

"So, you must maintain your study and your prayers as best you can."

"I intend to, Rabbi."

"That is good, very good, Yakov."

Even though I remain suspicious of his brother Pinhas, I ask the rabbi to convey my gratitude for his help in obtaining the teamster position.

"Indeed, I will. You know, my father had a business as a contractor to the government. He ran it with my uncle, his brother. They were contractors supplying things like timber, tools, grain, leather, and so on for construction projects and as war materiel for the army. Did your father tell you?"

"Yes, he did. I think you did too. Anyway, I am aware."

"Pinhas took over the business a few years ago. He has many connections inside the government, including the Ministry of War. And connections to other contractors, as you would imagine. They call him Pyotr, by the way, which I think he favors. But I still call him Pinhas."

"He must be a trusted man to live in St. Petersburg."

"Yes, you or I could not live there without being harassed every once in a while. We do not fit into the hierarchy like Baron Günzburg and his associates. My brother, however, moves freely in such circles. When I published my first book of commentary, I stayed at his home while the Imperial Censor reviewed the manuscript. It took weeks. I will have to go again when I finish my current project, God willing."

"God willing." I clear my throat. "There is something I wish to explain, Rabbi."

"Of course."

"My conscience is troubled."

"Oh?"

"I have done something . . ." I hesitate, searching for the appropriate words. "Something improper. I wasn't thinking. I may have hurt someone, a friend. It was a betrayal, as a matter of fact, and I feel ashamed." I realize that the way these words come out, I am referring both to Avram and to Rivkah.

"Do you wish to tell me about this? What impropriety, my son?"

"It is just that I know I have inflicted pain, and I'm not sure how to begin repairing the damage. The details don't really matter."

Reb Epshtein leans back and strokes his beard, judiciously considering both my desire for help and my reluctance to elaborate. "Then you would prefer not to explain any of this, is that right?"

"Yes, it isn't important. What's important is that I inflicted emotional pain — and perhaps more."

"Everyone makes errors in life, Yakov. And when we do, we must make *teshuvah*, a return to the path of righteousness. You must repent, and repair the torn fabric of the universe. God requires it. But you know this, yes?"

"I know, rabbi. But I . . ."

"You don't know how to; is that it?"

"It's not an academic situation, Rabbi, like a discussion in the *beit midrash*; it's real. I know I hurt people, and I'm not sure how to rectify it."

"You've already taken the first step, my son, which is admitting your mistake," the rabbi says with an encouraging smile. He is looking straight at me, but I quickly lower my head and fix my gaze at my shoes. "Before you express your regret to God, you must ask for forgiveness from whomever you have wronged. *Teshuvah* and *selichah*, repentance and forgiveness. You must compensate this individual. And you must vow to never repeat the mistake. You must tell them this."

"What if the person I have wronged cannot forgive me? What if the shock of what I have done is too much?"

"Are you saying this person is not aware of what you have done?"

"For the moment, yes."

"Well, you must tell him, Yakov. And if you are sincere, he will forgive you. It is God's command. Do you remember Leviticus? 'Do not hate your brother in your heart.' And if your friend forgives you, God will forgive you as well. I am quite certain of that."

I contemplate the simplicity of this formula. As the rabbi outlines the process, it is not as onerous as I had imagined. But can I do this? Not right away, not today. If I find Avram alive and well, the stain may already be cleansed. I will have to seek Rivkah's forgiveness too. Then perhaps I can forgive myself. How likely is it, though, that Avram will survive? That is in God's hands, not mine.

"You see, Yakov," the rabbi says, "God provides a path."

"Yes," I say dully, knowing that the path will not be evident or smooth.

"Before you go," he says, "let us recite the Hashkivenu together." The prayer is one of my favorites, which he knows. We chant in unison. The rabbi's voice is strong, mine less so.

> *Grant, O God, that we lie down in peace, and raise us up, our Guardian, to life renewed. Spread over us the shelter of Your peace. Guide us with Your good counsel; for Your Name's sake, be our help. Shield and shelter us beneath the shadow of Your wings. Defend us against enemies, illness, war, famine, and sorrow. Distance us from wrongdoing. For You, God, watch over us and deliver us. For You, God, are gracious and merciful. Guard our going and coming, to life and to peace evermore.*

"Amen," I say softly, echoing the rabbi.

As I rise to leave, I am moved to ask, "Rabbi, do you think the Ottoman Turks have such a beautiful prayer, a prayer asking God to defend them against their enemies? We invoke His support but so do they. They must. What does God do with all of these conflicting entreaties? Soldiers on both sides of the battlefield will beseech Him, each one seeking victory or protection. How does He pick?"

Reb Epshtein frowns, shrugs, and lifts his palms upward as if to say, "Who knows?" It is what the rabbi always does when confronted with an impossible mystery of life, a question no living soul can answer. Even Reb Epshtein knows when to retreat.

I have been concerned for days that Father has apparently done nothing to inform the Zaltsmans, despite our agreement that the wedding cannot go forward. The situation is fraught. Over the last few weeks, Father has grumbled incessantly about how and when to break the news to the jeweler that I would be leaving Navahrudak for a two-year supply job. But I knew he would eventually fulfill his promise. If Father had intended to skirt this responsibility, he would not have said a word.

Just as I decide to confront him, Father returns from an excursion in a sour mood, and announces to the four walls, "Alright, I told Zaltsman."

"And?" my mother asks.

"You think Zaltsman is overjoyed, Galya?"

"But what did he say?"

I am standing with them in the kitchen, though my father addresses only my mother, as if I am invisible.

"He screamed at me. What else, Galya? I had to defend myself."

"In the jewelry shop?"

"Don't worry, there weren't any customers. I waited until the shop was empty."

"What, he attacked you with a weapon, his fists?"

"No, no, no, not that."

"What did he say?"

"He said a lot of things. One thing was that this never would have happened if I hadn't listened to Yakov's objections. He said I should have insisted on going forward with the wedding when the arrangement was first made."

I cannot hold my tongue.

"And did you say to him that the arrangement was made without considering my preferences at all, Father? Not at all? And that I am the one whose life is going to be changed? What if I have another bride in mind? Someone I have strong feelings for? What then?"

Now I have gone too far. Confusion and suspicion etch themselves across both my parents' faces. For a moment, they stare at me, mute, uncomprehending. My father speaks first.

"What are you saying, Yakov? Now you are going to pick your bride? Or maybe you already have a bride we know nothing about? Which is it?"

Because I am about to leave home, I feel emboldened. This is an unusual moment of defiance for me, and though my voice shakes, I plunge ahead.

"I know all the traditions, Tatte. Maybe it made sense in your time, but things are changing. If Mindl's father wants to blame me for all of this, alright, I accept. You can tell him it's my fault. But if you and Mother are blaming me, well, that is not right. You know I resisted having a marriage arranged, or rather forced upon me. And I haven't changed my mind about that. And what about Mindl? She should also be resisting this forced arrangement. Maybe she has another boy in mind, someone she already knows. Maybe it's best for her to resist a life completely planned by her parents."

My father does not take this well. Pointing an accusing finger at me, he speaks loudly, building to a crescendo, "I should have sent you to speak to Zaltsman so you could say the same thing to him!" The first "you" is loud, the second is louder, and the "him" booms like thunder.

As usual, Mother wants to hasten a truce.

"Yudel, enough of this! What's done is done. Your son is leaving for Odessa. If Mindl Zaltsman is heartbroken, well, there is nothing we can do about it now. It's the fault of the Tsar! When Yakov returns from his job, maybe she will be unmarried, and maybe Yakov will again see what a wonderful girl she is."

"What's done is done," Father says sourly.

Without any hesitation, my thoughts turn to Rivkah. Maybe I will see her again when I return from my job as a teamster. Maybe she will forgive me. Maybe her interest in me will equal my interest in her. It is all up to me though. She will never forgive me unless I ask for forgiveness and give her a reason to grant it.

The morning before I depart for Odessa, my feelings for Rivkah again swell. Mother finds a sealed envelope under our door when she begins her morning routine in the kitchen. It is addressed to me and must have been delivered during the night, though I heard no shuffling of feet. I had no reason to think that Rivkah would reply to the letter I slipped under her door. I solicited no reply. Yet, to my surprise, she has responded, and I find myself fixated on each word, phrase, and serif.

My Dear Future Rabbi Yakov Leibovich,

Your supposition is quite correct; my brother has been called into the Imperial Army. He came home briefly and told us, soon before he was escorted to his barracks in Minsk. My mother and I shed many tears, first at seeing him and then at the thought of his required service in the army. As you might imagine, our concern for his safety and wellbeing is great, yet he believes the army will improve his general situation, which was quite poor on the streets of Navahrudak, from his description. You seem to have had a good instinct about this change in his attitude.

I am grateful for your offer to look after him as best you can should you come across him in your future travels. Will you be supplying his infantry division, the Fourteenth? I pray for his safe return, and for yours as well, even though from our last encounter it was plain to see that your memory of me was poor! If your memory clears, and you are able, I would welcome correspondence from you, though I may not have a means to find you to send a proper reply.

In our future communications, we must vow not to address each other with such formality. You shall call me Rivkah and I shall call you Yakov. Do you agree?

Most sincerely,
Rivkah

I can barely absorb all that this letter conveys. Behind its rough penmanship is a clever and fluid mind. How does a penniless girl who scrapes for everything she has display such free-spirited directness and wit in a letter she herself has set onto paper? It is as if the boundaries of convention mean little to her. She is unafraid of risk, and I feel even greater envy of her freedom and boldness. Apart from my private meanderings into secular matters, which offer a taste of free thinking, I see myself as ordinary, and of late, irresolute. After all, tomorrow I will board a train for Odessa and, most likely, return home to become exactly the person my parents and rabbi imagine and wish me to be. I cannot explain why — perhaps Rivkah Eizenberg is the unwitting catalyst — but I am beginning to question whether such a narrow, predictable pattern for my life is the best course.

4

The train car bound for Kiev and Odessa is packed with Jews in black frock coats and fur hats to ward off the mid-January cold. They jostle and gesticulate in conversation, or sit listlessly on wooden benches. They are mostly tradesmen, I presume, but there are also coughing children wrapped in blankets and women draped in woolen capes and scarves. At approximately the required time of day, I chant daily prayers to myself, eyes shut, lips fluttering with Hebrew, head bobbing in rhythmic praise of the Eternal God and Creator. The pious men among us do the same, though not in synchronization. It is every Jew for himself.

The temperature dips below freezing overnight and rises to barely freezing during the day. Snow and ice cling to the tracks, slowing the locomotive and causing the trip to stretch hours beyond its schedule. When the train finally pulls into Kiev with a piercing whistle, I am not surprised to see scores of soldiers with knapsacks milling about on the platform, smoking cigarettes. Bulging stacks of equipment, neatly arranged and lashed together with canvas, stand behind them. The soldiers are everywhere, gripping the straps of their muskets. I realize that in the time I have been on the train, war might have been declared and I would not have known it. I make my way into the station to buy food for the leg to Odessa and to look at the soldiers' faces. Who are these young men descending into the jaws of war? Do they look like me? Can I see myself among them? Is one of them Avram Eizenberg? They don't look particularly frightened, only weary and bored, and so young. I glance at every face, searching for Avram. Perhaps he is among the ones with scarves covering their faces against the cold. I ask one of them if the war has begun. He laughs sourly, as if I have asked whether his boots are lined with mink.

"War? I don't know about any war, Yid. We've all been invited to a big banquet in Bulgaria. How lucky we are! Maybe you should come."

"I'm not sure I was invited," I reply as I move on.

It will hardly be a banquet. Before departing Navahrudak, Father lectured me about the Balkans. The Ottoman Turks control the region, but have had to put down uprisings in Serbia, Bosnia and Herzegovina, and Bulgaria. The newspapers in London, Berlin, and even New York carry reports of ghastly massacres of Bulgarian Christians by Turkish irregulars. Russia has already fought two wars against the Ottoman Empire, and unfortunately, a third seems just over the horizon.

"The Tsar is making it look like a Russian crusade to save the poor Slavic Christians," Father told me contemptuously. "Do you realize how much Christians like making war, Yakov? They are bloodthirsty. If they didn't have the Jews to harass and demonize, it would be someone else. The Tsars always want a bigger and more powerful empire, every one of them. This Tsar knows he can't stand up to Disraeli and Otto von Bismarck, but he thinks he needs to for some reason. His lust for power is the problem, but he insists on hiding his real reasons, so everything can be justified based on the Church."

When father gets wound up, his face reddens and the veins in his neck engorge. This is such a moment. "The newspapers talk about Russia hoping to gain a port on the Mediterranean. But do you hear the generals or the Tsar admit to such a thing? Never! He wraps himself in the garb of his supposedly superior religion; it's an abomination." And so on.

By the time the train pulls into Odessa Station, my bones ache. It is mid-morning, and the sun shines brightly, reflecting off the surface of the Black Sea and the whitewashed buildings along the shore. The instructions from Varshavsky are in a pocket inside my coat, pressed against the letter from Rivkah Eizenberg. I find myself reciting phrases to myself from her note — "You shall call me Rivkah and I shall call you Yakov." I retrieve her face from my memory, how she looked at me, her jaunty smile. Though I have driven a wedge between us, I can't put her out of my mind. The idea of her, the ideal perhaps, is seductive.

When I reach the offices of Greger, Gorvits, Kogan & Company my bright, hopeful mood darkens. I had imagined a respectable institution housed in a sculpted stone building, but instead I find myself standing before a drab wooden storefront. My heart sinks. The front door emits a loud squeak as I pull it open. Facing me is a rotund, bearded clerk sitting at a massive desk strewn with papers. He glances at me. Behind him, with his back to the door, a younger clerk operates an electrical telegraph machine. The room smells of cigarette smoke and unwashed laborers. Both men wear skullcaps. Is this my new employer, I ask myself, feeling a pang of regret and wariness.

"Looking for work?" the older clerk asks impatiently in Russian, looking up again at me in the way a practiced pickpocket sizes up a bumpkin.

"I was instructed to come," I say, giving my name.

"Ah, let me look at my registry." He pulls open a thick, alphabetized ledger.

"Yakov Leibovich, you say? From where?"

"Navahrudak."

"Near Minsk?"

"Yes."

"Wait, wait. Hmmm, I don't see any Leibovich."

"But I have a letter from Mr. Varshavsky."

"Varshavsky?" The clerk's eyebrows arch as if I've uttered an obscenity. The telegraph operator swivels to see who has invoked this name. I set my satchel on the floor and reach beneath my coat to hand over the envelope.

The clerk leans back in his chair, revealing a belly the size of a washtub. He strokes his beard, adjusts his skullcap, and stifles a belch as he reads. I stand immobilized, my heart pounding. Is there a mistake? Does this man even know who Varshavsky is? Has Varshavsky forgotten about our arrangement? Will he summon the police to escort me to the nearest army barracks or to a prosecutor's office to be charged with desertion?

"I see you are the Chosen One, Leibovich," the clerk smiles as he switches to Yiddish and flashes a mocking grin. But his tone suddenly turns dark. "Do you think you will be treated like royalty here? We have no royalty in this business, Leibovich, just people willing to earn every kopek."

"I will earn everything, sir."

"Good, because there won't be any earnings except for exemplary service. Mister Varshavsky might see something promising in you, Leibovich, but you will have to prove yourself. Do you understand?"

"I will, sir."

"Good. Keep the letter, you might need it. I'm Kaminsky. This is Lifshits." He jerks his thumb backward toward the telegraph operator, whose face remains obscured. "Take off your coat and hat, we have work to do. I'm expecting recruits every hour today."

I am on guard; only my father addresses me so imperiously. My impulse is to defend myself, but I know the wiser course is deference.

When the clerk stands, I can see he is built like an ox, all muscle, even beneath the washtub. Kaminsky's shoulders, chest, and arms are solid. A large samovar rests on his desk amid piles of loose papers, ledgers, books, rubber stamps, and a cash box.

He escorts me to a storage room where I hang my coat and hat and deposit my satchel. Kaminsky guides me to a chair beside his desk. Sitting down, I realize how weary I am, and wonder if I will have enough focus to commit his instructions to memory.

"Well, Leibovich. Here is what you need to know. Remember everything. This is only a recruiting office. The main depot is on the outskirts of the city next to the railroad. You passed it coming in from Kiev on the train. Did you see it? Never mind. Later, you'll go there and find Benatar who runs the depot. He's a Sephardic Jew, an unusual man, who knows draft animals of all kinds: horses, oxen, buffalo, mules. And he knows how to maintain a wagon. If you treat the horses well, they will treat you well. If you abuse them, well . . . just don't abuse them. Understood?"

"Of course."

"Good. Now, the letter says you work in accounting."

"Not really."

"No? Don't worry, I will give you all the necessary information. You can count and write numbers, yes?"

"Yes."

"Good. Not many people I see are literate, so it's a good start. See this ledger? We keep a record of everything we are hauling, everything. What we pick up goes here. Every cart and wagon has a number. What we deliver goes here. Every train of wagons has a trainmaster. He works with our network of buyers. You have to count each item we carry. It's just numbers, Leibovich. You can count? You'll be fine. If I pick up a cartload of fodder, for example, I put it here, with the date and the place. And when it's delivered, I put it here, with the new date and the location. You see? Don't lose track of the calendar or where you are, or there will be hell raining down on your head. They can accuse us of fraud. There is nothing more they would like than to find evidence of fraud, understand? We are Jews, you know."

"Yes, of course."

Kaminsky is issuing directives so rapidly that I must force myself to pay attention and absorb. I can feel my anxiety spike.

"So if we're hauling something in wooden cases or crates, you put down how many. If you don't know what it is or can't see everything, just put an estimate, a good and honest estimate. But listen carefully, Leibovich. Never overestimate what we haul; do you understand? Never overestimate. We don't want to be delivering less than we say we're hauling, for obvious reasons. We Jews live in a bubble of suspicion."

"Yes, yes, of course."

"Good. You will be an accountant and a teamster at the same time. Don't tell anyone, but the pay is better. You get paid once a month in cash. Don't squander it on vodka. I don't smell any on your breath. Keep it that way."

"How many carts and wagons are in a train, sir?"

"Scores, sometimes hundreds. It goes for miles. The trainmaster and his deputy will tell you everything. Usually, you start at the front and count while all the wagons pass; sometimes you have to count in the camp at random. Don't lose track. You shouldn't, because all the carts are numbered. There might be two accountants, and in that case, you'll split the work. That's up to Benatar. The trains carry food for you, and there are cooks. It won't be like a Sabbath meal at home served by your *bubbe*. Was your grandmother a good cook? Mine was."

I am about to answer, but he doesn't seem interested.

"It will fill your belly, that's all that counts. You won't starve, trust me. Any questions?"

"Mr. Kaminsky, sir, I've heard there might be thieves."

"Thieves? If a teamster steals anything, we shoot him! Simple!"

I must have looked puzzled or perturbed, for Kaminsky asks, "What do you think we should do to a thief, Leibovich?"

"I meant if the train of wagons is attacked by a band of thieves along the route."

"Oh, marauders. Don't worry. True, there are thieves everywhere, but each train has an escort of mounted Cossacks assigned by the Ministry of War. They are well-armed, ruthless, and know what they are doing, believe me. They will deal with bandits quickly, I assure you. They know what to do, and don't hesitate for a second. But we also give you a knife, you know, partly to protect yourself, unless you already have one. Did you bring one?"

"I don't own one, sir."

"You don't own one. Well, okay, Benatar will give you one, as well as a sheath. Keep it hidden, but use it when you need to. Do you understand? Take charge! Be a man! What else do you need to know?"

"I do have one more question, sir."

"Out with it."

"Where do these trains of wagons go? How many days' travel?"

"Listen, Leibovich, where we go is a secret. A secret! You understand?"

"Yes, yes, you can trust me."

"I can trust you? How do I know that? You've been here less than an hour!"

I look at him sternly. "Because I am a man of my word, Mr. Kaminsky."

"Fine, it's okay." He lowers his voice, looks at me directly, and raises a chubby finger toward my nose, "If you open your mouth about what I'm about to tell you, I will personally drive a knife into your bowel and slit you open for a vulture's meal, you understand?"

"Yes, sir."

"Then listen carefully." Kaminsky leans even closer. "This firm — we call it 'the Partnership' — has been awarded a big contract, very big, from the Commissariat of the Imperial Army. The army is preparing for something, Leibovich, and we must be ready to supply them. Do you know how big the Imperial Army is? I'm certain you don't; no idea, right?"

I venture a guess, "One-hundred-thousand men?"

"Hah! Let me tell you. Forty-eight divisions of infantry, eight brigades of rifles, forty-eight brigades of artillery, seventeen divisions of cavalry, engineers, field hospitals — more than a million men in all! You see how big? A million men, Leibovich! Right now, many of these divisions and brigades are preparing to leave their barracks. I can't say how many. Never mind, they all have their own quartermaster. But the supply system has been in complete chaos in recent years. It's an utter mess, terribly managed. The Commissariat is corrupt and broken; ask any soldier, they know. So, when the army moves, it's our job to follow behind with everything they need: food grains and biscuits, ammunition, boots, coats, tents, fodder for the animals, medical supplies, extra bayonets, tools — everything except women, you understand?"

"Yes. I understand, but . . ."

"Quiet, Leibovich. Have you seen the newspapers?"

"I've seen the headlines about the Balkans, if that's what you mean."

"Have you ever been to Roumania, Leibovich?"

"I'm not sure. I mean, I'm not sure where it is exactly."

"No, just a boy from Minsk, just a half-baked Jew. Don't worry, when you meet Benatar, you can ask for a map. He doesn't hand them out like candy. If you are intelligent and he trusts you, he might give you one. And you seem intelligent to me. You are not far from Roumania right now, Leibovich. Do you realize? When you get a map, you'll see it."

"Is it the Balkans?"

"Leibovich, please. You are sworn to secrecy. Don't even mention places outside of Russia. If you read a newspaper you can trust, you can see for yourself what's going on. I'm not sure how many you can trust though." Kaminsky lowers his voice again, "The Slavic Christians are revolting. The Turks are brutal, killing everyone in sight. It's a bloodbath in Bulgaria, a bloodbath. Read and you'll understand. The Tsar is going to put an end to it once and for all."

He reaches into the cash box and hands me two roubles, then a white form where he has written my name. "We're done here. Hire a carriage to the Greger depot on Stepova Street," he instructs. "Whatever you do, stay clear of the Greek neighborhood south of us. The Greeks are killers. They get drunk and attack Jews. When you get to the depot, ask for Benatar and give him this form, you understand? He will get you some food and a bed. You'll need it because you're going to be working hard. You look like you could use some sleep. Go."

"Yes, sir." I gather my things, nod to him, and make my exit. But before I look for a carriage, I steal some time to meander along the streets of Odessa to take in the city. It is huge and alive. I happen upon an establishment I did not know existed. It looks like a bookstore, but all the materials in the window and on the shelves are periodicals and newspapers, journals of every sort. It seems to be an idea shop, for it sells news of the world, commentary on politics and the arts, even journals of engineering, trade, and farming. The shelves burst with ideas, and the variety is astonishing. I count publications from more than twenty countries in a dozen languages — Asian, Slavic, Middle-Eastern, and European languages, including Yiddish, Hebrew, French, English, Greek, and German. There are even technical and medical journals. Facing the wooden display rack, whose angled slots reveal the dominant news or essay on each front page, I spot a Yiddish paper with the chilling headline, "Horror in Bulgaria."

For a few kopeks, I procure a copy of *The Advocate*, a Hebrew newspaper I've been curious about but never read. It favors the Haskalah, the same Jewish Enlightenment that my father denounces. Although my family is traditionalist in our religious observance, just as Reb Epshtein is, we do not adhere to the teachings of any narrow Hasidic sect. My father is skeptical of all the reformers pulling European Jews in different directions, but also of certain Hasidic strains he says are based more on rabbinical personality cult than Judaic doctrine. As I've said, he believes the most fervent Hasidic rabbis too often popularize and cheapen Kabbalah by selling its mystical aspects to the ignorant and superstitious masses. Only Minsk's Chabad sect, with its intellectual approach to the Jewish faith, wins my father's grudging respect; but we do not count ourselves as Chabadniks.

I've heard Father sneeringly dismiss *The Advocate's* view, which is aimed at the modern Jew who embraces the Enlightenment. But I buy the paper anyway, as a quiet act of defiance. I also find a copy of *The Dawn*. One of my private joys in recent months has been reading the essays of Peretz Smolenskin, *The Dawn's* editor. He chastises both the Hasidim and the Enlightenment assimilationists for undermining the unity of the Jewish people. Smolenskin is also a novelist. That is how I learned about him. I borrowed one of his books from a friend at the *beit midrash*, passed along furtively, and when I finished reading the final page, I realized for the first time that a novel can be at once mocking, dark, original, and comedic. It was a revelation.

As I hand my coins to the news vendor, I ask the impossible. "Do you carry *Die Allgemeine Zeitung des Judenthums*?"

"Of course!" the man bellows, his belly shaking beneath a stained vest. The incredulous look on his face asks, "Would a reputable news vendor in the great and cosmopolitan city of Odessa fail to carry the premier Jewish journal published in German?"

I joyously fold all three newspapers into my satchel, feeling as if I have just acquired a box of the most delectable assorted chocolates. This will likely be my last chance to nourish my mind for many months. The newspapers may fray and yellow, but if I can keep my personal journal safe, it won't matter. My journal is my idea shop.

Even in the cold, the Partnership's depot emits odors of manure, burlap, and feed grains. One of Benatar's assistants grabs my white form and tells me to wait. Close by are separate sheltered pens holding draft horses and oxen, mules and chickens. I peer inside the dark, low-ceilinged barn. It is a vast building with thick posts holding up the roof. Large wagons and smaller carts sit on the straw floor, along with extra wheels. Tools of every sort rest against the walls: pitchforks, axes, saws, and hammers, along with pulleys and hay hooks. In a corner that opens to the outdoors, two smiths in aprons work at a forge. Canvas covers hang from hooks on the wall, and dozens of empty and half-full gunny sacks line the perimeter. The assistant directs me to a spartan but clean wooden dormitory, heated by a single wood stove. The cots look thin and fragile.

I learn quickly that the depot's master, Binyamin Benatar, is a force of nature. On my second day, Benatar delivers a stern welcome address to the latest group of teamsters.

"When your axle breaks," he declares, glaring at us, "the train does not stop. Understand this. The train does not stop. So if you don't want to die frozen, lost, and hungry on a lonely road in the middle of nowhere, I suggest you pay close attention. When I am done with you, you'll know how to fix it and catch up with your mates."

I befriend Temkin, his deputy, and learn that Benatar served during the Crimean campaign in the Imperial Army's Division of Intendance Transport, the overseer of supply trains run by the army and its subcontractors. Benatar knows every hurdle and pitfall of feeding and clothing an army on the move. There are dozens of teamsters, and it is Benatar's job — indeed, his passion — to impart every skill and nuance so that we are prepared to an exacting standard. As I think about the task ahead, I realize that the commissary officers in each Imperial Army division will be at the mercy of Benatar's proficiency as an instructor. He is demanding, impatient, and occasionally short-tempered, but also impressive in the breadth of his knowledge. Temkin whispers to me, "All the recruits fear him, but he knows how to instill confidence, you'll see."

And see I did. He instills confidence by requiring repetition, insisting that we master each skill, no matter how long it takes — repairing wheels and harnesses, sewing canvas coverings, swapping axles, righting an overturned wagon, feeding and watering the horses, properly securing cargo. We do everything again and again until Benatar is satisfied; often, he is not.

By my estimation, roughly a third of the teamsters in the depot are Jews. The faces of the rest look no different from those of the soldiers on the train platform in Kiev, though some look much older and wear the clothing of peasants. Beyond the barn and dormitory, the depot opens onto a huge staging area with its own rail siding. Two enormous warehouses sit on the edge of the property, both with sliding doors that admit wagons and carts. Each day, cargo trains and straining wagons enter the depot to deliver war materiel and other crated goods to the warehouses. Other wagons and carts arrive empty, waiting to be packed. More wagons are being built inside the barn. The arriving carts must be repaired, the animals fed and watered, and supplies inventoried and packed for the journey ahead. We do all of this.

It surprises me, but after two weeks at the depot, I begin to feel at home with the physical work, the sweat, even the pronounced smell of the animals. I have never experienced any of it. I poured my youth into the joy, mystery, and textual tedium of a dialogue with God, while privately consuming the secular ideas of Smolenskin, Goethe, Darwin, and Voltaire. For my entire youth, I knew almost nothing of manual labor. It is tedious and difficult at times in camp, to be sure; but it is also gratifying to overcome my awkwardness and begin feeling my physical strength. As my musculature improves, so does my confidence.

The canvas cots are pushed so close together that the only way to climb in is to slide up from the foot of the bed. I fashion a pillow by rolling up my frock coat. One night, I dream I am floating inside the *beit midrash*, above the benches, listening to an overheated debate while embracing a Torah scroll. As I float along, the scroll magically transforms from a cylinder of stiff wood and parchment into supple flesh. I am whispering prayers and burying my face between a woman's breasts. I pull away and look. It is Rivkah, staring through those magnetic eyes. She asks, "Will you return?"

I have been avoiding a response to Rivkah's letter, not knowing what to say, but the dream nudges me to finally respond. Despite my concern that Rivkah will not forgive me for what I have done to Avram, I cling to the thin hope that I have misjudged the situation. That is the power of my regard for her. I want her companionship and feel compelled to convey at least a hint of my allegiance.

Dear Rivkah,

My natural inclination is to address you with all the respect you are due, yet, as you can see, I have taken to heart your request that we address each other with less formality.

As I am working each day to prepare for my new duties with the supply company, I am unable to spend as much time as I would like describing my strange new surroundings. I find that I am adapting well to them, however.

I am pleased to have the information from you that your brother is now attached to the Fourteenth Infantry Division, and that he senses his new life might be a welcome change from the difficult circumstances in which he found himself in Navahrudak. I pray for his safety and wish only to have the good fortune of encountering him one day soon.

Rest assured that my memory of you grows stronger each day.

Fondly,
Yakov

With the letter in hand, I seek out Temkin, the wheelwright and carpenter who has served at Benatar's side for years, to ask how I can post a letter to a friend at home. To my astonishment, Temkin explodes.

"You think you are someone special, Leibovich? You are no better than anyone else!" he spits. "No one sends letters outside of this farm! Not you, not anyone. Spies are everywhere. You tell someone what goes on here and they talk to someone else, and before you know it, everyone knows where the supply trains are; even the Turks know. We don't talk about anything. Benatar explained this, didn't he? You want to send a letter? No, no letters! Don't ask again."

Listening to Temkin's diatribe leaves me despondent. It also tells me that knowledge of my arrangement with Varshavsky has spread far beyond Kaminsky's dusty storefront office in Odessa. This is the only explanation I have for Temkin's suddenly frigid reception. Does everyone know my business? Does everyone know why I have an arrangement with Varshavsky? Defeated and confused, I fold the letter to Rivkah and hide it at the bottom of my satchel.

By the end of my first month, it seems that every hired hand in camp is itching to begin whatever we are being so rigorously trained for, and morale begins to suffer. All of us are weary of repeating the same tasks. Whatever dangers might lie ahead have become nearly irrelevant. I am as deflated as any of the teamsters, watching the warehouses fill with supplies and new horses enter the pens, while we tend empty wagons and shovel manure in the rain.

Then, on the first of April, as if sensing the limit of our collective frustration, Benatar summons everyone — the teamsters, wheelwrights, warehousemen, and trainmasters. He stands majestically on the bed of a wagon, stares everyone into silence, and speaks with characteristic verve.

"The Imperial Army of the South is massing one hundred miles from here, at Kishinev in Moldova," Benatar begins, shouting to reach the back rows. We glance at each other, noting silently that he has broken his own rule and divulged a specific location. "This is no longer a secret to Russia's enemies. The Emperor is happy to let the world see the Imperial Army and to fear it, as they should. As you must all know, the reason for our work here is that the Turks are slaughtering Christians across the Balkans, and the Emperor is determined to protect these Slavs, our brothers."

His neck veins are bulging, and his hands slice through the warm air.

"So, we expect the Imperial Army to move into Roumania soon. Beginning tomorrow, every man will be assigned a wagon." He emphasizes the words "every man" and "tomorrow" by raising his voice to a fearsome pitch. "Every wagon will have a number and be assigned a complement of supplies. When you load up at the warehouses, make sure the accounting clerk has a record of what you're carrying. Whatever it is — fodder, rifles, boots, medical supplies — no one moves without an accounting. We have two clerks for this train. Litvak will take the even-numbered wagons and Leibovich the odd-numbered ones. Make sure they do their jobs. When the wagons are loaded and the supplies accounted for, we will move out. Prepare yourselves, men! And may God be with each one of you."

I am finally assigned a wagon, Number 17, and two horses. It is newly built and has a strong wood frame rising from the bed, which will hold medical supplies in wooden crates and leather pouches. An oiled tarpaulin will keep everything dry. At least, that is the hope. It has been a rainy spring, and I expect the tarpaulin to be an essential piece of equipment.

I examine my horses carefully, now knowing the signs of breakdown and ill health; but both animals seem strong and unscarred. I stroke them on the hips and muzzle, touching them in a way I could not have touched any animal during my days in Navahrudak. Horses no longer frighten me. To my delight, I find them companionable, even endearing. Examining the wagon's structure, the hitch, and the wheels, I recognize that I know my way around the equipment and feel a surge of self-assurance. The cautious young rabbinical student who stepped off the train at Odessa Station is a receding memory. My world is different now, and so am I.

In two days, all the wagons are packed at the warehouses. Our trainmaster, a taciturn veteran named Stepan, inspects Number 17 with an air of intimidating exactitude. I wait for his verdict. He straightens up, brushing off his weathered hands, and addresses me with a commanding expression.

"We don't trust just anyone with medical supplies, Leibovich," he says. "Guard these with your life, because someone else's might depend on it."

I promise him, and in doing so, I also promise myself. If I am going to be a teamster, I intend to be a good one.

Two dozen Cossack guards, impressive horsemen armed beyond all reason, ride into the depot, their faces bronzed by the sun. They make their own camp and keep to themselves.

Early the next morning, the order goes out to hitch up the horses and oxen. By midday, Benatar is shouting at us, "Let's go! Let's go!" The dusty chaos of the depot gives way to an orderly line. Everyone knows our destination is the Moldovan capital of Kishinev, not far from the Roumanian frontier. Nothing is a secret any longer.

On the day before we are to arrive at Kishinev, the Cossacks suddenly direct all the wagons off the main road into a flat, fallow farm field, wild with untended grasses and flowers. Russia's Army of the South needs to pass us on its expedited march to the Roumanian border. Standing on the seat of my wagon, with a perfect view of the road stretching forward and backward, I watch row after row of soldiers and horses, an entire division, fill the air with dust, song, and exhortations. My horses snort and pull at the grass. I scan the faces, searching for a soldier I might know, Tsipershtein perhaps. I recall the contours of Avram Eizenberg's face to see whether anyone looks remotely like him.

Unexpectedly, a company dominated by Jews marches past. I have never seen so many Jews in uniform. It is jarring and strange. I can see their ritual undergarments, the knotted fringes peeking out from their belts. Some have sidelocks tucked behind their ears. Many of them have removed their forage caps in the heat, revealing their skullcaps. How do they exist? Do they pray before battle in Hebrew? I wonder.

After the infantry, specialists march past: artillery, cavalry, sappers, engineers, telegraph operators, railroad builders, and bridge-builders. Then, the field hospital teams march by, and any romance of war shatters. The sheer size of the medical corps — thousands in uniform, including

Jews — reminds me that some of the marching soldiers will be wounded or maimed, and some will land in shallow graves, or be left for the vultures.

When the Tsar himself arrives at Kishinev to inspect his forces, the darker reality of our situation descends on us all. He declares war against the Ottoman Turks on April 24th. The Eighth Corps marches swiftly across the border at Ungheni, and our massive supply train falls in behind. The road is rutted from the passage of the heavy artillery. At the Prut River, our wagons cross an elaborate, gleaming steel bridge, completed only three weeks earlier under the direction of a French engineer. A plaque shines with his name on it: Gustave Eiffel. Fully a quarter of the wagons and carts on our train are empty. The Partnership's network of agents in Roumania, many of them Jewish merchants and middlemen, is procuring local grains, dried meat, and biscuits to be loaded at Bucharest.

Beyond the Prut River, the tableland of eastern Roumania is lush with fields of buckwheat, interrupted only by a few stands of forest. Our wagons skirt the Carpathian Mountains, whose small rivers enter the plain of Wallachia and feed into the Danube. Grateful for the horses lashed to the front of my wagon, I give each of them a nickname. They are my closest companions now; we depend on each other. One I call Yitzchak, after the Kabbalist mystic Yitzchak Luria, and the other I call Zalman, after Reb Schneur Zalman of Liadi, founder of the Chabad sect. From my bench atop the supply wagon, I exhort my team — "Come on Yitzy!" "Let's go, Zalman!" — and when it's time to unhitch, I find myself whispering endearments to them. A whip rests in a holder beside the wagon bench, but I never resort to it and don't think I ever could.

In our camp outside of Bucharest, I hear two startling pieces of information: first, the Russian Army is sending only two-hundred-thousand soldiers to fight, one-fifth of its full strength, and second, the Turks have superior weapons to those of Imperial Russia.

"Superior to the Imperial Army's?" I ask our trainmaster, startled and confused.

Stepan laughs and shakes his head at my naiveté. "The Turks have been spending money, boy. We still have outdated bronze artillery, but they bought Krupp steel breech-loaders from Germany. It was in the newspapers, which you probably don't read. And the Turks went to America and bought a deadly .45-caliber rifle for their infantry. It's called the Peabody-Martini. It has a much longer range, something like two-thousand yards. In Russia, we still use the old Berdan, which is nothing more than a converted musket."

I embarrass myself again by asking whether our wagon train can supply two-hundred-thousand soldiers. Now, the trainmaster and his assistants laugh out loud.

"In our train alone? Do you think this is the only supply train in Roumania supporting our army? We have more than three-hundred-thirty wagons and carts in this one train, Leibovich. Multiply that ten times, then you have enough supplies for two-hundred-thousand men at war. "

I am struck anew by this immense undertaking. For the first time, I consider the fact that victory for Imperial Russia is not assured. I think of my parents and the worry they must feel reading news of the looming battles in Bulgaria. I am not anxious, knowing I will remain far from the front lines, but I know they must be afraid for me.

I come across a Cossack who is about to ride to the village of Cornice and is willing to help me without raising any alarms. A month ago, I wouldn't have risked angering my employer by trying to send a letter. Now, I feel a calm assurance in my abilities and inner conviction. I hand the Cossack a handful of kopeks to post two letters for me, the one I had written to Rivkah at the depot in Odessa, and a hastily penned note to my parents:

Dearest Parents,

All is well, thanks be to God. I dare not mention where we are except that it is near a lake and under the stars. The days are hot and the nights cool. We have seen many soldiers pass, and we will trail behind at some point. I have two horses and a wagon full of medical supplies to manage. The horses are cooperative. I have done my accounting and filled out my ledger. The trainmaster is knowledgeable. The other teamsters come from all walks of life. Many are Jews, and some are my age. I say my morning, afternoon, and evening prayers, and so far, we have kept the Sabbath, and the kosher rules as best we can. But I do not know where we will go from here and what the conditions will be. I am not afraid, and you should not be afraid for me. I often recite the Birkat Hagomel: "Blessed are You, Lord our God, ruler of the world, who rewards the undeserving with goodness, and who has rewarded me with goodness."

Your loving son,
Yakov.

After a supper of barley soup and biscuits, I wrap myself in my coat to ward off the chill and watch the stars glimmer above through the wispy clouds. I pull out my journal, moved to write about how this work, this place, and this experience have fulfilled me in unexpected ways. It is a prayer of sorts:

> *"In these moments of serenity, I feel the true paradox of God — both the empty space of the universe and the manifestations of a Divine Force that lives within all things and inside the great emptiness. I see more clearly now why Kabbalah does not describe God merely as a heavenly parent creating and guiding all with His hands, but also as the Infinite Light, Ohr Ein Sof, the formless and transcendent essence. Strangely, here in the middle of what seems like nowhere, I am feeling this essence, if not seeing it. I feel closer to the Ohr Ein Sof than ever. I must tell Reb Epshtein that I no longer think it is the wisest course to wait for the arrival of the Messiah in flesh and blood or some other corporeal guise. Forgive me, O Lord, for this is surely sacrilege, according to some. Instead, I have concluded that I must prepare myself to help create a Messianic Age that will reside in each human soul. This experience in a new land was meant to be! It is an adventure like none before. All the commentaries in the beit midrash have not prepared me for this journey of the spirit. I feel stronger and wiser this night than I have ever felt. Thanks be to God."*

Carefully, I return my journal to the bottom of my satchel and store the bag beneath the tarpaulin behind my wagon bench. It is a good habit, this housekeeping task, for in minutes, a rainstorm moves in and begins pelting us. It only gets worse as the minutes pass into the darkness of night, forcing me to huddle beneath a damp piece of canvas on a bed of grass under my wagon. I cannot sleep under these dispiriting conditions. In my misery, I lose all sense of decorum and curse God — not the formless and mystical Ohr Ein Sof but the demanding and vengeful Father whom I have awed and feared most of my young life.

5

It is the 16ᵗʰ of July in the year 1877 by the Christian calendar and 5637 by the Hebrew one. I have now been away from home for half a year. The long train of wagons to which I am assigned, having crossed the treeless expanse south of Bucharest, rattles across a reinforced pontoon bridge at a leisurely pace to reach the Bulgarian shore. I walk the wooden planks, pulling Yitzy and Zalman forward gently so as not to spook them as we cross the slow-moving Danube River. Beneath the surface, sturgeon, pike, and carp wander. Above, geese and grebes gracefully patrol the shoreline. The air in my lungs is clean and sweet, and the sun is warm. If a war is being fought on the opposite shore, no one on this bridge would know it.

Looking out at the Bulgarian landscape, beyond the phalanx of Russian guards puffing on cigarettes at the edge of the riverbank town of Sistova, I see a hilly and forested terrain, a welcome change from the monotonously flat and empty plains of Roumania. Somewhere in these woods, I imagine, my medical supplies will save a life. I wonder whether Avram Eizenberg is here already and whether he will be spared, and that makes me think of his sister and whether I will be spared her wrath.

I stop to inquire with the guards about the whereabouts of Russia's Fourteenth Infantry Division. "Ah, the Fourteenth," replies a white-bearded veteran, a voluble soldier whose eyebrows flutter as he speaks. "The Fourteenth was the first across, in late June. Twelve battalions, seventy companies, twenty-five thousand men under Dragomirov, and that crazy officer Skobelev. The man wears a white uniform and rides a white stallion — I don't know how he isn't cut down immediately. I was in the Fourteenth myself, until they ordered me to stay here to guard the bridge. I do what I'm told. The Fourteenth is a strong division, led by skilled generals, I'm proud to say."

My eyes open wider. "Do you know Avram Eizenberg in the Fourteenth? Or Yisrael Tsipershtein?"

"Never heard of them. There were some Yids like you, from Minsk, in the Second Brigade, First Regiment, and Fifth Battalion, I think. Didn't know any of them or fight with them. Don't know what wave they crossed under, or if they're even alive. They were good though. I heard the Jews were tough. You want to know? Find Captain Nikolayev. I remember he led them, some of the Yids at least."

I ask about casualties in the battle to cross the Danube, and he tells me three-hundred Russians died and five-hundred were wounded.

"Heroes of Russia, every one of them. You will see some of the wounded from other battles coming north on the road you are about to travel. We've seen many."

It is a sobering recounting. I wonder if, like my father, Avram was wounded and sent home already. It would be a blessing. But in a division of 25,000, it seems only remotely possible. May God help me if he was killed.

"Where is the Fourteenth now?" I ask. "Do you know?"

"They marched to Tirnova, but they could be anywhere now. Crossing the Balkans or in Constantinople, for all I know!"

I thank the soldier and share a chocolate I picked up in Roumania. Our train rolls on toward the town of Byala, thirty miles to the southeast. We will deliver a small amount of supplies there, then advance deeper into territory once controlled by the Ottoman Turks.

The Bulgarian roads are in far worse condition than those in Roumania. Just as the guard predicted, we encounter ambulance wagons heading north with scores of wounded and sick soldiers. I cannot help but stare. Some are bandaged or wear splints; others are prone and lifeless without visible wounds, but weak, perhaps from gastrointestinal disease or malaria. I watch each wagon pass to assess the condition of the soldiers until I cannot look anymore. One of the wounded boys wears sidelocks tucked behind his ear and a skull cap on his head. It is not Avram. His arm is in a sling, but where there should have been a hand, there is nothing but a bloody stump. It is a train of misery on its way to the bridge, then a field hospital north of the Danube, and eventually back home to Odessa — if they make it that far. They are suffering, and I cannot understand why God allows it.

After only a day, the supply train moves south toward Tirnova, where I hear disappointing news: the Fourteenth has moved on, dispatched to a place called Plevna. From the opposite direction, the wounded keep coming.

"Everyone is marching to Plevna," an officer tells me, forcing a stream of cigarette smoke through his nostrils. "The Turks have taken the city with an army in the tens of thousands — forty to fifty thousand, I heard. Word is, they marched through the night while our forces rested. Damn them. Complete incompetence. Now, the Turks have dug in. It's not good for us, especially because their rifles are lethal at long distances. A bad situation."

I ask why Plevna matters.

"Our flank is exposed. They have enough soldiers at Plevna to attack any column of ours heading to the Balkan passes. So we have to crush them. There's no choice. And we will, we will. The Turks are exhausted. But it will take time, and bayonets, I'm afraid."

As I unload medical supplies at a sprawling field hospital, I see ambulance wagons entering the town from the south. The soldiers lie on the wagon beds, wincing and moaning with each turn of the wheels along the macadam. A Jewish doctor hops down from one of the wagons to help bring stretchers into the field hospital. He looks drawn, weary, with his skullcap askew and his pants stained with blood.

When he exits the hospital, our eyes meet.

"Have you seen the Fourteenth Infantry Division?" I ask.

"They're at Plevna, like everyone else."

"Have they been fighting?"

"I don't know. I believe they just arrived. I know one of their battalions was assigned to help the Sixteenth block supply lines at Lovtcha."

"By chance do you know Avram Eizenberg?"

"Who?"

"A soldier, Avram Eizenberg."

"No, unless he's dead. I only know the dead and wounded. Don't ask me about the living."

I stop asking questions. This is positive news though. If Avram was killed, this doctor would know it, wouldn't he?

Disgorging our supplies at Tirnova takes two days. I am barely able to sleep, there is so much work. The accounting is exhausting. I have to search for wagons being unloaded, then race to note the items being delivered. It is impossible to be everywhere at once, and chaos rules. However, I take Kaminsky at his word: if you don't know, estimate.

When our wagons are empty, we must return to the Danube's north bank for fresh supplies. Soon before departing, I hear a barrage of raw swearing a dozen wagons ahead. Stepan and an officer of the Imperial

Army are engaged in an intense argument. Hands are waved and voices raised. I step down from my wagon to see what the commotion is about. The army is demanding that Stepan assign twenty of our covered wagons to transport wounded soldiers north to Sistova. The trainmaster is willing, but only if a doctor accompanies the patients. "We are teamsters, not nurses," Stepan sneers. The officer barks, insisting that all the doctors are needed at the front, and the wounded will survive the trip. A more senior officer arrives and threatens to inform the commissariat in St. Petersburg of the Partnership's refusal to transport men he calls, "heroes of the war to liberate the Slavs."

Stepan throws up his hands and relents. "Some of these men will die without a doctor," he grumbles. The officer shrugs.

My wagon is among those chosen to carry casualties. I should have known. Stretcher-bearers place six wounded soldiers on the bed of Number 17, along with extra canteens and a few rations. Four are clearly in fragile condition, conscious but in obvious pain. Three wear bandages that look as if they have not been changed in days. The odor inside the wagon is pronounced. I cannot tell whether I am sensing unwashed bodies or the onset of gangrene, or both.

One of the wounded resists, telling the stretcher-bearers, "I'm not riding with a Yid!"

"You don't get to choose," an officer says. "They're all Yids."

I forgive this soldier. I forgive all of them. How can I not forgive them? I am supposed to be wearing the boots and uniform of a soldier myself. I should have faced the danger they faced. Instead, I am a teamster. The only assaults I have faced are the pungent excretions from Yitzy and Zalman.

The deep ruts on the road out of Tirnova seem to have no effect on my cargo. The soldiers sleep. That evening, as the wind picks up and clouds sweep in, the temperature drops. Stepan tells us the train will continue through the night unless a storm kicks up. I can see that one of the soldiers in my wagon, still on a stretcher, shakes with chills. I see the face of a boy my own age. He is bandaged around the stomach, and his skin is pale, almost translucent. I take a wool blanket from a bag behind my seat and offer it to one of the men still capable of reaching out.

"Put this on him," I say.

Just before dawn, the train stops to give the horses a rest. We have made good time; the field hospital at Sistova is only two hours away. My back aches. I grab my canteen and climb down to check on my passengers.

As I peer inside the wagon, one of the soldiers says, "Vadim is dead." He turns his head toward the boy on the stretcher with the stomach wound.

"What do you mean?" I ask in momentary confusion.

"He's dead. You can look."

"How do you know?"

"I know."

I still don't understand. He was alive during the night. I saw him. The boy was alive. I loosen the bolts on the wagon's rear gate and let it down, then hoist myself up. The boy's face is a pasty gray, his expression fixed. I kneel, then lean down to touch the side of his face with the back of my hand. His skin is cold, and I pull away quickly.

"The papers are in his coat," the soldier tells me, staring blankly toward the back of the wagon into the breaking dawn. "I fought with him at Shipka Pass. He was a good soldier, brave."

I glance again and pull the blanket up to cover the frozen expression.

"I'm sorry," I say.

"Never mind," his comrade replies. I can see this soldier's misty eyes. His face is fixed, and he trembles. He will weep for his friend as we go on. He doesn't need my permission.

I walk back to the front of the wagon and run my hand down Yitzy's muzzle, blinking away my own tears. This is war; did I need to remind myself? This is what happens when arrogant men miscalculate. I clamber onto the wagon seat and pull the journal and pen from my satchel. The dawn's clouds are feathered, and just enough light remains to compose an entry:

> *I am driving a team of horses in exchange for a chance to survive this war. And God willing, I will survive. I have to wonder though, where is the young soldier who took my place? In which trench does Avram Eizenberg sit tonight, or which grave? What kind of chance will he have to survive and return home? Will he end up like the boy named Vadim, whose body lies in my wagon and whose friend cannot hide his grief? Or will he return home a whole human to a grateful sister and a loving mother? If he does not, what will I say to Rivkah Eizenberg?"*

We cross the Danube six times in three months, with no end to the cycle in sight. Re-stocking in Roumania turns noticeably difficult. The prices of goods rise, and the quality declines. Some of the hay hauled to our encampment at Alexandria, twenty miles north of the Danube, rots on delivery. A sampling of the dried meat nearly goes rancid. The replacement boots have soles half as thick as the original boots issued to Russian soldiers. It is hard to know the condition of the fresh medical supplies hoisted in wooden crates and leather pouches onto my wagon. Whatever their quality, all of it will be needed, for the war does not seem to be going as the Tsar and his generals had planned.

In early fall, we prepare for a seventh passage south across the Danube. Word in camp is that, despite the well-known resiliency of the Russian soldier, two Imperial Army attacks on the Ottoman stronghold at Plevna have failed. I begin to accept the inescapable: this war will grind on for many months. The Tsar is mobilizing more Russian divisions, according to Stepan. None of this is a good sign, and nothing in this harsh new reality suggests that I will see my family or Rivkah Eizenberg before spring.

From what the Cossack scouts tell us, Russia's only option is to surround the garrison at Plevna and starve the Turks out. We prepare to go to Plevna for our next supply drop. Although it sounds dangerous, delivering supplies directly to the front lines does not frighten me, not now. I have developed a protective shell of confidence. My instincts for self-preservation are sharper, my anxiety more contained. I focus exclusively on each day's challenges.

Our wagons depart Alexandria on October 18th and cross the Danube at Nikopol, directly north of Plevna. There is no pontoon bridge. Instead, individual ferries carry the wagons across, as a cool wind sweeps the Danube from the west. The summer birds have departed. Plevna is a two-day ride on a road that hugs the Osam River. Tomorrow, we will halt in a thinly wooded area five miles north of Grivitza, an enclave held by the Turks, which lies just outside of Plevna. Tonight, then, may be our last night sleeping without interruptions.

The next morning, as I quietly chant the morning prayers, Stepan runs up to my wagon. "Leibovich! Hey! They need medical supplies!"

"Where?" I ask in a near-whisper, as if the enemy listens from behind every tree.

"At Lovtcha. I'll send a Cossack with you. It's not far, but you'll have to wind around the edge of town to avoid the front lines."

"Is it dangerous?"

I realize instantly that I've asked a damnably foolish question. Stepan's shoulders sink; he has lost any patience he might have held in reserve. "We're in a war, Leibovich! We have a job to do! You want to quit? You can quit. Go ahead, quit! You can march home to your mother. I'll find someone else."

"No, no, I just . . ." My words falter. Stepan is looking straight at me with a piercing scowl. I signal to him with my hands that everything is in order.

"Good," the trainmaster says. "Take ten minutes to tighten everything up on the wagon. Get some food, and take extra water from the creek. Get there as fast as you can. I'll bring the Cossack."

My heart pounds as I strap everything down on the wagon and check the wheels and axles. The horses have been fed. I race to the stream and fill four canteens. Inside the crates on the wagon are gauze dressings, splints, crutches, blankets, sheets, medical kits with scissors and forceps, vodka, morphine, chloroform and ether anesthetics, and surgical saws. At least that's what the labels say. I pray they are accurate. Each crate bears a prominent red cross, announcing that the contents are for compassionate uses, not brutality, as if the combatants discriminate. I am now on a life-saving mission, and I sense that at least one life is at stake, maybe many. The Talmud and Mishnah teach that whoever destroys a soul is considered to have destroyed an entire world, and whoever saves a life is considered to have saved an entire world. So, I will try to save a single life.

The Cossack is waiting when I return from the stream. Like the other guards, he wears a black sheepskin mouton and a high-necked wool coat, the *chokha*, with rows of rifle shells sewn onto the front of each breast. He looks to be twice my age and carries himself as if he has had ample experience as a soldier. Fixed to his belt is a dagger-like bayonet, and his sword is held by a shoulder strap that crosses his chest. The muzzle of his bolt-action Berdan rifle points toward the ground, its leather strap anchored at one of his epaulets. He looks me over, up and down, as I stow my canteens.

"Another Yid," he remarks under his breath. His tone is neutral, neither derisive nor warm. For this, I am grateful.

The Cossack's horse, a black Don from the steppe, pulls at his bit. I peer back at the rider for a moment, measuring the situation, then check each of the wagon's canvas straps.

As I work, I reply, "We both have a job to do." Then, I look up at him. "My name is Yakov Leibovich."

"Neschadymenko," the Cossack responds. "I am ready. It's forty miles. Let's go."

I mount the wagon wearing my wool frock coat, black hat, and the pair of leather gloves I was issued in Odessa. We move quickly under an overcast sky amid a wind that stirs and rustles the nearly barren trees. In late October, I expect cold, but the wind forces me to replace my hat with a wool scarf, tied beneath my chin and around my neck, that covers my head, skullcap, and ears. The plan is to make Lovtcha the following day, the 23rd of October, just outside the Russians' near-encirclement of Plevna. We will stop only once to rest the horses and have a meal. The road along the Osam River is rough and takes us close to the Balkan foothills. We skirt the Turkish enclave of Grivitza as artillery thunders in the distance, then head east to avoid the front lines. Initially, the terrain is flat. We pass untended farm fields, two abandoned villages, and patches of woods. Apart from the bursts of war over the hills, it is quiet and barren along the road. The Cossack says nothing to me. I see no animals, wild or domesticated, and no civilians. The wind has died.

A few platoons of Russian soldiers march past in the opposite direction. They all look worn and weary as they escort a dozen walking wounded and carry others on stretchers hoisted to their shoulders. Empty ammunition carriages follow, along with damaged pieces of rolling field artillery. The Cossack stops, dismounts, and speaks to the soldiers to understand any dangers we might face on the remainder of our journey.

Neschadymenko rides back to my wagon. "The route to Lovtcha is clear, but we need to be careful. Do what I say. There's a protected clearing ten miles on where we'll rest."

At the clearing, I pull grain from a sack at the back of the wagon to feed the horses. The soft grass is a luxury compared to the wooden wagon bench. As Neschadymenko builds a fire, I try to engage him in conversation.

"Where are you from, Neschadymenko?"

"It doesn't matter."

"I'm from the Minsk region, Navahrudak. We might be neighbors."

"No, we're not."

A moment of silence extends before the Cossack speaks again.

"I come from Horlivka, near Donetsk, in the steppe. We are peasants, and we are Christians, not Mohammedans. We know how to defend ourselves."

I'm not sure what to make of this response, but I take a risk. "So we worship the same God."

Neschadymenko stirs the fire's embers with a stick. "We leave in an hour."

When we enter Lovtcha, I can readily see that the town has been transformed into an armed Russian encampment. Lovtcha is bustling with soldiers and rolling artillery pieces. Cavalrymen tend their horses as guards march Turkish prisoners to the northern section of town. The prisoners look filthy and cold. A few smoke haphazardly rolled cigarettes. A kitchen wagon ladles soup and pours tea, but only for the Imperial Army. Dogs roam the streets, sniffing for morsels of discarded rations. A wiry Jewish sutler has set up in the town square, offering exotic foods and personal supplies, including cigarettes, from his one-horse wagon. I wander over and speak to him in Yiddish. He is from Bucharest. I conclude that, as dangerous as hawking wares in a war zone seems to be, he is an astute businessman offering in-demand items, mostly for the officers, who have a greater ability to pay than any rank-and-file soldier. He is surely making a handsome profit.

Neschadymenko returns with a warm loaf of black bread, from a field oven tended by an army baker, and tears off a piece for me. I've not eaten such delicious bread in months; it brings a smile to my face. Also, I privately celebrate the transaction with Neschadymenko as a triumph of tolerance. I nod to him in thanks.

"Let's go," Neschadymenko commands. "The field hospital is close by."

The hospital is a converted two-story residence that has sustained artillery damage, but its roof remains intact. Outside its walls, exhausted Russian soldiers pass cigarettes or spoon groats from copper cups. Many are bandaged, their legs, arms, torsos, shoulders, even faces, wrapped. Some stand with crutches. I pull the reins, engage the wagon's brake, and hop down to find out who is in charge.

Inside the compound, more wounded lie on stretchers under blankets amid an odor of putrefying flesh that forces me to pull my scarf over my mouth. An eerie silence pervades the house. An officer in a soiled apron walks down the stairs toward the entrance, in front of two soldiers carrying a stretcher with one of the dead.

When the officer sees me, he is stern. "This is a hospital. What do you want?"

"I'm delivering medical supplies. My wagon is just outside. Can we unload?"

"Alright, wait, I'll find the doctor."

Even with the scarf over my nose, I am fighting waves of nausea. A doctor wearing a surgical smock spattered with blood enters the foyer, exhausted. I notice a skullcap.

"What is your name?" he asks.

"Leibovich, sir."

"Leibovich, listen." The doctor's voice is raspy and strained. "Almost everybody who survived has been treated, so for now we have what we need. But our forces at the front, north of here, are desperate for bandages, splints, and pain medication. We don't have enough wagons to bring the wounded here. You have a wagon, yes?"

"Yes."

"Does it have bandages and splints? Morphine?"

"Yes, sir, everything."

"Good. You need to go there right away. It is a place called Tuchenitza, near the town of Brestovets. I'll get a Cossack guard to escort you. But you have to go right now."

"I have a Cossack guard, sir. We can leave right away. I just need a map."

"Tell him Tuchenitza. You don't need a map." He points directly up the street. "Follow this road, it's the only one leading to Plevna. Just keep going straight, no turns. General Skobelev's forces will intercept you on the road. I'm sure of that. It's due north, fifteen miles or so. But go now."

"Yes, sir."

"You can be there before nightfall, God willing."

"Yes. Praise be to God."

The doctor extends his arms, placing both hands on my shoulders as a loving father might to a son. "Thank you," he says earnestly. "Thank you."

I nod and turn to leave, my eyes welling with tears. I have not heard a single expression of gratitude since leaving Minsk — not from Stepan, not from the soldiers I encountered, not from the wounded I carried. How is it that a man who must take off the limbs of soldiers hour after hour, without rest, bloodied and sweating, can take a moment to acknowledge the smallest contribution of a mere teamster hauling medical supplies? Where does this unsolicited act arise from? Is kindness learned from parents and teachers? Or does this quality reside within us like a seed of goodness planted by the Omniscient One? Why does this seed lie dormant for so long, only to emerge in the worst circumstances? I compose myself quickly, lest Neschadymenko notice.

We are going to support Skobelev's division, I tell the Cossack. When I mention the name, he smiles broadly.

"I fought with him four years ago in the desert when we captured the Khanate of Khiva," he tells me. "It is east of the Caspian and west of Samarkand. He is a skilled strategist and warrior who knows how to fight a war."

The road to Brestovets is flat for a time, then turns hilly. Messengers gallop past in both directions, leather pouches bouncing at their sides. Neschadymenko presses ahead at a pace I find difficult to maintain. He is worried about the horses on the hills but pushes them anyway. I can see my horses' breath in the chilled air. My senses are on alert, but I feel increasingly at ease riding with Neschadymenko, a man whose instincts have been honed in battle. He will not betray me; I'm sure of it. Occasionally, he rides ahead to scout or stops and peers into the woods, sniffing the air for trouble.

After nearly two hours on the road, Neschadymenko gallops back to the wagon from a scouting foray. The sun hangs low on the horizon.

"Guards ahead. They will direct us."

Soon, more than fifty Russian soldiers, on both sides of the road, come into view. Two search the wagon without a word, then start marching into the woods to the east. Neschadymenko follows on foot, one hand pulling the harness with Yitzy and Zalman. His own horse is tied to the rear of the wagon. There is no road or trail, and the terrain is rough but passable. We climb through the trees to a wooded ridge, weaving through outcroppings and stumps. To the west, I can see the lowlands. We hear voices and the rustling of boots on forest debris as we enter a clearing. To the right lay scores of wounded soldiers on blankets, perhaps eighty of them in various states of consciousness. Some moan or plead for water. There is no time to consider this tableau, nor any time to absorb all that a battlefield presents to the senses. But for five seconds, I am frozen, staring.

An officer and a handful of infantrymen stride briskly toward the wagon.

"What do you have?" the officer demands loudly.

"Everything: splints, bandages, morphine."

"Good. We'll unload. You can stay the night and return in the morning. Unhitch your horses and tie them over there."

The soldiers assigned to carry the wooden crates and leather pouches have their faces mostly obscured by woolen scarves to protect against the cold (that or they are trying to protect their nostrils from the smell of open wounds and death). I hop down from the wagon and pull my scarf down to wipe the grit from my face and take in the cool mountain air. Suddenly, a hand grasps my arm.

"Yakov?"

I turn, thinking it is Neschadymenko, though the Cossack has never used my given name. Staring at me in the fading light, with a look of doubt and curiosity, are eyes I recognize through the smudges of battle. It takes a moment for me to grasp the image. The soldier answers my question before I have a chance to ask.

"Avram Eizenberg," he announces.

I am momentarily stunned, unable to react. I stare into his eyes and manage to say his name.

"Avram?"

He grabs my shoulders with both hands, as if to keep me upright, and asks, "In the name of the Almighty, how did you end up here?"

6

Avram's bent eyebrows are just as I remember them. His beard is full, his eyes dark, and his body muscular from the labor of soldiering.

I look at his face. "Thanks be to God, you are alive."

"We can talk about the random fortune and misfortune of battle when I've finished unloading," he says, smiling and tapping me on the chest with one hand. "Wait here."

Avram joins the other men hauling crates of painkillers and dressings into the cluster of wounded, where officers pry open the containers and tend to the suffering. Two men remove a limp soldier on a stretcher. He is dead, an awful wound to the chest. I wonder where they are taking his body or whether burial is even possible at the front lines. Is there time to bury the dead or say a prayer for their souls? I watch Avram, alive and nimble, return for another armful of supplies.

Half an hour passes as I watch a dozen officers toiling over the fallen. Avram returns to the wagon with a complement of soldiers carrying several unopened crates, which they slide back onto the bed of my wagon.

"We don't need all of this," an officer explains. "We've taken what we can carry. You should take the rest back tomorrow."

"To Lovtcha?" I ask.

"Yes. And you'll have to take a few of the wounded on your wagon. They'll survive the night."

"I'm not a doctor."

"None of us are doctors," he says tartly.

Avram shrugs. "Never mind. I'll help you load stretchers in the morning. You know, you saved lives today, the lives of my comrades. Do you realize?"

"Maybe. I need to unhitch the horses."

After I feed Yitzy and Zalman, Avram finds me and places a hand on my back.

"Come with me. You can meet the Yiddish Brigade of Marksmen over a fine dinner under the starlight."

"I'm not sure I'm hungry after seeing the aftermath of battle."

"You'll get over it. You have to, or you quickly lose your wits. "

"What is the Yiddish Brigade of Marksmen?"

"A joke. We Yids of the Sixteenth Division stick together. But I'm serious about the marksmen part; these boys know how to shoot."

I've never heard a Jew utter the epithet "Yid," even as a joke. War turns so many things upside down.

"I've been looking for you, Avram, but your sister told me you were in the Fourteenth Division, not the Sixteenth."

"My sister? You saw Rivkah?"

"Yes. I can explain. There is so much to explain. We need time."

We walk up the hill to a grove of trees where the soldiers are encamped, weapons and men leaning against trees.

"We have time," he assures me. "At least tonight we do. I was in the Fourteenth when I left Minsk. But they transferred some of us to the Sixteenth under General Skobelev for a special mission to complete the encirclement of Plevna. So far, it's going well, but we have more to accomplish. Did Rivkah ask you to look for me?"

"As I said, there's a lot to explain. First, though, tell me how this war has gone for you. Are you maintaining your health, your sanity?"

"I'll tell you after you meet the marksmen. They're good men. This is our own little yeshiva."

He guides me to a clutch of soldiers sitting on the forest floor with blankets around their shoulders. I notice for the first time that Avram is wearing the skullcap, the *yarmulke*, he had previously abandoned. Some of the soldiers have sidelocks that merge with their beards or are tucked behind their ears; others have none at all, having cut them off in violation of the Biblical command. This is a new phenomenon for me; everyone at the *beit midrash* had full sidelocks, and beards if they could grow one, but an army camp is not the same.

"Men!" Avram announces. "I want you to meet my yeshiva friend from Navahrudak, Yakov Leibovich."

One of the soldiers pipes up, "You must know my brother, Yitzchak Levin."

"Are you Kalman?"

"Yes, but you're among friends. I won't report you for spitting or taking God's name in vain. Just make sure you return the favor."

The promised home-cooked meal consists of cold black biscuits, accompanied by lively tales of wartime danger and hormone-fueled lust. War, as I say, turns everything upside down. The men look exhausted, but seem to find energy in their reminiscing about life in the Imperial Army. Kalman introduces everyone: Aaron, Shmuel, Eyzer, Lev, Yehudah, Geyrshom, and Leon. I am surprised to learn that the men are allowed to adhere to Jewish rituals, including daily prayers. Like me, many wear the fringed *tallit katan* undergarment, although not Avram — he gave it up years ago. During morning prayers, if they aren't on a march, they take the time to wrap the *tefillin* on their arms. Lev tells me he carries a miniature Torah scroll in his knapsack, encased in a hand-sized capsule.

"We just celebrated Simchat Torah because our commandant is a tolerant man," Avram says. "We told him we intended to dance around Lev's little Torah and sing its praises to mark the completion of the year's readings. He shrugged and said, 'I don't care. Dance if you want.' The other men in our unit looked at us like we were lunatics. To tell you the truth, we are lunatics!"

"And do you keep the Sabbath?" I ask.

"If we can. We do it together. I had forgotten about the Sabbath for a long time. It's a good tradition for a soldier though. If we are in camp, it calms us to have a day of rest and meditation. But it's not always possible. Are you able to keep the Sabbath, Yakov?"

"As you say, it's not always possible. I have a hard time keeping track of the days. God will forgive me, I hope."

"Don't worry, he knows you are trying. He told me so!"

Kalman clears his throat and addresses me, "You knew Yisrael Tsipershtein at the *beit midrash*, right?"

"Yes, of course. He was drafted last November. Have you seen him?"

"We've seen him. Avram can tell you, if he cares to."

No one speaks. Eyes move to the distant trees or the leaves covering the ground. There is an ominous moment of silence. Then, Avram turns to me. He doesn't address the others, only me, and softly.

"Yisrael is buried not far from here. He was killed on the eleventh of September."

My gut sinks and the air escapes my lungs. "My God. How do you know? Was he in your unit? May God keep his soul."

"He was in this unit. Yisrael and I walked every step together, " Avram says wistfully, looking into the dark forest. "But his time arrived. So many soldiers died that day — scores, hundreds I think. It's hard to speak about such butchery. We try to put it out of our minds. But you can't completely."

Avram and I talk late into the night, whispering after most of the men have curled up with their blankets to sleep. I can see how much he has matured, even blossomed, as he tells me about his days beside Tsipershtein. As difficult as it is, I can tell he wants to recount the events that led to Tsipershtein's death, to honor him.

"You know Tsipershtein and I recited Torah passages together at the *beit midrash*, just as you did. We were in the Fourteenth together, and we renewed our friendship."

A memory prompts him to laugh to himself before he continues.

"Yisrael was miserable at first. He was just a shtetl boy, you know, with no understanding of the mechanics of army life, let alone life in general. I tried to teach him — me, the vagrant, hah! Unfortunately, I knew something about boots that don't fit and filthy clothing and meals of hard rusk biscuits. I was living on the streets, living on vodka mostly. Did you know? Well, now you do. Yisrael was my army apprentice, I suppose. I showed him how to pad his boots and conserve the water in his canteen. He was carrying so many unnecessary items in his haversack, heavy things when you added it up. I forced him to get rid of two kilos of junk, items he didn't need and never used. He couldn't clean his Berdan or fix his bayonet or use the sight on his rifle when we marched into Bulgaria. I had to show him everything, poor boy."

"Did he learn?"

"Sure. The most important thing I told him was that he had to shrink his definition of daily personal needs, to live with nothing, or at least the barest essentials. It wasn't easy for him."

"The way you had been living in Navahrudak, I suppose."

"Exactly so. I was an opportunist when it came to survival. You have to be a crafty opportunist to survive. I told him, 'Yisrael, you have to put away your old life in the shtetl and yeshiva. Pretend you were never there. The only thing that counts is surviving today, just today.' Eventually, he started to understand. I miss him though, I really do."

"It's not easy to put all of that behind you."

"It's not. He kept quoting the rabbi. Reb Epshtein says this, Reb Epshtein says that, Reb Epshtein says that to study Talmud is to have a conversation with God. Tsipershtein said he couldn't stop having a conversation with God. He was a smart boy, spiritual and smart. You must believe the same thing, right?"

"I suppose I do."

"You're deluding yourself, Yakov. I'm glad if God speaks to you. He doesn't speak to me; or maybe he just stopped speaking to me. But I am a Jew, I know this. I have no conversations with God, but I am a Jew. I stopped wearing a *yarmulke* when I was on the streets, but in the army, when I met these boys, I put it back on my head. I'm proud to be a Jew, and I wanted the other men in the unit to know I was one of them. I don't wear the *yarmulke* because I think it protects me or that God has commanded me. I just wear it. But I don't put the *tallit katan* under my uniform. I don't need to wrap myself in God's laws. I'm not having any conversation with Him. Do you know what speaks to me, Yakov? There is something." He laughs to himself. "Do you know what really speaks to me? A voluptuous woman. That speaks an entire library to me."

I cannot help but laugh. "We agree, my friend. But I don't think you really believe this. You are saying daily prayers with the marksmen, right?"

"Sometimes I do. I enjoy the company of these boys — well not boys anymore, but good men. They're all from Minsk. You heard their first names but they have family names, too. And we're a family here. Let's see, there's Litman, Bernshtein, Fridman, Kaganovich, Frimovich, Shteinshnaider, Dubrovski, Fuks. I think that's it. We were on the train together to Odessa, all of them, plus Tsipershtein. At first, they couldn't stop talking about Torah and Talmud and Europe's most influential rabbis. Drunk on God, they thought they were at a rolling yeshiva. They got over it though. Life in the army, life in battle, sobered them up. It happens quickly. Two weeks in Bulgaria and they were joking about how many pages a pocket prayer book needs to stop a Turkish bullet, and whether it's kosher to eat dried-meat rations alongside biscuits that taste like granite."

"But the commanders let you live as Jews in the army. Is that right? It seems so."

"Dragomirov commands all 25,000 men and 600 officers in the Fourteenth, so we never lay eyes on him. What he thinks of Jews, I don't know. We don't even see our battalion commander. We're just one small company, Company B, 5th Battalion, 1st Regiment, 2nd Brigade. All our orders come from our company commander, Captain Pavel Nikolayev. He's a decent man, whose eyes remind me of my father's. Why would he make life difficult for the Jews? We're maybe a fifth to a quarter of the entire division! Jews! Imagine. We obey orders, and Nikolayev leaves us alone. He's the one who let us buy the little Torah scroll in Odessa, and who let us celebrate Passover and Simchat Torah. We just have to maintain discipline and try to look fearless, though we have many fears. But we have to put them aside. Yisrael did, eventually. Should I tell you how he died?"

"If you can."

"We'll see. He was with me all the way to the end. We crossed the Danube together in an early wave and survived that first battle by the grace of God. Once he figured out how to lock the bolt on his Berdan, he was fine. He talked to himself in Hebrew, and kept saying '*Chazak ve'ematz*, be strong and courageous.' He prayed as he fought, and he addressed his weapon with Yiddish endearments. It was beautiful. Tsipershtein was one of a kind."

Avram begins to choke up.

"Avram, I'm sorry. There's no need to go on."

"It's okay, it's okay, I . . . I want to. Actually, I feel strong and purposeful in the army, so I felt strong enough to help Yisrael. I thought it would be better for me to die in uniform than in some state of madness and squalor in Navahrudak. That's what it was, you know, madness and squalor, until I came to the army. Nikolayev kept calling us "Heroes of Russia!" But we knew we weren't. Yisrael died near here, in the Grand Assault. Except, it wasn't so grand. We marched from Tirnova and arrived on the first of August. He really believed he was going to die, he sensed it; and I kept telling him he was wrong. I told him how a year ago, I wanted to end my life in the gutter. I wanted to lie in the open street and just expire. I told him he was wrong about death, but it turns out he was right."

His voice trails off. I say nothing. Avram composes himself and goes on.

"I now see how foolish it was, my so-called life. I just wanted Tsipershtein to know he wasn't alone. You know what he did? He gave me his pocket prayer book. He reminded me of the important passages and what they meant. I was glad about that little connection to my old life at the *beit midrash* — not to God, but to some of the traditions."

I try to read his face. Though Avram's voice is clear, he looks only at the earth at his feet or the midnight sky.

"Yisrael died at Lovtcha. There was a lot of shelling from both sides. The Turks were preparing to retreat, but we couldn't let them take their artillery with them. You can't do that; you try to seize it. So we stormed their last redoubt. The Turks are good fighters, and their rifles are lethal at long distances. Nikolayev gave the order to push forward with bayonets. It's so hard to follow an order like that, but you must. So we were running, right up the hill, across trenches, right into their fire from the redoubt. I could see the flashes of rifle fire. I have to say, I was frightened by the bullets coming right at us. But I kept shouting at Yisrael to stay with me. It was madness, Yakov, hell, total chaos. I killed two men that day, one with my bayonet, in the redoubt. I shot the other one in the back as he tried to run away. Imagine. In the back. I can't even describe it. I remember feeling so cold even though it was so warm that day."

Avram pauses again to gather his thoughts. I know he is about to describe Yisrael Tsipershtein's end. I can see his face, and his expression full of pain.

"I looked around and Yisrael wasn't there. All of a sudden, I couldn't find him. I dropped my rifle and ran down the hill from the redoubt shouting his name. The injured and dying, men the Turks had just cut down, were everywhere. How was I still alive? I have no idea. You had to step over the wounded and dead. I found Yisrael in a trench. He had taken a bullet right to the chest, but he was conscious. I tried to stop the bleeding. I talked to him. 'Look at me,' I said. 'Look at me, Yisrael.' He said something about a relationship with God, but I couldn't make it out. I think he was telling me I had to have a relationship with God, or maybe that I had to remember him to God. And he said, 'It hurts, Avram.' And that was it, that was the end. He just said, 'It hurts, Avram,' and he just died in my arms. He died in my arms, Yakov. What could I do?"

Exhaustion and sorrow written across his face, his head drops to his chest, and he sobs quietly. I touch his shoulder, not knowing what to say or how to comfort him, except to just be with him.

"I'm sorry. I'm sorry, Avram. I'm so sorry," is all I can say.

He exhales deeply and wipes his face on his sleeve, then turns to me. "Here I am going on and on, and you haven't told me anything, Yakov. I need to know. How did you get here? And when did you see Rivkah?"

I realize this is the moment, and I must tell him the truth about everything.

"Back in Navahrudak, I was still studying to be a rabbi with Reb Epshtein. And I was supposed to be married to Zaltsman's daughter."

"Mindl Zaltsman?"

"Yes, Mindl. They made the arrangement, all without talking to me. But I was drafted in the lottery, and my father was fanatical about keeping me as far away from the army as he could. Obsessed. You know he was wounded in Crimea years ago. Of course, I should have refused all of his scheming, but I didn't. He enlisted the rabbi, and the rabbi arranged for me to work as a teamster and accountant for this supply company instead of entering the army. It's a Jewish firm, and the Ministry of War even approved the switch, but I'm not sure why. That's how I managed to avoid conscription even though my name was called."

"So, you were drafted in the lottery."

"Yes. The wedding had to be put off, and I'm glad. I feel nothing for Mindl, and she probably feels nothing for me. Who knows? I barely remember her. In any case, I have to tell you there is another young woman who interests me quite a lot, a young woman in Navahrudak. She is intelligent, and even reads Hebrew and Yiddish. She has a wry sense of humor, and, well, I think she is quite beautiful."

"You always had more luck than I did," he says.

"With girls?"

"No, getting out of the army. But who is this girl? You like her a lot, don't you."

"Avram, it's your sister."

"Rivkah? Really?"

"Yes."

"But how did that happen, Yakov? She didn't tell me anything about this!"

I don't detect anger in his reaction.

"I met her by chance. She remembered me, but I barely recognized her. She has grown up, you know."

"Ah, a woman now, right?"

"Yes, a woman. I am embarrassed to say it, but I have dreamt of her."

"A pleasant dream, I hope."

"Yes. I told her I would try to find you and make sure you were safe."

"In the dream?"

I laugh. "No, in a letter, just before I left Navahrudak."

"I visited Rivkah and my mother before I left. They knew I was going into the army, and must have been frightened for me."

I allow an awkward silence to pass.

"There is something I need to tell you, Avram."

"My mother, is she ill?"

"No."

"Then?"

"You were not conscripted. You shouldn't even be here carrying a weapon. If Rybakov told you you were drafted, he lied."

Avram lets out a belly laugh. "Oh, I know, Yakov. Believe me, I know I wasn't supposed to be in the Imperial Army at all. You must know from Rivkah what a bad state I was in, living on the outskirts of Navahrudak, drinking and stealing food. I was like an animal. I used to make my own vodka in a still. Why would the Tsar's army want me?"

Avram looks up, as if searching for stars.

"I think the army saved my life. It's ironic, isn't it? I had no will to live when I left home. I felt bad about not helping my mother and Rivkah, but I had no will to be with them or with anyone. I see now that I was suffering from melancholia. It was a very bad life, barely a life at all. Then Rybakov found me. It was soon before the Christian New Year. He pretended my name was chosen in the lottery, and took me in. But I found the official draft list inside his house and searched for my name, and it wasn't there. I didn't question it, because he treated me like a son. He took me in and fed me a delicious mutton stew and warm bread that first night. I can still taste it. We even had schnapps."

"You knew you weren't conscripted? Why did you go?"

"I stayed with Rybakov for a fortnight and began to feel renewed. He is a good man, Avram. Before I left for the barracks, he admitted to me that he needed me to fill his local draft quota. That was it. He said someone was ineligible, probably a kid who failed the physical, and he had to make his quota. I didn't hold it against him. By then, I was looking forward to being in a warm barracks and not having to steal food. He told me the good parts of army life and it sounded fine. And it has been fine. Just as I said, I think Rybakov saved my life. On the street, I was just waiting to die, Yakov. Understand that I wanted to lie in the rain until my body merged with the mud. And Rybakov picked me up and cleaned me off. Maybe I was like the son he never had; I don't know. But I think I gained some purpose when I entered the army, some self-respect. I'm part of something now. It was as if I suddenly wanted to live. It's crazy though. Here I am, watching my friends die."

Out of respect, I wait for him to finish. But I need to correct his view of Ivan Ivanovich Rybakov.

"Listen, Avram, you don't know the whole story, and you need to know it," I begin. "You replaced someone, that is true. But the person you replaced wasn't someone who was ineligible, it was me. You replaced me, Avram." I begin to choke on my words. "I'm the one who dropped off of his list. Do you see? I was supposed to go into the army, but when I got this job, they took you to fill my place. Do you understand? You replaced me."

"Well, maybe it's a good thing."

"No, no, no, you don't understand."

I've explained this badly. I can feel the guilt pulling my shoulders in and pressing against my neck, like two hands to the throat. I can barely speak. I have to push the words out of my mouth.

"Let me start over. I need you to understand this."

I tell Avram about my conscription notice in mid-November, my father's fixation on getting me out of the army, Reb Epshtein's intervention, and the arrangement with the rabbi's brother in St. Petersburg.

"I thought it was all set," I tell him, "but then Rybakov found me and demanded I give him the name of another Jew to take my place on his draft roster. He threatened me, saying if I didn't give him a name, he would publicly shame me by revealing in the newspapers that I was evading the draft. He said, 'a Jew for a Jew.' I had to give him the name of another Jew."

Avram is gently nodding. "So you gave Rybakov my name."

"No. I mean, yes, but not your name exactly. That old policy of drafting kids by religion was supposed to have ended. But Rybakov revived it to fit his needs. I had no idea where Avram Eizenberg was or what your circumstances were. I thought you were in Minsk or something. I didn't even know that the young woman I was flirting with was your sister at first."

"Then you didn't give Rybakov my name."

"Not the name, no. It's complicated. My father happened to know there was someone living on the streets, a young Jew, he told me. Father had been to the neighborhood making deliveries, close to where you were living. We didn't know who you were though. We couldn't see your face and didn't have any name at all. We didn't know it was you, Avram. And this is the crime of it, the true crime of it."

I'm starting to unravel. "We didn't even try to see your face. We didn't want to. We just gave Rybakov your location. We told him to take that kid living on the streets, that no-good kid, that animal. We gave you up."

I try to control myself, but tears fill my eyes, and my voice begins cracking.

"I told Rybakov to take the Jewish vagrant living at the end of Sverdlova Street. I went to his house and told him exactly where to find you."

"I see." For the first time, Avram is absorbing what I've done to him. He is quiet for a time. I await his verdict, his judgment, his wrath. But I hear nothing. His head is down, deep in thought for what seems like an eternity.

I speak again, "The Book of Splendor says that when the Messiah comes, even the perfect Jew must repent. I am far from perfect, Avram, and the harm that I have done to you is terrible, even if unintentional. But repentance starts with telling the truth, and I'm trying."

Avram finally responds. His voice is dull. "I wasn't supposed to be a soldier, but you made me one."

The weight of his words hit me. "I must make *teshuvah* for all you have endured, Avram. I must confess and repent. I just hope that someday you can forgive me."

Suddenly, he turns to me, animated, pointing a finger to the sky. "Listen, Yakov. I just told you the Imperial Army saved my life, didn't I?" He looks straight at me and speaks with a strong voice. "It makes no difference to me now. Why would it? I would have been living in the mud on Sverdlova Street right now! Or dead from too much homemade vodka. So don't feel sorry for me. When I tell you I'm happy, Yakov, believe it. Right here, right now, I'm happy to be in the army. So stop feeling guilty over this; I forgive you."

"But the war isn't over, Avram. You are the one wearing a uniform and carrying a rifle, not me. You are a target of the Turks, not me. Sure, you've survived until now, but you're the one still risking his life!"

"Well, that's true," he concedes. "The war isn't over. In fact, we're moving out at midday tomorrow. We're close to the edge of the Turks' artillery range, but we will fight them." He leans in and whispers with an air of cockiness that reminds me of the Avram I remember from yeshiva, "I'm a smart soldier, Yakov. I know how to take care of myself. And this is a life, after all. I feel alive. You see that? At home, I would be dead or as good as dead. After all this is over, we can meet in Navahrudak. You'll be the shtetl rabbi by then. And I'll be the Conscription Officer after Rybakov retires! How about that?"

"I wish it was that simple." I have taken in his argument that he is better off in the army. I wonder if he is right. Did I do Avram a favor? Is he alive today, or more alive, because my father and I turned him in to Rybakov? It sounds thoroughly irrational. And though I can't accept it, at least morally, the fact is that the army may be a blessing for my wayward friend. I can see that with my own eyes. What I did to Avram was wrong, could never be justified, and requires restitution; but I am beginning to feel my obsession with guilt and repentance easing. He even said it: he forgives me.

Yet Avram isn't the only person affected by my acts. I've hurt Rivkah too, and her forgiveness may be the most difficult to earn. If Avram comes home, everything is solved. How can I guarantee that he comes home?

I brush aside the dry leaves in front of me. "There's something else I have to tell you, Avram. Rivkah knows nothing of this. She doesn't know that I gave you up to Rybakov. When she finds out, or when I tell her, our relationship — whatever it is — will end. I know it. I don't deserve her."

Avram frowns as if I'm making a simple matter difficult.

"It can be our secret, Yakov. Forget it. Don't worry."

"Avram, I'm not asking you to keep it a secret. You've already said you forgive me, and I'm deeply grateful. But I need to seek Rivkah's forgiveness, too, though she'll probably want to beat me. I wouldn't blame her."

"Why don't you let me tell her?"

"No, I should be the one."

"But will you tell her the real truth about my life?"

"Which is what?"

"That I'm better off in the army than I would have been brewing vodka under a leaky canvas roof on Sverdlova Street."

"I hope that much is true. But the war doesn't seem to be ending anytime soon. You are vulnerable, Avram. And I put you here."

"Okay, you can tell her. But I'm going to write her a letter. I owe her that. She needs to hear my voice and hear that I am restored. She can share the letter with my mother. Can you buy an envelope and post it when you get back to Lovtcha? Would you do that for me?"

"Yes, if you want, Avram. Of course I will. I know they'll both be glad to see a letter from you, overjoyed in fact."

I wander back to the wagon, find my fountain pen and ink, and strip a few blank pages from my journal. When I return and hand them to Avram, he asks me about Rivkah.

"I've always thought about my sister as a kid, a youngster, a child. I don't see her as a woman, but I guess I've been blind. She is a woman, of course."

"She was struggling when I saw her last," I say. "Working to bring in a little cash. Do you know what I see? A very beautiful young woman. And she's incredibly intelligent; do you see that?"

"Not many girls want to learn to read Russian or even Hebrew. My father got her a tutor. I suppose it's rare. You said she is smart, and I have to agree."

"Her personality is rare too, Avram; isn't it?"

"Spicy."

"Yes, spicy. I suppose that's her way of flirting."

"She flirted with you?"

"I think so. What do I know? Before I left, I told her I would try to find you and care for you somehow. It was the least I could do."

"Care for me?"

"I want to get you home, Avram. You're not supposed to be here. The only way your forgiveness means something is if you come home alive."

He scoffs, "Oh, shall I write a little note to General Skobelev saying 'Good luck with your war, sir, but it's getting too dangerous for me and I'm going home?'"

"No. But we could trade places. An even trade: I was supposed to be in the army, so I become the soldier I was drafted to be, and you take up my duties as a teamster. Then, eventually, you find your way home to Navahrudak. Your mother and sister need you, Avram. And from the looks of things, you are ready to help them. You've rid yourself of your desire to dissolve into the mud."

"Trade places? You are fantasizing, Yakov. It doesn't work like that. Why would you do such a thing? You think this is the way to gain Rivkah's forgiveness?"

"I'm not thinking of Rivkah, now. I'm thinking of you, and God's judgment of me."

"I need to get some sleep now, Yakov," Avram says in near disgust. "So do you. Maybe your sanity will return in the morning. I'm going to write a letter to Rivkah and leave it for you at the wagon. Look for it in the morning."

"Just think about it, Avram. Think about a trade; that's all I ask. Sleep on it. It's only fair. Good night, may God keep you safe."

I search briefly in the dark for Neschadymenko but do not find him. He must be asleep somewhere. I spread my blanket on the leaf-cushioned earth beneath my wagon and say a prayer for Avram and for myself. I pray for the soul of Yisrael Tsipershtein and whisper the Mourner's Prayer. Even though Avram has absolved me, I pray again for Avram's safety and for God's acceptance of my repentance once I have made restitution. I feel exhausted, physically and emotionally, borne to the safe harbor of sleep on the mysterious chemistry of my own hopeful words.

7

Dawn filters through the wheel spokes, as I awaken beneath my wagon to the squeaky songs of birds piercing the cool, dry air. Nature holds me in a blissful embrace until I hear the horses stir and whinny. Only then do I remember I've been asleep inside an Imperial Army encampment at the front lines and within range of Turkish artillery batteries. This is the cauldron of war, and I must prepare my wagon to carry the wounded. I don't know where I can wash, and the horses will need to be watered. Must I say my morning prayers? Last night's prayers came easily. They are a burden today, but I stand beside the wagon, stretch my back, yawn, and grudgingly comply with God's commandment.

As I look for my hat under the wagon bench, I see my fountain pen atop folded sheets of paper. It is Avram's letter. There is a note on the page facing up; "Private. Please mail to Rivkah," it says, atop the mailing address for the alley dwelling. I am curious about its contents but restrain myself. I flatten the letter inside the pages of my journal and return it to the bottom of my satchel.

The soldiers begin to stir, including the wounded. I wander up the hill, closer to the tents, and find Avram sitting on the ground pulling on his boots. I kneel beside him and lean in to whisper.

"Have you thought about my proposal? It would allow me to make restitution. I need to do it, Avram. Please. It's a commandment of *selichah*."

"I don't know anything about this commandment," he says without looking at me, though I know with absolute certainty that he is aware of the rules of *teshuvah* and *selichah*.

I won't let him feign ignorance. "I know you know the five elements of repentance. Reb Epshtein taught both of us, didn't he? Recognize that you have sinned, be remorseful, and halt your sinful actions; right? And you must confess and make restitution. I've fulfilled some of these, but certainly not restitution. Do you see that I need to do this, Avram?"

Avram only shakes his head and purses his lips as he looks away. "Don't be a fool, Yakov. We're not swapping jobs. Forget it. Did you find the letter?"

"It's in my satchel. I'll take care of it as soon as I return to Lovtcha." Though I know he won't listen, I try one last time, perhaps half-heartedly. "You know it would be a just outcome if you went home and I put on the uniform I was supposed to have worn in the first place. It's simple fairness, isn't it?"

"You are more of a fool than I thought." He turns to me with a piercing, angry look. "I don't need anything from you, Yakov, including your restitution. We're not turning back the clock and starting over. Just do your job, and I'll do mine."

I start to protest again, but he cuts me off.

"It's that important to you, isn't it."

"Yes," I say in a barely audible whisper.

"Alright. You want to make restitution? Do this: find a way to help my mother when you get home. If you have a few extra roubles, you can make a gift. Or help her with something she needs done. She needs help more than I do, Yakov. Just do something kind for my mother. That's all. Then God will forgive you and you can go on with your life, and I can go on with mine. Can you do that?"

He is stubborn, and there is nothing else to be done.

"Of course, I will find your mother and help her. This, I can do."

"That settles it. We're done. Just do that and go on with your life. It'll all be fine." He grasps my shoulders and breaks into a broad smile. "Are you satisfied, Yakov? Because I have to pack up now. We're striking camp. And you have to get out of here. You need to hitch up your team and get back to Lovtcha, the sooner the better."

"I'll miss you, my friend," I say earnestly, "And the Yiddish Brigade of Marksmen. Tell them goodbye for me. Maybe I'll see you again on my next delivery. Will you take care of yourself?"

"I always do."

We embrace, and I make my way back to the wagon. Neschadymenko is tying his horse's reins to a hook on the sideboard.

"I've watered the horses," the Cossack advises. "The wagon's only half full, so take down the braces and the canvas. We'll be less of a target. We have room for three wounded. We need to get them up and get going."

I begin untying the canvas and removing the wooden braces. At the direction of an officer, the two of us carry three wounded soldiers on stretchers to the wagon and get them settled for the ride to Lovtcha alongside the remaining crates of supplies. I leap down again, pull on my leather gloves, and stride toward the horses. As I untie Yitzy and Zalman from a tree, the sharp sound of war gives me a start. Three explosions in rapid succession — boom! boom! boom! — shake the forest at the camp's perimeter, jarring the wagon and spooking the horses. I need all my strength to hold them steady as they buck.

When I turn to see where the shells have fallen, I'm surprised to find the smoke coming from far down a wooded slope, farther than I had imagined, as the noise was deafening. Our departure is now urgent.

"Steady, steady, let's get you hitched up."

Two more explosions resound in the woods. Neschadymenko helps me secure the horses to the hitch as they snort, pull, and dance. The animals know there is danger.

From the back of the wagon, one of the wounded soldiers cries weakly, "Get moving!"

"Get on!" Neschadymenko shouts at me. Another artillery shell explodes. It is much closer and alarmingly loud. Shaken, I clamber onto the wagon seat, check my gear, and grab the reins. We have to act fast. Just then, I hear Avram shouting from behind me. I turn and see him running down the hill toward the rear of the wagon, his backpack already on his shoulders.

"Go on!" he yells, waving his arms. "Get out of here!"

I turn and shout back, "I'll see you on the next delivery!" Neschadymenko mounts his horse, and we start moving out of the clearing toward the opposite slope, where we had entered. The horses are jittery and difficult to control; they try to bolt. In an instant, we veer left, and one of the wagon's front wheels lodges between a boulder and a fallen tree. The horses jerk side to side while I try to lash them with the reins, but we are immobilized.

Avram runs to us and begins to push the wagon from behind. "Try it!" he shouts. Neschadymenko dismounts and pulls Yitzy's bridle to urge the team forward. "Get us out of here!" a soldier on the bed urges plaintively.

I shift left on my bench to leap down so I can free the wheel. Before I can stand, though, I feel a screeching, thunderous blast behind me. A violent, sweeping force throws me to the ground, stunning me. I cannot move. My shoulder is in pain. Slowly, I open my eyes. The horizon is turning. From below, I see the horses rear up. Then I see Neschadymenko crawling toward me.

"Are you hurt?"

For a moment, I don't know how to answer the Cossack. I feel no obvious pain besides my shoulder, but I still cannot move or speak. Then, everything comes back into focus. I regain my senses and rise to my hands and knees. "I'm alright," I say weakly. Another shell explodes, farther off. I swivel to locate the smoke and notice a soldier sprawled on the ground behind the wagon, lying on his stomach with his face turned away from me.

"Wait!" Neschadymenko commands. "I'll go."

I ignore him and crawl back toward the soldier. There is a gaping, ugly wound at the back of his head. Only then do I realize it is Avram Eizenberg. His skull is torn open, and blood pulses from the wound. The leather knapsack on his back is undamaged. Only his head is shattered. It is awful. A sharp pang of nausea grips my midsection. I hurl myself onto my friend's back and press both hands over his open skull, as if my hands alone can protect his mangled brain and save him. I hear myself shouting, "No! No! No! No!"

There is no surviving such a ghastly wound. Still, I try to will my friend back to life. Tears flow down my cheeks as I press the back of his head, but the blood rushes through my fingers. "Come on, Avram!" I yell, as if trying to command his body to expel the shrapnel and re-inflate his lungs. My face is distorted in horror. I don't think I have ever felt raw panic until now. Another shell lands in the distance.

"Come on, Avram! Come on!" I shout again, but my voice is weakening. "Please, God. No."

Neschadymenko stands over us. "You can't help him, Leibovich. He's gone. We have to get the wounded out of here."

My vision is blurred and my ears are ringing. The panic subsides, and I lift my hands, wet with his blood. Avram does not move.

"Come on. He's gone," the Cossack says again.

I rise to my knees, turn away from the lifeless body of my friend, bend again, and heave out what little food was in my gut.

"It's over. Let's go," Neschadymenko commands.

Another artillery shell explodes, and another. Both fall where the wounded were camped, tossing up a shower of earth. I look up at the Cossack. There is no thought in my mind, no reasoning, no control. Only powerful instinct. It courses through me like a torrent from a burst dam, as if my soul has seized the reality that I have caused this tragedy and is shunting me onto an unimagined but necessary new path.

"You go," I shout back at the Cossack. "Take the wagon and go! Get these men and supplies to Lovtcha! I'm staying!"

Neschadymenko looks at me oddly. "Have you lost your mind? You are coming with me!"

I begin to stand. "No," I say firmly. "I'm staying. Just get out of here!"

Neschadymenko grabs me under the arm and lifts me upright. "We don't have time for this, Leibovich. Get on the wagon!"

With a defiant glance, I jerk my arm free and walk to the front of the wagon. "Help me free this wheel."

The two of us loosen the tree partly embedded in the earth near the boulder, and lift the front side of the wagon just enough to free the wheel.

"Get us out of here," one of the wounded pleads again.

Neschadymenko grabs Yitzy's bridle and guides the wagon onto a clear path. Another shell explodes on the slope below— then another.

"Let's go!" the Cossack shouts. "Get on!"

For the first time in my life, I feel the exhilaration of unrestrained free will. I know with absolute certainty what I must do and what I will do. "I'm not leaving!" I shout back. "I'm staying! Do you understand?" I reach up for my satchel and toss it to the ground. It holds everything I own. "Get out of here!"

Neschadymenko stares at me, shaking his head in disgust. "Stay, then." The Cossack turns and attaches a leather lead to the hitch holding Yitzy and Zalman, mounts his horse, and turns to glare at me again. "You are a fool, Leibovich, a damned fool."

"Go!" I shout.

Neschadymenko leads the wagon through the smoky woods and down the slope toward the road to Lovtcha. I spend only a moment watching him depart before turning back to look uphill at the Russian encampment. The last group of infantrymen moves out, using trees as cover. They aren't moving away from the artillery fire though. Strangely, they are moving toward it. I hear the crack of rifle fire in the distance and realize that the shelling has abated. I am shaking and cold, but there are no tears now, no emotion at all. I feel strangely calm, in the grip of pure, instinctive determination. I cannot say whether I am experiencing the delusions of trauma or sober obstinacy. I feel purposeful, almost desperately so, and as fervently connected to my task on this earth as I have ever felt, but without God or reason.

I pull a shirt from my satchel and wrap it around Avram's bloodied head, then remove the coat and uniform from his body. I know what I must do. I take the body of my friend by the feet and drag it into the indentation in the earth where Neschadymenko and I lifted the fallen tree. I can still hear the rifle fire, but it's farther in the distance and muffled. I remove my coat, blouse, trousers, and fringed *tallit katan*, then carefully drape the *tallit* atop Avram's body, a shroud of honor and protection. I slip on Avram's uniform, tucking the trousers into my boots and donning his Imperial Army coat. I latch on his belt, bayonet sheath, ammunition pouch, and canteen. I scoop and push loose leaves and forest detritus onto his remains. It is a shallow grave, hardly a grave at all. The *tallit* lays partially visible through the leaves, sticks, and earth, announcing that the body of a Jew lies here. It will have to do; I have no time to do more.

If I return to Navahrudak — perhaps I do not deserve to — I want to tell Shayna and Rivkah that I saw to Avram's burial. I will tell them where he is buried and the prayers that were spoken. I will tell them that I lovingly draped my own *tallit katan* over him.

When I complete the abbreviated interment, I place three heavy rocks at the head of the shallow grave, one on top of the other. I recite the Mourner's Prayer in Hebrew, the Kaddish, and the Psalm of David, " . . . Even if I walk in the valley of the shadow of death, I will fear no Evil . . . and I will dwell in the house of the Lord forever." But I do not linger.

As horrible as the situation is, my duty to Avram, at least for today, is done. Nothing will bring him back, nothing will salve the pain that his mother and sister will feel. I know that Avram's absolution won't dilute my responsibility, my culpability.

More rifle fire echoes through the woods. I pull my long knife from my satchel along with a few garments, my journal, pen, and prayer book, including Avram's letter to Rivkah, and place the items inside Avram's knapsack. I roll up my black coat and place it inside as well; it will serve as an extra blanket. I crush my black hat and push it into the knapsack too. After pulling the knapsack onto my shoulders, I return to the spot where Avram fell and find his army campaign hat several feet away. Ignoring the blood stain at the back, I pull it on over my skullcap, then toss my satchel toward the grave of my friend, imagining that in death he might use it on his final journey.

I feel the full weight of Avram's knapsack as I stride toward the abandoned camp. A rifle leans against a tree. Was it Avram's? It doesn't matter. The Berdan is heavier than I imagined. I've watched Neschadymenko clean his own bolt-action Berdan. I will fire this one if I need to, and learn to use it correctly and keep it clean. Holding the gun, I'm overcome by a strange mix of invulnerability and hopelessness. Will an artillery shell or bullet find me? It doesn't matter; I don't care. I imagine, for a brief moment, taking a small cylinder of burning metal to the chest and dying in the hills of Bulgaria as the fulfillment of God's plan for Yakov Leibovich. I neither think about the days ahead nor care. This is what I must do. I should have been here from the beginning, not Avram. I was the one conscripted, not Avram. I was the one called to duty. I was the one who found a way out, at the expense of my friend.

I pull the rifle strap over my shoulder and walk in the direction I saw the infantrymen take less than an hour before, back down the slope toward the trenches and the Ottoman artillery emplacements. My eyes are cast to the horizon. I will find his unit — Shmuel, Eyzer, Kalman, and Lev. Was it the Sixteenth Division? It doesn't matter, whatever their called, I'll find them. As I walk, I feel neither hunger nor thirst nor weariness. I am thinking about *selichah* and about the meaning of restitution, and about the generosity of Avram's forgiveness and his assertion that he was far better off in the army than on the streets of Navahrudak.

Tiny puffs of smoke from rifle fire are visible ahead, but I hear nothing, only the sound of my own feet crushing the dry leaves on the forest floor. I wonder if I am watching Turkish or Russian fire. Though it is too far away to tell, it seems that the foot soldiers of the Imperial Army are attacking a new ridge, for I see no cavalry. Artillery fire begins anew, this time from the Russian side, with its distinctive rumble and whoosh. Ahead, I catch a glimpse of a white horse and rider galloping through the forest. It is the insanely fearless General Skobelev racing across a trench line like a god of war, bending the Sixteenth Infantry Division to his will. I wonder if I will find Lev, Kalman, and the others — if they've survived. Do they know that Avram is dead? They mustn't, and I must tell them. I must tell them how he died, too. Maybe they are immune to death and shock and depression, or merely lost in the intoxication of battle. With this thought, my determination to find them redoubles.

Walking among the trees, I can now see the Turkish earthworks and the Russian advance, a brutal confrontation with shouting and bayonets flashing. Russian uniforms race out from behind trees, bushes, and outcroppings. Men fall to the ground in their tracks. Artillery rounds explode on the Turkish line, sending dirt and smoke, and body parts, no doubt, into the smoky air.

"Stop!" I hear the shouted command in Russian. I turn to my left. Three soldiers wearing Imperial Army uniforms are pointing their rifles directly at me.

"Lay the rifle on the ground!" one of them orders.

I comply but shout back with the only explanation I have, "I am a Russian soldier! A replacement! A volunteer!"

"Stay where you are! What unit are you with?"

"The Sixteenth!"

"The Sixteenth is a division. What unit?"

I have forgotten Avram's unit, so I say: "Avram Eizenberg's unit!"

"Stay where you are."

Two of the soldiers lower their weapons and step toward me.

"Who is your platoon captain?"

"I don't know. I'm a replacement for Avram Eizenberg. He's dead. He was killed this morning."

"What do you mean 'replacement'?" one asks skeptically.

"I was the teamster who came yesterday on a wagon with medical supplies, from Lovtcha. But I was supposed to be here, in the army, not ferrying supplies. Avram Eizenberg replaced me. It's too complicated to explain. I'm wearing his uniform. I can fight. Avram was killed by artillery fire, but I can fight. I can take his place."

"How do we know you're not a spy?"

"A spy? But I'm Russian!"

"You're a Jew, yes?"

"So are Lev and Kalman and Geyrshom. There are many Jews in the Sixteenth. I met them. Go and ask them. Ask their commander. I remember the name now: Nikolayev."

The three soldiers whisper among themselves. A gangly corporal with dark eyes addresses me, "It's okay, come with us." He picks up my rifle from the ground.

"What is your name?" he asks.

"Yakov Leibovich."

"Okay, Leibovich, listen. You're now with us. We're in reserve for this attack, patrolling the rear. We know Nikolayev, but we're in a different unit. Company A, Sixth Battalion. We can be ordered to the front line at any time; so stay ready. Can you shoot this Berdan?"

I lie, "Yes, but I need to get better."

"Never mind, you'll learn quickly enough. The Turks will be shooting at you, and you will need to shoot back. I'm going to report you to Captain Sidorov. He's our company commander. He will decide what happens to you. You haven't been trained. So, it's not ideal."

"I can learn."

"It had better be quick. We're at the front."

They escort me to Captain Mikhail Sidorov, a large-boned officer with a scar at the crease between his nose and cheek. He questions me closely about how Avram died and how I came to be wearing a Russian uniform with a private's stripes. He searches my knapsack. Then he walks off, telling me he must confirm that Avram is not with his unit. When he returns, he pulls me aside for a private conversation. He points a stubby forefinger at my nose.

"You can stay on one condition," he tells me sternly. "The moment you become a burden — you can't keep up, or lose your Berdan, or fail to follow orders — I will personally strip the uniform off you and kick you out, eh? I'll send you on your way in your Yid coat. Is that clear?"

"Yes, Captain. I just need a soldier to show me the best way to clean and load the Berdan."

"Alright, I'll assign someone. And your name will go on the company register at division headquarters. I expect you to fight like every courageous soldier in the Imperial Army. Do you understand? We are going to fight all winter if we have to, so prepare yourself. From what I hear, Eizenberg was a good soldier. Be like him. But the minute you stray or hesitate, you will be out and on your own. I won't tolerate a single slip."

I do what I am told. For days, while two Russian detachments labor to seal the encirclement of Plevna to keep supplies from reaching the Turks, I dig trenches and rifle pits using little more than the copper pot clipped to Avram's knapsack. It's backbreaking labor. The company is routinely working under fire, though we take care to remain outside of the Turks' rifle range. Their artillery, we are told, has been destroyed, so it is only the bullets that worry us now. On November 7th, Captain Sidorov orders us to prepare for an assault on the Turks the following day. That night, considering my situation, I reach into the bottom of my knapsack and feel for Avram's folded letter to Rivkah. My curiosity is strong, but I know it would be another betrayal to open it. I pull my hand free.

Dawn breaks, and we are enshrouded in a thick blanket of fog, perfect staging for a surprise assault. Today, I must creep up a hill toward the

Turkish positions with fixed bayonet, then sprint through the fog to attack before the enemy can prepare to defend. This is Skobelev's plan, and these are my orders. I am ambivalent about the threat. Part of me wants to survive, but another part of me seeks only an end to my sorrow and self-pity.

I will accept my fate, however it might be administered. Let God decide. And why not? Everyone else seems to be willing to place their lives in His hands. Shall I remain inscribed in the Book of Life? All I ask is that the verdict be rendered quickly and cleanly. If I am to die in today's battle, racing directly into the maw of enemy fire, or tomorrow's battle, or the next day's, dear God, let it be swift and sure.

We are one-hundred yards from the Turkish line. With visibility low, artillery fire from both sides has ceased. From my position, I can see General Skobelev mounted on his white charger. Behind him is a flag-bearer carrying a Cossack lance, a yellow silk banner at the tip. I ask the soldier next to me what the banner signifies. It is from Skobelev's desert battles of four years ago, he tells me. The general rides slowly among the ranks, ordering us to capture as many of the Turks' rifles as we can. The Peabody-Martini is far superior to the Berdan, he reminds us.

"Comrades, are we going to win today?" Skobelev shouts.

A lieutenant responds, "We will, Excellency!"

"Remember," Skobelev says, "this is not about bravery but rather discipline and obedience. Tomorrow, the band will play a waltz in the Turkish trenches; I guarantee it. For now, though, we have our bugler."

Skobelev dismounts, removes his cap, and crosses himself. The soldiers around him respond in a wave of pious gestures, invoking God's protective shield. One stands motionless; he must be the other Jew, or perhaps a silent nonbeliever. The prayers end, and the general signals the attack. We are up. I hear a stampede of boots, my own among them. We run through the fog for perhaps half the distance to the enemy line before rifle fire erupts. The Imperial Army bugle pierces the fog.

I dart through the mist, crouching over but with my eyes forward, listening to my heavy breathing and wondering if I am capable of plunging a bayonet into the flesh of a Turkish soldier. Indistinct figures come into view. I see the general himself swinging a sword. I feel as if I am witnessing my own nightmare. I hear the distinctive sound of a different bugle, a Turkish one. The soldier to my left stops short and collapses. This shocks me into realizing that the Turks are trying to end my life. It is them or us. Now, I can hear the Turks' cries from up the hill and the clash of metal amid the crack of rifle fire. I'm still running. I know I am alive but cannot understand how it is so. The edge of the trench appears. I leap. A Turk stands just in front of me, his sword poised to slash a stunned Russian. I thrust my musket forward, plunging my bayonet into the man's side and holding it as he screams in pain.

I hear Sidorov yelling. "Pull it out, man!"

I must have killed the Turk, for he is on the earth and still. I drop to my knees to withdraw the bayonet, feeling spent and nauseated. The battle has lasted just twenty minutes, and before me lies a tableau of slaughter, the floor of the trench strewn with bodies, and stretcher-bearers tending to the wounded — the Russians but not the Turks. In the distance, I hear pained moaning and understand more deeply how narrowly I have escaped death. Sidorov assigns me to help march captured Turks down the hill, where they will be escorted to Lovtcha by another Russian platoon. I have not fired my rifle. Rather than the exhilaration I thought I might feel, I walk in an uncomprehending daze.

When I return to the top of the knoll, the mist has lifted and sub-freezing air is moving in. Needles of ice begin to form in the trenches as we huddle together with little more than our eyes exposed, waiting for the counterattack that Skobelev has assured us will come. I wave off the offer of a cigarette. When I look north and west from the heights just captured, I can see why the battle of the Green Hills had to be won. Through field glasses, our detachment can watch the movement of Turkish troops along a wide stretch of land all the way to the edge of Plevna.

It isn't the end of the battle for this knoll. Just as Skobelev predicted, Ottoman units attempt to retake our position on the 10th, 11th, 15th, and 19th of November. Despite our exhaustion, we repulse every attack with barrages of rifle fire from well-fortified trenches and earthworks. Some of the soldiers now use the Peabody-Martini rifles, but I failed to pull one from the fingers of a dead Turk and am left with my Berdan. Helped by soldiers in my unit, I can now load and fire purposefully: aim, brace for the rifle's recoil, squeeze the trigger, pull the bolt back to eject the spent shell, find a new bullet, reload and lock the bolt briskly. When there is a lull, I clean my weapon. Maybe it is Avram's rifle; I will never know, but I think it must be.

The Turks are good marksmen. When a Russian soldier is killed, often from a silent bullet to the head, we bury him in the trench and erect a crude cross. I wonder if my own body might lie one day beneath a cross on some unnamed Bulgarian hill, mistaken for a Christian. It surprises me how little I care if there are other Jews in Company A. Being in a trench in freezing weather with other soldiers is an equalizer. I meet a soldier named Lebedev, a Christian from the western bank of the Volga, near Tsaritsyn. We strike up a conversation after he sees me struggling with my Berdan. He offers to instruct me in the finer points of marksmanship, and I accept. Lebedev is using a Peabody-Martini along with all the Turkish ammunition he can carry.

The Turks are too far away for us to know if any single bullet we have fired has found its mark. We are nearly blind in that respect. But the point is to spray the entire area. "Give them a curtain of fire, men!" Sidorov shouts whenever a Turkish attack begins. As far as we can tell, this tactic works. For the most part, the Turks remain in their trenches.

Late on November 14th, word spreads through the trench that Grand Duke Nicholas Nikolaevich, the Tsar's brother, has sent a letter to the Ottoman commander at Plevna, Osman Pasha, forwarded under a white flag of truce. The message purportedly states that Osman's fate is sealed by the encirclement, and he therefore has no choice but to surrender. We learn later that the Turkish general quickly and politely declined, allowing blind military honor, or foolhardiness, to overcome more sensible and humane inclinations.

For nearly a month into early December, it seems that all I do is dig fortifications and road networks, under increasingly harsh conditions. Snow and sleet fall as the stalemate endures. Strong gusts of wind sweep across the knoll on most days, and it is worse at night. I see almost no wildlife. We consume biscuits and tea heated above brushwood fires inside the trenches. On the occasional sunny afternoon, we pass cigarettes or break into song. During one of these brief respites, I smoke my first crudely rolled cigarette. I'm not sure what to make of the experience, but at least I have joined the others in this wartime ritual. There is no time to pray, nor do I know which day is the Sabbath. I have given up caring. Each afternoon, for less than an hour, our artillery units lob shells toward Plevna. General Skobelev walks the trenches to keep us informed and bolster morale. He must know how demoralizing it is to watch fellow soldiers ill with exposure or dysentery being escorted down the hill on stretchers. This is not how I wish to die. I envy those who take a bullet to the forehead.

Often, the conversation in the trenches turns to women. Lebedev, who looks to be in his late twenties, asks if I am married or have been with a woman. At first, I avoid him, but my defenses break down when he tells me about his wife and child in tender, endearing terms.

"This war saved me from a marriage I had no interest in," I confess.

"It was arranged, yes?"

"By my father and the bride's father, an old tradition I can do without."

"So you have no experience with women, yes?"

"None that I care to discuss."

"Ah. Is there someone else, then?"

"Maybe," I shrug. When I think of Rivkah, I feel both wistfulness and trepidation. "There is someone, but I made a mistake and hurt her, and if I survive this madness, I need to apologize and hope she'll forgive me."

"Are you in love with her?"

I don't know how to answer. I hardly know what love is.

"It's more of a longing," I say.

"Tell her the truth. Why not? It will show you respect her. You can see these soldiers have no respect for women. At least not here, in the middle of this living hell. Do you respect women, Leibovich?"

"I don't know. I think so."

"You think so? You either do or you don't. And if you do, you have to treat them like an equal person, no?"

"Did your father treat your mother as an equal, Lebedev?"

"I never knew my father, you see. My mother was everything, and I respected her and so did everyone else in town. She was a good example. So, I don't treat my wife like a slave. She has my respect. That's it. That's the only way. Now I ask you again: do you respect this girl, Leibovich?"

"Yes, I do respect her."

I begin to better understand my attraction to Rivkah, how awed I am in her presence: awed by her determination to survive, her jaunty humor in the face of hardship, her beauty, her self-reliance. I can see that it's not in her character to be subservient to me or any man. Why would I want her to be, because of tradition, because that's how my father acts? I think of my own mother. She deferred to my father to maintain peace in the home for all of us, not because she agreed with his insistence on obedience.

That night, huddled in a trench next to Lebedev, I dream again of Rivkah. She is walking away from me, and as hard as I try to catch up to her, I cannot. My legs won't work. The worst of it is that I don't sense if she even knows I am trying to reach her. She is aloof. The dream brings me no pleasure. I awake as confused and anxious as when I closed my eyes.

On December 6th, a messenger arrives from another company dug in farther along the knoll. I know him; it is Avram's friend Lev, one of the Yiddish Marksmen.

"Lev!" I call. "Peace be upon you. Do you remember me?"

"What? Avram's friend, the teamster! We thought you were dead!"

"It's me, Yakov Leibovich. I'm not at all dead."

"What are you doing here in uniform?"

"I'm in Company A now."

"A soldier? How? I thought you ran supplies. And what happened to Avram? We lost him."

"I'm sorry to say, but it happened the day we broke camp at Tuchenitza. He was killed by artillery."

Lev shakes his head. "Oh, hell. Hell. May God be with him. But why are you in uniform?"

"When Avram was killed — I saw it myself — I went into shock or something. It's too long a story to tell you now. I just decided to go in his place to fight. I took his uniform, and a musket. Maybe this is his Berdan. But what made you think I was dead?"

"Kalman told us, maybe a month ago. He went back to the camp with a platoon to dig up ammunition we buried."

"I don't understand."

"Kalman said he saw your body and satchel. He could see the fringes of your *tallit katan*. I think he recognized it."

"Oh my. They were mine, but I put my *tallit* on Avram's body and left my satchel when I took his knapsack. He's buried there, not me."

"I'm sorry, but I have to go or I will get frostbite," Lev says. "Maybe I will see you again, God willing."

"God willing, Lev."

That evening, I attempt to warm my fountain pen in my hands so I can add an entry to my journal, but my limbs lack any warmth at all.

"It is deathly cold," I write. "My hand is shaking and my penmanship is suffering."

For the first time, I set on paper my recollection of the death of my yeshiva friend, not because the images will never leave my mind — surely they won't — but in case Rivkah asks to know. So she can read it and I won't have to describe it to her. I don't think I can explain the circumstances of his death without breaking down.

I also write this:

> *I don't seem to care anymore whether I live or die in this uniform. I will do my duty, just as Avram would have, and place my fate in the hands of Almighty God. I will live or I will die without fear.*

Then, a new passage addressing my father:

> *Father, do you see that you have caused a terrible tragedy? You and I are both to blame. Why didn't I insist that your arrangement with the Partnership should not go forward? Why did I not think about how and where the conscription officer might fill his quota? Why did you have to bring Reb Epshtein into all of this, and why did the rabbi encourage you? Did you not see the injustice of it? Surely, the rabbi saw the injustice of giving up the vagrant. Did Reb Epshtein's brother not see the injustice? Did the Ministry of War not see the injustice? Avram has forgiven me, but I doubt that God has. Avram only wants me to help his mother, Shayna, if I can. But he is dead. May my effort at restitution be acceptable to Him. May Avram's family forgive us, and may his sister Rivkah one day have compassion and forgive me.*

Lebedev nudges my boot. "What are you writing, Leibovich?"

I look up. "A letter to myself, so I remember what I have seen and what I have promised myself — what my father should know if I don't return to Russia alive."

"We will return, Leibovich, you'll see. But we might not go home as heroes."

$$8$$

My extremities are numb with cold as a ray of bright midday sunshine pierces a cloud and illuminates our trench. It is the 8th of December. I am alive, but I don't count it as a blessing. I must flex my fingers and toes to keep warm, or at least to keep blood flowing and to know I can still move them. I have taken to marching along the trench so that my heart fills every vein and artery along my limbs. It is tempting to imagine this place, the Green Hills, at a different time of year. When I stand to my full height and peer over the edge of the trench I see the undulating forest and limestone cliffs surrounding us and, on cloudless days, the valley below and the azure Tuchenitza River. Winter and war have taken their toll on these woods. But in the fullness of summer, if I ever see another summer, this must be a glorious landscape. Today, the kind of glory borne of bravery in battle is the last thing on my mind. I am on a meditative walk, devoid of thought, when a messenger hustling through the trench shouts, "Leibovich!"

"Here!"

"Captain Sidorov needs to see you urgently," the courier says, catching his breath. "Come on."

My rifle and gear are already on my back, so I follow immediately, weaving through a phalanx of shivering comrades in arms, uncertain of my fate. Fear pulls my chest inward. My mind is racing. Will I face a false accusation of spying and be arrested or executed? I realize there is no use in speculating, but what have I done? What slander or false insinuation about me have they received?

When I arrive, my captain is standing, addressing several men, trying to bolster morale by delivering optimistic reports on the disposition and disarray of the enemy. He turns, looks me over, and asks an odd question.

"Leibovich, do you still have the garments of a Jew? I saw them in your knapsack."

"Yes, but they're soiled."

"Don't worry about that. Come with me."

We walk along the knoll and reach the entrance to a mud hut lit by candles. Sidorov ushers me in. Before me are three officers, including General Skobelev himself, sitting on a bench fashioned from a tree trunk. Streaks of mud cover his once-pristine uniform, but his full beard remains elegantly trimmed. Oddly, he seems to be cheery amid the icy cold.

"This is the Jew I told you about, Excellency," Sidorov announces.

"What is your name, Private?" the general asks in polished high Russian.

"Leibovich, sir."

"Am I correct that you are new to Company A and a man of some daring, Leibovich?"

I hedge, "New to Company A, sir, yes."

"Good. I have a mission for you, Private, but you must first tell me if you wish to volunteer for it."

Confused, I consider asking what the mission entails, but I think better of this, realizing it would instantly brand me as timid and unworthy. What would Avram have said, I wonder?

"Whatever will advance our cause," I respond. I can feel myself shivering. It is impossible to know if it is panic or just the damp, penetrating cold.

"Good, Leibovich. I want you to remove your uniform and put on the garments of a Jew. You speak the language of the Jews, yes? You speak Yiddish?"

"Yes, general."

"And are these your personal boots? They're not the boots of a soldier of the Imperial Army."

"No, sir. They are my own boots, sir."

"That's fine. Alright then, Leibovich. Your mission is crucial to our cause. Do you understand?"

"Yes, Excellency."

"Listen carefully then. You are to impersonate a Jewish peddler. A Cossack will escort you to the east road, and wait there in the woods for your return. You will enter the road and walk toward Plevna in the open, in daylight. We will give you a sack to carry. Inside will be delicacies in tins, some soap, some Liebig meat extract, and Roumanian cigarettes. You are to be an itinerant trader, a Jewish sutler. Do you understand?"

"Yes, sir."

"Speak only Yiddish. It is the only language you know. Carry no item issued to Russian soldiers except this fine watch." He hands me what appears to be a jeweled watch. "You took it from a dead Russian. You are a Polish Jew. Do you understand? They won't shoot a Polish Jew who is just a trader carrying personal items for sale. Go into the town, into Plevna, and sell the tins for twenty-five or fifty piasters. Sell the watch too, and make the price attractive."

"Yes, general." It dawns on me that I will be walking directly into a Turkish military stronghold.

"Do you have any idea why we're sending you into the heart of Plevna, Leibovich?" Captain Sidorov asks.

"To collect information, sir."

"Yes, but what kind of information?" the general inquires.

"Well, I imagine, sir, to learn what I can about the disposition of the enemy's forces, their movements and general condition, to open my eyes and ears and see what I can learn about their current state and their fortifications."

Skobelev seems pleased.

"This is exactly correct. I can see you are an intelligent soldier, Leibovich. We have chosen wisely. When you arrive, you are to notice everything and take careful mental notes. I mean everything. Are the trenches and redoubts you pass teeming with soldiers? Are the men healthy and well-clothed? Do they have ammunition? Do they have rations? Are they calm or in chaos? Are they packing and loading wagons? Are they shivering in the cold? In what direction are they moving? Take in all that you see and hear. Seal it in your memory. Sell what you can from the sack in an hour, not longer, and then walk out the same way you came in, along the east road, carrying the empty sack. If the Turks don't seem to be watching you, stroll right back into the same woods. The Cossack will be there."

"Do you understand, Leibovich?" Sidorov barks.

"Yes, sir."

Skobelev speaks softly and more kindly now. "We need information, Leibovich. We prepared a sack for you; look inside. I'm quite certain these items will sell quickly in a town that must be close to starving. Now change your clothes, keep your boots on, and be on your way. We'll get the Cossack ready."

As I glance toward Sidorov, he turns to the general and declares, "A sound plan, Excellency. He will succeed."

"Yes, you will succeed," Skobelev says, standing and looking directly at me. "Thank you, my eagle, for serving the Empire."

"I will do my best, sir."

The panic I felt has all but disappeared, replaced only by resignation. I will either succeed or fail, return or be captured. Maybe I will survive, maybe not. It is fate or fortune or God's will; it doesn't seem to matter anymore. If I am found out, I am certain the Turks will torture me. This is my only source of anxiety. A bullet to the head, at close range, would be preferable. I can always attack one of them with my bare hands, and they will shoot me.

I suck in a deep breath and pivot, thinking about the Jewish sutler I met in Lovtcha, a man trying to make a little bit of money by taking large risks in the middle of a battlefield. I will take on his persona for this journey and bear the risks of marching directly into an enemy camp. I will create my own bit of theater. It's the only way.

From what I have heard over the years, the itinerant Jewish merchant is a marginal but familiar character in the larger drama of war. He appears at random in a town or village center, hawking an eclectic mix of personal items, exotic foods, and gadgets from a cart. Often, the merchandise consists of seasonal items. Lately, in the dead of winter, this means fur hats, lined gloves, and fine scarves. The Jews are aliens in the minds of both sides of this conflict, and thus are suspected of being loyal only to their own kind and their own strange religion. But I have to wonder: in Plevna, who can afford the delicacies I will carry? Surely not the rank-and-file soldiers, but only the officers. They must have cash; or maybe they will barter with war souvenirs and campaign medals. And will a younger merchant seem odd to them? I don't have any idea, and that is what makes this implausible mission intimidating. I am a rabbinical student, and perhaps a soldier. And though I see wandering merchants from time to time, I have paid little attention to their methods and peculiarities.

At the edge of the woods, I leave the Cossack's side and walk briskly along the eastern road toward the town, in my black hat and soiled black frock coat, head down but eyes alert, with a burlap sack over my shoulder. I try to act as if I have ambled into Plevna a dozen times before. No one challenges me or even looks my way. I am part of the landscape. The Turks either don't think twice about a Jew with a sack over his shoulder or are too busy to notice. But I notice them. As I get closer, I can see Ottoman soldiers packing up weapons and ammunition, apparently preparing to abandon their earthen ramparts. The Turks' trenches and redoubts are hives of activity. A few soldiers are fashioning dummy figures with Turkish uniforms, and leaning them against the ramparts in a crude attempt to fool the Imperial Army. Field artillery pieces remain in place. Soldiers are exiting the redoubts with their rifles and full equipment. This is the kind of information that General Skobelev will find of great interest.

In the cold, my breath forms clouds in the air. I wonder: is a Jew like a mosquito to these people, a nuisance to be ignored so long as it doesn't try to bite? Given what I have seen in every trench and redoubt, I consider turning back immediately and alerting the general as quickly as possible that the Turks are moving out. He should know immediately. And yet, orders are orders. If I am dispatched to the town center to sell the contents of a sack, that is exactly where I must go and precisely what I must do. If I admit to having turned back before reaching the center of Plevna, Sidorov and the rest will accuse me of cowardice, and harsh punishment will ensue. There is nothing to do but keep walking.

Plevna is a zone of shocking misery. Haggard-looking soldiers consume snow with their bare hands. The streets and buildings have suffered damage from the daily shelling by Russia's siege artillery. I pass a crowded mosque serving as a refuge for civilians. Sick and wounded soldiers with gaunt faces lie everywhere, wrapped in linen bandages or waiting alone to die. Mongrel dogs roam the alleys. On some streets, the smell of rot and death is overpowering. I reach what appears to be the central square bustling with wagons and carts being packed with supplies. I notice soldiers cleaning their rifles and sharpening their bayonets. Oxen are being assembled to haul the carts and wagons.

I set down my sack and begin to place its contents on a low wall that surrounds an administrative building. Even before I complete this task, soldiers and civilians begin to gather. They see a Jew and think, he must be selling something. The sack's contents are gone in thirty minutes of flashing hand signals and urgent swapping of goods for coins. An officer buys the watch, offering two lira. No one understands Yiddish, but a few of the buyers try German, which I understand perfectly but do little more than acknowledge with a nod.

There is no need to linger. I have seen all I need to see. Nothing is ambiguous. The Turks are leaving Plevna, either preparing an armed sortie toward the Russian line of encirclement in an attempt to break out, or planning a mass surrender. The surrender theory is dubious though, as soldiers preparing to lay down their arms do not sharpen their bayonets.

But would Osman tell his men he is going to surrender? They are definitely not planning to march east; the eastern positions are the ones being abandoned, and a majority of the wagons are facing west or south. I fold the empty sack and tuck it under my arm. The Jew has sold his goods. I hunch over against an icy wind, returning along the eastern road, head down. No one bothers a mangy stray dog or a darting rat, and such is the Jew to these people — a nobody, a nothing, another inanimate element of the near horizon. It is dusk as I glance back, before veering into the woods at the appointed spot so that the Cossack can find me.

By the time we climb back up the Green Hills to Skobelev's hut, it is dark. I am relieved I wasn't shot or taken prisoner, not because those outcomes are undesirable, but because what I have learned will surely please the general. I eagerly tell him and his officers what I have seen in rapid-fire, detailed sentences.

"Everything tells me the Turks are packing up and moving out quickly, toward the west or south," I conclude with conviction. The meticulously memorized scenes pour out, including the precarious state of the Turkish troops. I end my report triumphantly.

Yet, shockingly, my word is not good enough. The word of a Jew counts for nothing.

"If you are right," General Skobelev says in measured speech, "other trenches and redoubts are being abandoned as well, but all of this must be verified. Before I telegraph headquarters, we will immediately take a small detachment as close as we can to where you entered the town. Another detachment will probe from the south. Put your uniform back on, Leibovich. You are going with the scouts. We will soon know if you have told the truth or tried to deceive us."

I had entered the hut physically and emotionally spent. Now, I am suspected of treasonous deception. In a voice that must have betrayed my exhaustion and disappointment, I say weakly, "I have told the truth, Excellency." There is no response. Captain Sidorov escorts me out without a word of gratitude.

It is obviously no surprise to me that the scouting parties confirm everything I conveyed, and our forces see that the Turks are abandoning the southern redoubts as well. The general concludes that the enemy is about to attempt to break through the encirclement to the west. He immediately telegraphs headquarters, and assigns fresh detachments to seize the abandoned trenches with stealth and speed. New orders arrive for my unit. Before daybreak on the 10th of December, we and other units descend the hill and march five miles to the left bank of the Vid River, the likeliest point for the Turks to attempt an escape. I have not slept in more than thirty-six hours and march in a daze, hoping that Osman Pasha will surrender and allow Plevna to fall without bloodshed. I do not pray for this outcome, however. What is the point? Is the One and Eternal God, the *Ein Sof*, listening to the lone voice of a Jew in a Russian uniform who stabbed a man to death in a Turkish trench?

It takes hours of fighting before Plevna falls. Russian forces sweep into the town from the east and make for the western gates to prevent a retreat back into town. Other Russian regiments along the Vid take the brunt of the Turkish attack. Our division is shifted back and held in reserve, but when the fog and smoke lift, I can see that hundreds, maybe thousands, on both sides have fallen. By afternoon, word spreads that the Turks have surrendered their entire force, more than forty-thousand soldiers and officers. Another rumor circulates: Osman Pasha has been wounded. Hearing of the surrender, I do not rejoice. I have nothing left, no energy, no feeling. I sit against a tree and fall into a deep sleep.

Someone jars me awake with a boot to the thigh. How long I have slept is a mystery, though I do not feel particularly refreshed. It mustn't have been more than an hour. I look up and see Sidorov.

"Leibovich, wake up! You've been summoned by His Excellency, General Mikhail Dmitriyevich Skobelev!"

"What?"

"I'm taking you to the general's field headquarters. Get up."

"I haven't done anything wrong! I am a loyal soldier, captain!"

Can this possibly be my fate? Discarded or even punished, now that Plevna has fallen, by my own superior officers after working as a spy and following orders to the letter?

Sidorov responds coldly, "I would advise you not to disobey a direct order from your commanding officer, Leibovich."

"Yes, sir," I say glumly. Resigned to my fate, I stand and adjust my uniform. We walk for ten minutes, past hundreds of Turks under guard after placing their rifles on the ground. Sidorov says nothing during our march. We arrive at a farmer's hut surrounded by Russian officers and guards. Sidorov enters and immediately emerges with General Skobelev. His coat drapes over his shoulders like a cape, partly obscuring his muddy uniform. He looks haggard but purposeful. It is hard for me to read his face.

"Leibovich, stand here!" the general orders.

I am bitter and exhausted, and don't care what he does to me. "Yes, Excellency."

"Look at me!" he demands, and I obey. Skobelev then places both hands on my shoulders. Rabbi Epshtein made similar gestures when offering a personal benediction at the synagogue. But this handsome Russian general is no rabbi. He offers the briefest smile.

"In the presence of these officers," Skobelev declares, "I am awarding you, Private Yakov Leibovich, the Cross of St. George in the fourth class, for acts of distinction in battle. You performed brilliantly in your mission yesterday, Private Leibovich." He reaches into his pocket and moves to pin a silver cross onto my coat.

I glance down and ask haltingly, "Excellency, who is St. George?"

I can see Sidorov's chin drop to his chest and inhale sharply while his eyebrows arch. There is a stir among the other officers and a few snickers.

"Why, a Christian martyr, of course!" the general snaps, looking directly at me.

A pained look must have crossed my face. I stammer, "I . . . I don't . . ."

Skobelev suddenly pulls back, the medal still in his hand. "Of course, of course, you are not of the Eastern Orthodox faith."

"No, sir."

"And a Jew cannot wear such . . ."

"No, sir."

". . . icons venerating a Christian saint."

"I'm sorry, sir. I hope you understand, Excellency."

I see Captain Sidorov shoot me a stern look of disapproval, but he holds his tongue.

"Never mind, Leibovich," the general says cheerfully. He lifts one of my hands, turns my palm upward, and places the cross in it. "For a Jew, you performed with surprising distinction, and these men are my witnesses. The notation will go into the record of the division, and the Ministry of War will be informed. But you are hereby relieved of the obligation to wear the damned thing. Put it in your pocket, Leibovich, and care for it. One day, you will remember this moment and want to show it to someone."

Skobelev turns to Sidorov. "Captain, I expect you to inform Company A of this man's exemplary acts on behalf of the Tsar, but you needn't mention St. George. Is that clear?"

"Yes, Excellency."

"Now, off with the both of you. We have work to do!"

I manage an awkward salute. Sidorov grabs my arm. Within five seconds of departing, the captain sputters and sneers, "How can you be so insolent and thoroughly without gratitude, Leibovich? You're lucky he didn't shoot you on the spot! He didn't, but I might."

I can feel the weight of the medal in the pocket of my coat. How strange, a Jew with the Cross of St. George. I am bemused. I admit to myself that I feel a morsel of due recognition. Turning the medal in my fingers, I realize it is now my talisman and that Captain Sidorov cannot harm a hair on my head or chin.

This small satisfaction is brief, for the captain exacts his revenge by assigning me to hoist the dead, Turkish and Russian alike, onto carts and dump the bodies into the frigid Vid River. The wintry conditions prevent the stench in the fields and roadways from overpowering us. I work with my scarf across my nose and mouth alongside three Jews from another company. The work is gruesome and sickening.

"Shall we say Kaddish for these souls?" I ask.

One of the others replies, "Why proclaim God's greatness in the Mourner's Prayer amid this carnage? What would be the point of that?"

"I suppose because with each death we also pray for abundant peace."

"A waste of time," another soldier declares. "Let's get this over with."

Disposing of the bodies takes most of the day. Each Turk is stripped of .45 caliber bullets required for the long-range Peabody-Martini rifles. When the enemy soldiers were ordered to lay down their weapons as part of the surrender, some removed the bullets and stomped on them until the powder spilled out, but not all. Carts arrive to haul away usable weapons. Russian units seize thousands of the advanced rifles and enough bullets to wage war for weeks.

When the removal of bodies is complete, Sidorov assigns me to help guard prisoners. This is only slightly less ghastly. The town of Plevna now holds thousands of defeated and bedraggled men. We search each prisoner and march them into open encampments, or place them in houses that are still standing. There are no doctors to tend to the sick and walking wounded. There isn't enough food. I have never seen such collective misery, even in Plevna. The sick lie beside the dying and dead. Drinking water is scarce because the water in the Vid River has been contaminated by the bodies we dumped there.

Some of the Turks are allowed to dismantle their carts for firewood, but many perish in the cold. Morsels of bread are handed out, but little more. Bodies begin to fill the trenches dug by the Turks to defend the town, drawing flocks of carrion crows. I stand guard over the shivering men for hours, shocked by the conditions they are forced to endure. Each day, I pull a prisoner aside and slip him a black biscuit from my pouch. I can do little more for them.

I ask Sidorov why there is no food for the prisoners. Everyone was focused on the siege and no one thought to stock supplies for prisoners, he tells me. We barely have enough to feed ourselves. But he knows we should be treating the vanquished the way we would wish to be treated had we been in their boots. "They fought bravely," the captain says with a shrug. "It's war."

"What will happen when we leave?" I ask. "The Bulgarian Christians will take their revenge, won't they?"

"The world isn't perfect, Leibovich. We're going to march those who can walk to Bucharest."

That evening, beside a campfire, I am moved to write an entry in my journal. Rereading it, I see that it is among the bleakest I have ever composed:

> *The privation and cruelty sit in my gut like a wound that refuses to heal. It makes me feel that nearness to God is impossible. I never imagined such human misery as I sat in the beit midrash all those years with big books and big thoughts — all academic, divorced from the brutal reality of nature and man. I try to put it out of my mind, but I cannot. It is a living nightmare. We consume animals for food, but we never slaughter them with such cruelty. Why are the vanquished treated worse than animals? That is what I have seen this day. We are taught to be loving, joyful, and humble. Why did the Creator fashion a world where such unnatural destruction takes place?*

While working for the Partnership, I wrapped my arms in phylacteries in the mornings to fulfill the commandment and recited the *Maariv* prayer each evening. Tonight, I pull a blanket over my head and fall asleep without any veneration or fealty. Tomorrow will be a better day, I think. It must be.

$$9$$

With Plevna seized, a new front line opens in this brutal war, and it lies along a range of mid-sized mountains, the Balkans, whose snowy passes are still controlled by the enemy. Mercifully, Captain Sidorov orders us to prepare to march there. Ordinarily, such an order would cause ripples of anxiety within our ranks, but for many of us, certainly including me, it is a blessed relief. We are no longer required to watch prisoners perish like trapped insects. Company A's new task is to reach the Balkans, help secure a passage through the range, then spearhead an attack on the heart of the Ottoman Empire, all the way to Constantinople. As relieved as I am to be retreating from Plevna's horrors, it is clear that this new venture may be our most challenging encounter with the enemy.

Sidorov is characteristically blunt. Lieutenant-General Mikhail Skobelev has tired of his bureaucratic duties as the military administrator of Plevna. It is no surprise. He is not built for such a dreary assignment, and the war against the Turks is far from over. Although the Turkish garrison's surrender at Plevna has removed a stubborn obstacle to Russia's advance, word in camp is that the Imperial Army has been stalled on the northern slopes of the Balkans. Our Sixteenth Division will move sixty miles southeast to Gabrovo, Sidorov explains, where three generals, Skobelev included, are preparing an assault. Though Sidorev doesn't say so explicitly, the clear goal is to take control of the Shipka Pass. Beyond the pass lie flat roads that run directly to the Ottoman throne. Russia has again seized the initiative, but it is now January and conditions are extremely harsh.

"We are marching in winter and we will fight in winter," Sidorov bellows to the assembled company mustered under a blanket of thick, low clouds. "Pack rations, extra gloves, and woolens if you can find them. Everyone will be issued a Peabody-Martini rifle captured from the Turks, plus .45 caliber ammunition, plenty of it. We'll train with the rifle this afternoon. Kiss your Berdan goodbye, men, and learn to love this new weapon. But understand this: a rifle doesn't win battles, only courage and obedience will."

My comrade, Lebedev, insists that no army has ever tried a Balkans crossing in January. I have no reason to question his knowledge of such matters, as the Balkans are a mystery to me. I picture jagged, snow-covered peaks and icy ravines, where soldiers led by fanatical generals simultaneously duel nature and death. But I know almost nothing.

Lebedev seems to have been raised in the outdoors and is an obsessive pragmatist. "When we get to Gabrovo," he advises me, grabbing my shoulders in a show of brotherly solidarity, "take some rags or cloth and wrap your boots. And make sure you have a thick scarf for your head and ears. Take one from the dead."

I find myself studying Lebedev, my mentor, to learn important survival skills. He spends his day assessing his condition and deciding what he will need in the next twenty-four hours to remain alive. He cleans his rifle at least daily, repeatedly checks his rations, keeps his canteen full, and tries to sleep whenever we aren't on the move. And he tells dozens of jokes on long marches. Though frankly, I am in no mood for laughter. Lebedev knows this, but cannot help himself.

"Did you hear about the Hussar?" he asks me loudly, then answers without waiting for a response. "He's sitting on the edge of a bed, pulling on his boots, and the whore he's been with says to him, 'Haven't you forgotten about the money?' and the Hussar says: 'Madame, Hussars never take payment!'"

Everyone within earshot laughs heartily, a result that Lebedev craves. I cannot help but break into a grin. When I think about it, he is my only genuine companion in Company A, and I take all of his suggestions to heart. Before we depart for the Balkans, I jettison my black hat, which I've been wearing or carrying from the day I left Navahrudak. I lighten my knapsack contents to the barest minimum. I cut the thick sleeves off my frock coat and tear strips from a white shirt that I last wore while impersonating a Polish merchant inside Plevna. All of the clothing that signifies my membership in the race of the Jews is gone. I now only have my skullcap and sidelocks as signifiers. I practice wrapping my boots with the coat sleeves and shirt strips while thinking of Avram. He would have known about wrapping boots in winter.

Our column's trek to Gabrovo takes three days of steady marching. I walk rhythmically behind the field artillery, and conclude that winter is far more tolerable when we are on the move than standing guard over a compound filled with miserable prisoners. My mind begins to empty, and I feel something close to serenity on this march, at least until the Balkan range comes into view. While less daunting than the jagged peaks I had imagined, these wintry mountains are intimidating nonetheless. Gabrovo stands at the northern entrance to the Shipka Pass, a trail we must conquer at four-thousand feet above sea level. Flanked by steep slopes, the pass seems to offer us only one military option. Everyone in our unit girds themeselves for a frontal assault using cannon, rifle fire, bayonets, and ruthlessness. Suddenly, my sense of calm evaporates.

The looming trauma connects my mind to unfinished personal business: *selichah*. By now, I imagine, the Imperial Army has sent word to the alley dwelling in Navahrudak that Private Avram Eizenberg died heroically near Plevna in an artillery barrage. Perhaps they have handed Shayna Eizenberg a small death benefit that the families of fallen heroes are offered. I imagine Rivkah and her mother grieving. I see their tears and feel their heartache. It makes me recall Reb Epshtein's teachings on the concept in Jewish law of *mechilah*, forgiving a debt.

If a person is sincerely repentant and has shown repentance in word and deed, the offended person is obliged to forgive. What I have before me is not a matter of simple indebtedness, however. I want to ask Rivkah for something more. I want to ask her to be merciful, to understand my moral frailty, to see my flaws, to take pity on me, and to offer a deeper forgiveness. This is the true meaning of *selichah*. Am I worthy? I feel myself slipping into a state of fatalism and surrender as I prepare to march as an obedient soldier through the Shipka Pass.

What drives this man Skobelev, I wonder, and how is it that he doesn't fear death? No other officer wears such a conspicuous uniform. The men who served with Skobelev say he wears white as a challenge to his soldiers, to show them how to vanquish fear. It seems foolish and unnecessary. But I grudgingly come to believe that it works. The general is a beacon, and, bloodied or not, his men follow him. They obey.

At Gabrovo, the general addresses us from the side of a hill, shouting to make himself heard, "Do you recall, eagles, how we ravaged the Ottoman defenses at the Green Hills?" he bellows.

"Yes, Excellency!"

"The Turks ran like rabbits! And with God's help and your good discipline, we will give them a devil of a fight tomorrow on the Balkan peaks!"

"Hurrah!"

"Here is the plan, my eagles. Two other Russian detachments are here at Gabrovo. General Radetzky's detachment will push directly into the Shipka Pass toward the town of Shipka at the opposite end. Prince

Mirsky's detachment will advance over the mountains on the left flank. And we will advance over the peaks on the right flank. When we join with Mirsky's force south of the village of Shipka, the Turks will be in a vise, and we will finish them!"

Silence falls over the ranks like a curtain of doom. There are whispers. He said "over the mountains." We all heard it. Did he mean to say that two task forces will not be marching through the pass itself but across the uncharted peaks on either side, where no pass exists? It seems to be impossible, madness, an error.

Lebedev elbows me, covers his mouth with a gloved hand, and whispers, "I wonder how many of us will be left when we descend on the other side of these Balkan monsters."

"There will be no supply wagons!" Skobelev shouts. "Each man must carry four days of rations. You now have the best rifles in the world. Use them wisely, but know that the Turks have the very same weapon. We will bring a dozen field artillery pieces with us, and if the horses falter, we will push the weapons ourselves. Prepare, my eagles, to be victorious!"

Confused, wary, and skeptical, we break camp at Gabrovo the next evening, the 5th of January, and set out to subdue the bitterly cold mountain slopes, with fifteen-thousand men under Skobelev's command. Sidorov says it will take two days to cross the mountains. A joint attack with Mirksy's forces will commence on the morning of the 8th. As we ascend the northern slope of the Balkan hills, the air begins thinning and my lungs being losing their capacity to bring oxygen to my limbs. Fortunately, the Peabody-Martini is a lighter weapon than the nine-pound Berdan. The snow along the winding route gets deeper as we climb in a long, single, snaking column. I can only imagine the sappers at the front facing the immense challenge of moving the snow and clearing a path; I am too far back to see their Herculean efforts. The black sleeves of my frock coat cover my boots, fixed with rags knotted across the insole and at mid-calf. It is a brilliant suggestion by Lebedev. Along the way, I eat snow and black biscuits.

Within half a day's march, Skobelev abandons the artillery. It is impossible to move the heavy pieces, no matter how many men are assigned to heave the steel. Lebedev and I are among those who had put their shoulders to the task. Both horse and man failed, and the horse-drawn artillery is ordered to turn back. At the peak, a biting wind sweeps across the landscape as the sappers dig through ten-foot drifts, probing for ways forward with plausible footing. The deeper the snow, the more protection we have from the wind. Even so, my feet and hands are in pain, and I wonder if they are frostbitten. With my wool scarf wrapped around my head and face, the cold is as much the enemy as the Turks.

"Keep moving to circulate the blood," Lebedev reminds me. But I know this.

The soldiers who haven't wrapped their boots or whose gloves are insufficient are in visible pain. Still, we advance on schedule, at least until our descent at the southern face of the mountain, when trouble arises — the Turks are dug in at a line of trenches overlooking the descending path.

Sidorov is shouting, "Marksmen with a Turkish rifle, come forward!" summoning the entire company, for we all now possess the Turkish weapon. Lebedev and I take cover behind an ice-covered outcropping.

"The trenches are fifteen-hundred yards across the ravine!" Sidorov yells. "Give them a stream of lead, boys!"

To shoot blindly is a waste of ammunition. Lebedev makes sure we both take time to aim. The volleys last less than an hour. Through field glasses, Sidorov can see the Turks retreat to a new trench farther along the path, or possibly all the way to the redoubts we are likely to find at the bottom of the mountain. A village called Sheynovo lies immediately below us, and we must subdue Sheynovo to reach Shipka. We move on, descending through the night in an icy mist, and gather at the bottom, not far from a set of Turkish trenches. We are just two miles from the southern entrance to Shipka, but the Turks have chosen to make a stand at Sheynovo. Thousands of them wait in fortified earthworks, and we must defeat them to achieve our goal, Sidorov tells us. At midday, he issues final instructions: we are to move forward without firing, remaining in our lines until given the order to rush the enemy fortifications.

"It sounds like suicide because it is," Lebedev says bitterly.

Surely, my time has come. I try to manage my breathing to remain calm. Prayer seems pointless. We fix bayonets, as ordered. I look at Lebedev. His eyes are closed while making the sign of the cross over his chest.

"Thank you for your help these last days, my friend," I say to him.

"I will be at your side," Lebedev says. "This is now out of our hands, Leibovich. We will be brave; I know it."

My lips move almost involuntarily. Hearing the faint sounds of Hebrew, Lebedev glances at me, and says with a smile and a wink, "Don't worry, Yid. We are made of iron."

"Be patient, men!" Sidorov shouts. "Stay disciplined!"

The Imperial Army band begins to play. Unit banners rise. Thousands of Russian soldiers, many still in pain from the mountain crossing, move forward in fixed lines, entering what we know will become a field of fire from the Ottoman infantry.

I conclude that my life will end this day and convince myself that I am prepared to die. I want all of this to end — the cold, the pain, the misfortune, the stupidity, the poor judgment, the guilt about Rivkah and Avram. I want it to end today.

On orders, we begin to jog, bayonets forward and held low. Lebedev runs directly in front of me. I feel as if I am running inside a cocoon. I hear my own muffled voice mutter under my breath, "Take me quickly from this earthly prison."

We pick up the pace, and Turkish bullets begin finding my comrades. Our orders are not to fire back until given the command by bugle. My bayonet remains forward, but I doubt that I will use it. I doubt I will enter any Turkish redoubt today; it seems I will be gunned down before then. Band members fall, with audible changes to their rallying anthem.

I hear my own shaky voice again: "Don't make me suffer." For a split second, I see an apparition — Rivkah. Even in her tattered garb, she is disarmingly beautiful. But I am not in control. My legs are strong. I am running. But I am not in control.

"Don't let me suffer!" I begin to say out loud as I run, my jaw locked and teeth gritted, my arms still carrying the Peabody-Martini. Lebedev is no longer in front of me. Russian infantrymen are falling around me. Somehow, my feet keep moving.

I imagine a bullet penetrating my forehead. It is hot to the touch, but I feel no pain. I don't want to suffer.

The bugle sounds. The noise is deafening as gunfire erupts toward the Turkish line, and the screams and battle cries of soldiers running to their fate fills the air. My movements feel involuntary, as if I was watching myself from afar. I cannot control anything. Operating on pure instinct, I kneel and fire my rifle once, then push myself up. My eyes are filled. Is it the smoke? Am I weeping?

"Don't make me suffer," I say again.

I can't see much as the battle smoke becomes ever thicker. But I hear myself screaming. Sidorov appears in front of me, firing a pistol. Grabbing my rifle in both hands, I prepare to leap into the redoubt. How did I arrive in this trench, in this whirl of clashing metal, bayonets, and swords? Confronting the chaos, I whimper while swinging my rifle. I find myself face to face with the enemy, and emit a guttural shout as I swing the butt of my rifle into the face of a Turkish soldier. His eyes flash with anger, fear, and what seems like exultation. He appears to be twice my age. The force knocks him to the ground, face up. Swiftly, I lower my bayonet and plunge it deep into his midsection with a force I did not know was within me. I feel the tip penetrate tissue and begin to enter the rocky earth at his back; or maybe it is bone. I hear a deep, ugly groan. Not an instant later, my left shoulder is in excruciating pain. His bayonet has pierced me. I drop to the earth, scream, drop my rifle, grab my arm, and slip into unconsciousness.

When I open my eyes, a man is kneeling over me. I can barely see him. I begin to focus. It is Sidorov.

"I am dead," I murmur.

"Of course not, Leibovich." He opens my coat to examine my wound, sending another bolt of pain through my shoulder.

"Then shoot me. End it."

"Shut up, Leibovich."

"I'm ready to die."

He ignores me. "It went through muscle. Take this cloth and press it here. Let's stop the bleeding."

"It's no use."

"Stop it, Leibovich! Stand up! Get to the back of the redoubt and find medical help. That's an order!" Sidorov barks these commands as he grabs me under the arms and pulls me up, grunting. My knees lock while holding the bandage to my throbbing shoulder. Coming to my senses, I realize the battle is over, and that I have survived and will probably live.

"Where is Lebedev?" I stammer.

"Quiet! General Skobelev is negotiating the surrender of thirty-six-thousand Turks. Right now, Leibovich! They're laying down their arms. Walk to the back of the redoubt. You're not the only one wounded. There are medics. Get going!"

"Where is Lebedev, captain?"

"A hero, Leibovich, a hero," Sidorov says quietly, gravely. "He fought with courage and, like his comrades, is bathed in honor. Now, get to the medical area."

Lebedev is dead, and I feel utterly numb, my emotions pushed somewhere deep inside; yet part of me wants to find his body and recite the Mourner's Prayer. But for whom? For Lebedev? No prayer will restore his life. Shall I praise God for allowing a good and honest man to be taken from his wife and family? Shall I find his widow and his mother and explain his senseless death, and sing a blessing in their presence to the one and only Creator?

"Why?" I ask myself out loud.

Sidorov shouts: "Walk!"

Wincing as I hold the compress to my shoulder, I take five or six shaky steps in the direction Sidorov is pointing.

"Alright," I mumble. Before I can take another step, though, my knees give way and my neck swivels. My head drains, and I collapse to the cold ground.

How long I was unconscious, I do not know. A soldier revives me with smelling salts, an awful odor but one that awakens everything. I'm not sure where I am, only that I am lying on cold soil. They bandage me quickly and painfully, place me on a stretcher, and carry me down a hill to a medical tent. A corpsman administers morphine by needle, and the throbbing pain subsides almost instantly. I feel as if I am floating on a bed of air, dizzy and euphoric. My vision is blurred. They lift my stretcher onto an ambulance wagon and tell me I'm going back to Gabrovo via the liberated Shipka Pass. There must be scores, maybe hundreds, of other wounded Russians; but I can barely think. The morphine transports me.

I need more such injections over the next two days. Slowly, I gain enough stability to walk among those who have suffered wounds, many more grievous than mine.

After the journey back through Shipka Pass, I find myself inside the Gabrovo field hospital, which is nothing more than a large home commandeered by the Imperial Army. They are weaning me off the morphine, though I still have throbbing pain. Why was I spared? I ask myself again and again but have no answer. Why Lebedev but not me? I know I am undeserving. When I learn that a thousand Russian soldiers died and another four-thousand were wounded in the Battle of Shipka Pass, I feel disgrace. I did not deserve to live. Lebedev did not deserve to die.

They want me to stand, so I deliver food, water, and medicine as best I can with my one useful arm, the right. My left arm rests immobilized in a bulky sling. The shoulder aches constantly. I have no sense of whether or when I will be returned to my unit. I have no desire to return, nor any desire to go forward. On the fourth day at the field hospital, I realize my wound is not improving, but worsening, along with the pain. The doctor says the shoulder has become infected. It throbs terribly. For the next three days, I run a mild fever and remain in bed.

During this time, Doctor Chernin, another bearded Jew from the Minsk region, routinely sprays carbolic acid into the puss-filled gash, causing me to scream in pain. "It will fight the infection. This is the kind of pain that will help you," he tells me. I want only to be put out of my misery.

On the first day of this treatment, I rest on a straw mat on the floor and fall into a feverish sleep. In a dream, I see Lebedev telling a joke and then laughing at it. A hole in the center of his forehead seeps crimson-colored blood. This fitful delirium continues for two more days. I see Lebedev again and again. One night, dozing and still feverish, I see myself sitting in a trench. A woman's hands and arms slowly enter my wool coat and embrace me. She places her face against my cheek, sending warmth throughout my body, and whispers my name. In the dream, I ask: "Who are you?" She answers, "Don't you know me? I'm Rivkah." When I pull my head back to see her face, Rivkah places her hands on the sides of my neck. They are cold. She disappears, and I awaken shivering, even beneath two blankets.

When the fever abates, my shoulder remains painful, but the throbbing is less pronounced. Boots shuffle near my floor mat. A figure in uniform stands over me, offering a glass of tea. I recognize him; it is Neschadymenko.

"Sit up, lad."

I can barely speak. My voice is weak. "How did you get here?" I whisper.

"Never mind. Sit up and drink."

"I'm not sure I can."

"You can. Come on." The Cossack puts the tea on the floor to help me prop myself against the wall, then hands me the glass.

"Drink."

I taste the sweetness. "Where did you get sugar?"

"We delivered supplies here yesterday in a big train — five-hundred wagons. The army wants to advance rapidly now that we control the pass at Shipka. I heard you were wounded there."

"Yes, with a bayonet. How did you find me?"

"I asked for you when we got here. I've been asking everywhere we go."

"Is Stepan here? I'm sure he wants to place me before a firing squad."

"I told him what happened, Leibovich, the whole story about your friend, and so on. But he's angry, of course. That isn't why I'm here though. This has nothing to do with Stepan. I bring news. When Stepan heard I had found you, he handed me a letter from the Partnership. It's for you. Varshavsky needs you to come to St. Petersburg. He's gotten the army to change your orders."

"What?"

"Varshavsky has summoned you to testify before a State Commission of Inquiry in St. Petersburg. You're going to St. Petersburg as soon as you can travel."

"What's going on?"

"There's a problem. The army claims the Partnership is cheating, that it's all corrupt, you know, delivering low-quality goods, overcharging and embezzling from the State Treasury to line its own pockets, and all the rest that you can imagine. It might be true, for all I know; it might not."

I need a moment to absorb this. The sweet, warm tea has an immediate beneficial effect, strengthening my voice. "What does Varshavsky want from me?"

"He needs you because you were an accountant. You have to testify in support of the Partnership. Here, read the letter," the Cossack says reaching inside his coat and pulling out a Ministry of War envelope. Inside are two documents, the unsealed letter summoning me to St. Petersburg and a new set of army orders. I take a few minutes to read everything, trying not to move my shoulder.

"They're first sending me to Odessa," I say. "Then, I have to take a train to St. Petersburg. They need me there in two weeks." I look up at Neschadymenko. "What if I ignore this?"

"Don't be a fool, Leibovich. Don't be twice a fool. They'll punish you severely. Prison, probably."

"I can't go today. I'm in too much pain. Are you supposed to accompany me?"

"No."

"A shame."

"I must stay with the supply wagons. The train gets bigger every day, and we need to move quickly. They are marching to Constantinople. The Imperial Army is about to cross the Balkans. But listen, Leibovich. Stepan already sent your ledger to Odessa. He told me to tell you that a man named Kaminsky has it. Do you know this Kaminsky?"

"Sure, I know him."

"You must leave for Odessa soon, not today, but soon. Even a wounded veteran of the Battle of Shipka Pass must obey orders."

I smirk, "I killed one Turk."

"Good. It's one less."

I laugh, and it hurts. "You're looking at a hero, Neschadymenko. Reach into my coat pocket. I have a story to tell you."

The Cossack rummages through the coat and pulls out my Cross of St. George attached to a black-and-yellow-striped ribbon. "Where did you get this?" he asks accusingly, as if I'd lifted the medal from a dead Russian hero. It takes several tellings, each with layers of detail, and probing questions from Neschadymenko before he accepts the truth about my escapade as a spy for General Skobelev at Plevna. Neschadymenko can only shake his head. "A Yid with the Cross of St. George."

I lower my voice and confide in Neschadymenko that I wanted to die at Shipka, that I yearned for a quick death, a bullet to the brain. He asks why, and I explain my history with Avram and Rivkah Eizenberg.

"It is a simple story," I say. "I did something stupid and wrong. I betrayed my friend, without realizing the young woman with whom I wished to form a relationship was his sister. I hurt both of them, and one is dead, the one killed behind our wagon. He is buried there, and his sister will never forgive me."

The Cossack shakes his head disapprovingly. "You want to be a man, Leibovich? Where are your testicles? This self-pity of yours is ugly! Just tell this woman the truth, and tell her she belongs with you as your wife! This is your duty and it's her duty."

"I have no good reason to be standing on this earth and breathing this air."

"Straighten yourself out, Leibovich. Do the testimony with your chin high. You are a war hero! So be the man that this woman needs. It's not difficult."

It is an odd relationship I have with Neschadymenko. I never expected a Cossack to befriend me, but he has, and I am grateful. I know he means well, and I can't fault his approach, but I will need to gather more strength before taking any steps, timid or bold.

The gauze soaked in diluted carbolic acid contains my infection over the next few days, and Dr. Chernin tells me to prepare to be transferred to a hospital in Odessa. He even finds a clean uniform for me for the journey north. I insist on keeping my wool army coat. Before I go, I act on an impulse and enlist an army barber to remove my sidelocks. They have cascaded down from my temples since I was a young boy. I know that cutting them off is an affront to Jewish law and custom, a desecration in the eyes of some Jews. But I see it as an act of personal liberation. I no longer bow to the Biblical directive: "You shall not round off the hair on your temples or mar the edges of your beard." I no longer see this as necessary to my spiritual sensibility. The barber in Gabrovo refuses to take even a kopek for the act, which takes him less than ten seconds.

I travel to Odessa first by wagon, then ferry, then train. Russian engineers have built a rail line, from the Roumanian border near Odessa nearly to the northern shore of the Danube, to speed supplies to the front. I am going in the opposite direction in a nearly empty infantry car.

On my way to Odessa, I scratch out an entry in my journal with one awkward hand:

> *Is my piety diluted? I am certain others will say yes, that I am little more than a pagan now that my sidelocks are gone. I will answer this way: I am a Jew in the most important way, in my heart and soul. Yet, I sit almost broken by all that I have witnessed and all that I have caused. In my mind, I see the back of Avram's head, the horrible wound gushing blood. I see the face of the dead Turk who took my bayonet to the midsection. My wounds are to the shoulder and the heart. I have stolen a life and been given life renewed. Neschadymenko is right though. I must go to St. Petersburg to testify on behalf of the Partnership, and as soon as I am able, even if I am called back to the front lines, I must travel to Navahrudak and ask forgiveness from Avram's family, without flinching. This is the only testimony that truly matters. Can I do this in the grip of such melancholy? When I look at myself, I see a man who has failed at life and failed at death.*

10

It is mid-afternoon, and the February sun hides behind a blanket of rain clouds, when I step out of the Odessa Military Hospital in a clean uniform and a fresh sling. My experience on the ward was more painful emotionally than physically. For a week, a stocky nurse tried unsuccessfully to befriend me, but I wanted only to be left alone to stare at the patterns of peeling paint on the ceiling. I can't say exactly why I felt this way, other than the hellishness of my recent experience. Men, including my own father, are scarred by war, but some of my scars are of my own making. I am anxious about my future, I suppose, most immediately about seeing the rough-edged clerk Kaminsky and having to explain my truancy to him and Varshavsky.

I was supposed to meet Kaminsky at the Greger, Gorvits office as soon as I was discharged, but I'm not ready to fulfill that responsibility. Instead, I wander the streets, scanning newspapers, sipping tea, and ruminating. In the back of my mind, I wonder: will the army send me back to the front, regardless of these new orders that will take me temporarily to St. Petersburg? I feel uncertain about my future. Having been wounded, must I serve the full six years required of conscripts? Physically, I might be able to fight, but I have lost the will to do so.

When I testify for the Partnership, I want to tell the truth because I've lied to too many people. I don't want to be disloyal to Varshavsky, but in all likelihood, he will want me to lie in some fashion to absolve the Partnership. And he has leverage over me; at any moment, he can bend me to his will with threats of arrest for abandoning my wagon. Varshavsky is well connected, and I'm sure he could arrange my incarceration with a nod. I find it troubling that I so easily lied to Rivkah before the war but am now unwilling to lie to an Imperial State Commission.

At a set of granite steps leading to the Black Sea, I sit and pull the letter Avram Eizenberg wrote to his family from the bottom of my knapsack. It is wrinkled and smudged but otherwise intact after weeks in a bag that traversed icy Balkan peaks and crossed the mighty Danube. This is the first real chance I have had to post the letter, and it is time to honor Avram's wish.

At the post office near the train station, I buy a proper envelope and copy the address in Navahrudak that Avram left for me. On the reverse side of the envelope, I carefully write these words and hope they won't cause pain or confusion: "Written immediately before his untimely demise and posted by a friend." That should suffice. My curiosity about the letter's contents was aroused at Plevna, but now I have no interest in seeing what it says. The words will remain private. I stare at the envelope before mailing it. God willing, the message to his mother and sister will bring more comfort to them than anguish. I have kept my word.

Resigned to facing the abrasive Kaminsky, I amble to Osypova Street and the unimpressive offices of Greger, Gorvits, Kogan & Company. It takes an act of will to overcome my ambivalence and swing open the squeaky front door after more than a year's absence. The barrel-chested clerk sits exactly where he was when I first entered his realm, but he doesn't recognize me — how curious. Has so much time passed? Kaminsky smokes a strong, rolled cigarette. He seems thinner and even more harried than my last encounter with him; flecks of gray speckle his hair. I clear my throat to gain his attention.

"Tell me what you need, soldier," Kaminsky inquires brusquely, not bothering to look up a second time.

"I believe you have something for me, Mr. Kaminsky."

The clerk methodically marks his place in the ledger sheet he has been scanning and lifts his eyes, with an air of exasperation at being interrupted.

"And who might you be?" Kaminsky asks impatiently.

"Leibovich. Do you remember?"

He looks startled, bemused.

"No! Leibovich the runway?" Kaminsky sends me a piercing look, then pushes out his chair and stands, arms akimbo. "I knew they found you, but they didn't tell me you would show up in the uniform of the Imperial Army! And you cut your sidelocks! And what is this sling? Were you wounded by the Turk bastards? Or did the drunken Greeks get to you here in Odessa? Give me the whole story, Leibovich. And it better be the truth."

"It wasn't the Greeks, sir. I took a bayonet to the shoulder while serving with the Sixteenth Infantry Division."

"A bayonet? My, my. They told me you abandoned your wagon near Plevna, but I didn't know where you ended up. You'd better have a very good excuse for that behavior, my boy, even if you did take up arms on behalf of the Motherland."

"I have a good excuse, but I can't share it with you just now."

Kaminsky frowns and cocks his head to the side, nearly touching his cheek to his shoulder because his neck is so short.

"Mmhmm. It's all very suspicious. You'll have to explain it to Varshavsky, in any case, so I won't beat it out of you. For now, there is work to be done. Listen, I have your ledger. And Varshavsky wants me to explain this horrible mess about the Partnership to you, and why you're going to St. Petersburg. It's complicated and will take some time. But I'm swamped with work today, Leibovich. I can explain it all first thing tomorrow morning when I have more time. There is too much happening all at once. Besides, you need some rest, I'm sure. Come back tomorrow morning, alright?"

"Is it truly necessary to wait until morning?"

"Yes, it is! Okay, I'll give you some cash for your overnight. Just be here in the morning." He reaches into his cash box and places three silver roubles on the counter. "Get a room and something to eat. There's a small boarding house and a delicatessen just around the corner. The boarding house is nothing fancy, but it's clean. The delicatessen, though . . . is heaven. How do you think I got this?" he says, chuckling and grabbing his belly on both sides. "Come back tomorrow, Leibovich. We will conduct our business." He dismisses me with a flick of his hand.

The name of the delicatessen is Geshmak Kosherny. Despite the rich aromas of chicken fat and pastries that bathe the street outside, I have no intention of stopping for a meal. Nor do I wish to stay at the nothing-fancy boarding house. I have made an important decision. My goal this day is to loosen my inhibitions with vodka and procure a woman for a few hours, perhaps the entire night if it's not too expensive. Rivkah will never have me; I am certain of that. I stride past the delicatessen and head to Odessa's infamous waterfront district. Along the way, I buy a cheap bottle of vodka. I hear there are brothels on every corner at the waterfront, even Jewish ones. With any luck, I will be sufficiently intoxicated within the hour to rid myself of all my excuses.

Unlike Avram, I have little experience with alcohol. As I sit on a bench and pull strongly from the bottle, the vodka blindsides me. Within twenty minutes, I realize I am talking to myself. At first, it is a whisper. Eventually though, as I continue to drink, I begin berating myself in pungent terms for my personal shortcomings and questionable judgment. I address the Almighty, asking why He has failed to help me in my moments of weakness and indecision, why He has never come to my aid despite my love and loyalty. I am angry at God. I curse, and I don't care — let my Good Inclination be damned.

All of this melodrama results in tears. While ranting to myself about the absence of a merciful God and the foolishness of countless rabbis, I suddenly become extraordinarily dizzy. My head drops and I slide off the bench, landing on the cobblestones. I must have opened my forehead on the stone, because I feel a warm trickle above my right eye. My shoulder throbs. I am too inebriated to move and incapable of figuring out whether the dampness on my cheek is from tears, or blood, or the piss of a dog.

Half an hour passes, maybe more. A hand touches my back. Through the blur of inebriation, I see the face of a man in a dusty, padded cotton coat and fur ushanka hat with ear flaps dangling.

"Come on, soldier, let me help you," he says, trying to pull me up from beneath my good arm.

I groan in pain, "Go away."

"Don't be stubborn. You fell. Try to get up."

"Leave me alone."

"You've hurt yourself. Come on, get up." He again tries lifting me, and I manage to rise to my hands and knees. He holds a kerchief to my throbbing forehead. "Up to the bench," he urges me again. "You're bleeding. Come on."

This time, I press on the bench with my good arm to push myself up off the ground, if only to rid myself of him. I groan, "See? I can take care of myself." When I am finally seated again, barely balanced, he stands and asks, "You were wounded in the war?"

I look up and see him more clearly. He is young, perhaps my age, but with an older man's wrinkled eyes. He must have spent a good amount of time in the sun. His face is darker than mine and spotted. He smiles warmly and looks straight at me, as if willing a response despite my pathetic state.

"Wounded at Shipka Pass," I mumble in Russian.

"Where is that? Bulgaria?"

"The Balkans." I ask him tartly, "Do you need a geography lesson?"

My brain seems to be functioning, but I have trouble speaking. The vodka binge has left me disoriented, nauseous, and hungry all at once. My head still throbs, but my shoulder pain is subsiding.

"I heard about a battle in the Balkans, read it in the newspaper," he says. Though uninvited, he sits at the opposite end of the bench. "You can give me a geography lesson, though. Since I've never seen that part of the world, I could use a lesson. I've been living in the East too long."

I consider sending him away more emphatically, but a certain charming openness about him breaks down my defenses. I wonder what he means by "the East," but I am too woozy to inquire. I take off my campaign hat and run my sleeve along my forehead.

He has spotted my black velvet skullcap, which was under my army cap. "Ah, you wear a *yarmulke*, so you are Jewish, I see."

"From the Minsk region." I wonder if he is Jewish too, but tread lightly. It is hard to tell. There are no outward clues.

I ask: "Do you live in Odessa?"

"I'm from Tomsk. My name is Veniamin. May I ask your name?"

"Where is Tomsk? The East?"

"Now you are the one who needs a geography lesson," he says, laughing. "You can tell me about Shipka Pass, and I will tell you about Tomsk. Deal?"

"Alright." For the first time in what seems like months, I am genuinely amused. "Two geography lessons, then."

What is the point of mistrusting this stranger? He's not judging me, though he could have. And he seems kind-hearted.

"My name is Yakov. Why are you in Odessa, Veniamin?"

"I am on a long journey. Odessa is just one stop."

"And your destination is?"

"Paris."

"Oh, you have a long way to go still."

"I don't mean to intrude, soldier, but you were saying something about wanting to die when you were lying on the cobblestones. It's not the best of situations, you know. Something is troubling you, Yakov. Is it the war?"

"You wouldn't understand."

"I was never a soldier, but as you can see, I am asking just the same."

"You weren't drafted? That's lucky."

"Not drafted. I suppose I'm lucky no one has been firing bullets at me, but I've been traveling for months on poor rations, so maybe I can sympathize with the life of a soldier to a small extent. I can see you are an intelligent fellow. Why are you so despondent, Yakov? Do you have to return to the front?"

"The war that matters is in my soul," I laugh mordantly. "I made a bad error a year ago and hurt someone I care about, a woman. I don't think she will forgive me though."

"I see."

I'm starting to feel revived, possibly by the conversation. Something intrigues me about this young man. I turn to him and announce, "I'm starving. If you help me walk back to Osypova Street, I'll buy you a meal and some tea and cake. I know a place. Help me up."

"It would be my pleasure."

We stumble back to Geshmak Kosherny. Veniamin carries a large satchel with a strap over his shoulder and takes my knapsack as well, saying he wants to earn his dinner. The restaurant is invitingly warm. The steaming pots widen my nostrils and help clear my mind. I buy a bowl of a rich chicken stew for each of us, my first home-cooked meal in a year. The woman tending the counter places a fresh slice of black bread on each plate, and my new companion carries them to the table. It is too difficult to remove my coat with an immobilized shoulder, so I keep it on. The soup is a balm to my hunger.

"What happened at Shipka Pass?" Veniamin asks.

I answer cautiously. I'm uncomfortable reliving the nightmare of war, and my acquaintance doesn't press me for details. I buy tea and cake for both of us and learn about Tomsk, on the river Tom, west of Irkutsk in Siberia.

"This is what I meant by 'the East,'" he says. "Tomsk is a trading center for grain, butter, spirits, and gold. I was born in Kiev, but moved to Tomsk with my family at a young age after gold was discovered. My father owns a mine there. We were a well-off family, especially compared with the workers in the mines."

"There are many Jews in Kiev," I remark. "Is there a *yarmulke* beneath your ushanka?" Then, I ask in Yiddish: "Are you a student of Torah and Kabbalah?"

"I know both. Although I am Jewish, I have more secular interests. We spoke Russian at home in Tomsk. I can understand some Yiddish, but speak it poorly. My father made sure I was tutored at home in Hebrew,

Torah, and the great philosophers. He insisted on it, though there was no *beit midrash* in Tomsk. My father is a businessman first — the owner of a mine, after all — but he is also a scholar. In that respect, I am lucky. But we disagreed on politics. Maybe he shouldn't have opened my eyes to philosophy. It gave me the ammunition to be rebellious."

As he speaks, I can see how thoughtful Veniamin is, how deliberate, how humble. His upbringing is entirely new to me. He describes himself as an acolyte of the socialist writer Pyotr Alexeyevich Kropotkin, who transited Tomsk on geological expeditions in Siberia. I have never heard of the man. Kropotkin crossed paths with Mikhail Bakunin, he explains, who had introduced Kropotkin to an obscure tract called *The Communist Manifesto* by a German economist named Karl Heinrich Marx. I have not heard of Bakunin or Marx, either, and I feel my ignorance. Veniamin calls Marx "a radical thinker," a Jew whose book was recently translated into Russian. It is an essay on class struggle and worker exploitation by the owners of capital, he explains. My head has nearly cleared, and I sit in rapt amazement as Veniamin expounds upon political and social concepts with the same command and eloquence that a venerated rabbi might employ to explain Torah.

"You have heard of the Age of Reason, I suspect."

"I'm afraid I have lived an insular life, apart from this war."

"Never mind. It's a movement to free man from narrowminded religious practices and our enslavement to dynastic rulers. This is what created America, yes? It allowed the French to throw off the chains of royal entitlement. Think about it: one day it will topple the Russian Empire, too. Please take no offense, Yakov, but how obedient are you to what the rabbis are telling us? We should be emancipating the Jews from all the Tsar's stifling restrictions, and I think the emancipation of the mind must go with it. Believe in the Torah if you wish, but blind obedience to rabbis clinging to mystical superstition doesn't help. Why wait for the Messiah, Yakov? It's up to us to build a society where everyone can breathe. That's all we're trying to do."

"I'm sorry you're a non-believer. I don't think I can ever let modernism crush my faith. I believe in emancipation, Veniamin, but not if it empties my soul."

"No, no. I am a Jew, but I won't cling to the past and never imagine a better future. There are revolutionary Jews, you know. Read Heinrich Heine. Do you know any German?"

"Yes."

"Then read him. Heine despises censorship, including self-censorship. He said: 'Where they burn books, they will ultimately burn people too.' To free ourselves, we have to open our minds and act. Ideas are nothing if they can't be transformed into action! This is what Kropotkin teaches. When I heard him, everything made sense. I realized that my father was exploiting the mine workers. It was awful . . ."

"Everything Kropotkin said made sense to me," Veniamin continues. "I realized that my father was exploiting the mine workers. It was awful. I grew up with everything I needed, and it all came from the labor of these poor men. He fed the workers dirt and they ate it. We had some arguments, my father and I. I challenged him, but he would have none of it. So I ran away to Irkutsk and took odd jobs for a while. Kropotkin was in Irkutsk for a time, too. He was born into nobility and served in a Cossack brigade of the Imperial Army. Such an unconventional life, such a genuine adventurer. I think it rubbed off on me; I know it did. He also advocates for voluntary collective farms. You would find him interesting, I'm sure. He writes on the ethical philosophy of anarchism."

"What is a collective farm? And anarchism?"

Veniamin is expanding my knowledge in great leaps. "Collectivism is the natural state, you see — the group is more important than a single person, yes? And anarchism? Ah, more difficult. It is the only effective way to resist an entire, brutal social system. The foundations must be brought down before you can rebuild. It sounds violent, but it doesn't have to be."

I'm not sure what to make of this philosophy, though I sympathize. Veniamin is persuasive. I keep asking questions as if I am back in the *beit midrash* analyzing the commentaries of the sages, only with the windows wide open to the fresh breeze and fresh ideas. He explains what it means to be an anarchist and a socialist — to attack a power structure that exploits workers to enrich itself. Some of this mystifies me. All of it is idealistic, and therefore alluring, but at the same time so revolutionary that it must be outside of what could ever be real — impossibly idealistic. I was an idealist once. At least I felt I was. But I doubt that I still am.

As I listen, I begin to understand how much I have missed pure learning while feeding horses and marching across the Balkans in boots wrapped with cloth. I was in service to the Tsar and his empire. Maybe I was also in service to the Russian power structure and the Russian exploiters. I don't know.

In Irkutsk, Veniamin says, he met descendants of the Decembrists, another group I have never heard of. The Decembrists were anti-slavery revolutionaries rounded up in 1825 after they attempted a coup in St. Petersburg, he explains. They were forced into exile. Hundreds of them, including Imperial soldiers, were transported from St. Petersburg to Irkutsk and Tomsk.

"They wanted to bring the American Revolution to Russia," he tells me. "Can you imagine? And maybe even build a Jewish state! What courage it must have taken."

There already is a Jewish state, I think to myself sourly. Or rather a prison: the Pale of Settlement.

"A Jewish nation? It is a fantasy," I tell him.

"Only if we refuse to make it a reality," Veniamin counters.

I have no answer to this, so I change the subject. "Why did you leave Siberia to come west?"

"This man Kropotkin traveled a great deal, but he is now a hunted man. The Tsar doesn't like anarchists, as I'm sure you can imagine. Kropotkin was arrested in St. Petersburg a few years ago, but he managed to escape to Switzerland. I know where he is now, and I'm going to see him. I am on this long journey for a reason."

"Kropotkin is in Paris then," I say, "and you are his disciple — and a socialist. Is this right?"

Veniamin considers my characterization for an extended moment, deep in thought. He looks up at me with piercing eyes and says emphatically, "Of course, I am a socialist. The world must change, my friend. That is a certainty. We cannot continue as a just society with so much inequality and exploitation. We must change it. The Paris Commune was only a beginning; there will be more."

"I agree about the need for social change; but how? And what is the Paris Commune? I guess I was too young to know."

"Not at all. Just six years ago, French guardsmen from the working classes chose socialism as the path to a better future. Radicals and women seeking equal rights joined them. They wanted to ban child labor and keep the government and the church separate. They took control of Paris for a time."

"I was surrounded in the trenches by men who had no respect for women, and it felt vulgar. But I also had a friend who loved and respected his wife and told me I must treat women as equals. Women are worthy of being exalted, Veniamin, but I'm not sure perfect equality is helpful. Their role is nurturing the family, isn't it?"

My friend smiles. "Nurturing, yes. But why should women be used? We all must be prepared to challenge the existing order, to take radical steps. We have to repair the damage of class exploitation, and equality for women is one place to begin. Women are not lesser beings, Yakov. Women are not a lower class. Women will one day be equal to men. It is inevitable. Maybe your friend should think about joining our cause."

"Maybe. But he's dead."

"I'm sorry."

Changing the subject, I ask, "How does someone so young become a revolutionary?"

"I suppose it's from seeing what was happening in my father's mine with my own eyes. Kropotkin just placed all of it in perspective. He says history has many layers, and we must be willing to peel all of them away without fear of what we might learn. I admit his vision is very enticing to me."

"But how are you managing to travel such a distance? Irkutsk must be three thousand miles away, maybe four-thousand from Paris"

"The only train from Irkutsk went east to Chita. So I traveled by riverboat and ferry on the river system, then by trade caravans. I worked as a cook's assistant and cabin boy along the way. I'm determined to reach Europe, and am nearly there. Some of the Jewish traders and importers helped me. I owe them a large debt of gratitude."

"Do you realize how far you still have to go to reach Paris?"

"Of course I do. But I have met so many interesting people along the way, which makes the journey worth it. I never had the benefit of the *beit midrash*, but my travels have not been dull. I love to think and to learn and to debate."

"So did I, once," I say. "It seems so long ago. My life has changed."

"Your life may have changed, but I don't think your mind has. How could it? You are you!"

When the evening began, I thought how poor my luck must be to have taken a bayonet to the shoulder in a ghastly battle. Now, I am beginning to feel something I haven't felt for a year — the stimulation of thought, a need to understand, an excitement, as if connections in my brain dulled by war have resumed their proper functioning. I realize how astonishingly well read this man is, in everything from philosophy and politics to gold mining. And he's a natural conversationalist. We would certainly have been friends at the *beit midrash*, staying after yeshiva for hours to argue and debate. Veniamin seems to know intuitively how curious I am and that I thrive on such intellectual challenges. I needed to be reminded of this as I lay drunk and despondent on the cobblestones.

I buy another cup of tea for us, and thank him for his commentary on socialism, anarchism, and the rights of Jews in Russia, not to mention women. He tells me he never learned much about Kabbalah and inquires as to my views. Without parroting rabbinical analysis or esoterica, I convey what I can about the Kabbalistic interpretation of the mysteries of life — its explanation of Creation out of the formless, eternal, and infinite *Ein Sof;* the ten guiding attributes of the supreme force called God; and the mysteries of Being and Nothingness.

To hear myself teach these words triggers strong memories. "Have you heard of the Hebrew thinkers Cordovero and de Herrera?" I ask. "Both of them framed Kabbalah in philosophical terms. This was new. It was more than mysticism. And I'm sure these Kabbalists influenced the great heretic Spinoza. Do you know Spinoza?"

Unsurprisingly, Veniamin knows Spinoza was excommunicated by Amsterdam's Jewish elders for his perceived heretical views.

"The essence of Spinoza's philosophy was really no different from Kabbalah," I tell him. "Both argue that nothing existed before God, that God determined the laws of Nature, and that the physical manifestation of God is Nature itself. Amazing, isn't it? Not long ago, a German rabbi named Philippsohn — he is my Kropotkin — wrote a vindication of Spinoza. It was quite bold of him. I admired him for that."

Veniamin listens sympathetically, luring me into confessional. I tell him I am questioning my plan to become a rabbi. I reveal the sad story of Avram Eizenberg and my connection to his sister. I tell him I've dreamt of Rivkah. I tell him everything, and I know he is worthy of my trust. As I listen to myself, I see the tarnished relic that was once my sparkling plan to become an eminent rabbi; after all, how does a drunken soldier with no sidelocks command a community's respect? I tell him this too.

Veniamin smiles and shakes his head, "You are more of a philosopher than a rabbinical student, Yakov. Philosophy nourishes you. I can see it in you because it nourishes me as well. You can tell I was hungrier for conversation than soup and bread. I see in your face that you have returned from the dead. You should think about what kind of life you really want to lead. Don't let anyone else decide for you, my friend." He pushes back his chair. "Now, I must go. Thank you for the meal. I usually go to the train station and buy a ticket so I can sleep on the benches. The police don't bother me, and it saves money. Besides, I really do have to catch a train. I'm going to Warsaw. Do you have a place to stay tonight? You can come to the train station, if you want, though it's not the most comfortable."

"I'm going to a small hotel nearby, so will say goodbye now. I feel much better, in body and spirit, thanks to you. I wish you a safe journey, Veniamin. God be with you."

It has been more than a year since I departed Navahrudak. How I have missed conversation like this! It is not that my experience and travel as a teamster have been a waste, far from it. Yet, I now see how much the war has taken from me, how it drained me of vital currents and left me so uncertain about my future that I fell victim to emotional inertia. Tonight, I feel as if a spring has reopened inside of me. Veniamin saw my future better than I did. An angel descending majestically from Heaven could not have influenced me more. I am re-awakened.

It is already mid-morning before I remember with a start that I am supposed to meet Kaminsky. I dress without washing and race down the creaking stairs of the boarding house and out to the street.

Kaminsky is irate when I race into the office. "Where have you been?" he screams. "I was ready to call the Third Section secret police!"

"I overslept, Mr. Kaminsky. I was exhausted."

"Don't repeat this behavior in St. Petersburg, Leibovich, or the Partnership's agents will find you and make you wish you hadn't."

Kaminsky loves to exert his will over people, as a father, a teacher, or a tormentor — whichever he deems most effective. In graphic terms, he explains why the Partnership needs me to testify.

"The firm is the target of Russian nationalists who hate the Jews. Hate us! Newspapers in St. Petersburg wrote repeatedly about supply shortages during the important battles in Bulgaria. Liars! They make this shit up! They spin tales of men subsisting on half-rations packed on donkeys instead of wagons — if you fight in the mountains, you bring donkeys! Tales of missing tea and sugar, poor-quality forage grains, and thin boots that fail to protect against frostbite. Gross exaggerations! The correspondents kept up a steady drumbeat. Lying bastards! Because the Partnership is mostly managed by Jews, the people who hate us leap at the opportunity to bellow loudly. Their essays demand answers! These nationalists complained that there was embezzlement and profiteering at the expense of Russia's heroic men in uniform, but guess what?! Not one instance was explained! Not one specific allegation! No evidence! None! Someone said the Minister of War himself, Miliutin, called Andrei Varshavsky a 'Jewish crook.' The real crook always calls someone else a crook! Am I right, Leibovich?"

Rather than waiting for an answer, he tells me that the manufactured outcry against sinister Jewish conspirators left the Tsar's government little choice but to create a Commission of Inquiry.

"Propaganda always works when everyone keeps their mouths shut. So here we are," the rotund Kaminsky concludes. "We have no choice but to fight this slander."

He looks at me, leans in, and lowers his voice, "Tell me, Leibovich. What did you see? Are the ledgers accurate? Were there shortages? Embezzlement?"

I tell him the truth. It is my first rehearsal for testimony to come. The gist, I tell Kaminsky, is this: I didn't witness corrupt transactions, but the quality of some of the supplies did worsen, especially goods acquired in Roumania, as the conflict wore on.

He asks, "Did the Partnership's agents in Roumania bargain corruptly to fill supply quotas?"

"It's possible," I tell him, "but that had little bearing on the goods ultimately delivered. There were so many other factors. Heavy rains and flooding in Roumania's fields rendered some of the grain unusable, and the trainmasters refused to accept forage shipments that were obviously rotten. Grain prices fluctuated wildly. The roads were poor in Bulgaria, slowing everything down. Winter ice hampered the wagon trains even more. The influx of reinforcements suddenly expanded demand for supplies. It was impossible to keep up. No one could have done better. No one," I conclude emphatically.

"Most importantly," I continue, "the supply wagons were held back on purpose during key battles, including at Shipka Pass, because the generals wanted to travel as light and fast as they could. A wagon would never have made it across the Balkans on the path Skobelev's detachment took. I should know, I was there. One soldier told me the same was true at the Battle of Lovtcha weeks earlier — the army didn't want to be slowed by hauling supplies in bulk. Yes, there were complaints from Intendance Officers when we made deliveries to army encampments. But they all demanded items of low priority, like tobacco and tins of meat, while the Partnership insisted on giving priority to basic grains, rations, and medical supplies, as we were contracted to do. This was our job! My trainmaster, Stepan, told me once that some of the camp officers forced him to pay kickbacks just to allow the empty wagons to depart for Bucharest to pick up fresh supplies. Imagine! When winter roads became impassable, I heard that Varshavsky himself asked the army to provide transport assistance and was refused. Is this true? Did the army make it impossible to properly supply them?"

Kaminsky listens and writes furiously, jotting notes for a report to St. Petersburg, while occasionally pausing to scratch and stroke his beard. Lifshits the telegraph operator enters. We nod, though I doubt he recognized me. Kaminsky is deep in thought.

"I don't know about this rumor," he says finally. "What I do know, Leibovich, is that you are the perfect person to testify." He shakes a lecturing finger at me, "Do you see why, Leibovich? You must go to the Commission in uniform! You have the credibility of a soldier and you can show your ledger. I've looked at every page. It is precise and legible. You did your job very well, very carefully — better than anyone! And the man who took it over from you followed your example. Of course, I don't know how accurate it is; but it looks accurate, that's the important thing. I'm going to give you a couple more ledgers, good ones, to take with you to St. Petersburg. You can deliver them and explain exactly what we did. It was entirely correct. Everything was documented. Just tell them to look at the ledgers!"

His desire to see me testify in uniform makes sense. "Perhaps I should wear my Cross of St. George to the hearing," I tell him, imagining myself standing before the generals on the board of inquiry while wearing an Imperial Army commendation medal.

"Don't make jokes," Kaminsky spits.

"It's not a joke, sir," I say, indignantly.

I reach into my coat and slap the silver medal on the desk in front of him, its ribbons splendidly arrayed.

"Don't fool around," Kaminsky retorts, dumbfounded but curious.

"General Skobelev himself awarded it to me on the battlefield. Ask the Ministry if you like." I recount how I earned it the night before Plevna fell — as a Jew impersonating a Jew in order to spy on the Turks, the black hat and frock coat, the Yiddish, the tins of meat extract, the cigarettes.

Kaminsky leans in, engrossed. His skepticism dissolves.

"Even better!" he declares. "Even better! A decorated soldier! A spy for the Tsar! I misjudged you, Leibovich. Your decision to abandon your wagon at Plevna — a rash decision, mind you — is now a stroke of luck! Genius! I have to message Varshavsky immediately. He will have trouble believing what I have to tell him, but I'll explain that I have seen this medal with my own eyes."

I have less than a week before I am due in St. Petersburg. To meet the schedule, I must leave Odessa for Kiev by train the next day. Kaminsky has already purchased the ticket. He hands it to me along with a satchel containing three supply train ledgers, including my own. I will need to speak with the Partnership's barrister, who is preparing testimony to defend the firm. Kaminsky writes down the lawyer's name and address in St. Petersburg and hands it to me.

On my way to the train station the next morning, I stop at the journal and magazine shop. The news is jolting: the war is over. The Russians and Turks have signed a treaty at San Stefano. The great bulk of the Imperial Army crossed the Balkans and reached Adrianople, just a five-day march from Constantinople. The Turks retreated to defend the Ottoman capital and sued for peace, agreeing to hand Bulgaria its independence and turn over Armenia and Georgia to Russian control. At least I won't be sent back to the front. One great source of my anxiety has suddenly lifted. But so many others remain.

11

The lawyer I am to meet in St. Petersburg is Samuel Shaikevich, an amateur violinist and a Jewish barrister of some prominence, who, according to Kaminsky, will defend the Partnership's record before the Commission of Inquiry "with absolute cunning." This put me on my guard when I heard it, and I remain on my guard as I pull the card from my pocket to confirm I am at the correct address, No. 17 Glinki Street, across the Moyka River and past the ornate Mariinsky Theatre. Arriving at the polished wooden door, I notice his name listed on a shiny brass plate and push it open.

Shaikevich is a short, sturdy man in his late fifties who doesn't look as if he can play the violin tenderly, or at all for that matter. His fingers are impossibly fat. The second-floor office smells of cigarettes, and the shelves behind his desk bulge with files and dusty memorabilia. He is clad in a fine suit and waistcoat that holds a pocket watch with a gold chain. I judge my own Waltham watch to be superior, though mine has no chain. He offers me a glass of tea, which I eagerly accept, hoping it will calm my nerves. Until this moment, I have never met a lawyer.

"Before you swear an oath to tell the truth before the Commission of Inquiry," Shaikevich begins, "I want you to understand the financial stakes here. They are quite large. Are you aware, Private Leibovich, that the Tsar's government will soon suspend all payments to the Partnership?"

"Whatever the stakes, I will tell the truth," I say earnestly.

"Fine, but everyone has his own truth, young man. If you are a barrister, you learn this quickly. There are shades of gray everywhere; nothing is black and white in the law. One word doesn't define the truth. Many different words can convey the same truth or obscure it. So we must be very careful how we say things. Do you understand? I will help you, of course, but you need to heed my counsel."

"I can do that, sir," I say, although I am not at all sure what Shaikevich means by "shades of gray." The Torah has no such shades, if Reb Epshtein is to be believed. Yet if God's Word is God's Word, why does Judaism rely on endless pages of rabbinical commentary, written across centuries, to interpret the Almighty? I prepare for a lesson in the law.

"You can do that," Shaikevich repeats. "Alright, that's good, young man. Everything will become clearer as we talk about what you need to say in your testimony."

I shift in my chair uncomfortably. It is a peculiar phrase: "what you need to say." Am I to answer questions from the board of inquiry extemporaneously or present a written statement? For the moment, I know nothing. It is a worrisome beginning.

"Did you ever hear of the army's Provisions Department, Private Leibovich?"

"No, sir."

"Then I will tell you. It was a completely ineffective and inept office, run by incompetents. As a result, soldiers starved, died of scurvy, and so on, during the Turkish war of 1828 and in Poland in 1830. Now, in the Crimean campaign, at Sevastopol, things improved, but the Department was full of embezzlers, and the supplies were often rotten, biscuits with mold and worms and probably worse." Shaikevich makes a face, as if he has bitten into a live rat. "You know what happened? All the soldiers got a gastrointestinal disease. So, after the disaster of Crimea, General Miliutin instituted a change. He created an office called the Chief Commissariat. Unfortunately, nothing changed but the name!" The lawyer waves his outstretched hands for emphasis.

"I see," I murmur.

"You haven't seen anything, Leibovich. Let me finish. The army always had contracts with Jewish purveyors, merchants, here and there. Why? Because so many of the barracks were in the Pale of Settlement. Supplying all these barracks during times of peace was the easy part. Now we come to this war against the Ottoman Empire, an enormous undertaking. You know Varshavsky, yes?"

"I know the name but have not met him."

"You will meet him today. He is coming here after lunch, and will be speaking to you as well. When the Tsar decided to protect every Slav within reach, the army summoned Varshavsky because he already had a contract to supply all the transport carts. The Army needed a much bigger contract, though— much, much bigger. They needed to supply all of the battalions going to Bulgaria."

I nod, though I'm still confused about the connection this has to my testimony.

"So, everything got complicated, Leibovich."

"It was a big project."

"Big, you say? Not big, Leibovich — monumental!" he exclaims, his hands flying into the air again. "So big that Varshavsky helped create an entirely new partnership to handle everything. No one has ever done this before. Do you know who the investors are, Leibovich?"

"Not really. Greger, Gorvits, and Kogan, I suppose."

"Yes, of course, of course, that's brilliant. But there's two more. Kogan and Varshavsky own forty-five percent. The rest, fifty-five percent, is owned by Greger and Gorvits and an investor whose name is private. I will say the name, but it is strictly private — strictly. Don't make me send my henchmen for you."

Shaikevich leans toward me, so close I can see the spittle on the edges of his mouth, and whispers, "General Nepokoichitskii." Then he leans back. "Do you know who he is, Leibovich?"

"I'm sorry, but . . ."

"Of course not. You were in the trenches, probably living in filth. Not in the elegant tents of the headquarters, eating caviar and drinking fine vodka. Nepokoichitskii is the Chief of Staff to the Tsar's brother, Grand Duke Nicholas himself!" Shaikevich again leans toward me and lowers his voice, "And by the way, he arranged the contract!"

The lawyer sits back again and resumes his bombastic monologue, "So, I'm telling you we already have a friend in the Army hierarchy. Is he going to fix everything? No. But we have a very good and influential friend. He can tell us what he thinks the commission will want to hear. In other words, Nepokoichitskii will tell us what we have to say to get this inquiry behind us."

I try to steer the conversation to what I "need to say" in my testimony.

"Am I to answer questions from the commission?"

"We will get to that. Be patient. You will provide the information that we discuss, and you will not wander into pointless issues. And if Nepokoichitskii is unable to secure the desired result, I am working on another avenue, a very interesting connection. Can you guess who that might be?"

"I'm sorry, no."

"Of course not! No one knows!"

We have now veered into the absurd. I remain silent.

"You aren't curious who this is?"

"Well . . ."

"You have heard of Princess Iurevskaia, I am sure."

"Well . . ."

"The mistress to the Tsar! You know who the Tsar is, Leibovich, I hope."

"Of course I know, sir."

"Well, this is so confidential that they will slit my throat if it gets out, but I have a friend on very good terms with the Princess — very good terms, indeed. And believe me, the Tsar pays attention to what his mistress says, very close attention."

I begin to wonder whether the lawyer for the Partnership will ever ask me what Kaminsky asked in Odessa: what did you see and hear in Roumania and Bulgaria? What was your experience? What is the truth? Instead, I am seeing the outlines of either a conspiracy with corrupt intent or a farce. Is this Commission of Inquiry real? Does it seek real answers? Is the Partnership's lawyer interested in real answers? I begin to feel manipulated. It isn't clear whether anyone — the Partnership or the Commission or the Army — wants the truth to come out. I see I'm losing control, or never had any. There may need to be compromises. The important thing is that I avoid outright lies. Either I will be generally faithful to the truth or I will leave. This is what I tell myself, at least — generally faithful. It is easy to place stakes in the ground, but somewhat harder to respect all of the boundaries when the stampede begins.

Shaikevich calls in his assistant and orders a lunch of herring and vodka, but all I can think about is the imminent arrival of Varshavsky. I had not prepared mentally to meet him and am dreading the encounter, knowing I will need to explain my actions in Bulgaria to the man who agreed to hire me as a favor to Pinhas Epshtein. He will ask why I quit my service to the Partnership, without any warning in the middle of a supply delivery, and why I failed to return to the wagon train. These are not unreasonable questions, after all.

When Varshavsky strides into Shaikevich's office, he says nothing. He is wider, balder, and shorter than I had imagined. His clothes fit poorly, and he seems to waddle from side to side as he walks. An impressively full mustache droops on either side of his mouth. He looks rushed or disturbed, or both. I am on my guard as I rise to greet him. Varshavsky ignores me and extends his hand to Shaikevich.

"Samuel, I assume you have imparted to this soldier the reasons his testimony is required."

"Indeed I have. But perhaps you might reinforce our position. Be my guest."

Varshavsky turns to me, and the interrogation begins.

"So this is the famous Private Leibovich," he sneers.

"Yes, sir."

"By all rights, I should be the one demanding testimony from you about your delinquency, not this gratuitous Commission of Inquiry."

"I understand, sir."

"I doubt that you understand, Leibovich. Do you realize I could bring a legal process against you for breaking your employment contract? For endangering your Cossack guard and our horses? For delaying the timely return of our wagon train to Roumania to re-supply?"

"If I might explain, sir."

"All of a sudden you are in the Imperial Army — the very army you begged me to help you escape! Did you fulfill your obligation to the Partnership? No! Whom did you think would take your place managing the accounting ledger? And now you are some sort of hero, I hear. Is that what you think, Leibovich? You are a hero?"

"No, sir."

"I should hope not. Anyway, you will do what Counselor Shaikevich asks of you, without fault or hesitation, or the consequences will be severe and you will regret the moment you wavered. Do you understand?"

"Yes, sir, but if I might explain."

"Never mind, Kaminsky said something about the Cross of St. George. Where is it?"

"In my pocket, sir."

"You are to wear it! Make it visible to all. It doesn't belong in your pocket. Do you understand? "

"Yes."

"Right on the outside of your coat or on the leather strap across your chest, whichever is more prominent."

"Yes, sir."

"Let me see it," he demands.

I remove the medal from my coat pocket and hold it out toward him in my palm, but he does not take it. He leans forward, as if sniffing an *hors d'oeuvre*. I can feel his breath on my hand.

"Alright, put it away for now. Just keep it safe until you testify. Something else: do you know how much money is riding on the outcome of this inquiry, Leibovich?"

"I'm sure it's a lot, sir."

"A lot? Samuel, tell the young man, would you?"

"The government is threatening to withhold more than three million roubles."

My eyebrows arch and my shoulders stiffen.

Shaikevich reaches for a piece of herring with his fingers and drops it into his mouth. "There's something else at stake in these hearings," he says, munching through the tender fish. "At stake for the Jews. Everyone wants to believe the Jews are weak, disloyal, unpatriotic cowards, that we care only about financial gain even at the expense of our own army, and that we'd rather live in complete separation from society than mix with non-Jews."

"It's false," I say.

"Of course it's false!" Shaikevich shouts, his hands rising up. "False from dawn to dusk!"

"Many Jews serve in infantry divisions," I note. "They fight and die like everyone else; I've seen it. But we still aren't allowed to become officers."

"We're going to change that," Varshavsky says with cold certainty. "I never should have agreed to the arrangement that Pinhas Epshtein wanted, never. I should have refused. I should have told Epshtein that every drafted Jew must serve, that Jews in the Pale must show the Tsar they are loyal if they want to win equal rights in this Empire. I made a mistake with you, Leibovich. I learned my lesson."

I have often wondered whether it is better to show loyalty to gain one's rights, or to withhold it until the rights are granted. I ask, "Wouldn't more Jews serve willingly if they were treated as equal citizens of the Empire?"

"Don't be naive," Varshavsky says, flicking an outstretched hand. "You give if you want to get." I wonder if he sees how his biting remark cuts both ways.

He shifts uncomfortably in his chair and winces. "This whole thing has given me dyspepsia," he mutters. "We need a vigorous defense, Samuel, nothing less. I will not have the Partnership smeared. We are fulfilling our contract with the Tsar under extreme conditions."

"And you will have a vigorous defense, sir," Shaikevich assures him. "The best money can buy!"

Varshavsky turns to me. "You will be an important witness for us, Leibovich. This is the only reason I'm overlooking your insolence. You quit on us. But now you wear the uniform and have even been wounded, I hear. There will be sympathy for you. And you also drove a wagon for us and took inventory. They need to hear a voice they can trust, someone with standing. But they are going to ask: why did you quit the Partnership and put on a uniform? We need an answer, a trustworthy answer."

"I suppose I could tell them something resembling the truth," I say.

Varshavsky leaps in, apparently without listening to my response. "Here is what you will tell them: you saw that the army was well supplied at Plevna, and that it needed men with carbines more than it needed bread because, militarily speaking, things were not going so well. So you volunteered. And eventually the general asked you to walk into Plevna as a spy, and you did. That's what Kaminsky told me. Is he right?"

Varshavsky is intimidating, and to disagree with him would carry serious risk. I doubt he would hesitate for a second to launch a legal process against me if he could not win my cooperation. I swallow hard, trying to hedge my response. It doesn't seem to come out as I intended. I reply, "In general, I suppose, yes."

"And then you fought bravely, intending to return to the Partnership until you were wounded."

"A very good response," Shaikevich interjects. "I like that. But will they inquire about how he came to be working for the Partnership in the first place?"

"It's irrelevant," Varshavsky declares. "The Army has no record of our arrangement to remove him from the draft list. Only the local Conscription Officer knows and is in a position to reveal this. But the Army will deny it vigorously because they supposedly make no exceptions to the draft. The Conscription Officer would be humiliated, so he will remain silent. The commission will only ask Leibovich why he quit the Partnership, not why he joined it."

"The arrangement to keep me out of the army never should have gone forward," I say. "I know that now. And I'm sorry I acquiesced."

"Never mind that," Varshavsky says. "Did you quit the Partnership because the general wanted a spy?"

"It wasn't quite like that."

"Wasn't it? Kaminsky told me General Skobelev needed a spy!"

"Allow me to explain," I say.

"Alright, so explain," Varshavsky demands, sitting back in his chair impatiently. "Go right ahead."

I knew it would come to this. I feel cornered. I have no choice but to tell the story of Avram Eizenberg, the Jew forced into the Army to replace another Jew — to replace one who arranged to have his name stricken from the conscription list. I proceed to tell Varshavsky and Shaikevich about my yeshiva mate being picked up from the gutter and forced to serve in my place. I explain exactly how Avram was killed near Plevna, the circumstances, the blood, the guilt.

Varshavsky and Shaikevich listen in silence.

"It was wrong, of course — a terrible injustice," I say, my voice quavering. "I couldn't have that on my conscience. He had a terrible wound to the back of his head. He must have died instantly. I will never forget it."

I stop to contain my emotions.

"Alright, alright, enough," Shaikevich interjects. "You can't tell the commission any of this. You tell them what we agreed. Nothing about this Eizenberg boy; understood? If you tell them about this other Jewish boy, you will have to tell them why he was serving in your place. We don't want that; we can't have that. You tell them you volunteered because you saw how badly they needed men to fight. You had just delivered medical supplies for the wounded. You had done your duty. And then Skobelev needed you to act heroically and walk straight into the enemy camp and you did. They will be transfixed!"

Varshavsky nods. "Nothing about Eizenberg. Do we agree on this, Leibovich?"

"I suppose it's the only way," I sigh.

"One more thing," says Varshavsky. "Tell me how you were wounded. We need to hear about that."

"A bayonet struck my shoulder at Shipka Pass."

"A battle, I presume," Varshavsky says.

"Yes, a serious battle in the trenches. We stormed a Turkish redoubt."

"Good. You still have the shoulder bandaged?"

"I had my arm in a sling for several weeks, but it's fine now. I keep just a small bandage on the wound now."

"A sling? Perfect. Wear the sling, Leibovich. You're not fully healed, are you? Wear it to the commission. Do you hear?"

"Well, I no longer need it . . ."

"Just wear it. You have a little pain, don't you? Of course you do. You wear the sling. No excuses!"

Now I know what I "need to say." I must act convincingly in this bit of political theater. The script has been handed to me.

The Commission of Inquiry convenes inside the neoclassical Senate building, an immense structure housing Imperial Russia's administrative bureaucracy. As a boy, I had seen an engraving depicting the building, but the reality of the structure overwhelms me and deepens my anxiety about my impending testimony. At the commission's inaugural meeting, I sit stiffly in the audience of an ornate hall, a small white sling at my wrist. The nearby seats are occupied by journalists. As the hearing opens, we all are subjected to endless monologues, as one commission member after the other pontificates about the gravity of the questions before them, and demands satisfaction on behalf of the Empire's valiant forces on the front lines.

From the very start, the Army's representatives, all wearing impressive uniforms decked with medals and ribbons, make it clear that much more than the Partnership is on trial. The Jews are on trial as well — all the Jews of Russia. And for one reason: the Partnership is run by Jews.

I am aware that one of the Partnership's public owners converted to Eastern Orthodoxy. Another is of Greek extraction. Two are Jews — Kogan and Varshavsky. Those facts, imparted to me by Shaikevich, do not seem to matter. From the very beginning of the hearing, the Partnership is characterized as an entity of the Jews, by the Jews, and for the Jews. In the Army's opening statement, it is taken as common knowledge that Jews routinely engage in corrupt, unscrupulous, and cutthroat behavior in their dealings with non-Jews. The Army's logic is distorted but nonetheless put forward with complete audacity: because all Jews are known cheats, these specific Jews must have cheated. And there is more. The commission is well aware, the Army's lawyer states, that Jews care little about the Imperial Army and the brave men who risk their lives to defend the Empire. The Partnership has one and only one purpose: profit. Its contractors are embezzlers. Of course they are! They are Jews! All of the Army's flaws in its current campaign against the Turks are attributable to the hardships visited upon its soldiers by these ruthlessly deceitful suppliers — these Jews.

As the bombast echoes off the lavishly gilded walls and ceiling of the hearing room, the journalists and essayists occupying wooden benches and chairs bend over their notebooks, scribbling furiously.

I listen to all of this in utter exasperation, but I mustn't allow my pique to rise to the surface. Surprisingly, as the Imperial Army and Commissariat officials pile outrageous accusations, one after the other, Varshavsky grows increasingly confident of a positive outcome for the firm.

"Just wait," he says. "Many of the Army's assertions about the Partnership's responsibilities bear no resemblance to the contract both sides signed in early 1877," he tells me. "So far," he points out, "the Army has presented no direct evidence of bribery, extortion, embezzlement, or other malfeasance, and Shaikevich will point this out with devastating clarity. The Army is vastly overstating its case, without facts, and this provides an exit door for the commission to eventually squeeze through — though not before excoriating the Partnership for what will turn out to be minor missteps."

As Varshavsky predicted, the pivotal witness for the Partnership is Army Private Yakov Leibovich. In Varshavsky's scenario, I am an entirely sympathetic figure — a wounded Jewish soldier, wearing the Cross of St. George for heroism, calmly explaining how the Partnership carried out its duties, its care with ledgers and books, and the mitigating circumstances of its flaws in Bulgaria, where unexpectedly harsh conditions conspired against the swift and sure delivery of goods. I am managing to hand the commission a public rationale for absolving the Partnership, especially if its members come under pressure from General Nepokoichitskii and Princess Iurevskaia.

Before my first appearance, Shaikevich spends several days drafting an official statement for me to sign. I must read a summary of the statement to the commission, in person. And I will need to answer their questions in public. I practice reading the statement with Shaikevich. The lawyer has taken some liberties with my story, as I expected, cleverly adding a melodramatic gloss. Yet it turns out to be what I needed it to be, generally faithful to the basic facts. I tell myself that General Skobelev himself would not disagree. Is it a rationalization? Maybe, but I have no choice.

When it's finally time for me to speak, I stand before the commission members and begin my testimony. I can tell from the reaction among commission members and the audience, especially the press, that my public recollections of the day I delivered medical supplies to the encampment at the front have an impact. The story is gripping, at least in Shaikevich's version.

"I saw the infantry being torn apart by artillery shells and shrapnel," I tell the commission. This is true, after all. "The Turkish guns found their mark. It was my duty to help."

The commissioners watch me carefully as I explain in detail my role in the fighting, then my espionage foray into the enemy stronghold at Plevna, and my bayonet wound in the Ottoman trench at Shipka Pass. The Cross of St. George, which I had refused to wear in Bulgaria, is now pinned to the breast pocket of my coat. I keep my arm in the white sling. I try to be articulate and use precise Russian words. My voice is firm. As Shaikevich instructed, I am deferential and respectful. I have learned my lines and delivered them well.

No one on the commission questions my work as a soldier. The topic the commissioners wish to examine carefully is my role as an accountant and teamster on the supply routes in Roumania and Bulgaria. Shaikevich foresaw this and prepared me well. Fortunately, the questions put to me come from the commission members, and not from the Imperial Army's corps of barristers and officers.

"How often did prices from middlemen fluctuate?"

"I wasn't directly aware of pricing, but from what I heard around camp, the bad weather played havoc with grain prices."

"Why did you deliver rotten forage?"

"My own wagon held medical supplies. But I know the harvest was very poor because of heavy rains that I myself witnessed. It was unnatural and excessive; you cannot quickly forget such downpours. No grain crop in the region would have been unaffected. We had little choice but to deliver the grain we had, as there was no other grain to be found."

"What percent of the teamsters are Jews?"

"I don't know exactly. Many are, but many are not."

"Did you ever demand payment from Army officers for the delivery of medical supplies?"

"Never, of course not. I saw the stretchers and ambulance wagons going north. I could see with my own eyes how much the army needed medical supplies. I did my duty."

The day after my appearance, I scan the newspapers to see what is filtering to the public, what facts and what slant. Shaikevich saves all of the articles. Every paper is covering the hearings with a pronounced slant, and every one of them writes about the testimony of the Jewish private who was an accountant for the Partnership. I suppose it makes for a compelling drama in the writers' eyes, though I fail to see how. There are only two tacks the newspapers seem to take: they either belittle me as a fraud and a liar controlled by the Jews, or they glorify me as a hero and a patriot. Neither is true, but it doesn't seem to matter to these frustrated novelists. To my dismay, the preponderance of the reportage falls into the first category: Private Leibovich as fraud. There is nothing I can do about this journalistic sewer except to stop descending into the filth. So I stop reading it altogether. I can't stomach it.

The residence of Pinhas Epshtein, the rabbi's brother, sits half a block from the Mariinsky Theatre in a stone townhouse on Offizierskaya Street. It is a three-minute walk from Shaikevich's office. I had inquired with Varshavsky if I might visit Mr. Epshtein, to thank him for arranging a job for me at the Partnership and, frankly, to explain why I abruptly left my teamster role to fight in Bulgaria. "I believe I owe as much to the man," I told Varshavsky. Pinhas Epshtein might slam the door in my face. If so, he would be justified. I will take that chance.

"What you do with Pyotr is your business," Varshavsky tells me. "Go right ahead. But you had better be respectful."

I intend to be, so I make my way to Offizierskaya Street. A housekeeper answers the door.

"I am a student of Mr. Epshtein's brother, the rabbi of Navahrudak," I say nervously. "Might I have a moment of his time? It's very important."

"And whom shall I say is calling?"

"Yakov Leibovich. He arranged a job for me. He will know the name. Tell him, the boy from Navahrudak."

I wait just inside the front door, examining the foyer's elaborate furnishings, particularly a grand mirror with a frame of inlaid wood in a checkerboard of shades. I can see that war has been good for Pinhas

Epshtein's business. A man in a dark vested wool suit and blue cravat enters the foyer. I notice the resemblance immediately. The same wide, intense eyes as the rabbi, with dark bags beneath them.

"They told me you would be coming to testify at this absurdist show trial," Pinhas Epshtein says. He skips any form of greeting and does not extend his hand. This puts me on edge.

"Yes, Mr. Epshtein. So far, I have survived, sir."

"What can I do for you, Leibovich, that I have not already done?"

It is intended as a dagger. "I just wanted to explain to you why . . ." I stammer.

Epshtein finishes my sentence. ". . . why your father arranged your exemption from the army — at a considerable price, I might add — only to see you throw it all away?"

I am momentarily disoriented. What price is he referring to? At the price of my father's time? His anxiety? Or was it what it sounded like, an exchange of cash?

"I wanted to explain why I joined the army. There is a specific reason."

"Whatever it is, you don't have to explain it to me. But you might want to explain it to my brother, your rabbi, and to your father."

"I certainly intend to. I didn't mean to disturb you, Mr. Epshtein."

Epshtein softens, "Never mind." He lifts out his pocket watch and glances at it. "Well, I want to find out how the commission testimony is going. And you are a long way from home. Come in. I should have invited you in. We can have tea."

I bow slightly and follow Epshtein into an immaculate drawing room off the foyer, lit by a central system of gas lights that I have heard about but never seen. Epshtein is a man of means; this much is clear.

"Tell me about the commission, Leibovich. You have given a statement, yes?"

"Yes. And I testified this week, and answered questions — a lot of questions."

"I heard about some of the accounts in the anti-Jewish press. It disgusts me. They are vermin. But tell me this, do you think this commission is inclined to destroy the Partnership, or will it be a slap on the wrist?"

"I'm not a good judge, but Master Shaikevich thinks he can avoid the worst. He has important contacts."

"He told you about Nepokoichitskii?"

"Yes, and another."

"Another owner?"

"No, a contact with some influence." I take care not to say more.

"Shaikevich has contacts everywhere. The man is shameless. Do you know how he makes these contacts?"

"Not really."

"Cash. He hands out attractive incentives in fresh roubles to make lawsuits disappear. The causes of action disappear miraculously. And where does he get so much money? He charges clients enormous sums. I am certain the Partnership had to promise him tens of thousands of roubles."

I see an opening to have him address the question that is suddenly gnawing at me. "And you received a cash incentive from my father to allow me to work for the Partnership?"

"Of course," Epshtein shrugs. "It certainly was not an exorbitant sum. Just enough to convince my friend at the Ministry of War to support the arrangement. Did you think I kept the money?"

"Well, I assume . . ."

"You assume? All of the roubles went to a contact of mine in the Ministry — all of it. I don't squeeze money from my own brother. This is how it works, Leibovich. It has always worked this way. We wouldn't be paying incentives to do business with the government if the thieves in the Ministry didn't demand bribes."

"I see. Yes, of course. Was it a lot, though? I mean, my father couldn't afford . . ."

Epshtein waves me off, "That's not important. He knew what was required. And he didn't pay a kopek more than what was necessary."

This revelation lands as acid in my gut. I turn and look out the window onto Offizierskaya Street, bewildered and disappointed. Until now, I had been feeling considerable guilt, but now it is both guilt and shame — and even deeper anger at my father.

I pivot to Epshtein. "I suppose your brother the rabbi served as a middleman for this."

"This what."

"The financial incentive, I mean."

"My brother and I communicated by letter. You can ask him whatever you want. He had no financial gain from this whatsoever, if that's what you're suggesting."

I can see that Pinhas Epshtein is unwilling to divulge any details of the transfer of funds. The details hardly matter. At the very least, the rabbi knew he was drawing my father into an arrangement that would likely require the payment of a bribe. If my father acted out of love, it is a peculiar way to teach a child to seek justice, to love mercy, and to walk humbly with God.

Pinhas Epshtein must be sensing my turmoil. He changes the subject. "Tell me, Leibovich, do you need to remain in St. Petersburg until the Commission completes its work? Or will you be required to return to a barracks somewhere? Thank God this war is over."

"Yes, thanks be to God. I don't yet know what is next. Master Shaikevich told me only to remain in St. Petersburg until he hears from the Ministry of War."

"Ah, but you realize he doesn't need to hear from the Ministry. If he pays the right person, he will receive the desired answer. I would suggest you tell Shaikevich you wish to return to Navahrudak. He can make it happen."

A return to Navahrudak is certainly necessary. I feel a powerful urge to confront my father and console my mother, who had no part in the fateful decisions he and I made. I want her sympathy too. And I must try to understand why Reb Epshtein abetted the needless death of one of his former yeshiva students who was never meant to be in the Imperial Army. The rabbi, too, should be ashamed.

"I'll tell you what, Leibovich," Pinhas Epshtein continues. "I'll buy you a train ticket to Minsk so you can go home."

"It's generous of you, sir, but I must wait for orders from the Imperial Army."

"Yes, of course. But as I say, the lawyer you are dealing with is quite influential. But never mind. I wish you luck, Leibovich. And remember, your father was doing what any good father would do. Look at you, you're alive, aren't you?"

When I think about it, I have to conclude that, yes, I am more than alive. Thanks largely to Veniamin, my sense of who I am has re-emerged, with improved confidence. I feel more mature, capable, and purposeful than I felt back home in Navahrudak, or on the cold cobblestones near the Odessa waterfront. Oddly, my experiences in St. Petersburg — with

Shaikevich, Varshavsky, and the grandiose Commission of Inquiry — have proven to me that I am worthy of respect, including self-respect. Why not wear the Cross of St. George proudly? I earned it, after all. An esteemed general pinned it to my chest, or tried to.

As for my future, nothing is clear. The war is over, and I am at a crossroads: I will either be ordered to resume my military service or be allowed to return home to Maya Street, where I face wrenching confrontations with my father and Reb Epshtein, as well as a painful conversation with Rivkah Eizenberg. My heart is swirling with powerful impulses — duty, retribution, fear, and love.

12

My testimony before the Commission of Inquiry has turned out to be an education, not only in legal matters but also in the political arts of grandstanding, half-truths, and subterfuge (with an additional lesson in the laws of unintended consequences). Shaikevich, for example, was certain that my testimony would demolish claims in the newspapers that Imperial soldiers were suffering at the hands of the Jews. Yet my testimony seems to have had the opposite effect. I have unwittingly emboldened the anti-Jewish press. Their odious accounts of the inquiry, with me as anti-hero, are clearly damaging the cause of Jewish emancipation.

It saddens and angers me. I picture my father reading about my testimony and burning with indignation that his son is the focus of a wave of nationalist hysteria. As much as I want and need to liberate myself from my father's influence, it is upsetting to realize that my acts may be weakening the cause he has held so dear. Tolerance for the Jews in Russia seems as fragile as ever.

Even so, within the offices of Samuel Shaikevich, there is cause for celebration. When I return to Glinki Street, Shaikevich informs me the Commission of Inquiry has decided to pare its allegations against the Partnership to a few lesser charges: the delivery of substandard goods, charging inflated prices, and a form of malfeasance bewilderingly labeled "general inefficiency." The panel of judges will dismiss the more serious charges of fraud and embezzlement, thankfully. Shaikevich believes the firm will be paid much of the money it is owed, though probably not all. The government might still claim the Partnership is at fault for supply shortages. But he and Varshavsky say the firm, while not fully vindicated, has escaped the worst outcome.

Before we have a chance to celebrate, Shaikevich hands me a sealed letter and counsels ominously, "I suggest you open it immediately."

It is addressed in elaborate script: *Private Yakov Leibovich*. It must have been delivered by messenger. I turn the envelope over and find a blue wax seal and an embossed name. It is the personal stationery of Baron Horace Günzburg. The baron is inviting me to tea the following afternoon.

Shaikevich takes the liberty of peeking over my shoulder. "Do you know who this is, Leibovich?"

"I just know he is very wealthy and very influential. I read an essay by him in the Hebrew press a few years ago."

"Quite so. Baron Günzburg is rich, but the wealth of his esteem in the Jewish community and in the connections he has to the Tsar and the government far exceed his worth in gold; I assure you of that."

The first reaction I have is wariness, followed by confusion and slight alarm at the idea that one of Russia's richest men wants to see me. I am not comfortable in the presence of nobility and excessive wealth. It may be my father's influence, but it may also be my sense of myself and where I fit in the world.

I ask Shaikevich, "Why does he want to see a soldier with a scar on his shoulder?"

"Ah, Leibovich. You have so much to learn," the lawyer says, stroking his well-trimmed beard and smoothing his mustache. "You are now a hero to the Jews, and a villain to the hate mongers."

"I suppose. But the exaggerations are on both sides. I wasn't a hero."

"What matters is that people think you are!"

Shaikevich returns to his desk and lifts a thick stack of newspapers. He turns to me and holds them up in both hands, dramatically, as if presenting evidence.

"The testimony you gave and the story you told is now everywhere," he says, dropping the stack back onto his desk with a dusty thud. "You are the celebrated soldier-Jew, a hero of the Pale, a loyal son of Russia, and the bane of the bloodthirsty Turks! Well, to at least half of these beastly journalists."

"And the other half?"

"Ah, the other half." Shaikevich pauses before launching into a heated monologue. "Those are the filthy kopek newspapers. They write theater for the masses, entertaining little plays about stereotypes like the drunken trader, the helpless wife, the diseased tramp, and, of course, the greedy Jew. They think you are a conniving disgrace, if you really want to know — a liar of the first order trying to cover up monstrous financial crimes by the Partnership, a paid charlatan, a venomous snake. They have never trusted the Jews and never will. People say we are in an era of reform, but let me tell you, the people who hate the Jews are never reformed. Do you know about the murder case in the Georgian region? Once again, it was the blood libel — nine Jews falsely accused of killing a child to use the blood in preparation for Passover. The darkest days of the Middle Ages never ended! Shall I go on?"

"I am a Jew defending other Jews, so I am a target."

"More than that, you are a Jew defending rich Jews! You are a Jew defending proven parasites! This is the conspiracy they invent."

"I suppose the Tsar's reforms have amounted to nothing then."

"Not quite, not quite; in some areas, the reforms are a meaningful step forward. But the Russian people don't like to see foreign tribes making progress. They need someone to blame for their plight, for failed wars and empty cupboards. They resent the fact that you are literate, Leibovich, that you are intelligent. They want to crucify someone, and the scandal mongers and the hate mongers of the press are only too happy to help them."

"Then maybe I have provided them with more evidence of what they already believe. I shouldn't be proud of that."

"You must remember that none of this is the fault of any Jew. I'll tell you something about my own profession. Do you know that to practice as a Jewish barrister, I must apply to the Ministry of Justice? Not any Jewish lawyer can walk into a court in Russia and appear as a legal representative. A Christian lawyer can, but not a Jewish lawyer! Many of my colleagues have been rejected for frivolous reasons. They are well-trained lawyers but are forbidden to practice, so they give counsel privately, or write articles for legal journals as academicians of the law. The only reason I was allowed to represent you before the Commission of Inquiry is that I am approved by the Ministry. And I was only approved because I don't bring cases to trial that embarrass the authorities, the Tsar, or the government. That's the reason: I settle them privately, quietly; nothing is aired in public; no one is embarrassed. But this commission is different. Had you been an accuser and brought forward evidence of corruption inside the Army's own Commissariat, that would have embarrassed them. Instead, you merely defended a business."

"Is this why Baron Günzburg wants to see me, because I defended a business? I'm curious, is he a friend of yours?"

"Of course he is. And a client, although Baron Günzburg has numerous legal representatives. Some for personal matters and some for business. You have heard of the I.E. Günzburg Bank, I presume."

"Well . . . no."

"My, my, my, you need a longer lesson than I thought! The Günzburg family is the most esteemed Jewish family in all of Russia, Leibovich! You should know this. They are financiers and philanthropists, the greatest force for Jewish rights in our time! They made a lot of money collecting taxes for the Tsar's government on distilled spirits and tavern leases. That was thirty years ago. Our friend Varshavsky made money the same way, the vodka tax. They sign a contract with the government and pay a fixed sum into the Tsar's treasury, but they get to keep a percentage of everything they collect — magic! It has been the biggest source of income for the government, by far. But the tax collectors don't hoard their wealth. The Günzburg family has given huge sums to Jewish charities. And they speak out for Jewish rights, steadily and most of all respectfully — nothing militant or revolutionary."

"I admit, I'm intrigued. I will pay the baron a visit, of course. But what do you think he will want from me?"

"You, Leibovich, are what the baron would call a useful Jew, not a Jew who fails to contribute. Whatever he wants, I would strongly suggest you agree. He has a circle of friends and associates who are very influential."

"And if I refuse him?"

"Don't be a complete fool. Most people would give their left arm for a meeting with Baron Günzburg. These kinds of opportunities come once in a lifetime, no more. Believe me, I know."

The Günzburg residence is a stone mansion in the Empire Style at No. 17 Konnogvardeysky Boulevard, near the Neva River embankment. I stand across the street, just before the hour on the invitation, and begin to count the windows; but with there being so many, I give up. The homes of the wealthy in St. Petersburg are startling in their grandeur. Each is an architectural statement if not a work of art. Nothing in Kiev or Odessa or Bucharest prepared me for what I have found in the Russian seat of power. The Günzburg mansion is at least four times the size of Pinhas Epshtein's impressive home.

A butler asks me to wait in the sitting room, where I take in the sumptuous oil paintings and shelves of leather-bound books. I walk to one of the nearby shelves and scan the works: Spinoza, Maimonides, Pushkin, Yehudah Halevi, Gogol, Turgenev, Abrahim ibn Daud's *Book of Tradition*,

Moses Mendelssohn's *On the Civil Amelioration of the Condition of the Jews*, and Ricardo's *On the Principles of Political Economy and Taxation*. There are medical textbooks, Baudelaire, Flaubert, and *The Rules of Double-Entry Bookkeeping* by an Italian. I count works in five languages. The breadth of one shelf's works alone leaves me in awe, but also perplexed. I know only a few of the names. Who are these authors, and why have so many of them escaped my notice? Was I too absorbed in the Talmud, the Aggadah, and the teachings of the great rabbis at the *beit midrash* to see the wider world of knowledge around me? Have I been consuming dogma alone? I think of myself as an educated person, but now I truly grasp my insularity.

The butler escorts me into a second sitting room where Horace Günzburg stands with his hands clasped behind his back. He is in his mid-forties, my height — roughly six feet — and already balding. Wearing a finely tailored suit and highly polished black leather Balmorals, he is richly impressive and impressively rich. Günzburg smiles as he shakes my hand.

"Right now, you are the most famous, or infamous, Jew in Russia," he says with a gleam in his eye.

Having been in the presence of nobility before — certainly General Skobelev counts — I sense that humility is in order. "I am certain you are more famous, Baron Günzburg."

"Well, perhaps. Nonetheless, you have made a very good impression."

The butler places a silver samovar and two glasses in silver tea holders on a low table that separates us.

"What do you think of our city?" Günzburg asks.

"A city of great beauty and wealth, nothing like the small town near Minsk where I grew up."

"Ah, but you have not seen Paris yet, I presume. Next to Paris, St. Petersburg is quite ordinary. Perhaps you know, but our family bank has offices in Kiev and Paris."

"I just learned this."

"We have been very fortunate, blessed in fact."

I remain erect in my armchair, still wary, as Günzburg begins to explain why he extended the invitation.

"I asked my secretary, Mr. Levin, to monitor the public meetings of the Commission of Inquiry, and he returned with a very favorable report of your testimony and statement. He suggested we sit down together, and after hearing about you, I insisted on it."

"I did my duty. That is all."

"You are aware that I have strongly urged Jewish conscripts to serve in the Imperial Army without hesitation, and to serve honorably?"

"Yes. I read one of your commentaries in the Hebrew press."

"I'm glad to hear that. But something puzzles me, Private Leibovich. What compelled you to leave the relative safety of a supply wagon and put on a uniform? You immediately became a target. So I am truly curious. I cannot imagine that my friend Andrei Moiseevich Varshavsky was to be feared more than a Turkish bayonet. Was it really a sense of duty to the Tsar and the Fatherland? Or perhaps something else?"

I look cautiously into Günzburg's eyes. He stares back. Perhaps he knows something already. Perhaps he has spoken to Varshavsky or Shaikevich. For a moment, I feel locked in a corridor with no exit, obliged to answer his question, and truthfully.

"I would like to answer, sir. But first — and I mean no disrespect — would you mind taking a moment to tell me more about why a man as busy as yourself wishes to speak with an Army private from Navahrudak? I'm glad Mr. Levin appreciated my statement, but I was just presenting certain facts."

"I would be happy to, and I will take more than a moment. You should know a bit about me, and not just what you've heard on the street. Those who do not know me sometimes make false assumptions. I am aware that my reputation runs hot and cold in Jewish circles. But never mind. It's true, I have inherited all of this from my father. He grew up in a simple town, Kamenets-Podolsk, south of Navahrudak. But he studied hard. When he was only in his thirties, he was fortunate enough to win a contract as an *otkupshchik,* a collector of taxes for the imperial treasury from the vodka distillers and tavern owners in the region. Well, he succeeded, and he expanded. Are you aware that my father's company supplied goods and clothing to the army during the Crimean conflict?"

"I did not know. My father fought at Sevastopol though."

"Interesting. In any case, we have something in common: roots in the shtetl. We moved to St. Petersburg and opened the bank twenty years ago, and it has been a success. But my father imparted to our family more than business acumen. He made philanthropy a duty, and we have tried from the beginning to champion the cause of the Jewish people here and in the Pale. And we have made progress, I am happy to say. Perhaps it has arrived more slowly than some would like, but it is progress nonetheless. And that brings me to the reason I have asked you here. You are in a unique position, Private Leibovich, by virtue of your public testimony. Many people will listen to what you have to say. And that could benefit the Jews of Russia — or harm them, depending on how you use your influence. Your example is compelling, and I'd like to convince you to publish your views more widely, perhaps in the journal *Ha-Magid.*"

I don't know how to react to this surprising suggestion. For the moment, I avoid it.

"You asked why I left the supply company. You may think I joined the Army out of a sense of duty. It was partly that, but also for personal reasons. It wasn't only duty to the Fatherland, but also duty to myself. I needed to give meaning to my life so that it would be worthy of God's blessing. I was studying to be a rabbi, but so much has happened since I left home."

The baron interrupts me. "I'm confused. Did you see fighting the Turks as worthy of God's blessing?"

"No, excuse me, I'll explain." Over the next ten minutes, I run through the details of my actions during the bombardment at Plevna, based on the pain of knowing that Avram Eizenberg had replaced me as a draftee. And I explain why, after Avram's death, I felt I had to stand in his shoes: it seemed like a moral imperative.

Günzburg listens and nods soberly, his hands clasped together in his lap. "You are an unusual young man, Leibovich," the Baron says. "I take it you have been raised in the traditions of the Hasidim."

"Not directly. My father demanded strict adherence to tradition, but we did not follow the Hasidim, though I know Hasidic ways. I am personally sympathetic to the philosophy of Kabbalah, the Ohr Ein Sof, but not to the faith-healing and folk magic."

"I have another meeting shortly," the baron says, "but I want you to consider something, Private Leibovich. If I can help to move you from an active army role to a reservist role, would you consider coming to work at our bank? We would pay for your education, whatever you want to study, while you work in an accounting role for the House of Günzburg and perhaps write for *Ha-Magid.* You have at least a little accounting experience. Just give it some thought. You may hear from my assistant, Mr. Levin. If you choose to return to the yeshiva, I wish you all the very best, and know you will succeed. But I want to give you an alternative that would open many doors."

It sounds like a grand opportunity, and it has landed like a bolt of lightning. But I refuse to allow the flash to blind me. What of my other obligations in Navahrudak, to Avram's memory and to the fulfillment of *selichah*? What of Rivkah Eizenberg? What of my own ambitions, which are still forming? My instinct is to delay, using the same excuse I used when Pinhas Epshtein offered to buy me a train ticket home.

"It is kind of you, and I will give it some thought, but I don't yet have orders from the Ministry of War informing me if I'll be returning to the Sixteenth Infantry Division. I really must wait."

"I imagine that the Ministry will inform Samuel Shaikevich about your forthcoming duties, Private Leibovich. If the Commission of Inquiry has no further questions, I doubt you would be called back to active duty. I imagine they no longer need you in the infantry, and will more likely have you in the reserves."

"God willing, my days in the trenches are over, but I will wait to see my new orders."

When I return to Shaikevich's office the next morning, another letter awaits me. Looking at the envelope, I recognize the handwriting, causing an immediate pulse of anxiety.

> *Dear Yakov,*
>
> *I read an account of your testimony in St. Petersburg, and decided to convey to you our sorrowful news with the hope that this note will be forwarded to you. The Conscription Officer visited us a month ago and informed us that Avram was killed during an awful battle in Bulgaria. He died heroically. I know you have been looking for Avram, but you won't find him. My mother and I are so grateful for your efforts on our behalf and equally impressed by your bravery. I look forward to the day you are safe at home and able to resume your studies. It would mean so much to me to greet you upon your return.*
>
> *With fond affection,*
> *Rivkah*

I slump into a chair and stare at the page, reading the note a second time, and then a third. My anguish is acute. I shut my eyes. She knows nothing remotely close to the truth. Worse, she thinks Avram's death was heroic. Rybakov knew everything but chose to hide the reasons her brother entered the army. It is fortunate, in some distorted way, that he told Avram's story with a soothing gloss. The cold truth would have been doubly painful. Yet Rybakov's explanation will only make my eventual confession to Rivkah more shocking and distasteful.

I tell Shaikevich's office assistant that I'm feeling ill and cannot see the barrister today, and that I will call again tomorrow. It is the truth. I step onto the sidewalk, profoundly disoriented. I don't quite know where I'm going or which street to take. How did I manage to transit from an obscure *beit midrash* near Minsk and the certainty of a future as a rabbi to this?

In my youth, I envisioned myself as a teacher and revered rabbi in a town somewhere near Navahrudak, or even in Minsk. Yet my esteem for Reb Epshtein lies in ruins. My philosophical guideposts were always Kabbalah and Torah, but in the cruel trenches of Bulgaria, my reverence and piety have drained away. If anything, the discussions I've had with the young revolutionary Veniamin and his opposite, Horace Günzburg, have reinforced the precarious nature of my relationship with tradition. I feel awakened to the attractions of modern thought, but am not sure where I should now apply my energies.

I am quite certain of one thing, however: I must see Rivkah Eizenberg and share the truth about her brother's demise. The sweetness and intelligence of this woman is beyond description. How is it that she finds the will to write to me and the courage to say, "It would mean so much to me to greet you."? I sense anew that she is an unusually strong woman, with an inquisitive mind, wit, and dauntlessness.

For years, I imagined a wedding standing beside a young woman who would provide me with children, obey me, and keep a well-stocked kosher kitchen as obsessively as my mother does. That image has now faded. I have begun to understand better what attracts me to Rivkah: it is her audacity, her confidence, her determination. She's the opposite of subservient and I now find this alluring; it surprises me I could ever have thought otherwise.

I find a park bench and watch the sparrows dart through the trees, chasing one another, swallowing bugs, and pecking at berries, oblivious to the laws of gravity but adhering to those of spring. All at once, change, curiosity, and modernity pull at me; but is my real future in banking? It hardly seems possible. One thing is clear: the ground under my feet has shifted away from an unquestioning devotion to the God of the great rabbis. I have more earthly interests waiting to be nourished. I recall the cautionary words of the great teacher of ethics, Rabbi Yisrael Lipkin: "Spirituality is like a bird. If you hold it too close, it chokes. If you hold it too loosely, it escapes."

13

My courtship by the proprietor of the I.E. Günzburg Bank is in full bloom, and the evidence resides in two messages delivered by courier to the law office on Glinka Street. One is from Emmanuel Borisovich Levin, Baron Günzburg's Secretary for Jewish Affairs, who has invited me to his office at the suggestion of the baron "so that we might become acquainted." The other is an official envelope from the Ministry of War. Effective immediately, I am assigned to a reserve battalion. The wealthy banker is evidently using his influence to channel me into employment at the House of Günzburg.

"I told you," Shaikevich remarks, pointing a finger at me. "He has you in his sights, and is moving in to ensnare you. Don't resist, Leibovich."

Just as he sang the praises of Baron Günzburg, Shaikevich lauds Emmanuel Levin, and again warns me against wasting an opportunity to enter the Günzburg realm. Shaikevich cannot imagine why I might be ambivalent; yet, I am. Not only am I wary of the banking trade, I am also suspicious of any situation in which I might be manipulated to fulfill the aims and purposes of a wealthy man. At least Levin is not a banker. He is seeking a better life for Russia's Jews, a goal I share. I will see him, but with my guard up.

When I enter Levin's office sitting room, I find a man older and less elegantly attired than Günzburg. He is the picture of scholarship. Books overflow from his shelves, and pages of handwritten letters and notes sit stacked on his desk.

"Fortune has placed a bright light upon you, Mr. Leibovich," Levin begins. "Baron Günzburg asked me to speak to you, so that we might better understand how your presence at the bank could enhance our business as well as the condition of the Jews of Russia. A voice such as yours would be extremely useful in both regards. Shall we speak about the condition of our co-religionists? Are you, by chance, a proponent of the Jewish Enlightenment, Mr. Leibovich? The Haskalah?"

"I wish I knew enough to form an opinion," I say cautiously. "I was a rabbinical student in a town near Minsk when I began to work for the Partnership. I do not come from a wealthy family, sir. I had always intended to return to complete my studies, but there have been interruptions. I find myself more open to modern ideas now, and perhaps a different path."

"Ah, you have been exposed to life outside the Pale," Levin says, "to new cities and new people, to new possibilities, to the modern world and modern culture — but also to war, unfortunately. You've witnessed the need for travel papers, the suspicion by the police, the limitations imposed by the state on what employment you might accept and where you might live, the attacks in the press, and every form of hatred of the Jews. You are aware of this, now, firsthand."

"Sadly, yes."

"You are also aware, I assume, that Baron Günzburg is deeply committed to improving the lot of Russia's Jews."

"I am told it is so and have no reason to doubt it."

"And it is so. This is my role. I am his eyes and ears when it comes to Jewish affairs. Some conservative forces in the Jewish community view Baron Günzburg as a traitor, unfortunately, because he chooses to work inside the Russian system to secure reforms. Never mind that he keeps the Sabbath and has told his sons they will not inherit a single rouble if they ever leave the Jewish faith. Never mind that he is today helping Jews to buy land in Palestine."

"I did not know."

"So it would be to our advantage to have ambassadors who might reach out to these conservative forces of our religion — rabbis, for the most part — and help to convince them that the most effective path is incremental reform and modernization. We could tailor a position for you that would meet your needs, and the compensation would be attractive. You would work directly with me on Jewish matters, while learning finance and accounting at the bank. We need to convince Russia's Jews that accepting secular influences in education will help lift them out of poverty. Too many rabbis are suspicious of modern life. We promote the teaching of the Russian language, for example. We are believers in the Haskalah. We are not trying to force faithful Jews and the Hasidim to relinquish traditions, but simply to offer a parallel path toward secular knowledge. You don't have to give up anything to broaden your outlook and open your mind."

Levin's diction is flawless, as if delivering a lecture from memory.

I ask, "Do you believe full emancipation for the Jews is possible? It seems so remote."

"A difficult question. When the Tsar emancipated all of Russia's serfs — you were probably a young child at the time — there were high hopes. But the peasants were allotted too little land and had to pay off large loans to purchase additional land from the government. So of course, poverty and unrest in the lower classes remains. Emancipation of the Jews is similarly fraught with uncertainties, Mr. Leibovich. I don't like the word 'emancipation,' frankly. A person with complete free will who nonetheless lives in abject poverty can hardly call himself 'emancipated.'"

"I have to agree, sir, though I know nothing of economics and little more about politics. I am a student of philosophy and religion, raised on Torah, Talmud, and Kabbalah."

"But you speak Russian as well as Yiddish and Hebrew, yes? This is a great advantage. Perhaps you should learn German too."

"I already know quite a lot of German. I am not ashamed to say that I used to read Goethe."

"That's wonderful. Already a modern man! In any case, I urge you to study philosophy — Mendelssohn, for one. Do you enjoy writing, Mr. Leibovich?"

"I keep a journal but have never thought myself a writer."

"And why not? I recommend it. I have published a Russian translation of the Wisdom of the Fathers, the Pirkei Avot. But I spend most of my time drafting petitions to the government on behalf of Baron Günzburg. Anyone who works for him is exposed to a man who sees no limitations on human possibilities."

"I'm not sure I could give up our traditions of spirituality," I say. "Though I have withdrawn from strict adherence to certain practices. I suppose my war experience weakened my dedication. But I don't think allowing some practices to fall by the wayside diminishes me as a human being or as a Jew."

"Of course it doesn't! You say it so well! I admire individuals who resist the rigidity of all orthodoxies."

"I am grateful to you and the baron for seeing in me something of value, but I need to consider what I want my future to look like; and at the moment, I'm not sure."

"It needn't include the Army, correct?"

"I suppose you know I've been ordered to the reserves."

"I heard it was a possibility."

"I have important personal business to attend to in Navahrudak, so I need to plan."

"Here is what I ask, Mr. Leibovich. Think about what is being put before you, the many possibilities, and come back in a few days so that we can discuss your future. You must know the old saying, 'You cannot avoid that which is meant to occur.'"

Levin rises to escort me out, placing a fatherly arm around my shoulder.

"You have much to give to the Jews of Russia," he says. "We need someone like you."

Even before I turn to leave Levin's office, I admit to myself that I simply have no interest in accounting or banking. It is all so remote and unattractive. I just can't say this to Levin's face. I am not comfortable in the world of money, and am not a tradesman or shopkeeper. The world that Baron Günzburg inhabits, where he can travel at will to his bank in Paris, negotiate large financial agreements, and hire a man as impressive as Emmanuel Levin, is foreign to me, distant from my experience, and, so far as I can tell, lacking in creativity. I feel like a stranger in their presence. To pretend otherwise, to force myself to enjoy such work, would be an error.

Yet I also admit that returning to the *beit midrash* would be a step into the past. My disappointment with Reb Epshtein is too deep. My questions about God's place in the universe and in men's hearts have only grown. What, then, is my future? I could find Rabbi Lipkin and study ethics with him. I could improve my German, escape the Pale to Berlin, and enter a university to learn the philosophy of the Greeks, Voltaire, and Spinoza. I could study with Rabbi Philippsohn in Bonn. I could find work at a factory in Minsk or Vilna to make enough money for a steamship ticket to America, where I hear opportunities abound. I could even track down Veniamin in Paris and study at the feet of Kropotkin.

Before dawn, after a sleepless night, I sit by candlelight in the cramped lobby of the rooming house where I am staying and draft a letter to Baron Günzburg that I intend to place in the hands of Emmanuel Levin, so that he might read it as well. It is a letter of gratitude for their belief in me and for their generosity. It seeks their understanding, but explains that I'm not of their world and don't believe I ever will be. My overriding priority, I emphasize, is to return home and fulfill my obligation to the family of my friend who was delivered into the arms of God in the most unjust of circumstances. Surely, they will understand how important it is for me to complete my repentance. I think of Veniamin as I write. How different his notion of society is from theirs, antithetical even.

I smooth out my army uniform, and again make my way on foot to the House of Günzburg, where the lobby clerk informs me that Emmanuel Levin will not be able to see me without an appointment. It doesn't matter. I write a brief note on bank stationery and attach it to my letter to Baron Günzburg:

Dear Mr. Levin,

This letter to Baron Günzburg explains my position. I wish you the very best.

With gratitude for your kindness, Y. Leibovich.

I emerge from the bank lobby into a light mist descending from gray skies. I have not eaten since the night before, yet have no desire for food. As I walk back to my room, I wonder whether Baron Günzburg might contact the Ministry of War after seeing my letter and, out of spite, demand that my discharge order be rescinded. I have barely enough money to get home, but to return now to Pinhas Epshtein's home and ask for a small loan is out of the question. I will do what I must to make my way back to Navahrudak. If I need a loan, Shaikevich will help, unless he is too bewildered and angry at me for rejecting the baron's path forward. I will have to explain all of this to him, then pack my belongings and purchase a one-way train ticket to Minsk.

This is my life now. But it is mine alone. I know that my first duty is to Avram and Rivkah and their mother — and to my own sense of justice. I must return to Navahrudak. There, I will make my own choices, and God willing, they will be wise ones.

Outside the Minsk train station, I'm reunited with the eccentric coachman who encouraged my learning of German. His clouded eyes sparkle as he greets me like a proud father. It takes a moment to explain why I'm wearing an army uniform. But soon, I am in his embrace, feeling his bristly beard against my cheek, and taking in the foul scent of smoked fish and what I now recognize as vodka on his breath. He takes my wrist in a hand bent by years of gripping leather reins, and ceremoniously hands me his worn edition of *Die Allgemeine Zeitung des Judenthums*. To have this journal of commentary in my hands again is pure joy, and he knows it. When I look into the coachman's eyes and grasp his shoulders in gratitude, words are unnecessary.

This was my welcome after the interminable dull clacking of the train from St. Petersburg, which I managed to pay for with an unexpectedly large envelope of back pay from the Ministry of War that Shaikevich handed me when I went to say goodbye. My status as a reservist has not been revoked, and I wonder for a fleeting moment whether the extra cash was extended to me as an anonymous parting gift from Baron Günzburg. I will never know.

It is May already, and the air is warm. Groggy from lack of sleep, I step high into the musty coach bound for Navahrudak. Immediately, I peruse the pages of *Die Allgemeine*, for there is always a surprise within. This edition has an essay by the paper's esteemed editor, Reb Philippsohn, arguing that recent instances of hostility toward the Jews are a form of fanatical envy, "which does not grant the Jew even a single piece of bread." I also read a review of a recently published book, *The Jewish Robinson Crusoe* by Solomon Rabinovich, a fifteen-year-old Russian prodigy writing in Hebrew. O how *Die Allgemeine* awakens me!

The back page is filled with often-amusing advertisements, and one small headline catches my eye: *Editorial Assistant Position*. Reb Philippsohn himself is seeking an assistant at his office in Bonn to help publish his newspaper, "because of the failing eyesight of this journal's Editor in Chief." I wonder: would the rabbi consider hiring a young Russian Jew whose German is only patched together? I tear the ad from the paper, tuck it into my pocket, and re-open a book I purchased in St. Petersburg — an acidic work recommended to me by Avram Eizenberg, the autobiography of Moshe Lilienblum, *The Sins of Youth*. I am in the middle of the second section, entitled "Days of Darkness," a period in which the writer's interests shifted from the religious commentaries of his youth in Vilna to modern philosophy and literature. It is stimulating to see that a Jew steeped in Talmud can remain a Jew while studying secular topics that include politics, even socialism. Lilienblum wrestles with his place in a fast-changing world, and is furious that he has been robbed of a freewheeling youth and adolescence, and denied the right to make practical decisions for himself. All of this now rings true for me.

I need to keep this book hidden from my parents because some of it is radical, flying in the face of traditions like arranged marriages and superstitions that I increasingly question. My parents will not understand the works of a Hebrew and Yiddish poet, satirist, and literary critic urging the Jews to come down to earth and engage with modern life. That would be heresy. Baron Günzburg would probably approve, but Yehudah Leibovich will not.

A series of ruts in the road jar me awake. The Lilienblum book rests at my feet. I look out the window and realize I am nearly home. The carriage ride to Navahrudak has taken three hours, but I must have leaned my head against the side of the coach and fallen into a deep sleep. I need to wash and find clean clothes, but I'm not sure this will be possible.

If I first see my parents and stay the night at Maya Street, I will have to answer an unending number of questions, some of which are bound to veer into the complicated reasons I entered the Tsar's infantry. So I will instead go in uniform directly to the Eizenbergs' room on Volkava Street.

As soon as I step off the carriage at Market Square and say farewell to the coachman, I notice something is different. The town looks strange, even antiquated. I have been away for more than fifteen months. It's not that the storefronts, donkey carts, women carrying baskets of baked goods, and children holding hands are any different from when I departed — it's that I have changed. My frame of reference has been radically altered and now includes familiarity with much grander European cities: Odessa, Bucharest, and St. Petersburg. Navahrudak is poor and small, I realize, and the idea of marrying and remaining here no longer holds much appeal for me.

I wear the uniform of a soldier of the Imperial Army. This is not a requirement for a reservist, but I am comfortable in this guise, even with shorn sidelocks. I am no longer the earnest yeshiva student and don't wish to be known merely as the tinker's son. Mostly, though, I wear the uniform because I am going directly from Market Square to the Eizenbergs' room, and I want them to see evidence of my kinship with their son. He was a soldier, and I am a soldier. I want them to understand my time in the army as an homage to him, a form of sacrifice on his behalf. It is wholly inadequate and won't return Avram to his family, yet I feel it will lend credence to my account. When I tell them Avram seemed strong of mind and body, fearless, and full of humor, they will be more inclined to believe me.

The sun is bright and warm as I turn away from Maya Street, walking in the direction Rivkah had taken me when I carried the sack of pots for her so long ago. The weight of the moment dawns on me. Somehow, everything around and inside me seems heavier, as if my being has suddenly become a dense mass, requiring greater emotional and physical energy to move and think. I try to imagine an encounter with Rivkah, and wonder if seeing her face to face might cause me to waver. I mustn't let it.

The neighborhood changes from one street to the next. As always, the poverty of the homes and people increases the closer I get to the town's fringe. I smell the coal stoves and see the same patched roofs, dilapidated windows, and dusty streets without paving stones. I pass the tailor shop, where the old man told me a year ago to find Miryam Steklov. In a minute, I am on Volkava Street, and remember the woman who directed me there so long ago. "Sweet thing," she had said of Rivkah.

In the alley, I see the small window and stovepipe at the upper level of the shed and take the steps to the small landing, where I take a deep breath and gently knock.

"Mrs. Eizenberg?" I call through the closed door. "I am a friend of your son." There is no response.

"Mrs. Eizenberg? I apologize. May I take a moment of your time?"

The door opens a crack. Half of Rivkah's face appears.

"Rivkah," I whisper.

The door opens wider. Rivkah wears no scarf. Even in the poor light, I can see her hazel eyes and dark curls. I stare at her for a moment with mixed feelings: pure happiness and reverberating apprehension.

"Yakov? You've come home!"

"Yes. I came to speak to your mother and you. I have much to tell you."

"Of course. About your travels."

"About Avram."

Rivkah pauses, looks back inside, then turns to me again. "I'm sorry, but Avram was killed in the war. You mustn't have gotten my letter. I sent it to St. Petersburg when I read about your testimony in the Yiddish press."

"I know, Rivkah. I received your letter. I know about Avram. I was there when he died. That's what I want to talk to you about. That's why I've come," I say, feeling myself trembling slightly. Months of anticipation, and my words feel strange. I hear myself, but it is as if I am watching myself perform a duty, judging whether I am saying what I need to say, what I promised myself I would say.

"You were there?" The door opens fully. She glances again into the room behind her.

"Is your mother prepared for a visitor?"

"I'm sorry, Yakov. We rarely get visitors. I'll ask her." She steps back from the door. In the shadows, I can see that Shayna Eizenberg is in bed. Rivkah returns.

"Can you come in half an hour?"

"Yes, yes, of course. Half an hour.

"Thank you, Yakov."

I nod and move carefully down the steep steps as the door closes, feeling strangely buoyant. Seeing Rivkah's face has lifted my spirits. A year older, she seems taller and even more striking than I remembered. She smiled when she said, "You've come home." She looked directly at me. A confident woman, I could see the kindness in her eyes.

I walk back toward the town center, to a bakery I passed on the way, and purchase four honey cakes. Sitting on the edge of a stone wall and fortifying myself with one of the cakes, I think again about what I will say to the Eizenbergs. My anxiety hasn't fully receded, but I've received an infusion of courage, enough to realize I will be able to tell Rivkah the truth.

When I return to the alley, Rivkah's door is ajar. I knock on the jamb, and she steps into the light, now wearing a headscarf. I see Shayna Eizenberg for the first time. She is sitting up in bed, her back on a pillow against the wall. She looks thin and pale, but it's hard to know how ill she is. The two of them live in a single room with a small wood stove, two chairs, two beds, and a chest of drawers. A sack holding kitchenware that Rivkah means to repair and sell rests in the far corner. Two brass sabbath candlesticks sit atop the chest. A stack of well-used books rises nearly three feet from the floor. The light from the only window and a lone candle on the chest allows me to see their faces. Shayna smiles at me weakly.

"I'm sorry, I've not been well," she says. "The fever comes and goes."

"God willing, your health will return," I say, glancing at Rivkah, who sits near the bed. She has been looking at me from the side, but when I turn, she glances down.

"Mother, Yakov has brought us some honey cake," she says. "I will fix a plate and make tea."

"Yes, tea. Can you stay for tea, young man?"

"With pleasure, but I don't want to intrude." I pause before confessing, "I'm here to tell you what I know about your son."

"Rivkah told me," Shayna says. "We are grateful. The conscription officer came and gave us the news. He was kind, and gave us twenty roubles as a military family benefit. But he had no information about what happened. He said Avram died a hero in a terrible battle." Tears well in Shayna's eyes, and she dabs them with a handkerchief she grips tightly in one hand.

I lean toward Shayna in my chair and say softly, "Mrs. Eizenberg, I am profoundly sorry for the death of your son. He was my friend at the *beit midrash*. And I was with him when his soul returned to God. It was a terrible battle in Bulgaria; that is true. But I don't know how much you wish to know, I mean, of the details. It might be difficult. If you are willing, I would like to tell you and explain some very important circumstances."

"I spoke to my mother," Rivkah interrupts, "and she is prepared. Can you tell us, did he suffer?"

"No, he did not suffer. Of this I am certain."

"Thanks be to God," Rivkah says.

"This is where the circumstances get complicated. I know you will have many questions. May I start from the beginning? It will be easier."

Rivkah is tending to the tea. "Please," Shayna says. "Avram came to see us just before he was sent to his barracks for the first time. We cried, Rivkah and I. We begged him not to go, but he said it wasn't a choice and he knew how to take care of himself."

I accept a small glass of tea from Rivkah, who offers a brief smile as she hands it to me, along with half a honey cake. I begin to tell the difficult story, starting with the Navahrudak draft lottery a year and a half ago and the arrangement crafted with the aid of the rabbi's brother in St. Petersburg.

Rivkah interrupts. I hear her say, "We know what happened." But I fail to take this in fully or to question it. I am too intent on telling the story, which I have turned over in my mind dozens of times. Besides, how can they know what happened?

"This will be painful and confusing for both of you," I say, "but Avram wasn't in the draft lottery. He wasn't meant to be conscripted." I take another deep breath. "You see, I was dropped from the conscription list through a special arrangement, and the conscription officer, Rybakov, had to find another conscript to fill his local quota. I'm sorry to tell you this, but he forced me to give him a Jewish conscript to replace me. 'A Jew for a Jew,' he said. My father and I knew of a vagrant, but had no idea it was Avram. And, well, I told Rybakov where to find the vagrant, without knowing who it was. Do you see that Avram was never meant to go to the army?"

I take another deep breath and go on. "The arrangement I got myself into pulled Avram into something he wasn't meant to experience, and I am truly, truly sorry. And before God, I ask for your forgiveness. I never meant for Avram to be taken into the army. I didn't know where he was. But I gave up the vagrant, and I shouldn't have."

Shayna's hands are clasped in her lap and her eyes are cast down. I can tell she is struggling to hold back tears. Rivkah, however, is peculiarly calm.

"Yakov," Rivkah says firmly. "You cannot blame yourself for this. You mustn't." She bends forward in her chair and briefly places both of her hands on mine, a gesture that is both surprising and confusing.

"We know everything," Shayna says softly. "We have already forgiven you."

I stare at her, dumbstruck; I'm not sure I understand what she's saying.

"Didn't you hear me?" Rivkah asks. "We know all of this. We know you told the conscription officer about Avram, even though you didn't know it was him."

I turn to Rivkah, profoundly confused. "How do you know?"

"I received a letter from Avram several weeks after he died, in his own hand. I know it was from him. He told me he had met you at a place called Plevna, and you had explained to him how he came to be in the army."

"Ah, the letter, the letter! He handed it to me the night before he was killed and asked me to mail it. I never knew what it said. I mailed it from Odessa weeks later, while staying in the hospital there."

"Yakov, the letter explained everything," Rivkah continues. "Avram said you gave up the vagrant to the conscription officer but didn't know who it was. We are aware of this. He asked us not to blame you. He said he felt more alive in the army than he had felt in years, and that he surely would have died of too much vodka had he stayed in Navahrudak. He asked us to forgive you, Yakov. And we do. We have. We forgive you. Do you understand? The Russian state placed a terrible burden on you."

I am trying to comprehend all of this, but it is too much at once. I begin to cry tears of relief, and the cascade of great heaving sobs ripples through me. So much has been held inside of me for so long. I don't want Rivkah to see me like this. I cover my face in my hands and desperately try to compose myself. It only takes a moment.

"May I see the letter?" I ask hoarsely.

"Not now," Rivkah replies. "It has some personal things in it. Maybe another day."

"Then may I explain to you exactly how Avram died? It is important."

"Don't worry. Go on," Shayna replies. "I think we should know."

I wipe my eyes as I sit upright again. My voice is stronger.

"When I happened upon him near Plevna, Avram looked fit and happy. This is the truth. His unit had many Jews, and they were comrades."

"I'm glad he was happy," Shayna interjects.

"Yes. He was joking. There was energy in his voice. Some units from the Fourteenth Division were transferred to the Sixteenth, including Avram's. I managed to get my wagon up a hill to the unit's encampment. I was carrying medical supplies and could see they had many wounded and sick. Avram helped unload the supplies, and he just recognized me. It was a coincidence. We talked for many hours that night, and I met the Jews in his unit. He called them 'the Yiddish Brigade of Marksmen.'"

Rivkah smiles, "It sounds just like Avram."

"One of them was Kalman Levin, the brother of someone we knew at yeshiva. They carried a small Torah. And they tried their best to keep the Sabbath. I remember Avram was wearing a skullcap."

"He was?" Rivkah asks.

"Yes. And he told me about Yisrael Tsipershtein, a boy from Navahrudak who was in Avram's unit and unfortunately was killed that September. And I remember this very well: Avram told me how Rybakov came and found him shortly before the new year on the Christian calendar. It was six weeks after the lottery. He told me Rybakov eventually acknowledged that he only needed Avram to fill his quota."

"Avram told us he stayed for a time at Rybakov's house," Shayna recalls.

"And he told me that while he was there, at Rybakov's," I continue, "he saw the lottery list and his name wasn't on it. He didn't know it at the time, but my name was on the list. He wasn't bitter though. He said 'the Imperial Army saved my life,' and seemed to truly believe that. Before Rybakov came to find him, he wanted . . . well, he wasn't very interested in living."

"He was ill and despondent," Rivkah says. "We know this. He took my father's death so hard."

Shayna covers her face with her handkerchief.

"Avram was at peace in the army. Being among the other Jewish conscripts must have restored him. But the war hit us hard the next day. I was preparing to leave. Avram was at the camp, very close by. Artillery shells from the Turks started falling and the explosions were close. Avram came running down from the camp to help get me out, but the wagon got stuck. He was desperately pushing the wagon trying to get me to safety. A shell exploded just behind him, and it threw me off the wagon. When I turned back, I could see Avram on the ground."

I glance at Rivkah. Tears are running down her cheeks, but she looks straight at me.

"I am sure he died instantly," I say. "It was a large wound to the back of his head, from shrapnel. There was nothing anyone could do."

Silence fills the room. I am drifting in a moment of pain and relief.

"You mustn't blame yourself," Shayna says with a weak voice.

"I was supposed to be in the army, not Avram. I was supposed to be in that unit." I wipe my eyes again.

"God willing, his soul is at peace," Shayna responds. "That is all that matters now."

"You are generous, Mrs. Eizenberg. But I want you to know how badly I feel about this. I buried Avram on the hillside and said the Mourner's Prayer and the appropriate Psalm of David. He had a burial according to our traditions. I put my *tallit katan* over him."

Rivkah stirs. "You know, you didn't have to go in his place, Yakov. It was a terrible risk," she says, pain and loss written on her face.

"No one forced me," I say. "Everything I did from that point on was clear before my eyes."

Rivkah reaches out and grasps my forearm for a moment. My head sags. The steadying presence from Rivkah's touch, however brief, reminds me how mature she is and how much I admire her.

Shayna breaks the silence. "Thank God the war is over. What will you do now? Return to yeshiva?"

"I have to think. I loved the *beit midrash*, but all my recent experiences are pulling me away. I may go to Minsk for a time. I hear there are factory jobs. I could earn some money. Then perhaps I can go to a good university, or study somewhere outside the Pale, Germany maybe, or go to America. I don't know."

"I told Rivkah she should go to America," Shayna offers. "People in Market Square say everything is new there, that Jews can live without fear, work where they want to work, live how they want to live — unlike in Russia, unlike in the Pale. There is nothing here for Rivkah. She is a beautiful young woman, but there is no dowry and no man will have her."

"Mother!" Rivkah protests and looks at me, perturbed.

"What she meant to say," Rivkah adds firmly, "is that I won't agree to customs that require a girl's complete obedience to men, and assume that women are suitable only for bearing children."

"Rivkah!" her mother exclaims.

"I understand this, Rivkah," I say, trying to reassure her.

"As you can see, our situation is hard and I must work," Rivkah says.

"People cling to these matchmaking customs," I continue, "but they make no sense to me anymore. I agree with you, Mrs. Eizenberg. Your daughter is indeed beautiful." I glance at Rivkah.

"He is being polite, Mother," Rivkah says.

"Have some more tea," Shayna says. "It is a comfort to me to have you here."

"There is something else I must do, Mrs. Eizenberg. My repentance will not be complete in the eyes of God until I provide compensation to you."

"You don't have to repent, Yakov," Rivkah says.

"Avram suggested how I might do this when we met near Plevna. It was the morning that he died. I was telling him I needed to compensate him, that God requires it. And he told me he didn't need anything, but to think of something I could do for both of you. So, I must do that. Please understand. I have a plan that will provide you with some extra resources. Surely you can use it."

"But this is not necessary," Shayna says. Rivkah remains silent.

"It is not a choice, Mrs. Eizenberg. It is God's commandment. And I must honor Avram's wishes. Do you see?"

Rivkah slowly nods to Shayna, "It's alright, Mother."

"Well, then," Shayna says, "I will not prevent it. Rivkah works so hard to bring in extra cash. You can do this for her, not for me." She draws her hand close to her chest. "Thank you," she whispers. "I'm tired now. I need to sleep."

"And I must return to my parents' house," I say. "They don't know yet that I have returned."

"You came here directly from the coach?" Rivkah asks.

"Yes." I stand to leave.

"I'll come outside with you for a moment," Rivkah says, smoothing her long skirt. "Rest, Mother. I'll be back shortly."

Rivkah closes the door quietly. The sunlight is falling at a shallow angle and illuminates her face.

"You have shown us great kindness," she says, nervously fidgeting with her hands. "I want you to know, well, we hold no anger toward you. My brother's death wasn't your fault, Yakov. I believe that. And I know my mother feels the same way. Avram's letter made everything clear to us. Perhaps I can show it to you sometime."

I am overwhelmed with relief. I never imagined I would receive such generosity. It starts with Avram's letter. What magic he must have created with words on paper, what compassion! Rivkah is trying to release me from the pain she knows I feel, the pain I have carried inside for so many months. I try to reply but stammer, and look up to the sky. All I can say is, "Thank you." With the sun on her face, she turns her head slightly. I catch the luster of her eyes.

Rivkah is neither an intellectual nor a zealot. But she has surprised me by speaking out against arranged marriages. I can see in our brief encounter with her mother that she is even bolder, more self-confident, and more generous and kind-hearted than I knew. At times, her modesty overshadows her strength of character. Both qualities attract me. Looking beyond her threadbare clothing, I see a woman more beautiful than I had remembered. I notice every detail, the slender eyebrows and lips, the skin that seems to hold a permanent gloss.

I will be as boldly honest with her as she has been with me. "I wasn't being polite just now. You are a beautiful woman, Rivkah Eizenberg. Any man would be lucky to have you, dowry or not."

This time, I am certain she blushes. "I suppose you meant what you said to my mother," Rivkah says, looking away. "This is what Avram told me in the letter, the private part. He said, well, he said you have feelings for me."

She looks up at me. "Is that true?"

I lean down to whisper in her ear, "Your brother was perceptive." Then acting on impulse, I kiss her at the edge of her cheek and neck. Rivkah recoils. Her hand shoots to the spot. She looks at me, confused.

"I'm sorry," I say. "I shouldn't have."

Rivkah's hand slowly falls from her neck. I cannot tell if she is angry or surprised, or both.

"It's just that I'm not used to being kissed," she says, her eyes cast down.

"Forgive me."

"I have to ask: are you no longer thinking about Mindl Zaltsman?"

"Oh, no, not at all. I should have told you. There won't be a wedding"

Rivkah stares into the distance. "Do you mind if I ask what happened?"

"Many things: the draft lottery, the war, the supply job. It was a bad time for a wedding. My father called it off just before I left for the war. And I confess that I was quite relieved."

Still looking away, she asks, "It was a poor match?"

"Here is the truth, Rivkah. I never wanted it. I thought I wanted an obedient bride who would spend her days repairing stockings and cooking kugel. But I now realize that was foolish, pointless, and idiotic. I love my mother, but I don't want to marry someone just like my mother. I only agreed to the engagement because I was worn down by my father. He pushed and I got tired of pushing back. In the end, I was the obedient son, setting an example for my brother. I don't know why. But everything has changed, hasn't it? Everything."

I want Rivkah to tell me how relieved she is, how pleased she is. Instead, she places her hand on my forearm.

"I'm not sure you need to be forgiven for kissing me," she says with the merest smile. "But you must do me a favor. Can you help me carry my sack tomorrow from Market Square, like you did before?"

"It would be my pleasure. Shall I come to the square at noon?"

"Yes, come at noon."

"I will."

As I walk down the steep stairway, I glance back. Rivkah smiles at me from above. I make my way through the alley and turn toward my parents' home on Maya Street, feeling infinitely lighter and invigorated. My entire body is unclenched and at ease, and my stride lengthens, no longer restrained by anxiety. I smile to myself and shake my head in utter wonderment at my good fortune.

14

The *mezuzah* holding the Hebrew texts from Deuteronomy is missing a nail and hangs askew on the door jamb, as I knock at the entrance to 57 Maya Street, afraid I might frighten my parents if I walk in unannounced.

"Hello? It's Yakov!"

From within, I hear the crash of a kitchen pot and my Mother's voice saying softly, "Yakov. Yakov." She opens the door wide. I am not sure what I was expecting — joy and relief, perhaps. Instead, Mother's face is drawn and lined with worry. Have I done this to her, I wonder, over the past year? Has my absence caused such distress?

"Yakov, come here."

I set down my satchel and wrap her in a long embrace. "Yes, mother. I'm home."

My mother begins to sob. Her arms are tight around my back, and pull me toward her as if she might never let go. She is too short to wrap herself around my neck or shoulders. "I prayed you would come home. I prayed to God each day."

"Let me look at you, Mother." I loosen my arms and try to push her back from the shoulders, but she keeps me in a tight hug.

"Not yet, Yakov. I need to hold you." She is crying softly.

"Of course, Mother, of course. Please don't cry."

I look beyond her into the kitchen, which is oddly chaotic. The table is strewn with dishes and the sink holds dirty pots.

"I have something to tell you," she whispers.

I push back to examine her face, which is now damp and distended. She looks much older. Something is wrong. "What is it, Mother? Where's Father?"

She pulls me in again, her face burrowed into my chest. "God has taken him, Yakov. God has taken your father."

"What?" I pull back more forcefully and stare at her in shock.

Nodding, she attaches to my eyes. "We buried him in November, Moyshe and I. The rabbi told me the supply company didn't know where you were. I couldn't reach you to tell you."

"My God, Mother. What happened?"

"Come inside, my son."

We sit at the kitchen table. I understand now why it is strewn with dishes and utensils, and why the *mezuzah* at the door hasn't been repaired.

"Mother, this is terrible news. Please tell me what happened."

"It's been six months since he died. His heart failed, just stopped working. The doctor called it 'angina pectoris.' He thought you were dead, Yakov. We all thought you were killed until the rabbi read me the newspapers." Tears well up again.

"What are you talking about?"

"They told us you were dead, Yakov. What can I say?"

"Who did?"

"Kalman Levin's father came and read us a letter from Kalman, sent from a place called Lovtcha. It said you had died and he was sorry for the news. He said he found your grave and saw your *tallit katan* and your satchel, the one your father gave you. We tried to find out what happened, but no one knew."

"Kalman Levin? My God. I heard he thought I had died, but I didn't imagine it would come to this. I had no idea he would go this far. How could he? I heard from another soldier that he had seen my *tallit* on a body, but the body obviously wasn't me, Mameh."

"Yes, the letter said he saw your grave in a place in Bulgaria called the Green Hills, but he only described your *tallit* and satchel. And . . . and the next morning I found your father on the floor beneath his workbench." Tears overflow now, and I take her hand.

"Mother."

"It broke his heart, Yakov. It just broke his heart. He wanted so badly for you to live a good life and a long life, as full and as long as can be. When he heard you were killed, he couldn't live any longer. He couldn't."

"I just can't believe it."

"For three months, Moyshe and I thought you were dead. But in March, Rabbi Epshtein read us the newspapers about your testimony in St. Petersburg. We said it must be you, how could it not be? I was so confused. The rabbi contacted his brother, who confirmed you were testifying to the state commission. I wept tears of joy. But I decided to await your return. I knew you would come. I didn't want you to see this news in a letter or hear it from someone else. I needed to be the one to tell you, and the rabbi agreed with me. I'm sorry."

"Mother, don't apologize. I know why Kalman mixed up everything. It's not his fault, but he should have been more careful. It's . . . it's just a tragedy."

"Tell me what happened, Son? Why was your *tallit* on the grave of another soldier?"

"A good soldier died, Mother, a Jewish soldier. I placed my *tallit* on his body before burying him. He was a friend, and I was alone. All the other soldiers had left. I heard later from another soldier that Kalman had come back to the camp to retrieve ammunition. He must have seen the grave and recognized my *tallit* in the dirt and mud. He saw my satchel, which I had traded for a knapsack. It was a makeshift grave that I dug myself. I wanted the soldier to have a proper Jewish burial. The news must have been devastating for Father, my God."

"I never saw him so weak with pain and sorrow as the night we were told. I tried, Yakov. What could I do? We both had so much grief."

"You can't blame yourself, Mother. This is just . . . How did God allow this?"

Mother's face suddenly wrinkles. "Where are your sidelocks! You cut them!"

I frown, "Yes, Mameh. Please don't worry. I'm still your son. And I'm no longer in the army, even though you see me in this uniform, just in the reserves. I can explain about the sidelocks."

"May God forgive you, Yakov. You know what your father would have said. He would have asked if you are now breaking all of God's commandments, whether you worship idols and such. I don't ask this but I can hear his voice. What happened? I know you earned a medal. The rabbi told me. Did they make you shave? Thanks be to God that you are still wearing a *yarmulke*."

"I am a Jew, Mother. I wear a *yarmulke*. God knows if I am pious and faithful or not. Please don't worry."

Moyshe enters the front door, home from school. He has grown. Soon he will be a Bar Mitzvah.

"Yakov?"

"Yes, Moyshele. Come." We share a long embrace. My brother must sense my emotions, because he tells me, "Please don't cry."

Mother wraps her arms around us both. "You're alive, Yakov," she whispers. "That's all that matters, Moyshe. He's alive. Blessed is the Merciful God."

"Yes," I say softly, "blessed is the Merciful God." I know this is what I must say, but I wonder what mercy He showed to Avram Eizenberg or Yehudah Leibovich.

This is the day I had planned to confront Father over Avram's death, but now it is irrelevant. I try to calm myself by fixing the *mezuzah* and helping Mother clean the house, though my deep sadness cannot be erased. In the afternoon, we gather for tea, and I tell Mother and Moyshe about my work with the Partnership and the testimony in St. Petersburg. All Moyshe wants to know is how I came to be in the Imperial Army and awarded a medal for valor. Mother is less insistent, but is also curious about my unusual army experience. I move comfortably into the role of storyteller. It helps to push aside the anger I hold against Kalman Levin and the sorrow that his error, innocent as it may have been, has wrought. I stick to an account of my soldiering, because I don't want Moyshe to hear about the gruesome death of Avram Eizenberg. It is the barest of summaries.

"I was at the siege of Plevna delivering medical supplies last fall. They had lost a lot of men. It was difficult to see all the wounded and the sick. There were fevers and intestinal diseases. I was frightened, to be honest. The Turks were shelling us. I picked up a rifle and that was it. I met a general there named Skobelev, who asked for my help, and I gave it. I fought at Plevna, spied on the Turks by pretending to be a Jewish merchant, then fought again at Shipka Pass."

"We heard about some of these battles. You could have been killed," Mother murmurs.

"I was wounded at Shipka. Just my shoulder."

"How did it happen?"

"It doesn't matter, my shoulder is fine now. I was in a sling for a time, and they sent me to the army hospital in Odessa. It was infected for a time, but it healed. I was much luckier than a lot of the boys."

I turn toward Mother and ask somberly, "Do you know that Tsipershtein was killed near Plevna?"

"We know. So many people came to say the Mourner's Prayer at his parents' home and at the synagogue. The whole community was grieving for this boy."

Mother knows nothing of the scheme that unfolded before I left for Odessa more than a year ago, after Rybakov demanded a Jew for a Jew, but she will have to know eventually.

"Did anyone say the Mourner's Prayer for Avram Eizenberg at the synagogue?" I ask her.

"Eizenberg? Who is he? A soldier from Navahrudak?"

"Someone Father knew. Yes, he was from here, but not many people knew that." Anger rises inside me, and I don't want it to take over, so I tell Mother I'm going for a walk. I have to bring fresh air into my lungs and allow my disquiet to find equilibrium.

Out the door and onto Maya Street, I gaze up at the stars, wondering whether I should even mourn my father. Beyond Kalman Levin, I am angry at my father still, and angry at myself. Although the Eizenbergs have forgiven me in the most generous way, I realize that tragedy has compounded tragedy, all of it growing from a single act, in which I participated, that could have been prevented.

There is catharsis in the telling and retelling of grievous events. I have felt compelled to impart to others the trauma of Plevna, of Avram, and the battles that ensued, and each time it happens, I feel a lightening, like a coastal tide running out; but the tide always returns. I think about all of this as I lie on a mattress, awakening slowly to a faint scratching sound. I open my eyes, but for a moment, I don't know where I am. The surroundings seem dark and unfamiliar. I turn and see the first pale light of day through the window and realize I am home, on my mattress, with my army coat covering my feet. Moyshe's bed is empty.

The scratching is coming from my father's workshop. Was all of this a terrible dream? I descend the stairs and peek into the work area. It is Moyshe, playing with the gadgets and clocks and lamps, perhaps assuming that if he causes enough damage or clatter, Father will return to scold him, just like always.

I stand over him. "You miss Tatte, don't you, Moyshele?"

My brother shrugs. "Mameh cried a lot."

"Did you cry?"

"A little. Not much."

"I cried last night," I tell him, and it is the truth.

"I heard you."

"It's not a sin to cry when God takes your father."

"But why did He take Tatte?"

"I don't know, Moyshele. It's a mystery and will forever be a mystery." This is how I imagine Reb Epshtein would have responded.

I wrap an arm around Moyshe's shoulders. "Let's have some food. I will be here when you return from school." But Moyshe remains at Tatte's workbench.

In the kitchen, I heat water for tea and wipe my face with a damp cloth. I remember I left clean clothes in a cabinet a year ago, and go to retrieve them. Even as I prepare tea, I cannot seem to release my urge to speak to Father about Avram. I suppose he assumed he would never learn the fate of the besotted vagrant at the end of Sverdlova Street whose location I had divulged to Rybakov. Perhaps Father believed that had Avram not entered the Tsar's army, he would have died of vodka poisoning or cholera, a lost soul and a lost cause, one of those dull and useless Jews who never comes to the synagogue, and quits the *beit midrash* because it is too demanding and because God is too demanding.

Mother enters the kitchen, her voice is insistent. "Moyshe. Come and eat. You need to go to school."

There is silence at breakfast until Moyshe departs.

"I see you've put away the army uniform," Mother says.

"I found these clothes. They still fit, and it feels good. Mother, can we speak for a moment about the boy Avram Eizenberg, the one I mentioned last night?"

"I remember. How did your father know him?"

"Last night, you heard me say I volunteered for the army, but there is more to it, a great deal more. Avram was a friend of mine at the *beit midrash*. I know how he came to wear the uniform of the Imperial Army, and how he became a target of Turkish artillery. It was unjust. And I know how he died because I was there."

"Tell me, my son. What happened?"

"It's a complicated story, but you need to know that Tatte and I did something wrong — very wrong — to keep me out of the army. And as a result, Avram Eizenberg lost his life."

"Oh my."

I tell her for the first time about Rybakov's demand of a Jew for a Jew and father's plan to provide the location of the vagrant.

"Your father didn't tell me. How did you find out it was the Eizenberg boy?"

"I know his sister, Rivkah. A few days later, before I left for Odessa, I asked about Avram, and she told me he had left home months before and was living on the streets."

"You know, in your grandparents' time, the Jewish Council — the town's rabbis — paid kidnappers to find poor Jewish boys to go into the army in the place of boys from rich families. They hired kidnappers. Did you know that?"

"I have heard this."

"The rabbis had to fill the quota, not a conscription officer. It was terrible. Rybakov made this injustice continue."

"There's more, unfortunately."

I tell her about Pinhas Epshtein. "I know how it is that he came to arrange work for me with the Partnership. It wasn't out of the goodness of his heart."

"Oh?"

"Tatte paid a bribe, Mother. He paid someone at the War Ministry to keep me out of the Imperial Army."

"Oh, Yakov, it can't be! Your father would never . . ."

"You think not? The rabbi's brother arranged it and told me about it. Right to my face, in St. Petersburg. 'This is how things are done,' he said. Yesterday I went to see Avram's mother and sister, and I apologized to them. If Father hadn't paid to get me a job with the Partnership instead of serving, I'm the one who would have gone into the army, not Avram. He was innocent. Do you see?"

"But a payment? Where would he get the money for such a thing?"

"I don't know, Mameh. But I intend to speak to the rabbi about this. I just want you to know, Reb Epshtein is as much at fault as Tatte and me. The rabbi was part of all of this."

"But you can't blame yourself for the boy's death, Yakov. Where would the Eizenberg boy be today if you had gone into the army instead of him? Suffering, probably, maybe even dead from the cold."

"Or from too much vodka. Or maybe he would be alive, Mameh. May I just tell you about Avram Eizenberg? I need to say it."

Mother sits silently as I explain the wagonload of medical supplies and the Yiddish Brigade of Marksmen. I am speaking softly, slowly, feeling each word. "At Plevna, I told Avram how sorry I was and that I wanted us to switch jobs. He would drive the supply wagon and I would be the soldier; but he refused. I wanted to compensate him. He said if I wanted to compensate anyone for what had happened, it should be his mother, Shayna. The next morning we were preparing to leave and there was an artillery barrage."

I tell her how Avram died, how I took his uniform, how I buried him, and how I placed my *tallit katan* on his body. Mother's hand covers her mouth, and her eyes are shut.

"It was a gesture of respect. I found a rifle at the camp where his unit had been. And I went to find them. And they took me along as a soldier. So I became a soldier and I fought, and I didn't really care if I lived or died, to tell you the truth. Each time I thought about it, I knew how frightened Avram must have been."

I turn to look into my mother's eyes. They are still shut. Tears streak down both cheeks.

"Open your eyes, Mameh. I killed a man. I killed a man with a bayonet, a Turk. I saw his eyes just as I am looking at yours. I think about it every day."

She takes a moment to compose herself, and I wait. "Two armies at war try to kill each other, Yakov. Please, please don't torture yourself. They would have killed you too."

"Do you know why Avram left the *beit midrash*, Mameh? He quit a few years ago, not because of prayers, or Hebrew, or God, or the rabbi. It was because his father died of cholera, and he just fell apart. Avram's sister told me."

"Oh, the poor boy. But you know, Yakov, it was the Turks who killed the Eizenberg boy. You said so yourself. Do you see that it's not your fault?"

I hear her, but her words do not ring with conviction. She understands my sadness and guilt.

"Father tried to control my life for so many years," I say. "Then he paid someone to keep me out of the army. It makes me angry. But it's also my fault for letting him do it. I have to take responsibility for placing Avram at the front lines of a war. And if Father was alive, he too would have to take responsibility. You know the Torah, Mameh. Moses didn't want to go back to Egypt and serve as God's messenger. He didn't want to. He wouldn't take responsibility. 'And the Lord's wrath was kindled against Moses.'"

"I know. But this is in the past, now, my son. We all have to begin to look again to the future. It's the only way, isn't it?"

"Maybe you are right. But my repentance still requires that I compensate Shayna and Rivkah Eizenberg. That's what I'm going to do."

Initially, I worried about telling Mother the details of my plan for compensation, because I feared she would disapprove. But in the course of our extended conversation, I begin to see that she is less fragile emotionally than I had imagined. She has been without Father for half a year already, and I marvel at the depth of her strength and empathy. Rather than pour out her anxieties to me, she wishes only to relieve me of the pain she knows I carry. My idea had always been to sell a valuable possession and give Shayna Eizenberg whatever profit it might bring, but I see now that my own mother also deserves a share. If I can help two widows, I must.

"Mother, I've decided to sell my Waltham watch. This is how I will compensate the Eizenbergs, and there will be enough left over to help you and Moyshe. Please don't try to stop me."

"The good watch? Yakov, are you sure?"

"I'm going to take it to Dvorkin the clockmaker to see what he will give me for it."

"But I don't need anything, Yakov. Your father, may God bless him, saved money."

"No, Mother. I must do this my way."

I feel the warmth of her hand on mine, and I see in her eyes that she understands.

"Alright, Yakov. Do what you must. Do what God requires. But if you fulfill this, you must put all of your pain about the Eizenberg boy in the past. Please tell me you will free yourself of this burden."

"I will, Mameh."

What I mean to say is, I will try. But I know I will never be completely free of this painful chapter in my life.

At Market Square, much of the vendors' fare has already been picked over. Farmers offer early-spring produce, but the larger vegetables are gone. Many sell day-old and damaged produce, items that have not found buyers the previous day. It is a good day for bartering. Hagglers have brought used goods to sell and swap at the makeshift bazaar. Some come to hunt for bargains and pennyworths, items on offer from desperate or ignorant sellers. Many of the regular shoppers simply enjoy the sport of bargaining. Rivkah Eizenberg comes for survival.

The sun is high and warm. New growth on the trees and bushes has started to appear. I spot Rivkah sitting on an upturned crate. She is waiting, I assume, to see whether I will remember our rendezvous. A sack sits on the ground beside her, showing only a few wrinkles and ridges from its contents.

I approach her from behind. "Have you been waiting long?"

Rivkah stands, turns, and shades her eyes. "There is so little to swap or sell today," she says. "I've looked over everything."

I notice she is wearing a fresh, unwrinkled scarf.

"Do you come every day?" I ask.

"Most days. I can earn a few kopeks and find something that needs repair."

"So you are a tinker."

"If so, I am the worst tinker in the shtetl."

"Did you know that my father is a tinker and a watchmaker?"

I catch myself. My father is no longer.

"I shouldn't say he is a tinker. He was a tinker. I have something to tell you."

"And what is that?"

"When I went home yesterday, after I saw you, Mother told me . . . she told me that my father died six months ago, while I was in the army."

"Your father died? How?"

"He thought I had been killed and his heart just gave out. It happened the morning after this false news from Bulgaria, which, as you can see, wasn't true. News arrived in Navahrudak that hadn't been verified at all. It was all such a terrible, tragic mistake."

"Oh, Yakov, I'm so sorry."

In Hebrew, she offers "*Zikhrono livrakha.*" May his memory be a blessing. I have never heard these words from a woman.

"You know Hebrew, then?"

"Yes. And why not? My father taught me when I was young. Avram was at yeshiva, and there are no girls at yeshiva. My father was very patient with me, and I think he loved to teach me. But the lessons ended when he died. We couldn't afford a tutor. It was out of the question. So I taught myself. It's my little escape."

"It's unusual for a girl, and very ambitious."

"Do men think Hebrew is their private domain?"

"I suppose it shouldn't be."

"Never mind the Hebrew. Who told your father you'd been killed?"

I tell the story of Kalman Levin and the *tallit katan*. She can only shake her head in disbelief.

"How are you managing through all of this?" she asks.

"I'm not sure. There was friction between me and my father. He pushed me into giving up your brother to Rybakov, and I just let it happen. I'm sure I'll adjust. I just need time."

"What about your mother?"

"It happened six months ago, so she has had time to grieve. We had a long talk this morning, and she's steadier than I thought. I know the rabbi will help her. He liked my father, and I'm sure he feels some responsibility for her. So, I'm hopeful, and you needn't worry. Now, I came here to offer my help, correct? I will be disappointed if there is nothing in your sack to carry."

"I knew there wouldn't be. But you can walk with me anyway."

"Why don't we go to the castle ruins? It's not far."

"You won't feel embarrassed being seen with me?"

"Embarrassed? I don't pay any attention to the gossip."

"In that case, on such a nice day, I'm going to leave my sack in the bushes. We can get it later. Everything in it is worthless anyway."

We walk north, side by side but at a proper distance, up a hill to the stone ruins where a tower and fortress, once a stronghold of the King of Lithuania stood four-hundred years earlier.

"How is your mother feeling?" I ask.

"She is not getting better, but today was not so bad. She's had pain in her chest, but she had no fever this morning. She dressed and went for a short walk."

"Has a doctor come?"

"We have no money to pay a doctor, Yakov. They always demand payment. And they are expensive."

"I can help solve that problem."

"How, may I ask?"

"Do you remember I promised compensation, Rivkah? I will keep my word. I have a watch, and I'm going to take it to the clockmaker on Pushkin Street. I'll see what he will give me for it. It's quite beautiful. I've decided to give half the money to your mother and half to mine."

Rivkah stops, frowns, and slowly shakes her head at me. "Is this really necessary, Yakov? To sell something you love?"

"It is a requirement and the least I can do. I'm going tomorrow. I like this object, true, but it's only an object."

We resume walking. "I can see your mind is made up," Rivkah says, "so I won't try to stop you. You are going to Dvorkin's shop?"

"Certainly not Zaltsman's. He won't want to look at me."

Rivkah smooths her skirt nervously as I adjust my skullcap. Both of us are focused on the jagged assemblage of stones where a tower once stood. I remember the books that were stacked in Rivkah's room above the shed, and I ask her about them.

"Some are Yiddish, mostly little novels. I buy them used at the market. I love reading stories about other places, other people, cities I will never see." She pauses and looks away. "Can I ask you something, Yakov? Something personal?"

"You can ask."

"Have you thought about what you're going to do now that your army service has ended? I mean, after you earn some money, will you return to marry and have a family here? Or . . ." Her voice trails off.

Rivkah has pierced a secluded corner of my life, one shaped by the dreams I have experienced, including ones in which she appears. I have told Shayna, in Rivkah's presence, that I no longer believe the sole path before me is ordination as a rabbi. How should I answer now? Should I tell her that I was so despondent I wanted to die? That I met a young radical in Odessa who made me realize how much I care about learning? That I wish to study Spinoza? That I imagine learning and then teaching philosophy? Does she want to remain in Navahrudak to care for her mother, or fall in love with some older man in town, perhaps once or twice divorced and seeking to salve his loneliness? I am far from certain, but I tell her what I believe I feel.

"I don't think I can stay here, Rivkah. I need to see more of the world and learn more than Reb Epshtein can teach me. Even if I wish to become a rabbi, it will be postponed, and I will be studying elsewhere. I hope so, at least." I glance to gauge her reaction. She studies my face.

"In my heart, I want something more," I continue. "After I earn some money, I want to study at a university in a large city, to read modern philosophy, beyond Kabbalah. I would like to read in the sciences and politics, and perhaps write and travel to new places, maybe a great city in Europe, in Germany or England or France."

"Have you thought about America or Palestine?" Rivkah asks.

The question surprises me. When Shayna spoke of America, Rivkah offered no discernible reaction. I assumed she had no interest in America.

"Maybe," I hedge. "What do you think?"

Rivkah speaks in low but resolute tones as we both watch the warblers skitter across the grass in search of insects. "It is my dream to leave Navahrudak. I hope you won't find it odd, but I am a little bit like you. I want a real education. And I want to train and work. I've never told anyone this, but I want a profession. I want to be a midwife."

"Truly?"

"Yes."

"What about your mother?"

"That is why I call it a dream. I must care for her — and I will. But she wants me to go to America."

"She wants something better for you than she's had for herself."

"We've had arguments about marriage. For a time, she tried to make an arrangement, but I refused. I just refuse to be imprisoned by these traditions."

"You deserve better. I can see how hard it has been since the death of your father, and now after having your brother taken from you."

"It will be hard for you, too, Yakov. You need time to heal from your father's death."

"Have you read much about America, Rivkah?"

"I borrow the Yiddish newspapers or find discarded copies. Can I confess? You won't like this. I enjoy the essays about more rights for women. Since my father's death, I have always imagined I would work and earn a living for myself. It's not the normal path in the shtetl."

"But I do like it! I admire your determination, Rivkah. You are lucky to be able to read so well; many girls don't."

"Because we aren't taught. We are kept out of school, and it's wrong."

"Do you remember when your mother said you have no dowry? I thought, 'How unfair.' It's a foolish custom. Women deserve better."

"Do you really think so?"

"Yes. You can work and you can marry," I say with conviction. "I'm certain you will marry someday."

"Why are you so sure?"

I shake my head and smile at her. Feeling bold, I again say what I undeniably feel, "Don't you see how intelligent and beautiful you are?"

Raising my open hand to the smooth skin, I caress her cheek, and slowly lean toward her and place my lips against hers, lingering for a moment. This time, Rivkah neither flinches nor withdraws. I pull away gently.

Rivkah sighs as she turns away. "I can see you might feel something for me that I also feel for you. I have felt it for some time."

"I have dreamt about you, Rivkah. I told Avram about my dreams. Well, at least some."

"No wonder he wrote in the letter that you have feelings for me. I have the letter here. I wanted to share it with you, but I wasn't sure." Rivkah reaches into the pocket of her skirt, unfolds the sheaves of paper, and hands them to me.

Dearest Sister,

How strange it was tonight to see Yakov Leibovich enter our camp in the Bulgarian hills with a medical supply wagon. I know you remember him, because he told me you met recently. He thinks you are intelligent and pretty, but I will get back to that.

I am well. Military life suits me. There are moments of fear and danger, but so far I have managed to survive. I plan to live through this war and come home to be with you and Mother. I feel much better than I felt on the streets in Navahrudak. I know this will sound odd to you, but going into the army has been a blessing. I get along well with the other Jewish boys in my unit, and I have discovered many skills I did not know I had.

I know you are working hard to keep Mother safe and healthy, and I want you to know that I will never abandon you again. When I return, God willing, I will place my focus on helping our family.

Mostly, I am writing to tell you about Yakov. After he arranged his supply job, he and his father gave up my location to the Conscription Officer, Rybakov, so that I could replace Yakov on the draft list. At the time, Yakov had no idea that the vagrant they had betrayed was me. I can tell he feels much shame about this — too much in fact. He even tried to switch jobs with me on the battlefield, so that he would be a soldier and I would carry on his supply role. I told him this was foolish, as I feel very much at home in the Imperial Army. I do not think he believed me.

You must understand this: he is surely in love with you. I can tell. If the feeling is mutual, you should do everything you can to marry him, as he is a good man with a good soul. You must forgive him for betraying me. He had no idea it was me. I don't care one bit about these circumstances, because I now feel completely alive and would have surely succumbed to vodka if I had remained in Navahrudak.

I have given this letter to Yakov to mail when he can. I hope it reaches you without delay. I pray for the health and happiness of you and our dear mother.

With the utmost love,
Avram

I can barely speak. The generosity of Avram's letter overwhelms me. It is a beautiful lesson in forgiveness, offering a fresh understanding of how central the concept of forgiveness is to the compassion and grace that lies within every human soul. Maybe this is where God really resides.

I take a moment to read it again, then hand it back to Rivkah.

"Do you understand now why we forgave you, Yakov?"

"I never imagined he would speak to us like this from a grave in the hills of Bulgaria."

In silence, we stare at the ruins and the gathering clouds. Many minutes pass before Rivkah whispers, "You can kiss me again if you'd like, Yakov Leibovich. And this time, do not apologize."

15

As I approach the stone synagogue on Minskaya Street, I can already hear the sonorous voice of Reb Epshtein and the soothing words he will no doubt use to express his condolences. I will nod and thank him. But my mind is made up: I must speak the truth to him about the payment to the Ministry of War, to confront him and hear his response.

I've committed my questions to memory. The more I recite them to myself, the angrier I get. I don't know if I am transferring this anger to the rabbi because my father can no longer hear my voice or see the fury in my eyes. I will tell the rabbi I am grateful for his good intentions but must protest the manner in which his work with my father was carried out. I will tell him I met his brother in St. Petersburg and that Pinhas revealed that a bribe was paid. I need an explanation as to why he and Father kept so much from me. I want to see his face and assess his veracity.

In this state of anxious resolve, I make my way to the rabbi's study. He doesn't know I am coming, but I know his habits. He will be there. The door to his study is ajar, and I find him writing at his desk, head down.

"Peace be upon you, Rabbi."

"Ah, Yakov Leibovich! Come here, young man. I was worried it might be years before I saw you again."

He freezes. "But where are your sidelocks?"

"It is one tradition that God will forgive me for eliminating."

"What does this mean, Yakov?"

"Nothing, Rabbi. I am still Yakov. You needn't worry. I will not betray God. And I will not betray my fellow man."

"Well, we can discuss it later. The important thing is that we talk about your blessed father."

"I've been home for two days. Mother told me everything."

"How is she?"

"I cannot imagine what she has gone through. We've had some long talks, and I am pleasantly surprised by her state. She is sad but wants to look to the future. She is strong."

"Good, good. I want you to know that the heart of the entire community is with her in this difficult time."

"And I'm sure your kindness has helped sustain her. I have come today for a specific reason, Rabbi. I need to speak to you about some things that are troubling me, and it's not about the death of my father."

"Of course. This must be hard for you. I, too, have questions — so many questions. All the articles in the newspaper left so much unanswered. This is a good time to speak, so please go ahead. Is it about your future at the *beit midrash*?"

"No, Rabbi. I want to talk about last year, the arrangement that kept me out of the army."

"Ah."

I can feel my heart beating, and my hands are clenched tight in my lap.

"I'm grateful you were willing to help my father keep me out of the army. I know you had good intentions, the best of intentions, I'm sure. But things went badly wrong. I now see how much went on behind my back."

"On the contrary," he responds, with eyebrows arched and an edge in his voice. "I believe we kept you well informed. And we kept you alive!"

"Well, I met your brother, Pinhas, in St. Petersburg, and he told me that a payment was made to the Ministry of War to purchase special treatment for me. My father paid a bribe. Am I correct?"

The rabbi stares at me, frowning, then looks up for a moment. Ordinarily I would allow him to gather his thoughts, but today I'm not willing to wait.

"I wish to know, Rabbi, why the payment was made and why no one told me I was buying my way out of the army."

Reb Epshtein clasps his hands in front of him and rests them on his desk, as he always does before a grave pronouncement.

"Your father made no payment to the Ministry of War, Yakov. I can assure you of that," he says, emphasizing each word to give his statement finality.

"Why did Pinhas tell me otherwise?" Now, there is an edge in my voice.

"Calm down," the rabbi commands. "I'll tell you what happened. Your father, may God bless and keep his soul, made a donation to the synagogue in your honor, Yakov — a donation. Yes, I suggested this might be appropriate, and he generously complied. He wasn't forced. He paid nothing to the Ministry of War and nothing to Pinhas Epshtein. You see? Nothing."

"A donation," I say, skeptically. "Your own brother told me the Ministry of War had been paid an inducement and that this was how such matters have always been resolved. Do you know that, because you and Father arranged to relieve me of my responsibility to serve in the army, a boy from this town was sent in my place, and he is now dead? Did you know that? His mother and sister are grieving."

The rabbi looks surprised. "Who is this? Tsipershtein? His name was picked in the lottery, I believe."

"No, another boy from Navahrudak who was in our *beit midrash*: Avram Eizenberg."

The rabbi's surprise turns to irritation. "Wait, I remember the Eizenberg boy, but I haven't seen him in several years. He stopped coming to the *beit midrash*."

"I will explain, Rabbi. Please. The army has a draft quota. When I was relieved of my duty to serve, they needed another boy to replace me. Did you not think about this? The conscription officer, Rybakov, threatened us — threatened me, specifically — and forced us to provide a Jewish name as a replacement, which is not supposed to happen. He said if we didn't, he would tell the world about how I had avoided the army."

"I see. He insisted on a Jewish boy to go in your place, a despicable act."

"Yes. And Father knew of a vagrant in the northern part of town who had once worn a skullcap. 'A nothing person living by theft,' he said. We didn't know the name. I shouldn't have done it, but I gave the location to Rybakov. I agreed to this, so I am not blameless. But I learned later that the vagrant was Avram Eizenberg, a friend of mine. Rybakov took him as a new conscript, and he was killed in the war. I saw it, in fact. I witnessed it. I saw this boy die."

In sadness more than anger, I go on, "We should have known, Rabbi. This is what happens when men go to war, isn't it? It was entirely foreseeable. I feel ashamed about this, and if Father were alive he should be feeling shame, too. Now, I must compensate the Eizenberg family in order to repent. And I feel the need to confront Rybakov and tell him that his insistence on having a Jewish replacement was an abomination. He could have drawn a new name from the lottery pool at random and kept religion out of it. That would have been fair. But he was vengeful."

"Yakov," the rabbi says softly, sighing deeply. "You're right. But I want you to know it is not a disgrace to do regrettable things under such duress. This Rybakov, he forced you and your father to make a terrible, terrible choice. But I would counsel you not to confront Rybakov. If you do, he will take it out on all of us, Yakov. The state can punish an entire community. As for your father, he did this out of love. He did this to protect you. But you are right, I must say; we should have foreseen the risks. You are doing the right thing by seeking forgiveness from the Eizenberg family."

The rabbi nervously shuffles papers on his desk and strokes his beard. Clearing his throat with a deep rumble, he continues, "Now I must offer you an apology — an apology to you and to your father, may he rest in peace. I want to speak to you in confidence; this must remain private. But let the truth be healing."

The rabbi's face is red with anguish.

"It's true that I didn't tell you all that transpired, Yakov. I led your father to believe that his donation to the synagogue was a gratuity, something to compensate me for my time and effort to carry out the arrangement for you; but the payment was more than that. Your father was not aware at all, but I agreed to pass the money from your father to Pinhas, after he told me his contact at the Ministry insisted on an incentive payment. We didn't expect it, but it just happened. I had the money, the donation, and I passed it to Pinhas."

"I was right, then; it was a bribe."

"I'm sorry to say it, but yes. This is what was required."

In his confession, I see for the first time the depth of the rabbi's involvement. This is the man I revered for so many years as a paragon of rectitude. It seems I naively misjudged him.

"I never told Yehudah this," the rabbi continues. "He had no idea we paid the Ministry, none whatsoever. You mustn't blame him. This is the way things are accomplished in St. Petersburg and elsewhere in the empire, though it's regrettable. Many people bend the rules, especially when it comes to favors from the state."

"They are corrupt," I whisper in disgust.

"Corrupt or corrupted, yes, I'm afraid so. Your rabbi and your father were drawn into events that we frankly never imagined, but should have.

We should have thought carefully about how Rybakov would fill the quota I admit I knew he had. He has one every year. We didn't see the injustice that might befall an innocent boy. But, you see, Yehudah never told me about the vagrant. I can see why. If he had told me . . . well, I can't say I would have done anything differently. I just don't know. So I owe you an apology, Yakov. I, too, must repent and seek God's forgiveness, His *selichah*."

Having received the truth I had sought, my shoulders relax and my agitated breathing recedes. A quiet sadness comes over me, satisfaction and sadness.

"You taught me about repentance, Rabbi. And I have tried to repent for all of this."

"I am certain you have, son. And I am certain God will accept it."

"The night before Avram Eizenberg was killed, I told him the truth about how he was placed in the army, and I apologized to him. I offered to switch places with him. He would become a teamster and I a soldier, but he refused. Then, he was killed by an artillery shell. I came back to Navahrudak to seek forgiveness from Shayna and Rivkah Eizenberg, which I am happy to say they have given. But I must compensate them as well. Avram refused compensation, but he said if I wished to compensate anyone, it should be his mother. So I'm going to sell my jeweled watch, the prize. Do you remember it?"

"Yes, I do remember. A beautiful watch, indeed. I'm sorry you have to do this, but it's the right thing. Take the watch to Dvorkin. He will give you a fair price. I'm certain of it."

"This is just who I had in mind. We'll have to see what he offers. I'm going tomorrow afternoon."

"I will make sure the Community Fund helps this family, the Eizenbergs. I can speak to someone. I have heard that the girl begs in the square."

I look up, startled. "She is not a beggar, Rabbi," I say acidly. "She barters for things that are close to useless and polishes them or fixes them to make a little money, just like Father did. The Eizenbergs are poor and live very modestly, but are honest, kind, and generous. She is not a beggar."

"Excuse me, I did not mean any offense. And where is the father?"

"You don't know?"

"No."

"He died when Avram was sixteen from the cholera epidemic. Then, everything for this family collapsed. That's why Avram stopped going to the *beit midrash*. The father had been teaching Hebrew to his daughter, but that stopped too."

"So much sorrow in one family," the rabbi says, shaking his head. "God willing, you will receive a good price for the watch. I'm sure you will."

"May God grant me a good outcome."

"We have evening prayers in an hour. Before you go, Yakov, I must tell you something else. It's very important. Please stay for a moment."

Another rabbinical confession, I imagine.

He turns to me with a quizzical look. "May I ask: what did your mother tell you about your father's death?"

I shrug. "The morning after he heard that I had been killed, she found him slumped at his workbench. I guess the doctor said angina pectoris. His heart gave out. Why do you ask?"

"This is not untrue, not at all. But there is more to it. They did summon Doctor Shifrin, but it was too late. After the burial, though, the doctor confided in me. You are a mature young man, Yakov, and you should know everything."

The rabbi gathers his thoughts before going on.

"Your mother doesn't know the details, and it would be wise to keep this to yourself. Can you? She needn't know. It is a hard thing. It wasn't your father's heart, you see. Yehudah must have felt he had failed at something vitally important, that he had failed to protect you. When he heard you had been killed — an unbelievably tragic error — he felt this failure deeply, too deeply."

Everything comes into sharper focus, impossibly sharp. I know what the rabbi's next words will be, yet the story they will tell is abstract and incomprehensible.

"Yehudah poisoned himself, Yakov. Your father took his own life."

My emotions lock. There are no tears, only resounding shock. I find it difficult to breathe.

"Only two other people know, Yakov, Doctor Shifrin and me. Your mother was too distraught to hear this. There is no need for her to know; you must see that. But you are a man now, and I know you have seen death."

My head is in my hands. I look up. "How did he do this?"

"Dr. Shifrin found cyanide salts in his shop. He must have used them for his metal working and cleaning and extracting of gold. He probably kept it locked, but it was there. The drawer was open."

"Oh, God."

"There was no note or letter, no parting words, I'm afraid. He was distraught though. That much is clear from what your mother told me. Yehudah was a good and decent man. I know he pushed you to be excellent, Yakov, and you have been excellent. But he couldn't let you go to war. It was his absolute limit. When he heard you had died, it was a terrible blow, a shock he couldn't absorb. Such a tragedy."

"Yes, a tragedy."

"I pray for him and your mother, and for Moyshe and you."

"I know you do, Rabbi. I needed to know the truth. You know, Avram Eizenberg's father also died before his time, in the epidemic."

"It doesn't matter how. God receives all of His flock into His loving arms. We must look to the future now and not dwell on the past. I've told your mother this many times."

"And she has taken your advice to heart; I can see that."

"And what of your own future, Yakov? Are you ready to grow your sidelocks again, as the Book of Leviticus commands? And perhaps take a wife?"

Once, I would have hesitated to answer. Today, though, I feel liberated. "I have thought a lot about our marriage traditions. Everyone submits to them. But they are rooted in the past and not created with the future in mind, or the best interests of the bride and groom, to be perfectly candid. I will take a wife when I am in love with a woman who knows me and loves me in return — someone who is free to make a choice on her own, not a girl forced into a relationship."

I can see that my words sting Reb Epshtein. He looks as if he is suffering from severe dyspepsia as I dismiss a centuries-old Jewish tradition. For now, I have said enough. I do not feel it necessary to tell him I have already met such a woman.

I bound up the steps to Rivkah's room the next day, with my jeweled watch in my pocket and a fresh plan for the final step on my journey of repentance. One of us must carry the watch to Dvorkin and return with enough cash to deliver financial relief to two widows, Shayna Eizenberg and Galya Leibovich.

My optimistic mood is quickly dashed as Rivkah opens the door to the room atop the storage shed. She looks pale, and her eyes are red and puffy. I whisper, "What's happened?"

She shakes her head, "Wait a moment." She closes the door.

When she reappears, Rivkah is more composed and has a scarf covering her hair. I can see in the background that Shayna Eizenberg has the bedcovers pulled close to her chin. Her eyes are closed, and she coughs repeatedly.

"Mother has a fever again."

"You must be frightened."

"I am. I can't go out with you now, Yakov. But I'm glad to sit with you here if you wish. You'll have to tolerate her coughing. She is weak."

"I just came to tell you I'm going to the clockmaker today, to Dvorkin."

"Are you sure?"

"The sooner we can bring a doctor, the better. If I can get at least a partial payment today for the watch, we can summon a doctor right away. I want to take everything we get and split it between your mother and mine. They are both without their husbands."

"It would be such a mitzvah. What do you think you can get for it?"

"I'm hoping for two-hundred paper roubles. That was my father's estimate when he gave it to me. He bought it in Minsk, and he knows the value of such things. I want you to see it."

I remove the velvet pouch and slip the watch into my palm. Rivkah's eyes widen. "Yakov, it's beautiful, a treasure. Are you sure?"

"Yes, it's beautiful, but it's only a watch. Ask yourself: would you keep a watch or sell it to get a doctor for your mother?"

She nods understandingly.

"I have an idea if you are willing. There's a chance Dvorkin will give us more for the watch if you go to him instead of me. If you tell him the truth, maybe he will be more generous. He is one of the wealthiest merchants in town. Tell him you need to pay for a doctor for your mother and that it's urgent. He will look into your eyes and see God speaking to him. I will stay with your mother. Tell Dvorkin you can leave the watch overnight for him to examine carefully. He needs to look at the jewels inside, and he can be trusted. Explain that I will come tomorrow to hear his offer. Tell him my name, and say I'm a friend of your family. I'm sure he knows my father has died."

"It's a good idea. I'll go. Just wait here a moment. I want to give my mother some soup and tell her you'll be staying with her. Then I'll go to Pushkin Street."

Outside the open door, I can hear Rivkah explaining.

"We're trying to summon a doctor for you, Mother," she says softly. But I can tell Shayna is confused.

"You and Avram go together," Shayna says. "I'll be fine."

"It's Yakov, Mother." Rivkah motions to me to enter.

"Yakov?" Shayna asks.

"Avram's friend. See? He came here to tell us about Avram. Do you remember? He was in his army uniform."

"Yes, I remember now. A nice young man."

"And handsome, don't you think?" Rivkah says.

Shayna Eizenberg coughs, "Handsome, yes. Are you going to marry him and go to America?"

"Mother, I'm not leaving you. Besides, we can't afford such a journey."

"Whether you marry him or not, you should go to America, Rivkah." Her voice is rough, gravelly, and inhaling is clearly difficult for her. "What is there here for you? The Jews don't live in fear in America; that's what people say. The Pale is like a jail for you. You need a new chance." She coughs again.

"Rest, Mother. I have soup for you. Yakov is going to sit with you while I go to the clockmaker."

"Fine, but right now I'm weak, my dear. I need to sleep."

"I know, Mother. Eat something. Then you can sleep."

Shayna Eizenberg takes only a spoonful of soup before closing her eyes and lifting a hand to signal it is all she can manage.

Outside, on the landing, I remind Rivkah to accept nothing less than two-hundred roubles. "And don't worry about your mother. I will be here."

"I know," she says. Rivkah stands on her toes and presses her lips to mine.

"I have to go," she says. From the bottom of the steps, she glances up with a look that tells me unmistakably that she has deep and important feelings for me.

Re-entering Shayna's room and seeing her condition, I am convinced she is near death. Her face is sunken, her skin is nearly translucent, and her breathing is irregular. I wonder if a doctor can help her, but I know our effort with Dvorkin is a necessary step. In my mind, I have already relinquished the jeweled watch. It means nothing to me except as a means to repent. It no longer belongs to me. It belongs to Avram and my mother, and in their names, I say a prayer, asking only good fortune for Shayna Eizenberg's most deserving daughter and peace for both of our mothers.

I know Dvorkin only by sight — a wiry man with spectacles — and by what my father has told me about him, which is that he can be trusted. This is high praise from my father. When he said this about Dvorkin some years ago, it made an impression. Father had a tendency to believe the worst about people: they will steal from you if you give them half a chance. Dvorkin never fell into that sweeping category in Father's mind.

Yet when Rivkah returns, I learn that Dvorkin, though trustworthy, is not a trusting man. Her pique is evident.

"He must have thought I had stolen the watch," she tells me. "At first, he was so arrogant. He asked, 'How did you come by this?' I said it was a gift, and he wanted to know from whom. He wanted what he called 'proper origin.' Well, I got angry. I told him it was a gift to my mother and she was too ill to come herself. Then he asked, 'Would I know the party from whom this gift has come to your mother?' I have haggled many times for used items at Market Square, and this behavior is not new to me. He couldn't imagine how a poor girl comes by such a watch. He was certain I had stolen it!"

"But you convinced him?"

"You could say that. I told him you would come tomorrow to hear his offer and that you wanted to make a gift to my mother and to yours. As soon as I mentioned your name, his tone changed. It was remarkable. I told him you were the tinker's son, and suddenly he was relaxed, even warm. He said: 'Let's see what you have.' I think he was impressed by the watch's beauty, to be honest. When he saw it, I could see his eyes open wide to study it. I hope he can give us a good price."

"I'll tell him we must have partial payment right away. Your mother needs a doctor, Rivkah."

The mid-afternoon clouds part, and for a moment, rays of sunshine penetrate the window, waking Shayna Eizenberg.

"Is that you, Avram?" she asks weakly, still confused.

"It's Yakov," Rivkah says.

"Oh. Are you getting married?"

Rivkah and I glance at each other.

"Mother, where did you get that idea?"

Shayna coughs. She manages a weak smile. "You told me he was handsome."

"Mrs. Eizenberg," I say, "I'm leaving now, but I want you to know that what matters is not whether I am handsome, but whether your daughter is clever and beautiful. And I assure you, she is both."

Shayna smiles. There is more life in her than I realized. I stand, whisper to Rivkah that I will return the next day after seeing Dvorkin in the morning, and squeeze her hand in a gesture of affection and hope.

Dvorkin's shop on Pushkin Street resounds with a symphony of clicking gears and swinging pendulums. Each shelf is animated, and I anticipate the bells and chimes that will strike a crescendo at noon. A customer is just leaving. With his bristly gray eyebrows and beard, Dvorkin looks far older than I remember, but he is in good spirits.

"Come in, come in, my boy. You must be Yehudah Leibovich's son. I can see the resemblance. Am I correct? It is Yakov, yes?"

I acknowledge him somewhat warily.

"Good, good. And tell me about the young woman who came yesterday with the watch. I have seen her in Market Square. She said you were a friend, but maybe she is more than a friend?"

His probing annoys me. I can imagine how Rivkah must have felt.

"She is a friend, and I am helping her with this transaction."

Dvorkin grins. "She is quite beautiful!"

I do not take his bait.

"Have you had a chance to evaluate the watch, sir?"

"Yes, yes, I have."

"And the quality is very good, isn't it?"

"It is quite good. Do you know this is an American watch? The mark is Waltham, a good watchmaker. Do you know how many gems?"

"Maybe a dozen?"

"Thirteen. But how did the family come by it, if I might ask?"

"My father purchased it in Minsk."

"Hmmmm. Well, this watch is quite rare; not many of them were produced. So I can give you a good price, a fair price, more than fair, in fact."

"That is all we are seeking, a fair price."

"And you shall have it." His face opens to a broad smile. "I can give you four-hundred roubles. What do you think?"

I stand still, erect, and motionless. Whether he intends to pay in silver roubles, gold roubles, or paper roubles, the value is double the figure my father had mentioned. I am astonished. Four-hundred! How is that possible?

I ask: "In paper roubles?"

"Yes, paper, of course. Ha! In gold or silver roubles, four-hundred could buy the Empress a mansion and stables in the country! It could buy the entire Postal Savings Bank!"

Regardless, it is a fortune, and we have been blessed with immense good luck. It will be enough to provide Mother with an enviable account at the bank, and enough to move Rivkah and Shayna to proper housing and pay for as many doctor visits as are necessary. It is enough to go to school and learn midwifery, and enough to erase a guilty conscience.

"Let me consider the offer for a moment," I say, hiding my euphoria.

"Of course, young man. Take your time."

I turn my back to Dvorkin and cup my hands behind my back as I walk to the clocks on the shelves and pretend to examine each one carefully. All the while I am thinking: Rivkah, you are no longer destitute; you shall have new clothes and shoes and food in the cupboard.

I turn back to Dvorkin. "Well, I think it's an acceptable price."

With his bushy eyebrows arched, Dvorkin beams as if he is also delighted by the amount he can offer. "I thought you would find it attractive!"

"Just tell me how quickly you can make payment."

"Don't worry, young man. I can pay half right now, as we stand here, and the rest tomorrow. I will write you a proper receipt. Is that acceptable?"

"Of course, Mr. Dvorkin. Thank you. I'm sure that my friend Rivkah explained about her mother. It means we can summon a doctor immediately."

Dvorkin reaches to his desk for paper, ink, and pen. "I will compose a receipt for you and gather two-hundred roubles, which you can count.

I insist that you count it! Guard it carefully until you reach the savings bank."

Raising an index finger, the way the rabbi always does to emphasize a lesson, he insists, "You must take it straight to the bank, young man! There are thieves about."

With a thick envelope of rouble notes in my inside coat pocket, I ignore Dvorkin's advice and bypass the bank, walking directly to Rivkah's room.

Shayna Eizenberg is sleeping. When Rivkah hears the offer of four-hundred paper roubles, she gasps and nearly collapses. I grab her, and hold her tightly in my arms until she can look up at me.

"Are you sure?"

"Yes," I whisper.

"Oh, Yakov. I can't wait to tell Mother. How did this happen? I have waited so long for something good to happen, and now — for once, just once . . . after so much suffering."

"It is hard to believe," I say. "I don't fully understand it." I reach into my pocket and pull out the envelope of bills and flip through them. I show Rivkah the hand-written receipt, stamped with Dvorkin's lavish signature, noting that two-hundred more is owed tomorrow.

"I need to get a doctor, Yakov — a good one, not a magician or faith healer selling an elixir of ground roots, a real doctor. Can we?"

"What about Shifrin, the young one on Grodnensky Street? My mother told me he was trained in Moscow."

"I don't know any doctors, Yakov. I haven't seen a doctor since I was eight. Can you summon him?"

Having heard us, Shayna stirs. "He won't have a cure," she says in a barely audible voice.

"Just let him examine you, Mother, and take his advice. You need to see a doctor."

Doctor Leo Shifrin's office is less than a ten-minute walk. A woman I recognize from the synagogue — I can't recall her name — sits in his waiting room as he finishes with another patient. I can hear his voice faintly through the door. When he emerges, I rise quickly, smile at the woman in the waiting room, and speak with the doctor urgently. He is young, only in his late thirties, perhaps. I want to ask him about Father's death, but it's not the time or place, so I avoid introducing myself by name. I am here on a mission for a friend.

He looks at me with more than a casual glance, revealing he knows who I am. He places a hand on my arm and tells me, "I'm sorry, but I have a patient waiting."

The old woman rises gingerly from her seat, pushing herself up with both hands, adjusts her clothing top and bottom, limps toward us, and says firmly, "It's fine, Doctor Shifrin. Don't worry. You have an emergency, and I have only a pain in my leg. I can wait. I know this young man. Don't worry. Go."

She touches my forearm warmly, but I cannot recall her name.

Shifrin replies, "Are you sure, Mrs. Dvorkin?"

The jeweler's wife! What are the chances? Two mitzvahs in a single day! Two moments of good fortune and kindheartedness! Perhaps God has heard my prayers, after all.

"Of course I'm sure," she says, smiling at me reassuringly. I reach out and give her weathered hand a squeeze.

"May God bless you, Mrs. Dvorkin," I say.

Shayna is still feverish, but alert when I return with Doctor Shifrin. I descend to the dusty alley during the examination to give them privacy. The exam takes less than five minutes. When Shifrin descends, I pay his three-rouble fee.

"She has consumption," he says. "The daughter can explain."

Shifrin pauses and touches my arm. "My sincerest condolences, young man. I knew your father."

All I can do is nod. What else is there to say? Thank you for finding the cyanide? Thank you for keeping the truth from my mother and brother? And if I say to him: "I know about the suicide," how would he reply? There is nothing more to say. We share a glance.

"Thank you, Doctor. Good day."

I know little about consumption except that it is a disease of the lungs. When I re-enter the Eizenbergs' room, Rivkah sits slumped in a chair. I kneel beside her.

"I told him she coughed up blood a few days ago and that she eats almost nothing. He spent the longest time listening to her chest and her back."

"It's in her lungs?"

"Yes. He said there is a new name for the ailment: tuberculosis. It's contagious, Yakov. We have to be more careful. Don't be close when she coughs. He said it would be wise to keep the window open for fresh air."

"Are there drugs she can take?"

"No, nothing. He said to give her good nutrition and fresh air, and to summon him if she coughs up blood again. At least she's seen a doctor. Thank you, Yakov."

Shayna whispers hoarsely to Rivkah, "Don't worry. I will do my best. But you must look after yourself, Rivkah, dear. Go someplace new. Bring something new into your life."

"Stop, Mother. I am taking care of you."

Shayna motions for Rivkah to come closer, but I can hear their conversation.

"I worry about you, Rivkah," Shayna says. "You must have a life of your own. I want you to do me a favor. Go for a walk with the young man. He likes you, and you like him. I can tell. Buy something at the bakery and go for a picnic. I will be fine."

Rivkah sighs, "I can't leave you just now."

"I am just going to sleep, my dear. I'm not leaving this bed. Don't worry. You need some fresh air. Go for a walk; it will be good for you and will give me peace of mind."

"Alright, Mother. A walk will calm me. But promise me you will be okay."

"I promise, my dear. Take your time."

Rivkah looks at me for reassurance, and I nod my assent. A walk would do both of us some good. As we descend to the alley, Rivkah's emotions are clearly raw.

"I don't know how long Mother has," she says. She turns to me, grasping both of my hands. "I am falling in love with you, Yakov Leibovich. And I need you just now."

The words penetrate me swiftly and powerfully. My eyes remain fixed on hers. Relief and gratitude wash over me. Being needed by another person I admire and respect is as powerful a human emotion as I have ever felt.

16

At the edge of town, the street narrows to little more than a path through the trees and tall grasses. We are alone, in the warmth of spring, and my hand reaches for Rivkah's. Dappled light dances across the underbrush as it penetrates the trees. The branches are beginning to show the tiny buds of new leaves and the fruit to come. Everything around us is renewing, full of Creation, and it penetrates me. I feel as if I have reached a peaceful, verdant shore after a long and difficult journey on an uncertain sea.

We sit in a clearing and share a pastry from the bakery. Rivkah pulls off a piece and places it in my mouth, laughing at my awkward acceptance. The honey and nuts have never tasted better. We swap stories about growing up, about our parents and siblings, about our yearnings. They are happy stories, for the most part, though I notice that Rivkah speaks only of the years when her father was alive and says nothing about his death and its complicated aftermath. I was not so young when my own father died; I wonder what she must have faced in that cruel moment of youth, and how she righted herself. I don't really want to speak of my father's suicide. I want to push it all away, but I also need to share my world with Rivkah, to share everything, even the moments of pain.

"Do you remember when we walked together last year, just before I left for Odessa?"

"I carried your book of commentaries," she says proudly.

"You did. And you told me about Avram, and about how your father died."

"I remember our meeting as if it happened yesterday."

"So do I. We have some things in common, you and I, don't we? Our hope for a more peaceful time and a more peaceful place, our love for Avram, our idealism, our desire for an education, our widowed mothers."

"All of those."

"I told you about my father's heart, how it failed. I learned something important from the rabbi, but it has to remain between us, alright?"

Rivkah sits up, sensing the gravity in my voice and perhaps my distress. She takes my hand.

"Of course, Yakov."

"It wasn't my father's heart. Doctor Shifrin told my mother it was his heart, but he knew more. He and the rabbi know how he really died. He took his own life with a chemical, cyanide salts. He had it at his workbench."

Rivkah gasps and covers her mouth.

"They didn't think Mother could bear the truth. They didn't want her to have to cope with the gossip and the stares, I suppose. So she doesn't know. To her, and to everyone, it was angina pectoris."

Rivkah breaks down, stifling her sobs with her face in her hands.

"I had to tell you, Rivkah. I couldn't keep it from you."

She reaches out and pulls herself toward me in an embrace before her sobbing subsides. "It's all so sad, Yakov. But I know you needed to tell me."

I whisper, "It was hard for you, wasn't it, when your father died."

"A terrible time. Father was a carpenter and made beautiful tables, cabinets, and frames. He was an artist in some ways, but not a businessman. We were poor, but never uncomfortable; he made sure of that. And he paid for a tutor for me. Can you imagine? Then the epidemic came, and it was frightening. Cholera is awful. When he died, I remember closing myself off from everything. I didn't want to eat or go out to the market. I didn't want to see people, or play, or read. I was just a child and felt this had been done to me. Mother was in such pain, too, but she somehow had the strength to help me return to life. The worst was Avram. He was so melancholic. He left one day and we didn't see him again for a year."

"I'm sorry you never met my father," I say. "He was difficult and tried to control my life, and I resented it. But he meant well, and he was learned. He once wanted to be a rabbi, too, according to my mother, but the Crimean War changed that. He was wounded and came home with bitterness."

"Were you angry at him for what happened to Avram?"

"Very angry, but now that he's gone, I'm not sure what to feel. I am both angry and grieving. He was adamant about keeping me out of the army. It was an obsession, a burning obsession. When he heard I had been killed . . . it was just too much for him."

I also explain to Rivkah my anger at the rabbi and recount his confession for his role in buying my freedom from army service, the bribe.

"It's over now. Besides, Avram was happy, wasn't he? You said he was."

"Yes, he was."

To keep the warm memory of her brother intact, I tell her about our first meeting at the front lines near Plevna — Avram's jokes about the Yiddish Brigade of Marksmen and the playful banter as we huddled in blankets the night before he died. I tell Rivkah about my dreams, the frightening ones and the ones in which she appeared. I tell her about Neschadymenko and my wagon companions Yitzy and Zalman. For the first time in days, we both laugh. It is a release and a bond. I gather Rivkah's hand and kiss it gently. The stories and the laughter flow back and forth naturally, as we comfort ourselves from a shared pain.

Lying side by side on our backs, holding each other and looking up at the sky through the branches, I realize how much I love this woman. I turn to kiss her. She holds me in a long and passionate embrace.

Rivkah's hands find the back of my neck and pull me closer. Something has awakened inside her, a yearning for intimacy, perhaps, or for swift passage to a new life she has fantasized about.

"Don't be afraid," she whispers and begins to loosen her dress.

"Are you sure?" I ask, knowing instinctively that her response is a foregone conclusion.

"Yes," she says.

Any pretense of caution or propriety drifts away. We are both swept forward by an urgent desire to discover one another completely. Making love on the grass, partially clothed and fully consumed by our passion, she presses me close with an indescribable affection. When we finally loosen our grasp of one another, I see she is smiling, though tears are rolling down the sides of her face.

"Have I hurt you?" I ask.

"No, Yakov, no. Just tears of joy — and relief," she says, wiping her face with open palms. "I don't remember the last time I felt this happy."

When we return, still aglow, Shayna Eizenberg is fast asleep. Had she been awake, she likely would have sensed that something exceptional had occurred. For now, this intense moment of mutual generosity is ours alone.

Making my way to Rivkah's room the following morning, I spot her and Dr. Shifrin walking briskly along the street toward the alley. When I intercept them, I can see that Rivkah is overwrought. She tells me Shayna's fever is worse and that she has begun to cough up blood again.

"She seemed barely conscious this morning," Rivkah says.

We enter the room, and the situation is clearly dire. Shayna is as pale as I have ever seen her and does not stir.

Kneeling at her bedside, Rivkah whispers, "Mother, the doctor is here."

"Bring Avram," Shayna says softly, her eyes closed. A cloth at her chest is spotted with blood. "I want to see my son."

She is alarmingly thin and gives the impression of a person disengaged with life. The doctor dispenses with the formality of asking me to leave. He has difficulty examining Shayna because she can barely sit up. Shifrin's assessment is brief. He administers a teaspoon of Laudanum and hands Rivkah a bottle of the opiate.

"This will ease your mother's pain, calm her cough, and make her sleepy," he says. "It is not a cure. There is no cure, no treatment. Just give her a spoonful every two hours if you can. The only thing you can do is make her more comfortable. She is extremely weak. All you can do is ease her suffering."

When the doctor departs, Rivkah kneels again and lifts her mother's hand up to her cheek.

"Bring Avram," Shayna whispers.

"Yakov is here, Mother."

I kneel, too.

"Avram," she says, reaching out to grasp my arm. "Promise me you will take care of Rivkah."

Rivkah and I look at each other.

"Promise me," Shayna repeats.

"Yes," I whisper. "I promise I will take care of Rivkah."

Shayna's mouth now hangs agape, and her breathing becomes increasingly labored.

Dvorkin had been unnaturally cheerful when we received the second payment from him, as if he were presenting us with a gift rather than concluding a business transaction. We opened two accounts at the Postal Savings Bank, one in Shayna Eizenberg's name and the other in my mother's, making two deposits. I felt satisfied that I had finally made the necessary repair for acts I had agonized over for months. Yet now that I have carried out Avram's wishes and completed my repentance, I kneel beside Shayna's bed and wonder: has my gesture come too late for Avram's mother?

By the next morning, Shayna's suffering is over. Rivkah is awake, sobbing, when I arrive soon after dawn. She looks drained and disheveled. Her mother lies rigid and gray. She didn't last the night. I summon the Burial Society to bring a coffin, and they move the body to the cemetery. Rabbi Epshtein arrives with eight men from the synagogue to complete a quorum for the prayers. We recite the Psalms and the Mourner's Prayer, the Kaddish, at Shayna Eizenberg's grave, and Rivkah shovels fresh earth onto the plain coffin. Stoically, she pushes the earth onto her mother's grave, and the clumps thud emphatically against the softwood boards.

When the prayers are complete, Rivkah stands numbly, peering at the earth. The rabbi takes me aside and asks me to come to the synagogue to pray with him and "to speak privately" after the seven-day mourning period for Shayna Eizenberg, the *shiva*.

"We can talk about anything that interests you," the rabbi says quietly. "This has been a difficult time, and I want to offer my help."

My trust in Reb Epshtein is at a low ebb, and I sense he wants to know whether I will remain to complete my rabbinical studies. I accept his invitation on one condition, that Rivkah accompany me. I want Rivkah to hear everything. The rabbi is taken aback. It is an unusual request. As he strokes his graying beard, I fill the silence.

"There is nothing I wish to say that Rivkah cannot hear, Rabbi."

"She is not your wife," the rabbi counters.

I am either feeling bold or stubborn. "I am certain that in God's eyes we are completely devoted to each other and inseparable. She is my *bashert*; that is what matters. If you wish to talk with me, she must be there."

"Your *bashert*? You believe God has preordained your relationship with this girl, and that she is your soulmate? If so, you have much faith in God, more than I realized."

"I haven't given up on God, Rabbi. But we hardly show our respect for the Almighty by blindly accepting everything we tell ourselves to calm our souls."

"I see," the rabbi responds. "We can talk about this when I see you. Make sure Miss Eizenberg uses the women's entrance."

Rivkah has entered my world fully, and I am determined that she witness my conference with Reb Epshtein. She is my friend, confidante, and intimate, not a subordinate. Rivkah has displayed unusual autonomy and a desire to live her life unshackled by convention. I never thought I would find her strength of character so alluring, but it is.

The ritual *shiva* period for Rivkah's mother passes slowly for both of us. In keeping with tradition, she remains secluded and wears a torn blouse each day. I return to her with bread and hard-boiled eggs every morning, and we share stories from our families. I want to know more about her father and she about mine. Gradually, we turn from family to future. I want to learn more about midwifery and she about philosophy. We speak of our brothers, Avram and Moishe. I recount my secret self-taught lessons in German and my furtive entries in the journal I kept beneath the floorboards under my bed. Rivkah's sadness, palpable in the first days after her mother's burial, slowly lifts, yet I am struck by how few friends and neighbors climb the stairs off of Volkava Street to comfort her and help to lift from her shoulders the burden of mourning.

Toward the end of the week, Reb Epshtein knocks on the door to Rivkah's room. He seems stiff and formal, offering condolences in a manner that suggests he has pronounced the exact same words hundreds of times. The rabbi casually inquires whether we remain willing to see him in his study, and I assure him we do, reminding him that Rivkah will join me.

Despite Rivkah's frugality, I convince her at the end of the *shiva* week to take a small amount of money and buy herself a new dress before meeting the rabbi. She deserves something better than the drab and worn street clothes she wears. I picture her in a transformative moment, stepping into a fresh cotton dress and buttoning it before the small mirror that sits atop her chest of drawers. I'm certain that she too can picture such a moment.

When Rivkah arrives at the rabbi's study wearing a smartly fitted dress, she is nothing like the formless girl who stood frozen at Shayna's graveside just the day before. She allows herself to smile at me, and beneath her grief, I detect a level of pride that I have rarely seen in a person. I can tell the rabbi is surprised, for as he pauses to look at her, he forgets to greet her.

He quickly gathers himself and clears his throat. "Peace be upon you," he says, still looking at Rivkah.

"Peace be upon you, Rabbi" she replies, nodding.

The rabbi turns to me. "Shall I assume that Miss Eizenberg is aware of our last discussion about the conscription situation? And she knows of your father's death, of course."

"Yes, Rabbi. She knows everything that I know. Everything we spoke about."

"I see. Yes, well, secrets among friends are usually not a good idea." He addresses me, as if Rivkah were not present and I am the one who must answer for her. "I know Miss Eizenberg understands such difficult situations from her own experience. And I am grateful for her understanding that we speak here in confidence. Others need not know what the doctor determined after your father's death."

"She can tell you herself, I'm sure."

Embarrassed, Reb Epshtein turns to Rivkah. "Yes, I'm sure you do understand."

"I do, Rabbi," Rivkah replies. "I can keep a confidence."

"Good. Thank you."

He pauses and turns to me. "Before you left for Odessa, Yakov, you were one of the best students at the *beit midrash* in years. I'm sure you know this. You were conscientious, intelligent, inquiring."

I know what the rabbi is about to say.

"With another year of work, I'm quite sure I could convince the council to sign the papers for your ordination. You will make a fine rabbi. I know this was once your goal. But you seem to be wavering. May I ask what has changed?"

From the beginning of the war, I have considered this question many times. I speak cautiously but tell him the truth as best I know it. "I still feel inspired by Torah, by Kabbalah, and by the teachings of the great rabbis. Learning brings me great joy, Rabbi. And you nurtured that. I haven't decided to end my religious studies, only to wait a bit, to expand my intellectual horizons." I glance at Rivkah. "I think a lot about ethics, science, philosophy, and social reforms. I think about secular disciplines. And I have now traveled far beyond the Pale. I've met business people and intellectuals, people trying to improve the lot of workers and of women. I was in St. Petersburg and Odessa. I read journals and newspapers and leaflets that do not come to Navahrudak. And I should tell you, Rabbi, I have read many books and novels that would probably not meet with your approval."

Reb Epshtein frowns and holds up his hands, signaling that I should cease. "You don't need to tell me which ones. But I wonder, have you lost faith in the Creator, blessed be His Name?"

"Faith? No, Rabbi. It's just that I understand better the difference between blind faith and reasoned faith. God's realm is infinite. It is nothing and everything. If I want to cleave to God, shouldn't I understand His everything? How can I strive to be a better person and closer to God if I don't see, with deep knowledge, the true nature of His realm and how all of our actions affect His realm?"

The rabbi strokes his beard as if studying its shape with his hand. He still looks unhappy. "You need not remove yourself from the secular world when you devote yourself to Torah," he says.

"Torah is still important to me. But it has a way of clenching too tightly. I can no longer be consumed by Torah. I want the freedom to explore."

"If you do not become a rabbi now, what will you do?"

I look again at Rivkah, who is smiling at me, then turn back to the rabbi, who looks stern. "Rivkah and I have begun to speak about leaving Navahrudak."

"Does your mother know?"

"I intend to speak with her. I want to try to get established outside of the Pale, then send for her and Moyshe. They deserve something better, too."

"I know your mother, Yakov. She is a strong woman, and will have the help of the Community Fund, and my help, of course. She will manage. I'm certain of that. Where do you want to go?"

"I might wish to attend a university in Germany for a time, a secular university, a serious place. But I may need to take a factory job first to earn some money. Rivkah can speak for herself, but I don't wish to do anything or make any decision about my future without her."

The rabbi turns to Rivkah. "I wonder, Miss Eizenberg, do you wish to speak about any of these topics?"

She glances at me and I offer a nod of encouragement.

"It's not a traditional path for women, but I too want to educate myself. It should be normal for women." She glances at me again, perhaps wondering how much she should reveal. "I want to train as a midwife. I don't think either of us wishes to be a spectator to our lives."

"An interesting way to put it," the rabbi acknowledges. "And do you feel devoted to Yakov?"

Rivkah doesn't hesitate. "Completely," she says.

"Are both of you aware that Russian law forbids you to leave the Pale of Settlement? You can't just go where you want, when you want."

"Yes, but others have managed this, Rabbi," I reply. "If the war taught me anything, it is how to be resourceful and improvise, and that my fears can be overcome. I don't know where we will go yet. Rivkah's mother hoped we would go to America. But I have also thought about Germany, or maybe France. I confess that my knowledge is limited. And I know you read widely about such places. If you have any insights, we would be pleased to hear them."

"Everyone speaks about America, but it is a more challenging place for Jews than the stories we hear," the rabbi cautions. "One can find work there, of course. But you must undergo questioning and medical examinations when you arrive, from what I understand. The immigration officers want to know how you plan to earn a living. You would have to learn the language and customs. There is no official discrimination, like here, which is certainly helpful, but Jews can be targeted in America. A year ago, a Jewish banker in America, a man of wealth and standing, was refused a hotel room at a resort in the state of New York because he was Jewish. I read this. Do you see how such humiliation works even when there are no laws segregating people?"

"Yes, it lives in men's hearts."

"Exactly. So, you cannot venture into the unknown with a fanciful notion of what life will be like. I fear you know little of either America or Germany, Yakov — only that neither one of them is Russia."

"This is undeniable, Rabbi, but . . ."

He forges ahead. "They call America 'the Golden Land' and 'the Land of the Free,' but these are only labels. It is vast and rough. I read that New York is a warren of tenements and factories where anyone can get lost. What kind of job would you find when you don't know the English language? Whatever it is, the pay will be poor and the hours long. What university will accept you without language skills? They don't teach in Yiddish, Yakov. All of the Jews who emigrate to America have relatives there already, who keep them from making mistakes. Do either of you have anyone?"

"I'm afraid not."

"So, this will make you susceptible to charlatans and thieves. You cannot set up a business because you have no trade yet. They are building railroads in America. Do you want to work setting rail ties? Or delivering goods on carts in New York City as you did in Bulgaria? It's back-breaking work, I am sure. And you will be competing with the destitute Irish Catholics, who will work for almost nothing."

I resist mildly. "All of this may be true, Rabbi. But here we live with discrimination and injustice every day in the Pale. In America, you can work in any trade, become an apprentice, or start a business. You can own property. No one decides for you whether employment is permitted or not. You give yourself permission. I can even work and go to school at night. It doesn't frighten me. In Bulgaria, in the army, I learned to be resourceful. That's what it will take."

"Maybe, maybe," he says with a shrug. "So, should we speak of Germany? Why would you want to live there?"

"The universities, scholars, thinkers, and philosophers — the intellectual life. I am attracted to all of this, religious and secular. Do you think it is worse than America, or than Navahrudak?"

"At least the Jews in Germany enjoy what I might call 'civic equality,'" Reb Epshtein intones. "I don't believe the threat to the Jews is from the state and its laws, like it is here, but from the human heart. I'll give you an example. A book was just published in Germany by a prominent scholar of religion — de Lagarde is his name — that is so offensive I can hardly speak of it. He proposes to force every Jew out of Germany and send them to the island of Madagascar. And he is a highly regarded man! Imagine!"

The rabbi is shaking his head, pursing his lips, and scratching his beard. I can tell there is more he wishes to say.

"But the biggest difference is that Germany's Jews are ceasing to be Jews. They forget the commandments. They forget the Sabbath. They forget the kosher laws. They forget who they are! They assimilate. All of their knowledge of science leaves them in a spiritual wasteland. They care only about the so-called Enlightenment and they forget about the Laws of Moses. And as to the Jewish women in Germany — I have a cousin there, you know, and I have read about the Jews in Germany— in the wealthy families, the women there believe their children should dress and speak and play and learn just like every German child. How can this be good?

The Germans don't love the Jews, Yakov. They just keep it hidden. Don't think you can walk into any university you want and become a professor. I would just caution you to be careful."

I suspect he is correct that the assimilation of Germany's Jews has not changed the average German's suspicion of the Jews as a people. Hearing all of this, I feel a wave of discouragement.

"We are forever aliens in so many places, always viewed with scorn. I don't know where any of this will lead," I say.

"It's a good thing you don't know," the rabbi interjects, "because you'll have time to realize that it's not so easy without proper papers."

"As I said, Rabbi, I know about the necessary documents. But I'm sure you know that people cross the green border with the help of border runners all the time. If you are careful, you can do it."

"You probably have the money now to pay a border runner and bribe a border guard. Bribery, that's a requirement, unfortunately."

"Yes, I sold the watch."

"And I suppose the payment now goes to Rivkah as an inheritance, yes?"

"Yes, Rabbi," Rivkah says. "It's at the Savings Bank. I've spoken to them. But may I ask also about Palestine? I hear in Market Square that some people want to go there to build a new life. Do you know what it's like there?"

"Ah, Palestine is an even greater challenge if you are thinking about that kind of journey. It is very difficult. You must be prepared to be a farmer, to raise farm animals, and to live off the land. And not all the land is suitable for farming." He sounds resigned, almost plaintive in his tone. "Wherever you decide to go, Yakov, my advice is to not to give up on becoming a rabbi. It would suit you; I'm certain of that. You are unusually bright, and you are kind and generous with people. You listen well."

While I remain angry at the rabbi, at this moment I feel his generosity as well, and say, "I promise you we will think hard about this."

"I want the best for you, Yakov, and for Miss Eizenberg. I know you have reason now to doubt me, but I don't speak disparagingly of these places out of selfishness. I'm certain there are ways to thrive in America and in Germany. But it's not simple. Think about what I have said. Whatever your path, I am certain that God's blessing will shine down upon you both."

"We will gratefully accept God's blessing and yours, Rabbi, but we must all try to create blessings for ourselves — our own blessings."

"It is an odd way to put it," the rabbi counters.

When we depart, I turn to Rivkah and tell her, "We mustn't be demoralized."

"It's a bit frightening," she says. "Do we know what we're doing? Do we know each other well enough to go through such a complicated change without it crushing what he have together?"

I'm a bit shaken by Rivkah's words. I don't know what to say except, "I hope so."

17

The sobering conversation about immigrant life in America and Germany marks a watershed in my relationship with Rivkah Eizenberg. We both want to leave Navahrudak in our past, and she is as eager to build a new life as I am, and equally capable of making the difficult journey, even alone. Yet I sense that something is missing. Are we fully bound or cemented to each other? Is there a gap that neither of us can accurately describe? I worry that our idea of leaving the Pale of Settlement together took on a life of its own without the foundation or fuel necessary to sustain it. Perhaps we are ahead of ourselves because we have not overtly and forthrightly committed to a life together.

This comes to a head over tea as Rivkah and I dissect our meeting with Reb Epshtein. "Your mother wanted to send you to America with Avram," I remind her. "It is sad because she will never see what becomes of you. She didn't want you to be alone, Rivkah. She was trying to protect and guide you to the very last."

Rivkah toys with her empty glass and looks up. "I have managed so far, and I am sure I will continue to manage. I'm no longer a girl. I'm not helpless."

I sheepishly apologize, "I'm sorry, it's not what I meant. I know you're capable of making your own choices. Have you thought about America, though? Do you want to go?"

"I was waiting for you to ask. It's the question I need to answer most urgently."

"Please be honest, Rivkah. You won't hurt my feelings. Do you want to go?"

Listening to myself say those words, I know I am conveying what I believe Rivkah needs to hear — that the choice is hers, that she can control her own life. But I also know I don't want to give her the freedom to choose without me. In a selfish corner of my heart, I don't want her to do anything without me. I don't want my feelings crushed. To have Rivkah leave me now would be extraordinarily painful.

Gently, Rivkah turns the question around. "This is hard for me to say, Yakov, but so much depends on you. I feel closer to you every day. How could I not? But the choices in front of us are not small. Can I ask this question: how much does it matter to you if I go to America?"

I lower my head, feeling the weight of her question, then look into her eyes. "It matters more than you know."

I grasp her hands gently as if holding a wounded bird. "I want to be with you. If you only knew how much I feel for you. I have so much to tell you. It begins with us being together. If you wish to go to America alone, to make a new life for yourself, you should go. But you will break my heart. And if you truly want to go to America but you do *not* go — because of me, because you think I want something else — you will also break my heart. Do you see what I mean?"

For a moment, Rivkah is unable to speak. She places her arms around my neck in a tight embrace, and her voice cracks as she tries to reply. "Now, I must speak honestly," she says softly, releasing me. "I could never go anywhere without you. I don't care if I am in America or Germany, France or the most distant star in the sky; I only know I want to be with you. Wherever we are, we can be happy."

There is a long pause until Rivkah asks, "What do you think we should do?"

"I wish I had an answer. I feel a strong attraction to a place with great universities and an intellectual life, like Germany. The Jews there are reform-minded, and German law treats Jews equally. Women in Germany have certain freedoms too. They're not afraid to speak up and go to universities if they want. I think you could be happy there. But as the rabbi implied, the Germans are no more tolerant than others. They would probably step on the Jews like bugs if they were given half a reason to."

"We don't know anyone in America or in Germany, Yakov. But you speak German, and I can learn it. I'm sure you could go to a university there."

"So could you, Rivkah. There will be so many more opportunities than we have here. But that is also true of America, isn't it? I hear there are boundless opportunities. And your mother wanted you to go there. Do you ever think about that?"

"All the time. I remember it so vividly. We would have to buy steamer tickets to cross the Atlantic. They are expensive. And where in America would we go?"

"Only one place, New York," I say. "Thousands of Jews go there. I'm sure I could find work, but I'm not sure about a university. We would have to learn English. The biggest obstacle for us right now, whether we go to Germany or America, is that we don't have papers to leave Russia."

"But people manage to cross into Prussia and then Germany. How do they do it?"

"They pay runners or guides to get them across the green border. That's what they call it. You walk through the forests and fields, and you cross. And then the border runner might have to bribe the German or Prussian border guards. People do it all the time."

"And if we're caught?"

"I don't think the Russian border police care at all. They're glad to see the Jews go. But I'm not sure about the German police. I don't know what they will do. So, there are risks. Let me talk to some people. I can learn more about the border runners. If we go, it has to be through Germany, even if we end up on a boat to America."

Rivkah sits pensively. "It's still a risk I would take with you," she says. "Mother would be angry if we didn't try to leave Navahrudak." She looks up quickly, as if a thought has burst into her head. "Do you know anyone in Germany who might offer you work papers? I mean proof that you have work? So they wouldn't deport us?"

"I've been thinking about that. Do you recall I mentioned Rabbi Philippsohn in Bonn, the one who edits a journal that I read? He is looking for an assistant, or at least he recently placed an advertisement for one. I saw it on my way here from Minsk and saved it. But so much has happened, and I forgot about it. Then I discovered it just today in my pocket. Maybe it's a sign. He might have hired someone already. And if I write to him, we would have to wait for his reply; it could take weeks. He might say no, or might not reply at all, but maybe we should be optimistic."

Rivkah's eyes brighten. "Oh, Yakov, let's be optimistic! You must write him a long letter today! In German. Can you? You are such a persuasive person, with so much life experience already; I know you can persuade him. Tell him about yourself. I know he will reply; I know he will."

Infected by Rivkah's hopefulness, I immediately set about writing to the rabbi from Bonn. I have seldom felt such a wealth of purpose and energy. I find a quiet spot outdoors, along a wall at the ruins. Birds dart about, and the paper flutters in a light breeze as I write. The words flow easily, even in German. After ten pages, I re-read the biography I have crafted. To me, at least, it brims with earnestness, humility, charm, and self-awareness, not to mention the grim experiences of war. There is so much to say, but ten pages are more than enough. As I write, I realize how my years parsing passages in the Torah and the Book of Splendor at the *beit midrash* were insufficient to prepare me for all I have lived through.

In the year and a half I spent away from Navahrudak, I was exposed to unimaginable human extremes: cowardice and daring, savagery and compassion, abject hatred and immeasurable tenderness. These experiences have imbued the lessons of the Torah with far greater meaning, transforming what was once preparation for the rabbinate from an exercise of the mind to a molding of the soul. My relationship with God has evolved beyond a rote set of beliefs and rituals. Above all, I see how idealism has shaped me, and hope Reb Philippsohn will see that idealism in my words. He must.

I write my closing lines to Ludwig Philippsohn:

> *I wish only to devote myself to assisting you in publishing your estimable journal, and, God willing, I will have a favorable and timely reply from you. I propose to travel to Bonn immediately, assuming there are no unforeseen obstacles to my entering Germany. I assure you that I have sufficient resources to manage my own affairs and would expect compensation only in proportion to your assessment of my contribution to 'Die Allgemeine Zeitung des Judenthums' and your ability to reward my efforts on your behalf.*
>
> *With the utmost respect and sincerity,*
> *Y. Leibovich.*

I read all ten pages to Rivkah, translating to Yiddish as I go.

"He will say yes! You will see. He will see your character, Yakov! I know he will say yes."

"You are hardly an objective judge."

"I am partial, but I believe in you for a reason. You are a person of integrity, a mensch, a person with a solid core, Yakov. You may have left a boy when you entered Bulgaria, but anyone can see that you have returned a man, and a confident one."

It is the greatest compliment Rivkah can give, and it melts my anxiety. Whatever the response from Bonn, I tell myself, everything will be fine if I am with this woman.

"Did you mean it when you told Rabbi Epshtein that you didn't want to decide anything without me?" she inquires.

"I want to be with you, Rivkah, with all my heart, completely, as you put it. Do you see that? That means you must have a voice in my future, in our future. Do you know the great rabbi DovBer Schneuri? He said, 'It is the man who chases after the woman, for the soul of a man sees what he is lacking.'"

Rivkah laughs gently, "Two very wise men, you and Reb Schneuri."

"How long do you think we should wait for a reply?" I ask.

"It's already fall, and the nights will start getting cold. Maybe we have a month to wait for a reply from Bonn. In any case, I need to give away my mother's clothing. I will give them to the Community Fund. I want to look for our family memorabilia. And I must pay the rent."

"And buy a new wardrobe for yourself," I add. "Clothes to travel in: a decent coat, a well-sewn scarf, and sturdy shoes. You can afford those now, Rivkah. And you'll need them."

"It is hard to believe, but yes, I can afford a few items."

I promise her I will find out what I can about the border runners, how they operate and what fees they charge, who can be trusted, and who is experienced. I will need to travel to Minsk to make inquiries, and I will look for a leather portmanteau for her.

"I'll post the letter to Reb Philippsohn today," I say, "and give my mother's home as the address for a reply. We'll just have to wait for an answer." I pause and look at Rivkah. "Are you sure you're prepared for this? Germany will give us a chance to grow and start a family, and to find our best future. But to get there, we will have to be determined, very determined, and quick-witted too."

Rivkah looks unperturbed, and hugs me. "It will be our odyssey. I am determined to do this, but you are the quick-witted one. We will go, and we won't look back."

I have never craved something more than to be at one with this woman, to merge every cell, every impulse, every thought with hers. My desire is both emotionally profound and, I admit, urgently physical. Its power seems to overwhelm me, dissolving my reticence and pressing me toward a conclusion that I've been turning over in my mind for days. I take Rivkah's left hand in both of mine and tenderly stroke it.

I whisper awkwardly, fixing my gaze on her eyes, "I care for you, Rivkah, so much. Do you understand?"

"I'm beginning to."

"I could imagine spending my life with you."

She raises an eyebrow, cocks her head to the side, and asks, "Is that a question, Mister Leibovich?"

I catch myself. "No, no. I'm sorry. I'm being a fool. What I really wanted to ask was whether — was whether you would be my wife."

Rivkah emits a peal of joyful laughter. "No arranged marriage then, Mr. Leibovich?" she asks with a radiant smile.

"Arranged, yes. But arranged by you and by me, Miss Eizenberg."

I pull her close again and hold her for a moment. "I fought my father for years about a brokered marriage. I was putting it off during my studies, but I still expected it to be arranged by others one day. Now, I realize I was resisting for the wrong reasons. It should only happen when two people know and love each other. I do love you, Rivkah. Will you have me?"

"Well, Yakov Leibovich," Rivkah says wryly, "only because you have become a partisan for the rights of women do I accept your proposal of marriage."

I am now the one laughing. "You shall have all the rights you want. I will tell you something interesting about Rabbi Philippsohn. He favors educating women and drawing women into all of the Jewish rituals. The Jews of Navahrudak, including my parents, would see him as a radical and a threat, but I don't. He's a genuine reformer who still believes deeply in Judaism. You would like what he has to say."

"If he dislikes the Russian laws that require a woman to have her husband's permission before going to school or taking a job, I am sure I will like him. But, listen, dear Yakov, I do want to leave Navahrudak. Mother was right. There is nothing for me here. And it's clear you want to leave as well. But your mother is now a widow, and she has Moyshe to raise. Have you thought about that?"

"I've been agonizing over it. I want to be a good and loyal son. In a crazy way, it would be my father's final vengeful act to force me to remain here in Navahrudak out of a sense of duty to Mother. As I told the rabbi, we could leave the Pale for somewhere safe and open, then send for Mother and Moyshe . . ."

"Your mother can emigrate if she sets her mind to it. Wherever we settle, perhaps we can bring them to a wedding; do you think? Then, they could come and live with us. A big family would be a blessing. My family was so small and only got smaller."

"I need to speak to Mother, and to Moyshe. He's old enough to understand. Mother won't try to dictate any of our decisions. She's not like that. I just want to prepare her for hearing about you, and to let her know we're thinking of leaving the Pale together for Germany. She needs to meet you, too. Would you do that?"

"Yes. I want to meet her, Yakov. It would be such a pleasure."

"Soon, maybe tomorrow, because I have an appointment this afternoon."

"What is that?"

"Nothing important, just about the army. Officially, I'm in the reserves. I'll let you know how my mother takes the news. Whatever her reaction, I know she will want to see you — to weigh and measure you."

"Literally?"

"Yes! If I know Mother, she will want to see if her wedding dress will fit you."

"So we will marry, yes, Mr. Leibovich? You will take me for a lifetime of adventure?"

"Yes, we will marry, Ms. Eizenberg. Two adventurers and a lifetime together."

This is our emotional cement, and it makes anything seem possible.

Returning to the residence of Ivan Ivanovich Rybakov is a necessary coda to the transgression I committed at the same spot on Kirova Street more than a year ago. The rabbi has counseled against such a confrontation with Navahrudak's conscription officer, but I cannot let it go nor absolve the man. There is nothing in the military reform law that calls for a Jewish conscript who slips out of the lottery to be replaced by another Jew. That corrupt system was to have ended, and I am compelled to say so to the man who chose to perpetuate it. I must say it to his face.

No matter how kind Rybakov was to Avram, my replacement should have been the next name picked at random in the lottery, regardless of his religion, not a poor vagrant snatched away because he was a Jew.

I am not going to confront Rybakov out of petty hatred, mind you. And I don't blame him alone — not at all. I am also responsible for the disaster that befell Avram. It was Rybakov, though, who demanded a Jew, and Rybakov who set in motion the events that ultimately led to Avram's death. There is no choice here. I must confront him to fulfill my duty to repair the just world that I yearn for.

Everything I've studied and experience has driven me to this conclusion: everything Reb Epshtein has taught me and everything I have learned about an ethical life from Reb Philippsohn, Reb Lipkin, Peretz Smolenskin, Reb Moshe Cordovero, Alonzo de Herrera, Johann Wolfgang von Goethe, and Baruch Spinoza; everything I have learned about *teshuvah* and *selichah*; everything I have learned about forgiveness from Avram and Rivkah Eizenberg; everything I have learned about war from Neschadymenko, Skobelev, Sidorov, Lebedev, Yitzy and Zalman; everything I have learned about pragmatism from Pinhas Epshtein, Horace Günzburg, and Emmanuel Levin; everything I have learned about courage and the consequences of shrinking from responsibility.

I knock loudly. Rybakov looks puffy and unkempt when he pulls open his creaking door. "State your business," the old man mutters, squinting to see who stands before him.

"Officer Rybakov, I am a friend of Avram Eizenberg."

"He was killed in the war."

"Yes, sir, I know."

"A hero in Bulgaria."

"Yes, I . . ."

"I don't know where the grave is, if that's what you are looking for."

"I know where it is. I fought in Bulgaria. But . . ."

"You fought? And they discharged you already?"

"I was wounded, and they sent me home. But I have been in St. Petersburg for a time on business."

"Wait, wait, what is your name? Is it Leibovich?"

"Yes, Leibovich, Yakov Leibovich."

"The tinker's son, I knew it. I remember you now. You gave me Eizenberg's name. Then you went into the army anyway and received the Cross of St. George. Is this correct?"

"You are correct, sir. But I didn't give you his name. And I shouldn't have given up his location. It was illegal what you did, demanding to have the name of a Jew. Avram Eizenberg's name wasn't in the Navahrudak lottery pool."

"What is your purpose here, Yid. To be insolent?"

My tone turns insistent. I have considered this moment, thought about the right words, and even practiced saying what I must say to him. "You forced me to give you the name of a Jew to fill your quota. You could have drawn lots, but instead you picked him off the street because he was a vagrant and a Jew. You thought no one would notice. And now he's dead. I saw him die near Plevna. His blood was literally on my hands, and it is on your hands as well."

His face having steadily reddened, Rybakov bursts, "Get out of my sight, you piece of manure, you filthy Yid. How dare you!" He is shaking his fist and the veins in his neck bulge. "You caused all of this, you and your meddling father, not me. You were drafted and you didn't go! You are a coward, a coward! That's the reason your friend is dead!"

I hold my ground and try, with difficulty, to remain calm. Rybakov has spoken a painful truth, which I have also thought about a great deal. Lowering my voice, I respond, "It is true I feel guilt and shame, sir, more than you know. But I never thought the selection of my replacement would be handled so corruptly. You threatened us, and should be ashamed. You are the one who chose to replace a Jew with a Jew. It's not in the law; it was your vengeful choice!"

"You'll pay for this insult, Leibovich. Mark my words: you'll pay. Now, get out!" he shouts, spitting with rage. "Get out!"

I step back to the street and turn away, shaking. To calm down, I remind myself that I have just fulfilled a promise to myself to speak of this injustice in the open and confront all of those responsible. *Selichah* does not require such a harsh confrontation, but for me, it was the final necessary act. Only now do I believe that my repentance, and my duty to Avram's memory, are complete.

I walk briskly back to Market Square feeling a thorn of self-doubt. Did I overstep? Should I have forgiven the old conscription officer? I quickly shake my head. No, allowing this injustice to go unanswered would risk perpetuating it. I could never do that.

I take the long way home to collect myself after confronting Rybakov. As I enter the front door at Maya Street, Moyshe is in the workroom polishing a lamp, for his absent father or perhaps as a meditation on life's tendency to leave us tarnished over time. I want to tell both of them —

Mother and Moyshe — that I am in love, but I find it's not an easy thing to say. The words are momentous. The three of us gather for a meal.

"I have a friend, Mameh," I begin. "She and I have grown close."

"A friend? A close friend?" Mother asks.

"Yes."

"And where is her family? Do I know her?"

"No, but she lives in Navahrudak, in the poor quarter. She lives alone. Her mother just died. There is no family."

"So that is why you have been outside of the house so much."

"Yes."

My mother quickly puts bits of information together. "Wait, Yakov, the Eizenberg girl? Her mother died?"

"Her name is Rivkah. And yes, she just buried her mother."

"Poor girl," Moyshe interjects.

"Losing a parent is difficult for anyone, Moyshe," Mother says, "but you can't carry grief with you forever. Life is what matters."

"Mother is right, Moyshele. Slowly, slowly, we are able to watch the birds in the sky and smell the flowers on the bushes, and feel God's grace."

Mother asks: "This girl, are you in love with her?"

Moyshe makes a face, as if he has just been forced to swallow lard.

"I think so, Mother. We have a very strong commitment."

"Then there will be a wedding?"

"Someday, Mother, someday. I think you agree that I'm old enough to make my own decisions about whom I wish to marry, when, and where, despite the traditions of our faith."

"Yes, Yakov, you are. And do you know what? Your father agreed. While you were away, we talked about when you might marry, and he told me something I never expected. I remember his words: 'All the marriage brokers can disappear from the face of the earth, and so can the dowries.' He thought about it and changed his mind. He agrees with you now. It surprised me, but that's what he said."

"And you, Mother, do you think I can choose whom to marry and where to live?"

"Whom to marry? Well, yes. Your father persuaded me. But where to live? What do you mean?"

"We will come to that. First, I want to tell you about Rivkah."

"Yes, tell me about this girl."

Moyshe is fidgeting. "Do I have to listen?"

Mother and I laugh.

I try to reassure Moyshe. "Don't worry, it won't be awful. You're almost an adult."

Mother comes to my defense, "Let Yakov finish, Moyshele."

"I have known Rivkah for a long time, ever since Avram and I were friends at the *beit midrash*. She is Avram's younger sister. We were youngsters, but of course she has grown up, and so have I. We met again, by chance, just before I left for Odessa. I had no idea whether I would see her again, but she made an impression on me. She's had a difficult life since her father's death. He died of cholera when Avram was sixteen and she was twelve or thirteen. It was a blow to Avram, and he left home. Rivkah took care of her mother, who just died of consumption. I went to see them before she died. And I apologized to them and gave Rivkah's mother half of the money I got for my watch."

"You could have given her all of it, you know. But just the same, I am grateful. The watch was more valuable than I imagined."

"It truly was a blessing what Dvorkin gave us — shocking, actually."

"God is looking favorably upon you and Rivkah. Can I meet this young woman? Can you bring her to meet me and your brother?"

"I want you to meet her and to see in her what I see. In all of my encounters with Rivkah these last few weeks, I have come to understand her qualities and intelligence. Her father tutored her at home before he died. She can read and write. And as I said, I think we have fallen in love."

"Will you wed at the synagogue here?"

I don't want to bring painful news to my mother, but there is no alternative. "Mother, please understand. Both of us feel our lives will be better somewhere else, outside the Pale."

"Oh." Mother looks down at the tabletop and wipes her hands nervously on her apron before looking up. "Why do you have to leave Navahrudak? You no longer have to be a soldier, so you can start a business, a publishing house or a newspaper or a journal, right here, and have a wedding. And if you decide you want to be a rabbi after all, there is no better place."

"Mother, at some point I need to leave the Pale because I am thinking of studying at a university, not just Talmud and Torah but secular subjects too. I want to know about science and literature, not just Yiddish tales and ancient discourses. Do you see that I have this thirst?"

"You have tasted new things. I can see that."

"Rivkah wants an education, too. She has aspirations, just as I do. It's one reason I admire her. She wants what is best for me and I want what is best for her."

Mother peers out the kitchen window for a moment. I wonder if she sees, finally, my need to explore beyond the confines of the shtetl and the legalisms of Torah and Talmud. I wonder if she understands Father's failure to encourage me to follow my own path, his stubbornness and narrow-mindedness. I wonder if she realizes that together, the rabbi and Father initiated the chain of events that delivered me to this moment, to this crucible.

"I hope you can come to love Rivkah as a daughter, Mother. And if we leave the Pale, I want to send for you and Moyshe, to help you leave and come to live with us. What do you have here except sad memories? In a few years, Moyshe will have to register for the conscription lottery, too. There are so many opportunities for a better life if you can take a small risk. Rivkah and I can help you do this. We're ready to take such a risk."

"I don't know, Yakov. I need time. Your father died half a year ago, and I feel much steadier today, but it's still a little overwhelming. He left us some money, and you have been generous, but I will have to find a way to earn money, maybe by tailoring or working at the synagogue. The rabbi has been so kindhearted. "

"I want something better for us, for Rivkah and for myself. Not perfect, but better. It's not here in the Pale, Mameh. Maybe it's in Germany or America. We want to see more open doors, but all we see in Russia are closed, narrow, and uncertain ones. We want to build a family, but outside of Russia."

"How soon, Yakov? When must you go?"

"Winter is a few months away, and we can't cross the border in winter. It would have to be before the snow. First, just meet Rivkah."

"Of course." Mother swallows hard and looks away in pain and resignation. I admit it hurts me to be the cause of more anguish.

When I arrive at Rivkah's room, she is wearing a new dress and has discreetly styled her hair beneath a new scarf.

"I was waiting for you," she says warmly.

"Rivkah, you . . ."

"I fixed my hair."

"Yes. I mean, no, it didn't need fixing. But you do look wonderful."

"Such a charmer you are, Mr. Leibovich. You haven't greeted me properly."

I embrace her and kiss her on both cheeks, and then on the lips. I linger until she pushes me away.

"This can wait," she says. "We have to see your mother."

I try to anticipate every possible source of anxiety that Rivkah might encounter when she meets Galya and Moyshe Leibovich, but she appears completely at ease while poking fun at my coaching.

"Disarm them with your candor and wit," I tell her. "This is your strength — to look people in the eye and acknowledge who you are, joyfully. Hold nothing back!"

"Nothing? What if your mother's breath is sour? Should I tell her?"

"No!" I laugh. "In that case, just flatter her. Whatever you say, she will be convinced. She and Moyshe will love you, as I do. One thing, however: it is best to speak of our plans to leave Navahrudak only in generalities. Mother will be afraid, and so will Moyshe. We don't want to say too much about the risks ahead."

"I see," Rivkah replies, arching her eyebrows and cocking her head. "So, we are leaving to go somewhere nice, where all Jews are welcomed with garlands and parades, yes?"

"Exactly, garlands and parades. We just haven't decided which of those many mythical places we wish to go first."

As we approach the house on Maya Street, I realize that Rivkah is serene and I am the one wringing my hands. I have to remind myself that Rivkah Eizenberg has withstood many trials in her short life with more grit and humor than I will ever possess. She expresses her emotions unhesitatingly, but I do not mistake this for fragility. Rivkah is resilient. Whatever arises, she will survive. It would have been much more intimidating had she faced Yehudah Leibovich as well. I'm certain Father would have prepared a list of questions about Rivkah's family life, upbringing, and religious habits, which in turn would have required her to relive her father's death and its aftermath. I'm convinced, though, that she would have won him over.

An aroma of warm gooseberry cakes infuses the house as Rivkah and I step inside. It is as neat as I have ever seen it. Mother's onetime habit of expending her frequent reserves of nervous energy by polishing, dusting, and straightening has returned. It is heartening to see, given the house's condition the day I first arrived home from the war.

The moment Mother sees us step through the front door, she offers her condolences to Rivkah. "Peace be upon you, and may I express my deepest sympathies on the losses you have endured."

Rivkah deftly puts her at ease. "Peace be upon you, Mrs. Leibovich. I want you to know that my brother Avram was happy in the Imperial Army," she says. "He didn't want to return to living on the street. He wrote us a letter telling us this. But you have also suffered a grievous loss, and I know it has been so difficult."

As Rivkah greets Mother, I see that the woman I plan to marry is luminous in her natural state of maturity, confidence, and optimism. My mother cannot seem to unfix her gaze. She stares at Rivkah, smiling warmly, but still staring as if a single penetrating look could unlock secrets. Mother, there are no secrets, I think to myself. Today, you will begin to know this woman as a daughter.

All Mother really wants is to know whether Rivkah will be a good wife and mother, according to Jewish tradition, including whether she will produce grandchildren. Rivkah understands this, and makes a point of mentioning that she wants to raise a family. These are the words Galya Leibovich longs to hear.

Gradually, Mother turns to the sensitive matter of our future. I remind her that we are thinking seriously about a life beyond Navahrudak, and that the destination, while not specific, falls to the west, outside the Pale and beyond the boundaries of greater Russia. This is still a painful message for Mother to receive, and an unmistakable sadness is etched on her face.

"I have sent a letter to an important rabbi to solicit advice about my further education," I tell her.

"When will you be married?" she asks.

"Soon, Mother. But we won't marry in Navahrudak."

"But why not, Yakov? I can see that Rivkah will make a lovely bride for you. Everyone can share your happiness. Your cousins from Vilna will come. Rabbi Epshtein can bless both of you."

"It's complicated, Mother. Rivkah and I have talked about it. It is not my desire to withhold the joys of a wedding, but Navahrudak holds many negative memories for both of us. The conscription matter is just one. Frankly, I am disillusioned with Reb Epshtein, as you know, and I would prefer to have another rabbi officiate our wedding. Also, Rivkah has had a difficult life here since her father's passing. She has suffered. Her brother and her mother have died, and she has no one now."

Upright and rigid in her chair, Rivkah looks at my mother, and tells her, "Mrs. Leibovich, we don't know yet how or when this will happen. My own mother could see that my future here was limited, and she told me many times how much she hoped my brother and I would go to America. She said it again just before she died. I don't know if that's where we will end up, but I know she sensed how much I needed to start afresh."

"I see," Mother says softly. "May I ask, when will you have children?"

"When we are settled in a new home," Rivkah says, glancing my way. "As I said, we do want children. It would be a blessing."

I grasp Rivkah's hand as I address my mother. "You know what The Book of Splendor says: 'A husband and wife are one soul, separated only through their descent to this world. When they are married, they have reunited again.'"

"I'm sure it is true," Mother responds, "but your father always quoted the Talmud. Do you remember? 'A man should eat and drink less than his means, clothe himself according to his means, and honor his wife and children beyond his means.'"

No one speaks. Mother stares at her hands. In a moment, she lifts her head and speaks to both of us, "You have my blessing and, God willing, all the blessings that a life together can offer. I know Father would say just the same."

"God willing," I say, glancing at Rivkah. I wonder, though, what my father would have really said following a conversation with me about taking responsibility for the death of Avram. I'm not sure he would have been as generous as Mother, but I will never know.

18

Rivkah and Mother peer down from the synagogue's segregated upper seating, while I lurk in the back of the men's section, as Reb Epshtein reads the prayers marking Rosh Hashanah. The ritual trumpeting of the ram's horn signals the opening of a new and unpredictable page in my life, and in Rivkah's, a blank space that we intend to fill on our own terms. As I stand and recite, I wonder when I will see a reply from Reb Philippsohn. Waiting has been nerve-wracking.

But the new year begins well. As soon as I return home to Maya Street, a bulging envelope is waiting. The great rabbi has sent an essay-length reply in German, written in the shaky hand of a man well past his prime. I summon Rivkah and translate the rabbi's words for her as I read them for the first time.

Dear Master Leibovich,

I have received a most disarmingly sincere, humble, and erudite letter from you applying for the advertised position of editorial assistant at 'Die Allgemeine Zeitung des Judenthums,' which is edited at my desk here in Bonn. I wish to convey my apologies for having taken so long to reply. Ill health has slowed my usually energetic approach to important tasks, and this, to be sure, is a very important task.

Your letter has been greeted with great interest, as I now find that having an editorial assistant is an absolute requirement for the future of my journal of ideas. I have spoken with a few suitably enthusiastic and intelligent candidates, and you, sir, are most certainly among the most enthusiastic and most intelligent. Therefore, I would be pleased to have you come to Bonn as soon as you can to take up this important role, as a trial while I assess your skills. If we both agree that your talents are valuable, I would be delighted to create a formal employment agreement.

"Do you see?" Rivkah exults. "I knew he would not be able to resist a person like you!"

"But he's not making a commitment, is he. It would be a trial."

"I'm certain you will impress him, Yakov. Don't worry. What else does he say?"

> *You have provided an excellent summary of your skills and desires to further your education, and I can tell you without hesitation that Bonn would be an excellent place for you to expand your knowledge. The University of Bonn has an outstanding reputation, and Jews are welcome! (Many Jews have pursued advanced studies at the university, serious scholars all, even including Karl Marx!)*

"Who is Karl Marx?" Rivkah asks.

"I didn't know until recently. He is a social reformer who sides with workers. He co-authored a pamphlet that attracts radicals and anarchists."

"What is an anarchist?" she asks.

"Someone who believes that the way people are governed now and the current economic arrangement between workers and owners is broken and must be discarded in order to create something new and more humane."

"Then I must be an anarchist," Rivkah announces with a laugh.

I return to the rabbi's letter.

> *We Jews have a great opportunity in Germany, much greater than in the Pale of Settlement, I'm afraid to say. Germany is a vibrant place. The history of Europe's Jews has been full of sadness for centuries, but now is the beginning of a new age. In Bonn alone, we had violent pogroms centuries ago. Jews were blamed for murders and even the plague. We were taxed and expelled. We had to build guarded gates on both ends of the ghetto, the Judengasse. Then Napoleon gave us full rights, and the community rejoiced and flourished. We built schools. We just opened a beautiful new synagogue by the Rhine. Five-hundred Jews live in Bonn now, and we are growing quickly. It is a wonderful city from which to publish the 'Allgemeine Zeitung.' I am certain that the future of a man such as yourself will be much brighter than in the Pale.*

"Who is von Goethe?" Rivkah asks.

"He lived a century ago. I read him when I was younger, and I feel some kinship with this man, as his life was not so different from mine. He studied law and abandoned it, then took up soldiering briefly, devoted himself to literature and writing, and fathered a child with a woman he would later marry. But I have no intention of waiting eighteen years, as Goethe did, to marry!"

"I don't think your mother would be happy waiting eighteen years, Yakov. Nor would I."

Rivkah's eyes widen as I explain Goethe's play *Faust*, about a man who sells his soul to the Devil in return for wealth and omniscience.

Reb Philippsohn's letter reveals detailed plans for changes to his journal and the role he expects his assistant to play. He also takes a full page describing the beauty of Bonn and the bucolic Rhine valley, as if he worries we might be tempted to remain in Berlin as we travel west.

Philippsohn uses the German word for beech forest: *buchenwald.*
"*Buchenwald,*" Rivkah repeats. "It sounds so lovely."

"Yes, I'm sure it is."

Rivkah asks, "Will you continue your rabbinical studies in Germany?"

"It was my entire goal in life for so many years. But my interest in secular topics, like philosophy and history, is now stronger."

"But after you complete your studies, could Reb Philippsohn become your new rabbinical instructor?"

"The more I think about it, the more I'm convinced I would be happier writing essays on topics of the day in his newspaper than in dissecting religious doctrine. Besides, he is an old man. I wish him good health, but I'm not sure how many years he has left. There is some risk in going to Germany. He's not really hiring me, but rather trying me out for a time. If he isn't pleased, what would we do?"

"I'm sure he will be pleased, Yakov. I wish there was just one place where we Jews could breathe, without worry or fear."

"It's not Russia; I'm sure of that. There are risks in Germany, but Bonn could work. I have to find a border runner in Minsk. They might know how difficult it is to get to Bonn from Prussia. We should understand that part of the journey, too. I think it's wise to begin planning for Germany."

"Yes, time is running out," Rivkah says.

I would like to offer ironclad assurances to her about Philippsohn and Germany. But the truth is, I cannot. Winter is just over the horizon, and we must set out soon. Despite our ambivalence, it is time to tell Mother that I hope to take a job in Bonn, and that Rivkah and I will leave in a few weeks.

As it turns out, Mother insists on having Rivkah join us for an evening meal, which offers a convenient opportunity to open a delicate conversation about our plans. I needed no further convincing after she offered to cook her beet soup and knishes.

When we return from a short walk, Mother looks content and cheerful as she bustles around the kitchen table making sure that every required dinner implement is in its proper place. She dotes on Rivkah and enlists her assistance in the kitchen even though everything is already prepared. I watch with a mix of surprise, satisfaction, and amusement. Rivkah glances my way with a knowing smile.

After the meal, Mother sends Moyshe to putter at Father's workbench, and pulls her chair closer to us. She has something important to say, but I haven't a notion what it might be. My impatience takes over.

"What is it, Mother?"

"Be patient and listen. I've been thinking about both of you these last few weeks, and I've talked to the rabbi. I know you're angry at him, Yakov, but he cares so much about both of you."

"I wish you hadn't . . ."

"Wait, my son. I know. But he is sorry for what happened, sincerely and deeply sorry. I know he is."

"Alright."

"There is something I want you to have," she says.

I'm certain she is going to present us with a family heirloom, like the sabbath candlesticks, or her wedding dress, to be re-tailored to fit Rivkah — or something else to convince us to remain in Navahrudak, like a set of kitchen dishes that we can't possibly carry with us into Prussia.

I know this much about my mother: she is a generous woman. I wish she would look after herself, but she is at ease and happy caring for everyone else in the family.

"I went to the Postal Savings Bank last week to inspect your father's account," she begins, a remarkable statement in that I hadn't known that Yehudah Leibovich had an account at the bank.

"He had some savings there," she continues.

I was aware of his bedrock frugality, but I had no idea that Father was paid enough for his services to put money into savings. Until Rivkah and I went to the bank to open accounts in the names of our mothers, neither of us had set foot inside a bank.

"I spoke to Mr. Popov, the general manager," Mother continues, "and he showed me the deposits in your father's name, which I inherited."

I am now utterly confused about Mother's intent. Rivkah's expression displays equal bafflement.

"It's not a large sum, but it's big enough to allow Moyshe and me to stay here, in this house. And you left us money from the sale of the watch. I know why you did it, Yakov, and I approve. The Community Fund has promised to help, too, if we need it. So, this is what I want you to know: we will be fine, Moyshe and me. Do you understand? We are not in dire need, so there is nothing to worry about. I'm going to take in some tailoring, anyway, to stay busy and bring in a little extra money. It would be good for me to stay busy. And Moyshe wants to polish some of the items Father left on his workbench, and repair what he can. He can start to earn, too. He wants to, and he enjoys it."

Mother is calmer and more confident than I have ever seen her. I lean over and place my hand atop hers as she speaks.

"So with a little extra money, I've bought something for both of you that I hope you will use," she says. "I mean for you to use it, so please don't fuss and protest, alright?"

She rises from the table and returns with an oversized envelope retrieved from a kitchen drawer.

"Open it," Mother urges.

Rivkah is looking over my shoulder as I reach inside and remove two Second-Class Letters of Passage from the Hamburg America Line for an eleven-day voyage to New York on the S.S. Suevia, departing from Hamburg on November 15th.

"Mother," I say softly, looking directly into her twinkling eyes. Rivkah places her hand to her mouth.

"It was my mother's wish," she says softly, as if to herself.

Galya Leibovich is beaming. "You should go, both of you, together. When you told me a few days ago, Rivkah, that this was your mother's wish, I knew what I had to do. This is God's will, too. I can feel it. If you really want to be in Germany, these can be returned and they will refund my money. I made sure of that at the bank. But I hope you won't do that. I hope you will make a plan to reach Hamburg and make this passage to New York."

"Mother . . ."

"Yakov, it would be so easy for me to tell you how much I need you to stay, and how much Moyshe needs you. But it's not true. We are fine and will be. We can manage. I will go forward in peace knowing that you and your bride can start a new life in a better place."

Tears well in Rivkah's eyes. "You can't afford this, Mrs. Leibovich."

"No, dear girl, I can. I made sure. That's why I went to the savings bank. I wanted to do this with all my heart. You cannot say no, Rivkah, my dear. I won't allow it."

The tickets carry much more weight than their thirty-five-rouble value. Mother is giving me permission to go, to marry, and to begin my own life in my own way. She knew the burden I was carrying, the guilt of leaving her and Moyshe. She also knew how much my father tried to guide my life. Her greatest gift is her acceptance of the inevitable rupture that every parent and child experience, some with rebellion and others with the serene knowledge that the laws of human nature always apply.

I rise and take my mother into my arms for an extended embrace, and whisper, "Are you sure?"

"Yes. I'm sure, my son. When you settle down, we can talk about whether Moyshe and I should come. Maybe it will happen. It's too soon to know."

I release her and ask, "What changed? I thought you wanted us to stay."

Mother smiles at me and replies softly. "What changed? Why, Rivkah. I can see she is a new kind of woman. She needs to spread her wings, just as you do. Did you know, Yakov, that I wanted another child? A daughter? Now, I have one. Rivkah needs to grow, just as you do. How can I deprive both of you? It would be cruel. You just have to promise me that I will have grandchildren someday."

"This, I can promise."

Rivkah's eyes are brimming with tears.

Our plan to emigrate to Germany is now upside down. As I walk Rivkah back to the alley off Volkava Street, we both wonder if my Mother's purchase of steamer passages is providential.

"Do you think she heard Shayna's voice telling her that America is where we must be?" I ask.

"Of course I do, Yakov. Well, not my mother's voice exactly, but maybe God's voice."

"Do you think He answers our prayers?"

"No, it's not like asking for candy and waiting to receive it. It's what we make of God's signs. I think He encouraged your Mother somehow. At least, she felt encouraged. Do you see?"

"Yes. Reb Moshe Cordovero was an important man in interpreting Kabbalah. He said: 'The essence of divinity is found in every single thing.' Maybe my mother and your mother were expressing this little piece of God within their souls. Maybe they focused on America because it is far away, a clean break from our current lives, a truly new beginning."

"We do need a truly new beginning, Yakov. I know Reb Philippsohn publishes a newspaper you love, but there must be newspapers in America, aren't there?"

"Some amazing ones, but only one is in Yiddish."

"One? But that is good!"

"You think so?"

"Yes! Why couldn't you work there? Is it in New York?"

"Well, yes. I don't know much about it, but it's run by a man named Kasriel Sarasohn, who emigrated from the Polish lands. You know who told me? The old man who drives the coach from Minsk. He reads everything. I think he said the paper is called *Di Yiddishe Gazeten*. I was so focused on Germany at the time, and on Reb Philippsohn, that I didn't pay much attention when he mentioned it. The *Gazeten* must come to Minsk in the mail. That's how the coachman knows it. I can ask him to get me a copy."

"You must! Couldn't you write a letter to Sarasohn?"

"I suppose so. Or as you suggested once, just go to New York and knock on his door. We would have to adapt to completely new ways in New York, wouldn't we? Forget the old ways and embrace the new; could you?"

"Of course I can. I am suffocating here, Yakov. I yearn for a new place. I know I told you weeks ago that it didn't matter where we went. But now, I think our mothers are guiding us and we should listen to them."

Mother's gesture has changed everything. As much as Reb Philippsohn's journal interests me, I can now see more enthusiasm for America in Rivkah's eyes. To fulfill her mother's wish would mean so much, and perhaps sustain both of us through the inevitable trials ahead. I think of my own mother too. I doubt she would have purchased the steamship passages if she could not see herself and Moyshe joining us one day in New York. I cannot argue with Rivkah's conclusion, but if we are going to America via Hamburg, we must act quickly.

"You're right, Rivkah. It would mean so much to your mother and to mine to use those Letters of Passage. I can write to Sarasohn right away, but I don't see any point in waiting for a reply. Everyone says America is a rich country, and if you work hard you can succeed. I could even start my own Yiddish newspaper, couldn't I?"

"You could!" Rivkah pulls me into her arms and holds on tightly.

"To America," I whisper.

She whispers back, "Do you think there will be anarchists in New York?"

The border runner I am searching for in a tightly packed neighborhood of Minsk is named Leon. The beadle at the synagogue wrote his name on a scrap of paper, along with that of a tavern he frequents, and handed it to me without saying a word. Though this source may seem unlikely, even I know the beadle's reputation for connections to the rougher side of life and to men who operate in the shadows of the law.

Leon is a guide who sells his knowledge of the frontier terrain and his skill at bribing local guards to look the other way. Within minutes of my arrival at the tavern, we are sitting on a park bench. Leon is muscular, swarthy, and has a head of wild hair. I quickly see that he is an intense and slightly arrogant man, one with whom I would not ordinarily wish to socialize. I am not interested in a friendship though.

"I do it once a month or so, never more frequently," Leon tells me. "It's because every trip requires planning and care. You'll make it. I guarantee it — unless you're careless, and you don't strike me as the careless type. Ask anyone around here about my experience. Ask your friends in New York about the Jews I've sent to all the ports of Europe. They'll tell you. Only once did we fail." His head head cocked proudly, he continues, "And anyway, the woman was sent back to Russia. That's all, not sent into detention. She's going to try again! And why not? I'm sure she'll get through, just as you will. If you can afford it."

Leon, it turns out, is not the runner, but the organizer and salesman. He works with his cousin, Maksymilian, who lives in the Polish territory near the border with Prussia. Maks is the real runner. But I cannot meet Maks before making a commitment and putting money on the table. Leon doesn't work any other way. I must take it on faith that Maks is as experienced and careful as Leon claims. How can I know? I have little choice but to go forward. If I trust Leon, I will have to trust Maks. This is only one of the risks of fleeing the Pale of Settlement.

"You will dress like ordinary Russians and buy two train tickets from Minsk to Bialystok," Leon says during a carefully detailed explanation. "I will give you forged identity papers before you leave Minsk. They are exquisitely done, true works of art. You won't find better. And that is where my job ends. When the train stops at Grodno, just before exiting the Pale, the conductor will check your papers for travel into Russian-controlled Poland. It is all part of greater Russia, but the Polish territory is a different administrative area. So they check, especially people they think might be Jews trying to escape. Fortunately, it is not an everyday occurrence for a Jew to be escaping. Every week, perhaps, but not every day. You won't have a problem; you wear no sidelocks, and the papers are impeccable. You are just another Russian traveler visiting family. You see how easy it is?"

I don't exactly see, and am moved to ask him, "The time it failed, was it the papers? Did they see that the papers were forged?"

"No, no, no, nothing like that. It was at the border crossing, not on the train. We didn't have enough money to pay what the guard demanded. It was a mistake for us to try, but we did anyway. It was an aberration; the guard was new. Don't worry. When you get off at Bialystok, you have to take the road north to Kolno, still in the Polish territory. Maks will meet you in Kolno, where he lives. I'll write the directions. You can walk to Kolno from Bialystok if you wish, but it takes twenty hours. If you have the money, take the coach. You should save your energy for the border crossing."

As I listen, I can tell that Leon has explained the route many times.

"From Kolno to the Prussian border is just a ninety-minute walk; that's it. And the terrain is flat, some farms but mostly woods. Depending on the conditions that day, Maks will either take you west of the road or east of it. Trust Maks; he knows what he's doing. The border is just a small stream, nothing at all to cross. You just take off your shoes and that's it: you're in Prussia. Then, you just have to avoid the road for an hour or so. After that, you can walk right along the road. Maks will explain everything. Don't worry. Once you're on the road, you can breathe; you're free."

It is a lot to take in, but I judge Leon to be sufficiently specific in his instructions. What can I do but feel confident that he has performed the service for which he is demanding a fortune? He wants fifty roubles. I choke at the price, then use a tactic my father employed many times, though it is risky.

"Fifty? We can't afford it," I say flatly. "I'm sorry I took your time, Leon. I will have to look elsewhere." Looking dejected, I rise from the bench and gather my things.

"So what can you afford?" Leon asks.

I shrug, "The most we can spend is fifteen apiece, thirty total. Otherwise, I really have to look elsewhere."

"Okay, fine. Don't worry, we can do it for thirty-five."

"You can make the papers perfect?"

"Sure, sure, the artist who makes the papers does all of them the same. They are exquisite. Trust me. They can be ready in one week. You can come when you're ready to make the journey. But don't come to the tavern. I don't ever keep papers there. You should come to my flat."

"Well, in that case, we have an agreement."

"Yes, a deal. I wish you luck, but you won't need it."

Leon writes his address on a slip of paper. I hand him twenty roubles. The remainder is to be paid to Maks when we reach Kolno.

As soon as I return to Navahrudak, I spread open a map to examine the route Leon mentioned: Navahrudak to Minsk to Grodno to Bialystok to Kolno. It seems to make sense. I estimate the distance between the Prussian border and the dock from which the S.S. Suevia departs. We can go by train to Warsaw, then Berlin, then Hamburg. I want Rivkah to see the map and to trace for her all of the steps Leon sketched, plus the route from the border to Hamburg. She must know everything. If anything happens to me, she must be able to go on.

I am not surprised by Rivkah's reaction. The distances are daunting, but she is still full of hope and infectious enthusiasm.

"We won't have to hide," she says. "We have enough money to take trains. They are quick, aren't they? I've never been on a train. What is it like?"

"Much faster than a coach or wagon, but not always so comfortable."

"Getting into Prussia will be the most difficult part?"

"Yes. But Leon promises excellent forgeries for our papers. We'll see what the artistic genius produces. And if Leon's cousin is as experienced as he is made out to be, we will make it, God willing."

"I'll think of my mother. She'll give me the will to go forward."

It is a bittersweet moment for my mother when I tell her that Rivkah and I will attempt to emigrate to America using the steamship tickets she purchased. She places both hands over her heart and smiles weakly, as she says, "You have made a good choice, Yakov. How soon must you leave?"

"Two weeks," I tell her. "We need to pack carefully, withdraw cash from the Postal Savings Bank, and say our goodbyes discreetly. It would not be wise to fuel gossip about an attempt to cross the border illegally. Not everyone can be trusted."

"Will you say goodbye to the rabbi at least?" Mother asks. "You really should, Yakov. He cares about you."

"I know he cares, and I'm sure he wants to repent for what happened to Avram Eizenberg, and for arranging a bribe to the Ministry of War. I confronted him, you know. He didn't cause Avram's death, but what

Father and he did pushed the conscription officer to demand the name of a Jewish replacement. I know the rabbi's upset about that. I could tell when I talked to him. It wasn't something he foresaw, but it all started with this corrupt plan."

"God will forgive him."

"Maybe I should forgive him; I don't know. He's asking for God's forgiveness, but . . . You know, Mother, I used to think that God scolds us and teaches us and uses His power of forgiveness only if we ask for absolution with a pure heart. That's what the rabbi taught us at the *beit midrash*. But it's such a narrow view of God: the Giver, the Taker, the Ruler, the King whose subjects must beseech Him to forgive transgressions. It doesn't any longer make sense to me."

"Then what do you believe?"

"That when we treat others with contempt or wrong them, we must seek forgiveness and try to compensate them for the harm we've caused. And we do it because it is right and just, not because we need to secure God's forgiveness or to appease Him. I have changed, Mother. The war changed me, just as it changed Father, and not just the war, but seeing new places and encountering people of different backgrounds in different circumstances. I want to understand and rely on my own instincts and ideas, not merely God's law and the laws of the great rabbis."

"Yes, I can see you have changed."

"I will be grateful forever for the *beit midrash* and all of the questions we confronted there and tried to answer. It taught me how to think. But many of the questions are just not answerable, even if having the answers would comfort us. When you step out into the world, as I did, you see how many other questions — an endless number of questions — must be asked and answered to understand the human condition. "

"Just don't try to persuade Moyshe to leave the *beit midrash*. He's just starting."

"Don't worry, I'll let him find his own way. I wish Father had let me find my own way when I was Moyshe's age, but I didn't have the courage to stand up to him."

"You found much courage. You are a man now, and I'm proud of you, and your father would be proud, too."

Her voice quavers slightly, and I reach out to her.

"I will write you letters, Mother, about New York and life in America, until you can come."

"I need to see how things go. I know this shtetl is too small a place for you. God willing, you will thrive and have children." She pauses a moment before changing subjects, "I want to visit your father's grave this afternoon."

"I'll come with you, Mother."

I walk slowly arm in arm with Mother and Moyshe, who has joined us after coming home from yeshiva. We stop at an unmarked mound of dirt. There is no stone yet for my father. Only the raw earth and sparse young grasses that mark a recent burial. Mother tries her best to appear serene. She lowers her head and grips my hand tightly.

"Yudel," she says. "We are here, your wife and your two beautiful sons, to tell you how much we miss you and to reassure you: everything is good; everything is okay."

She glances at me and manages a brief smile, while squeezing Moyshe's hand. "Your sons Yakov and Moyshe are here to have a moment with you, a loving moment. Yudel, I want you to know that Yakov is going to America with his soon-to-be bride Rivkah. She's a lovely girl. I have met her and I know you would approve." Her tone is almost cheerful. "They want to start anew, and Navahrudak has too many bad memories for them. Rivkah is alone, now that her mother has been taken. I want them to go to America, Yudel. I bought them steamship tickets. It's going to be fine. We're going to be fine. Yakov will have a new life. That's all. Rest, Yudel." By now, Mother's voice is cracking, but she quickly recovers her poise. "I've said what I need to say," she tells me.

"Take Moyshe, Mother. I'm going to stay."

As the two walk back, I stand alone before my father's grave and look around the grassy cemetery and its Hebrew headstones. I wonder if there is a stone for Yisrael Tsipershtein, but catch myself. His body must have been placed in a common grave somewhere near Bulgaria's Green Hills. If I could visit the grave of Avram Eizenberg, I would.

I look down and gather my thoughts. "Father, it's Yakov."

How long will I hold this grudge against my own father? I can't carry it forever, for my sake as well as his. Everything about what happened — to Avram and to Father — is tragic, but the tragedies will be compounded if there is no reconciliation. I have come to realize that the future can't seek its true path when it is tethered to recrimination and anger. As a boy, I tried to forgive my father's outbursts. And today? Doesn't the lesson of forgiveness that I explained to my mother apply now? I learned it from Avram, and from Rivkah and Shayna. Their generosity moved me and taught me.

"We've had disagreements, Father. You tried to guide my life carefully, and I resented it. I wish you had let me make my own mistakes and figure out what I wanted from life. And I wish we hadn't turned Avram over to Rybakov; I really wish we hadn't. He wasn't just a vagrant. I should never have let it happen. And I wish Kalman Levin had never gone back to Avram's grave and seen my *tallit* and my satchel."

My eyes fill. "And there's something else. I wish you hadn't felt the need to end your life, Father. I wish you hadn't." I look up at the sky. "But I forgive you, Father. I am opening the door and bringing you in. I forgive everything. I know you only wanted to protect me. I forgive you. I love you. But I know it's too late."

I say the Mourner's Prayer, the Kaddish, slowly, the way the rabbi must have done half a year ago at Father's burial. " . . . He who creates peace in His celestial heights, may he create peace for us too."

Mother's suggestion that I pay my respects to Reb Epshtein one last time has weighed on me. She knew I was incensed at his secret bribery scheme and that my esteem for him was damaged. I viewed him as a diminished, pitiable man trying to make amends. A few short months ago, I would have had nothing to do with him, so deep was my disgust. Today, though, I see strength in magnanimity. I suppose I have matured. The rabbi has seemed genuinely sorry. If I am willing to forgive my father, shall I not forgive Reb Epshtein? It costs nothing to forgive a man when he is in his grave. This will be different.

I will miss the stone synagogue on Minskaya Street, and the *beit midrash* where I spent endless hours in diligent study of rabbinical commentaries. I don't dismiss these fervent men of learning, though perhaps they devoted themselves with rigid scrupulousness to solving unsolvable mysteries. At some point, why not accept a mystery as mystery, and if you can't do that, dismiss it as nonsense?

When I knock at his open door, Reb Epshtein sits in a familiar bent pose, ink pen in hand, scratching purposely across the paper in front of him.

"What news do you have for me?" he asks cheerfully, looking up from his work.

"Rabbi . . ."

"Ah, something important, I see."

"And private."

"So private it shall remain. Close the door."

He directs me to one of the chairs opposite his desk.

"I have come to say goodbye."

"I see."

"Rivkah and I will be leaving Navahrudak soon, and if we're lucky we will escape Russia entirely. I tell you this in confidence."

"You need to escape this town? No, never mind. I understand. You need a bigger life. Where will you go?"

"Probably to New York, though we don't know a soul there."

"Ah, yes, the forbidden fruit of modernity. I thought you might choose Germany, but America will suit you."

"It's more than that."

"Yes, it is, I know. I keep interrupting you; forgive me. You know I wish only for God's eternal grace to shepherd you."

"It is good to have your blessing. But I'm afraid I need to ask more of you. Can you please look in on my mother and brother every once in a while and guide them through any storms?"

"This was always my intention. Your father dedicated so much of his love and his time to the synagogue. It can never be repaid fully, but I will try. You have my word."

"I'm grateful. You know, I have something of a confession, rabbi. I was quite angry with you about what happened."

"The Eizenberg boy."

"Yes, and the bribe. You have been a mentor for so long, and I felt betrayed. I'm sorry to use such a strong word. I hadn't intended to come here. I wanted to punish you by leaving without saying goodbye, the way a schoolboy sulks after receiving a bad note. I was angry."

The rabbi clears his throat and nods. "You had a right to be angry."

"But I also want to recognize your sincerity, Rabbi, and to tell you that I've felt your regret in my heart, so your apology is accepted with sincerity."

I feel my entire being lowering itself to a calmer, warmer, and more satisfying place. I feel peace. If this is the gift that forgiveness offers, I humbly accept it.

"It isn't easy for a rabbi to see his own shortcomings. Anyway, enough. May you have a safe journey and may God's blessing accompany you and protect you."

"I remember Numbers Six, Rabbi. 'This is the way you shall bless the children of Israel.' "

"See? You would have made a wonderful rabbi, my boy."

"You told me once: 'Every rabbi is a teacher first, and every teacher must first be a student.' I will be as diligent a student in America as I would have been here."

"I have no doubt."

He stands and summons me with outstretched arms. Our embrace is that of a reconciled father and son, and it feels good.

19

My clothes and boots are those of a common worker or student in the Russian hinterland. I have purchased a casquette cap to wear in lieu of my skullcap, and will tuck my pants into my high boots. I fold clothes into a new satchel along with my dog-earned journal, which also contains one of the folded Letters of Passage from Hamburg. Rivkah will carry the other. I will leave behind the pocket prayer book I took to Bulgaria. And though my father would surely have disapproved, I have trimmed my beard. I will be taken for an ordinary Russian, or Pole, or even a Prussian. I also pack a copy of *Di Yiddishe Gazeten* to read on our way to Minsk in the coach; then, I'll have to discard it. We will carry nothing in Yiddish on the train to Grodno.

I hold the Cross of St. George in my palm and consider its weight. Can I leave it in my parents' home? Moyshe might find it and lose it. I slip the medal into the pocket of my coat. It is a habit now. The medal survived a long journey from Bulgaria housed in a deep coat pocket. Shortly after my confrontation with Rybakov, I wondered if I should have tossed it at the officer's feet and disavowed it. I imagined saying to him, "This medal shows what the Jews do for the Tsar, and in return we are treated like dirt." But I didn't say it. Subconsciously, I must have wanted to keep the Cross of St. George as a hidden talisman, a phylactery.

Rivkah packs two dresses, underclothing, a few scarves, a second new pair of leather shoes, and a framed family photograph, from when she was ten, with her holding hands with her brother while her father's hands rest on her shoulder. She withdraws cash from the bank and splits it four ways. She and I will carry a quarter of the money in our coats and the remainder in our satchels. I will pack two other items that Rivkah does not know about. One is the knife and sheath handed to me in Odessa by the supply company. The other, carefully protected in paper wrapping, is the veil my mother wore at her wedding. She asked me to take it for Rivkah. I promised I would, but doing so didn't erase the sadness in her eyes.

On the day we are to depart, early in the morning, Mother packs food for both of us, enough to get us beyond Minsk. Rivkah has pulled the door shut at the room above the shed for the last time and walked to Maya Street with all the belongings she needs. We both are wearing our wool coats. The wind is brisk, and leaves tumble along the street.

The goodbyes were meant to last only a minute. This is the way I want it. But Mother holds onto me so long I beg her to release me, but not before whispering, "I will come for you." We leave behind reassuring words and a promise to send a letter from Berlin and another from New York.

I'm certain the eccentric coachman will be guiding our intercity coach to Minsk, so I prepare a cover story. As he tends his horses, I introduce him to Rivkah and explain that we are going to stay a few days with family. This is what we will tell the conductor on the train to Poland. We must be comfortable with this story and not depart from it. We settle into the cushioned seats of the coach, the only passengers. I squeeze Rivkah's hand, and she leans over and kisses me on the cheek. The future pulls us forward. It is a good feeling, strong enough to mask our trepidation. The team of horses pulls and jerks at their harnesses, familiar sounds to me now.

As the coach clacks along the road to Minsk, I notice a solitary horseman just behind us. I can hear the clatter of the hooves, but cannot make out a face behind the shadow cast by the rider's leather hat. The clatter is rhythmic and soothing, and I doze for part of the trip, trying to prepare myself for what lies ahead. When I awake, we have already arrived.

Minsk is a thoroughly modern city, with paved avenues, a municipal water supply, and three-story brick houses. I am comfortable here, but Rivkah finds it to be an overwhelming mass of bustling humanity. She was here once as a child, but has little memory of it.

Leon is home when I knock and immediately escorts us upstairs to a spare room behind a locked door. He reaches for a packet of papers stuffed behind a bookcase and hands me the forged identity cards, our internal passports.

"Take a look," he says confidently, as if he were showing off his latest fine art sketches.

When I remove the papers, I see that Leon has not exaggerated the artistic skill of his forger. The documents are on card stock, folded once to open like a small book. But everything is somehow worn and faded, making it seem like they have been carried in a pocket for years, including on rainy days. The stamps and text and signatures look authentic. Each bears the eagle, symbolizing the Empire of Russia, and carries a false name and the same false Minsk address. As I had instructed, the papers indicate that I will be traveling with a woman with the same family name. Rivkah can pass as my wife or as my sister. Seeing the quality of the identity cards sends a jolt of confidence through me. I feel certain the passage into the Polish zone of the Russian Empire will go well, but I still harbor worries about scrambling across the green border.

We stay the night in a small hotel near the train station, posing as a married couple. Our destination is Bialystok, via Grodno, and we buy two one-way tickets. At Leon's direction, I tell Rivkah to mention to the conductor that we are visiting her aunt on Zytnia Street in Bialystok. Leon even created the relatives' names. One, he confides, is that of a woman who died in Bialystok a year ago.

At Grodno, the conductor never even asks for a name. He opens the identity cards, seems to check our ages, and distractedly asks what our business is in Bialystok.

"We are visiting my wife's aunt." As planned, I feign a memory lapse and turn to Rivkah. "What was the street?"

"Zytnia Street," she says, smiling at the trainman.

The conductor closes the cards, hands them back to us without a word, and moves to the next set of seats. When he leaves the car, I lean over and whisper to Rivkah, "You were perfect!"

"If you only knew how queasy I was feeling," she replies.

A light rain is falling as we step off the train in Bialystok. It is early evening, and I find an inexpensive hotel for us close to the train terminal. The long ride has left both of us weary, but the anticipation makes it nearly impossible to sleep.

In the morning, we return to the station, and I find a coachman willing to take us to Kolno. As I bargain with the driver over the price, which seems impossibly high, another traveler offers to pay half, because he too is traveling to Kolno — a stroke of luck.

The village of Kolno sits in the hinterland, and the road there is poor and narrow. But the woods we pass are breathtaking; the autumn reds, oranges, and yellows form a brilliantly colorful corridor for nearly seven hours of travel.

Exhausted from a sleepless night, both Rivkah and I doze during part of the journey. The man in the coach with us keeps to himself. He looks to be in his forties and dresses like a Russian clerk. He asks whom we are seeing in Kolno.

"A close friend, and we have to return to Grodno in a few days," I tell him. When I ask the same of him, he is circumspect. "A business matter," he grunts.

Kolno is little more than a quaint crossroads with a church in the center. The sun is already nearing the wooded horizon when we arrive. Our quiet fellow passenger doffs his hat, bows to Rivkah, and disappears behind the old stucco church in the central square.

We follow Leon's directions and find the modest home of his cousin Maksymilian just two blocks from the church. The man who answers our knock is short and, like his cousin, muscular. He looks like a stonemason I remember from Navahrudak. Leon told us Maksymilian lost his wife in one of the cholera outbreaks and lives alone. As soon as I introduce myself, using the false name on our papers, Maks scans the street. Without greeting us, he asks: "Do you have the money?" Only after I assure him he will be paid and dig into my coat to show him the rouble bills does Maks open the door wide enough for us to enter.

"You can stay the night," Maks says blandly. "I will get some food for you. In the morning, I will explain the route. We will leave for the border after breakfast. You will be in Prussia long before the sun sets."

There is no warmth in Maksymilian's demeanor, but he seems to relax when he sees how weary we are and how reserved. He prepares a meal of fresh bread, cheese, and fruit, then sets up makeshift beds on the floor with straw and blankets. We are both hungry and desperately tired. Sleep comes easily. It is a good omen.

The morning is overcast; there will be no sun today.

"I feel queasy again," Rivkah says after awakening.

I embrace her. "You are nervous," I say. "It's an important day. I'm sure Maks will have some tea for us, maybe sugar too."

"Yes, tea will help," she says, "but I have no appetite for food just now."

Maks is already up and outside the small house. He walks in the front door, lights the kindling for the stove, and begins to heat water for tea. "It is good that we have clouds today," he announces. "Even better if it rains. The guards don't patrol in the rain. They're lazy."

"But I'm sure their vision is good," I remark.

"When they are sober," Maks replies. "If you want me to bribe the Russian and Polish guards on this side of the border, I will need an additional six roubles, three for each of them. They are bloodsuckers."

I give a start. "Six more roubles? Leon never discussed this with me!"

"He sometimes forgets. You can take your chances if you wish," he shrugs, seeming not to care whether we pay or not. "I will take you to within a mile of the border. I never go closer than that. There is no path, but you will see the notches I've left on the tree trunks. It will show the way."

Rivkah leans toward me and whispers that I should give the man the additional money. "We have enough," she says.

Maks is pleased to have the additional payment and insists on carrying Rivkah's portmanteau for our trek into the woods. The cool country air feels invigorating. The trees grow close to one another, forming a canopy above us, but there are also small farm fields to cross, many with grazing cows. We can hear the birds and sense the deer rustling through the underbrush.

Only a few minutes into our hike, Maks stops. "We will skirt a village called Wincenta and work our way toward the Pisa River for a short time," he explains. "It marks the border. It is very small, just a stream. I will leave you not far away and direct you to the riverbank. You only have to continue north along the bank of the Pisa until it bends sharply to the east. There, you must cross if it looks quiet. It is shallower at the bend. There is a sandbar on the near side. Will you remember these instructions?"

"Yes, but how deep is the river, Maksymilian?"

"No higher than your knees. When you reach the far bank, you are in Prussia."

"And remind me where we go from there."

I commit his instructions to memory. After crossing, walk east for a mile and find the road to the town of Pisz. Stay off the road for five miles or so, keeping the hills on the left. Then walk east along the only road. Pisz is a large town, not like Kolno, and there we will find everything we need. From Pisz, take a carriage to the nearest train station — unfortunately, he doesn't know how far the main rail line is. Trains will take us all the way to Berlin, then Hamburg. It sounds so simple.

As we walk, Rivkah begins to feel more like herself. The fresh air seems to help. She appears full of hope and to be thinking only of the future. Navahrudak is behind her, already a fading memory. I take her hand.

"We can stay a night or two in Berlin," I tell her. "It is cosmopolitan and beautiful, I hear. Then we can buy tickets for Hamburg."

"And I will tell this man Sarasohn he will be making a grave error if he does not employ you," Rivkah says sternly.

The woods grow thicker but the land is still flat. The earth feels damp and softer. Vines climb up some of the tree trunks. Fallen leaves carpet the forest floor. Maksymilian stops again and sits on an overturned tree trunk.

"We rest," he commands, placing Rivkah's portmanteau on the ground and pulling a leather pouch of water across his shoulder. He offers it to both of us, and we drink.

"This is where I leave you," Maks says. "I usually don't come this far. On my way back, I am going to pay the guards a visit so they won't bother with a patrol. They are always cooperative when they can bring home extra money." He points to the notches on the trees ahead and makes sure I understand the direction to the river. "It is only a hundred yards to the riverbank. Remember, when you reach it, turn right, then find the sandbar. Rest here for as long as you wish, but I think it might rain soon. I always take a different route home. Don't be confused. I wish you well."

Maks stands and awkwardly shakes hands before departing. He has left us the water pouch. We each eat a biscuit and take a few sips of water, conserving the rest.

"We will be fine," I say to Rivkah, smiling. Mostly, I am reassuring myself.

"You promised an adventure, Yakov Leibovich. God willing, we will see Prussia soon."

"Yes, God willing."

We are on our own now. The forest is quiet, save for the rustling of leaves and the call of an owl somewhere high in the branches. Rivkah sips again from the water pouch as I strain to hear the flow of a stream that I cannot yet see.

"Are you ready to get your feet wet?" I ask.

"Only to the knees, as you promised" Rivkah replies.

A light rain begins to fall through the few autumn leaves still clinging to the branches overhead. We gather our satchels and begin to walk toward the notched trees. The cuts, all at the same chest-high height, though not fresh, remain easily visible. I can imagine Maks carrying a hand-ax through these woods, marking the way. Fifty yards into our walk, we both hear a large animal galloping through the brush behind us. Frightened, Rivkah turns to look. I reach down to open the satchel and find my knife. But it's not an animal.

Someone shouts, "Stop! Police!"

My heart drops straight into the pit of my stomach, as a man races toward us with a pistol in one raised hand.

"Stop!" he demands in Russian.

We freeze. He slows as he approaches us, seeing that we are not running away. He wears a brimmed hat and a long dark Mackintosh. His pistol is pointed directly at us. I recognize this man. It is the traveler from the coach ride to Kolno. He is winded and his face is red. He stops and bends at the waist for a moment to catch his breath. "Don't move," he gasps. "You're under arrest, Leibovich. I know who you are, and you're not authorized to cross any border."

Rivkah drops to her knees as if she has been slashed at the back of her legs. My face tightens. "What is this all about?" I demand. I raise my palms to the middle of my chest, facing out. "We carry no weapons, so put yours away!" The raindrops suddenly become heavier. My exposed face and hands are wet.

"Officer Voronov of the Russian Interior Ministry police," he declares imperiously between pants and through heavy breathing. "I am taking you back to Navahrudak, Leibovich. You are under arrest, and you'll spend a long time in prison for this. Don't try to run."

Rivkah begins to sob. She is still on her knees. I can hear her choke out my name. Beyond feeling frightened, I am completely baffled. Why does a man travel all the way from Bialystok to Kolno to make a border-crossing arrest? I need an answer.

"You rode with us from Bialystok. Why? What difference does it make to you?"

Voronov is now a dozen feet from us, still pointing his pistol directly at my chest. He sneers, "You picked the wrong conscription officer to insult."

"So Rybakov sent you," I say dully. Voronov must have followed us from the moment we left Navahrudak. Perhaps he was the rider beside our coach to Minsk. He must know about Maksymilian. They probably know about Leon too. It occurs to me that my entire future, and Rivkah's, is turning to dust. A horrifying image passes before my eyes — a beaten man returning to Russia in chains and landing in a fetid prison cell. And what of Rivkah? What will they do to her?

She is still on her knees, the raindrops dappling her face and shoulders. "Please don't do this," she pleads to Voronov. "Why do you care about two harmless people in the woods? We have hurt no one."

I answer her question. "Rybakov sent him, Rivkah. The conscription officer. He hated the arrangement my father made two years ago. And he hates me."

"As I said," Voronov taunts, "you picked the wrong Russian official to insult."

Rivkah cries out, "I beg you!" She slumps farther to the ground, holding herself up with one hand. "I'm pregnant!" Her voice trails off. Between sobs, she says, "My child needs a father."

Shocked, I drop down beside her. "What?"

"My monthly flow is late," she replies softly, tearfully. "I feel it. I'm sorry, Yakov. I'm sorry."

"Enough!" Voronov shouts. He begins to walk toward us again, still pointing the gun.

"Wait!" I shout in desperation, again holding my hands up while I stand. Voronov stops.

"What did Rybakov tell you I have done? Explain that to me, at least. We haven't crossed any border, so what is my crime? What did he tell you?"

"It is a crime in Russia to avoid army service when you are drafted and healthy," Voronov says firmly. "You Yids know this."

"The Ministry of War approved it!" I respond with equal firmness. "Did he tell you that? I was in Bulgaria as a teamster delivering supplies at the front line, at Plevna. Did he tell you that?"

"I know all I need to know," Voronov says. "You were called to serve and you didn't serve."

"But I did serve! I did!" I blurt out everything that makes this moment absurdly wrong and all the evidence in my possession. "Didn't Rybakov tell you I served? Didn't he tell you I volunteered in Bulgaria? That I carried a Berdan with the Sixteenth Infantry Division? I fought at Plevna and the Shipka Pass under General Skobelev! Huge battles. Bloody ones. I killed Turks! Didn't he tell you any of this? Didn't he tell you I was wounded with a bayonet, stabbed at Shipka Pass, where tens of thousands of Turks surrendered? He didn't tell you any of this? I spent weeks under the care of army doctors. Didn't he tell you?"

Voronov doesn't move or speak. His face is frozen. He holds his pistol with both hands. It is still pointed at my chest. He stares at me and I look directly into his eyes. Rivkah is still on the ground, whimpering.

Finally, as if he were speaking to himself, Voronov mutters, "You have no proof." The rainwater begins to drip from the brim of his hat.

"Proof? You need proof? Look! Look at this wound!" I remove my coat and drop it onto the damp leaves. I remove two shirts. The cool rain sprinkles over the pale skin of my chest and shoulders. I rip off a piece of gauze I had taped over the scab at my shoulder to keep it clean.

"Do you see this?" The scar is scarlet red. "I fought with Skobelev and bled for the Tsar! It is in my military record! I buried Russian bodies at Plevna! Did Rybakov tell you any of that?"

"You have no proof," Voronov says again, inserting more conviction into his voice as his chin juts forward.

"But I do have the proof," I tell him calmly. I am no longer shouting. But I remain defiant. Still bare-chested, I slowly reach down for my coat while watching Voronov twitch. I lift the coat slightly and slowly slip one hand into a pocket.

"Stop!" Voronov shouts. "What have you got there!"

I lift my eyes toward him again. "It's not a weapon," I say, almost scoldingly, as if speaking to a child. My hand gently exits the pocket. I hold up the Cross of St. George and its yellow ribbons. My elbow straightens as I push the medal directly at the police officer.

"Look at this. Look carefully. General Skobelev himself awarded this to me the day Plevna fell. Do you see? A Jew with the Cross of St. George. Ask the Ministry. Ask Skobelev. I was on a spying mission for him directly into an enemy camp, directly into Plevna, and he gave me this award for valor. Even Rybakov knows this. It was in the newspapers. But I'm sure he didn't tell you. He didn't, right?"

I can see that my declarations are having an effect. Voronov's resolve might be cracking. Having regained her composure Rivkah watches me with a look of wonder, mouth agape. I drop the medal on top of my coat and put my shirts back on, shivering in the damp cold.

Rivkah has composed herself and addresses Voronov in a clear voice, as if she is speaking to a clerk in a shop. "Please don't shoot us," she says. "We are only trying to make a better life for ourselves. We deserve that. We can't die here, not in these woods."

"Who said I was going to shoot a woman?" Voronov responds without emotion. "Rybakov doesn't care about you. You can go to Prussia. I don't care. Go. He only cares about your friend here."

Rivkah begins to lift herself off the forest floor. She wipes her face and picks up her portmanteau. The rain eases to a light mist. I, too, wipe the rain from my face and start to put on my coat after laying the Cross of St. George at my feet. I can see that Voronov is telling the truth. He won't harm Rivkah. He only wants me. I speak slowly, addressing the officer. My voice remains calm.

"Officer Voronov. I'm going to escort my pregnant wife to the bank of the river, just there," I say in a firm voice, momentarily pointing to the rear. "We are going to walk slowly. She will cross the border. I'm going to leave the medal with you. You can keep it." I pick up the Cross of St. George and toss it low across the leafy ground. The medal and its yellow ribbons fall with a muffled thud just in front of Voronov's boots.

"If you want, you can tell Rybakov you shot me as I ran. The proof is lying at your feet. But I'm not going to run, sir. We're going to walk away slowly. The river is fifty yards. I need to get my wife and child across. That's what I'm going to do."

"Yakov? You can't," Rivkah says, looking at me with alarm.

But I quickly turn my face to the officer, trying my best to look utterly determined. "When my wife is safely across the river, I will walk back, and you can arrest me," I say to Voronov. "As I said, I'm not going to run."

"Yakov, no!" Rivkah says in an insistent whisper. I turn to her and embrace her tightly, whispering into one ear, "Trust me. I will never leave your side."

I release Rivkah quickly and turn again to Voronov, whose pistol is now aimed not at my chest but my belt. He reaches down and picks up the Cross of St. George, glances at it, turns it over, and glances again.

"We're going to the river now," I tell him. "She is pregnant, and I must help her cross."

I take Rivkah's hand firmly and pick up my satchel. She places the strap of her portmanteau on her shoulder. We turn slowly and begin to walk. Rivkah is trembling. A crow caws in the distance as the branches of the trees rustle in a light gust of wind. I set a slow, deliberate pace, squeezing Rivkah's hand tightly. Her hand is cold. We hear only the sound of leaves and twigs crackling under our feet. Voronov seems to be standing silently, though we don't dare look. We cannot hear him behind us.

"Don't turn around and don't stop," I whisper. I can see the gentle slope of the river bank now, twenty yards ahead. "Trust me, Rivkah. Just keep walking."

We come to the riverbank's crest. The undergrowth is thinner, and I can see the mud beside the river. It is little more than a stream, just as Maks told us, but the flow is rapid and the depth difficult to gauge.

Rivkah grabs my arm. "I won't do this without you, Yakov."

"I know. Trust me."

I slowly turn back to look. We have just crossed an acre of woods, and there is no one behind us. Voronov is nowhere in sight. He could be hiding behind a tree, but I see no hint of him. I scan the damp forest from left to right, listening and looking. Rivkah turns, too. The woods are quiet but for the chirp of a single bird.

"He's gone," she says softly. "You knew, didn't you."

"A guess, a risky guess. But I didn't think he would shoot us. Listen, before we look for the sandbar, tell me: are you sure you're pregnant? Are you able to go on now? Can you walk?"

"I'm pregnant. I can feel it, almost certainly. But, either way, I'm not an invalid, Yakov. We should go now while we have the chance."

Following Maks's instructions, we turn right along the riverbank, walk until the stream turns east, and look for the sandbar. I stop every minute to watch and listen. But still no sign of Voronov. After a ten-minute walk, we see the sandbar. I pull the knife from my satchel and trim a fallen branch to use as a probe for the depth of the river. The stream is quick. We remove our shoes, and Rivkah hikes up her long dress and ties it to her waist. I roll my pants legs up to my knees, and hoist the portmanteau and satchel above my head. Rivkah carries her coat. I instruct her to walk directly behind me and grab hold of my belt.

The water is dark and numbingly cold. As we wade up to our knees, the unmistakable sound of a single gunshot pierces the quiet woodland, but it is far in the distance. Both of us flinch and duck low. Is it Voronov? A hunter? The gunfire could not have been very close, but how can we know?

Feeling a surge of adrenaline, I say urgently, "Hold onto me!" as I begin to push forward across the rippling flow.

Rivkah shifts her hands from my belt to the side of my shirt. I feel the mud and smooth rocks beneath my feet. The opposite bank is only a few yards away, but the stream bed drops and the water rises quickly to our waists. Then the bed rises sharply again, angling to shallower water. There are no more gunshots, only the sound of our panting as we scamper up the opposite bank. I toss our bags up to a patch of weeds, then grab Rivkah's arm and pull her up onto all fours at the stream's bank.

"We have to get out of sight," I tell her, dropping the walking stick.

Ten yards in from the stream bank, and hidden by overgrown ivy and drooping bushes, we fall to the wooded floor and lay on our backs. Our feet are muddy and our clothing nearly soaked. We both breathe heavily. The satchel and portmanteau have survived the crossing, but my shoulder is aching from pressing the bags over my head.

"What was it?" Rivkah asks, reaching out to hold my arm. "The gunfire."

"He couldn't have been shooting at us. It was too far away. Maybe he wanted to expend one bullet that was meant for me. I was trying to give him a way out, Rivkah. A way to declare to Rybakov that he had fulfilled his mission, to give him credibility. And I think he took it. I hope he did. He has the Cross of St. George. I gave it to him so he could convince Rybakov he had killed me in the forest. He must have planned to let you go and bring me back — or shoot me if I turned and ran. It was just a guess. I was desperate. But we're safe now. We're safe. God has favored us."

"I hope you're right," Rivkah says. "I just wonder if he was shooting at Maksymilian."

I let out a long sigh. "I don't think we'll ever know. Maks took another route home for a reason. We must put it out of our minds. We have a long way to go."

A cool mist filters down from the canopy of the forest. Rivkah covers herself with her wool coat, which we managed to keep dry. The pounding in my chest subsides.

I turn to Rivkah. "If Maks is right, we are on Prussian soil looking through the branches of Prussian trees into a Prussian sky."

"Thanks be to God. I was sure he was going to shoot us both," Rivkah says. "I should have said all three of us. When he pointed the gun at us, I wanted to protect this child."

"You saved us, Rivkah."

"So did the general who gave you that medal," she says. "You will never see it again, but it served its purpose."

"He told me to keep it because I might want to show it to someone one day, and he was right."

In twenty minutes, we move inland through the woods and find apples to pick from a tended grove. We skirt other farms and fields, following the line of the low hills that Maks described. The rain ends, and a cool blanket of air settles onto the forest. We find a clearing to spend the night, and I recite the evening prayers and thank God for our safe passage. The apples are sweet and crisp. Rivkah squeezes my hand. She begins to sing. Her voice is pure. I lean back, look at the sky, and think how powerful Avram's forgiveness proved to be — and how calming it was when I summoned the strength to grant forgiveness at my father's grave and before the rabbi.

We sleep in the open, huddled together under patches of stars. We are weary but grateful to be together and to feel each other's warmth. I keep glancing through the woods to the horizon, looking for border police, but there are none.

At dawn, I again offer a prayer for our safe passage and for our new lives. Rivkah takes my hand. We turn east, find the narrow and pitted road to Pisz, and begin walking north.

Afterword

Although the Pale of Settlement imposed severe restrictions on Jews, the story told in this novel takes place at the peak of tolerance and Jewish liberties in Imperial Russia. Only a few years after 1878, the year of the story's closing chapter, conditions for the Jews in Russia's restricted region declined sharply. The Great Reforms of Alexander II, including military reforms, collapsed with his assassination in 1881. Even before his murder, more virulent strains of nationalism and xenophobia began to infect Russian life, and many of the incremental changes that had advanced the cause of Jewish emancipation withered.

The ability of Jews to attend universities was restricted. The military severely limited the number of Jewish doctors permitted in the army. The authorities also placed constraints on Jewish engineers, pharmacists, border guards, medical assistants, scribes, and artisans. And they rescinded permission for Jewish veterans to settle in the place of their military service outside of the Pale.

In his book *Imperial Russia's Jewish Question*, the historian John Doyle Klier concludes that one of the costs of the improved legal situation for Russia's Jews during Alexander II's reign was a harsh public backlash. "As Jews came to encapsulate all manner of conservative fears, a new strand of Judeophobia emerged based on fantasies and paranoia," Klier writes. These included an obsession with fears of a Jewish conspiracy to dominate the world, Jews as nihilists, Jews as vampires performing ritual murders, and Jews as corruptors of Christianity.

A month after the Tsar's assassination, anti-Jewish riots broke out in dozens of cities — the infamous pogroms. The destruction and killings, along with the relentless poverty experienced by many Jews in the Pale, launched a wave of migration that sent Jews to the Americas, Palestine, and Western Europe.

To see this novel as a depiction of Jewish life in the Pale across the entirety of the last quarter of the Nineteenth Century is to conjure a mirage. It depicts only a fleeting moment of hope.

<h1 style="text-align:center">SELECTED READING</h1>

A History of East European Jews,
Heiko Haumann, Central European University Press, 2003.

A Jewish Life Under the Tsars: The Autobiography of Chaim Aronson, 1825-1888, tr. Norman Marsden, Allenheld Osman & Co., 1983.

Bayonets Before Bullets: The Imperial Russian Army 1861-1914,
Bruce W. Menning, Indiana University Press, 1992.

Beyond the Pale: The Jewish Encounter With Late Imperial Russia,
Benjamin Nathans, University of California Press, 2004.

Conscription and the Search for Modern Russian Jewry,
Olga Litvak, Indiana University Press, 2006.

Czar and Sultan: The Adventures of a British Lad in the Russo-Turkish War of 1877-78, Archibald Forbes, Charles Scribner's Sons, 1894.

Gate of Heaven,
Abraham Cohen de Herrera, tr. Kenneth Krabbenhoft, Brill, 2002.

Hasidism: A New History,
David Biale et. al., Princeton University Press, 2018.

History of the Jews in Russia and Poland,
Simon Dubnow, The Jewish Publication Society of America, 1920.

Imperial Russia's Jewish Question: 1855-1881,
John Doyle Klier, Cambridge University Press, 1995.

War in Bulgaria: A Narrative of Personal Experiences,
Lieut.-General Valentine Baker Pacha, Sampson
Low, Marston, Searle & Rivington, 1879.

Jews in the Russian Army, 1827-1917,
Yohanan Petrovsky-Shtern, Cambridge University Press, 2009.

Major Trends in Jewish Mysticism,
Gershom Sholem, Schocken Books, 1941.

Sins of Youth, Guilt of a Grandmother: M.L. Lilienblum, Pauline Wengeroff, and the Telling of Jewish Modernity in Eastern Europe,
Shulamit S. Magnus, Polin: Studies in Polish Jewry,
The Littman Library of Jewish Civilization, 2005.

The Breakfast War,
Rupert Furneaux, Thomas Y. Crowell Co., 1958.

The Golden Tradition: Jewish Life and Thought in Eastern Europe,
Lucy S. Dawidowicz, Beacon Press, 1967.

The Manor and the Estate,
Isaac Bashevis Singer, tr. Joseph Singer et. al.,
University of Wisconsin Press, 2004.

The Russian Army and Its Campaigns in Turkey in 1877-1878,
Francis Vinton Greene, D. Appleton & Co., 1879.

The Russo-Turkish War of 1877: A Strategic Sketch,
Major F. Maurice, Swan Sonnenschein & Co., 1905.

The Shtetl Book,
Diane K. and David G. Roskies, Ktav Publishing House, 1975.

"The Sick and Wounded in the Russo-Turkish War,"
British Medical Journal, September 1877.

The World of Sholom Aleichem,
Maurice Samuel, Simon & Schuster, 1986.

World of Our Fathers,
Irving Howe, Harcourt Inc., 1976.

Paul Horvitz is a former newspaper journalist and financial writer in the United States and Europe. He was a reporter and editor at The New York Times, the International Herald Tribune, and Bloomberg News before joining a nonprofit investment advisory firm. Mr. Horvitz is retired and lives north of Boston. He is the author of *Agent of Intrusion*, a contemporary novel about state-sponsored hacking and industrial espionage. His other writings, including essays on politics and climate issues, can be found at *paulhorvitz.com*.

www.ingramcontent.com/pod-product-compliance
Lightning Source LLC
Chambersburg PA
CBHW061653190726
48289CB00006B/1854